THE SPIRIT DANCER
TESSA LAMAR NOVELS BOOK 5

KATHRYN M. HEARST

THE SPIRIT DANCER
Copyright © 2021 by Kathryn M. Hearst. All rights reserved.

This book is a work of fiction. Names, characters, businesses, organizations, places, events, and incidents either are the product of the author's imagination or are used fictitiously. Any resemblance to actual persons, living or dead, events, or locales is entirely coincidental.

Excerpt from BLOOD VOWS copyright @ 2020 by Kathryn M. Hearst

Worldwide Rights. Printed in the United States of America. No part of this book may be used or reproduced in any manner whatsoever without written permission except in the case of brief quotations embodied in critical articles or reviews.

Published by Wyndham House, Inc. July 2021

www.kathrynmhearst.com

Cover art designed by Crimson Phoenix Creations

Editor Holly Atkinson, Evil Eye Editing

Proofreader Book Nook Nuts Proofreading

❧ Created with Vellum

CHAPTER 1

A grad school professor once told me that change came from great insight or great pain—mine came in a shiny red sportscar and claimed he was my brother.

Standing in the yard, sandwiched between my two husbands, I replayed the previous three minutes on repeat. An unbelievably handsome stranger had driven up in a car that cost more than most folks made in a year—and that wasn't the weird part.

Mr. Tall, Blond, and Handsome had crossed magical wards that acted like an invisible fence…an invisible fence that surrounded our property and only opened for blood relatives.

The wards were meant to keep us, and the people we loved, safe from an ever-growing list of enemies. Yep. We're a paranoid bunch, but we came by it honestly, considering we'd tracked down a half a dozen serial killers, black magic users, and a freaking boo-hag in the previous couple of years.

Aaron folded his arms and gave my alleged brother his best intimidating cop-stare. "What did you say your name was again?"

"Killian, Killian O'Roarke." The guy looked like he'd just stepped out of a movie screen. To say I didn't see a family resemblance would be the biggest understatement in the history of understatements.

Then again, I had no idea what my father's side of my family looked like, so what the heck did I know?

"And you're my brother?" Not only did my voice quiver, but my dang Southern accent thickened to Scarlet O'Hara levels.

The hurt and abandoned little girl inside me wanted to throw herself into his arms and beg for scraps of information about her daddy, but grown-up Tessa couldn't risk it. Not until I had a DNA test or—better yet—divine intervention.

"That, I am." He glanced over the property. Emerald green eyes landing first on the house I shared with Bryson, Aaron, and our kids, then settling on the little pink cottage that belonged to my great-grandmother. "Sorry to show up and drop a bomb on you. Is there someplace we can talk?"

My manners warred with my common sense. It was rude to leave a guest standing in the middle of the yard, but there was no way I was inviting him into my home for sweet tea and a chat. Not until I knew he was who he said he was.

And therein lies the problem. How the heck do I figure out if he's telling the truth?

"It seems like a shame to waste such a pretty day." I motioned to a wrought iron table and chairs beneath an enormous live oak.

Killian gave the pink house one last look before following me to the table.

His interest in my great-grandmother's place set me on edge. We had two kids, two old ladies, and a newborn hiding there until we gave the all clear—*if* we gave the all clear.

The men waited for me to sit. Bryson and Aaron claimed the chairs on either side of me, and Killian sat directly across the table.

Unsure what to say, I dropped back and punted. "Let's start over. I'm Tessa, and these are my husbands, Bryson and Aaron."

"It's a pleasure to finally meet you and your spouses." If the news that I had two hubbies surprised him, he didn't let on. "Unfortunately, this isn't a social call. As I said, *our* dad is in serious danger."

Our dad. Our dad. My dad.

The words hit me like a two-by-four upside the head. Waffling between anger and tears, I held up my hand as if to stop the world, or my brain, from spinning. This man, whoever he was, didn't need to know how much his words affected me. "What sort of danger?"

As if on cue, his cell phone rang. Killian pulled it from his pocket, glanced at the screen, and frowned. "Excuse me. It's urgent."

"Of course." I waited until he walked a safe distance away before blowing out a breath. "Holy Moses kayaking on the Red Sea. I wasn't expecting this today. What do—"

Bryson held up a finger and whispered a privacy spell.

As soon as the soundproof bubble snapped into place, Aaron said, "I don't like it. How do we know he is who he says he is?"

While I agreed with him, I wasn't ready to dismiss Killian's claims. Not yet. Not when I'd potentially met a member of my father's side of my family. "We don't, but he *was* able to cross the wards."

"I should check to make sure they were not tampered with." Drawing a slow, deep breath, Bryson closed his eyes. A split second later, his magic caressed my skin as it spread across the ten or so acres we called home.

While I appreciated the fact he was protecting our family, I wished he'd hurry the heck up. If Killian was up to no good, he likely wouldn't stand by while we assessed his magic. But if he was telling the truth, I had questions—a million and sixty-two questions.

Bryson sighed, but his shoulders remained tight as bow strings. "The wards are intact, but Killian is locked and loaded with magic."

Aaron rubbed his arms. "That's coming from him? I thought it was Tessa."

"So did I…at first." Bryson met my gaze. "He may very well be your brother. The similarities are hard to ignore."

My brain stuttered. "You think Killian's magic is like mine?"

I'd sensed the same thing, but had chalked it up to wishful thinking. He didn't have the heat of the firebird—that part of me came from Atsila, my birth mother. Killian's magic was stormy and cold and reminded me of the part of myself that allowed me to talk to the dead.

Bryson nodded, but the lines between his brows told me he wasn't happy about it.

"Do you think he's telling the truth? That my father is in trouble?" I didn't know my dad, and the idea of finally meeting him made me dizzy.

"I don't know." Bryson took my hand. "But you'll never forgive yourself if you don't find out."

"She's not talking to him alone. I'm telling you, there's something off with the guy. One of us should be with her." Aaron shifted to the edge of his seat as if preparing to launch into action. His unease plucked on my already frazzled nerves.

Planting my hands flat on the table, I said, "*She's* sitting right here and can make up her own mind."

Aaron's frown deepened. "What do you want to do?"

"I have no clue." I wished I could let go of the doubt and give Killian a chance, but I'd been fooled before. I needed to know for sure he wasn't using some sort of Fae mind trick on us before I could trust him. "Is there a spell or something that will prove he's my brother?"

"Maybe, but we'd need time to research it." Frustration thickened Bryson's voice.

Aaron scratched his jaw. "Can you reach out to Charlie or Atsila to confirm his story?"

"I can try, but I'd have better luck tonight when it's quiet." I glanced back at Killian. Nothing about him seemed threatening, but I couldn't let my guard down. Not yet. I had more than just myself to think about.

Bryson split his attention between Killian and me. "It's your call, but you might want to get him out of here before Darlene and the others get here."

"Crap on toast." I'd forgotten about the family dinner to celebrate my cousin Tank's release from jail. The poor guy had witnessed a boo-hag running off with his wife's skin, been arrested for her murder, and then thrown in a maximum-security psych ward. He deserved a drama-free dinner, or as drama-free as it could get with Darlene at the table.

Aaron slung his arm around my shoulder and leaned me close. "I know how much finding out about your dad means to you, but we need to proceed with caution."

"Spoken like a true police detective." Nuzzling into his side, I whispered, "I love that you get it, and I promise. I'll be careful."

My men exchanged yeah-right looks.

I absolutely hated it when they ganged up on me, but in this case, I understood. Had it not been for the fact the Queen of Nosy-ville was coming for dinner, I would have put my maybe-brother through a Q&A session that would have made the Spanish Inquisition seem like a game of Go-Fish. "I'll get his number and arrange a meeting when we can all talk in private."

"That sounds like a reasonable plan, but are you sure you're willing to let him leave before you get some answers?" The concern in Bryson's eyes warmed me from head to toe. Sometimes it felt like he understood me better than I understood myself.

Their support gave me the courage to do the right thing, even when my inner-child wanted to hurl herself at Killian and beg him to stay. "I'm sure."

"Let's make it quick. Darlene and Stone will be here any minute." Bryson dissolved the privacy spell and nodded toward my maybe-brother. "He's finished his call."

Presenting what I hoped was a picture of a happy family, or at least a united front, we watched as Killian walked back to the table. Unfortunately for me, the closer he came, the more I second-guessed myself.

What if my dad is in serious danger? What if I am the only one who can save him? What if he dies while I'm dragging my feet about Killian? Could I ever forgive myself?

"Sorry about that." He met my gaze. "Court business."

Court business?

Aaron perked up a bit. "Are you a lawyer?"

"Not even close. Perhaps proper introductions are in order." Laughing, he bowed with an honest to goodness flourish. "Killian. Killian O'Roarke, second of the *Leipreachán* clan and advisor to Caoimhe, Queen of the Aos Sí."

I glanced between Bryson and Aaron, unsure of what Killian had said, let alone how to respond. His California accent had morphed into the thickest brogue I'd ever heard.

Aaron shrugged.

Bryson, however, narrowed his eyes.

Fat load of help they are.

I recalled the Aos Sí were the Celtic version of Fae. Bryson and I were Nunnehi, or the Cherokee variety. Then again, if Killian and I shared a father, that'd make me…a what? Did it work like dog breeds? Was I a *celt-okee?* A *chero-tic?*

Thankfully, Bryson interrupted my visit to crazy-town. "I'm familiar with the *term* Aos Sí—"

"It's another word for Sidhe, right? The rest of what you said went over my head." I realized I'd not only cut him off, but I sounded as uneducated as I felt. "We aren't usually so formal. What with titles and all."

The space between Killian's brows wrinkled for a split second before he plastered on his Hollywood smile and plopped into his chair. "Forgive me. English isn't my first language. I suppose you could say I speak *Fae-glish.*"

Be it my nerves, or temporary insanity, I laughed. Loud. Hyenas had nothing on me. Sure, his joke was dumb and racist and he spoke English just fine, but once I started giggling, I couldn't stop.

Aaron rested his hand on my shoulder, likely in an effort to calm me down.

Bryson ignored my borderline hysteria and continued to stare at Killian.

"Let me try again." His accent changed to nondescript American. "I'm Killian O'Roarke. Son of Liam. Second of the Leipreachán clan, and advisor to the Queen of the Aos Sí."

Liam. My dad's name is Liam.

Questions zinged around in my head. *What's he like? Does he know about me? Of course, he knows about me. How else would Killian know who I am? Why did he stay away my entire life? Where is he now? What kind of trouble was he in?*

My brain screeched to a halt.

Wait a cotton-pickin' second. Did he just say I was half-leprechaun? Half Celtic-Fae I could handle, but little folk with pots of gold and rainbows? Not so much.

Aaron, God love him, scratched the side of his head. "You're a leprechaun?"

Killian's smile melted into a bland indifference. "Yes, but as you can see, the legends have it all wrong. We are not short, nor do we wear funny hats and green shorts, and we keep our gold in banks, not pots."

It'd taken me a while to accept the fact I was a fairy who happened to shift into a flaming bird, but this…this would take some getting used to.

Killian motioned in the general direction of my deflated baby bump. "You were pregnant in the photos on the website. Where is the child now? I would very much like to meet him."

And just like that, my suspicions formed an ice wall that would make Jon Snow and all of the Night's Watch drool with envy. No one, and I mean no one, outside of the immediate family went near my baby. Bryson, Aaron, and I had been warned Quin was powerful, and that kind of magic would put him in danger.

"I don't think that's a good—"

Bryson interrupted me. "Exactly what sort of trouble is your father in, and why is it that Tessa is your last hope?"

Before Killian could answer, my mother's little blue Prius came up the drive. Even from across the lawn, I could see the whites of her eyes as she stared, first at the Lamborghini, and then at its owner.

Hurricane Darlene was about to make landfall.

CHAPTER 2

I hooked my arm in Killian's and pulled him to his feet. If we moved fast, I could get him into his fancy car before Darlene inserted herself into an already-complicated situation. "It's best if we continue this conversation another day."

"With all due respect, the circumstances are quite urgent." Killian turned and went wide-eyed.

I couldn't blame the guy. Most folks had the same reaction the first time they saw Darlene in all her leopard print spandex glory.

Bryson and Aaron exchanged glances, though neither spoke, it didn't take a PhD in male psychology to know they didn't give a crap about the situation or urgency.

"Tessa Marie! You come back here and introduce your friend to your Momma." Darlene's voice hit a pitch that rivalled a cat with its tail under a lawn mower.

"Mom?" Killian glanced from the charging woman to me. "Atsila is your mother, correct?"

"It's a long story. Until recently, Darlene thought I was her biological daughter." The doubt I had about Killian melted away a little more. Precious few people knew Darlene wasn't my biological mother, and fewer still knew my birth mother's name.

Darlene stopped a couple of feet from us. Lips pursed, she took Killian in one slow inch at a time. Considering the man was as tall as Bryson, the appraisal bordered on obscene. When she glanced at me, she bugged her eyes. "Honestly, Tessa. Where are your manners?"

"Momma, this is Killian O'Roarke. Killian, this is Darlene, my mom." I had no desire to go any further down Introduction Road. For one, it'd been a little over a week since she'd learned I wasn't the child she'd given birth to. I didn't know how she'd react to finding out he was probably my brother.

"Killian..." She fanned herself and glanced away. The coy routine was so *not* Darlene. I had the feeling something was up. Something I was going to hate.

He flashed her what I was quickly learning was his fake smile. "It's a pleasure to meet you in person. You're...you look exactly like I pictured."

In person? What he expected? What the heck?

Aaron's expression went from curious to what I called his cop-face —hard and blank. "You two know each other?"

Darlene waved her hand and flubbed her lips. "We've spoken on the phone once or twice. I'd hardly say we know each other."

Stone, my stoner stepfather, joined us with my baby brother in his arms. He glanced from his wife to Killian and back. "Is this the guy you've been talking to day and night?"

My mother dipped her chin.

I planted my hands on my hips and waited for someone to explain themselves.

Stone said, "Look, man, I practice a nonviolent lifestyle, but I'm not stupid. What do you want with my wife?"

Killian looked my stepdad over, from his Grateful Dead T-shirt, to his baggie jeans, and Birkenstock sandals. Rather than addressing Stone, he turned back to me. "She introduced herself as your manager when I called the number on the website."

Aaron groaned. Bryson scowled. And I stood there unable to form a single syllable.

Killian furrowed his brow, only this time, he didn't try to hide his confusion. "You know, *The Wonderful Witchardly World of Tessa Lamar.*"

When Darlene had learned I wasn't her biological child, she'd handled it better than I'd expected. I mean, finding out that the child you'd gave birth too died, and your uncle switched your real daughter with his grandchild was traumatic—learning said grandchild wasn't human could make anyone snap.

Darlene, being Darlene, hadn't snapped. She'd sorted through the news and focused on what would benefit her—namely, the bit about me being a fairy. She'd glommed onto the idea that people would pay big bucks to consult with a real fairy. Thus, the *Wonderful Witchardly World of Tessa Lamar* website had been born.

What she'd failed to realize was that by putting my heritage, and contact information, on the internet, she'd given every whack-a-doo, human magic-wielder, and psychopath a giant, flashing neon arrow pointed at my house.

"Honestly, Tessa. I don't know why you're so mad. I thought you'd be thrilled to meet your brother." Darlene clung to Stone's arm. Not like a drowning woman holding onto a life preserver, this was more like a gladiator holding a shield—a human shield.

I had no doubt she'd sacrifice him to save her own hide. Too bad for Stone, because I was about to rip her shellacked hair from her head. "Someone called and claimed to be my brother, and you didn't think it was something you needed to tell me?"

She gave me a bless-your-dumb-heart look. "I didn't want you to be disappointed if he turned out to be full of baloney. How was I supposed to know he wasn't some loony from the internet?"

Aaron arched a brow. "Did you give him the address?"

"Not exactly." Darlene toed the ground like a scolded child. "He saw it on the website."

Stone, the most nonconfrontational person I'd ever met, stepped away from Darlene. "You promised to take the website down."

Her lower lip quivered. "I was going to, but with all of the drama and murders…and then the new grandbaby…I forgot."

"When was the first time he called?" Stone wasn't having her excuses, which made me love the guy a little more.

Darlene exaggerated a sigh. "A few days before Quin was born."

"That was over a week ago." Bryson shook his head.

"You've known about this an entire week?" In a moment I can only describe as temporary insanity, I lunged for her.

Thankfully, Aaron grabbed one side and Bryson grabbed the other. Between the two of them, they managed to keep me from serving a minimum of sixteen years without the possibility of parole.

"Whoa there, settle down. I'd hate to have to arrest the mother of my children." Aaron chuckled, but it lacked his normal humor.

Though he remained quiet, Bryson's calm, steady magic slid over me until the angry red haze lifted.

For the life of me, I would never understand Darlene. Deep down, I thought she meant well, but her schemes caused me trouble on a regular basis. Case in point, that dammed website. On the other hand, two potentially good things had come from the ordeal—a brother and a father.

Killian stood a few feet away, watching the goings on with an expression I couldn't quite decipher. It reminded me a bit of Aaron's cop-face, only with a heaping helping of horror.

I had no clue where he was from, but judging by his fancy car and clothes, he didn't rub elbows with country-folk very often. He had to think he'd stumbled into a redneck nightmare. Then it hit me.

They'd been talking.

For *days*.

What about our so-called father? Where had Killian's sense of urgency been then? Lord in Heaven, he could have gotten all sorts of information about me from Darlene. She could have blabbed all of my secrets—including Atsila's name.

I needed time and privacy to sort it all out. He might be Fae, but that didn't mean he wasn't some loony from the internet—nor did it mean he was my brother.

After drawing in a cleansing breath, and exhaling nice and slow, I said, "Momma, you and Stone go to Gram Mae's. Tell her to serve dinner without us. We'll be in as soon as we say goodbye to Killian."

"That's nonsense. He's obviously your brother. The least you can do is invite him for dinner." She made doe eyes at Killian. "You are her brother, right? You sure as heck don't dress like a psycho-killer."

"I'm sure Ted Bundy's victims thought the same thing the first time they met him." I realized I'd insinuated my alleged brother was a serial killer the moment the words fell out of my mouth.

Killian's expression turned as cold as the magic coursing through him, but it warmed when he glanced back to Darlene. "I'd love to stay for dinner."

Thunder rolled overhead and dark clouds filled the bright blue Florida sky. Odd considering the forecasters had called for a sunny day. I couldn't help but wonder if my alleged brother was monkeying with the weather in hopes of forcing me to invite him inside.

Not freaking likely.

"Not tonight." In no mood to play games, I drew my spirit animal to the surface. Aaron was right. Brother or not, something was definitely off with the guy. The sooner I got him out of there, the better.

Likely sensing my magic, Bryson and Aaron followed suit. One way or another, Killian O'Roarke was going to leave.

My great-grandmother stepped out onto her front porch. "Tessa, I hate to interrupt, but I figured the coast was clear since Darlene and Stone didn't come in…"

The last thing I needed was Gram Mae insisting on meeting Killian. She'd take one look at his Hollywood smile and bully him into staying for dinner.

"Go back inside, Mae." Bryson spoke without taking his attention off me and Killian.

Never one to follow orders, Gram Mae hurried down the steps and across the lawn before coming to a stop a few feet from us. "Killian…my goodness. Is it really you?"

"*A Mhóraí?*" He took a tentative step toward her, then another, and another. "It's been too long."

"Sixty years." Mae choked out a sob and threw herself into his arms. "I thought I'd never see you again."

I had no idea what he'd called her, but it was obviously a term of endearment.

Stone tilted his head. "Mae's your grandmother?"

"Since when do you speak—" Darlene waved her hand. "Whatever it was he just spoke."

"It's Gaelic. *Mhórai* means grandma." Stone furrowed his brow. "But sixty years? The guy doesn't look a day over twenty-five."

It took some mental gymnastics, but my brain managed to pull off a double round-off twist and land on the truth. "My god. He's really my brother."

Darlene barked out a laugh. "I told you so. And it looks like I'm not the only one whose been keeping secrets."

CHAPTER 3

The million and sixty-two questions I had for Killian had grown exponentially. Heck, I had about the same number for my Gram Mae. She'd obviously known about my brother. It wasn't a stretch to imagine she'd known my father's identity all along. The fact she hadn't shared the information with me, even though I'd asked at various points in my life, hurt like battery acid on road rash.

Gram Mae pulled back from Killian and gave me a sheepish smile. "The three of us should talk."

Ya think?

Biting my tongue to keep from sassing her, I nodded.

Darlene cleared her throat. "Don't you mean the four of us? I'm the one who found him. I should be included in the conversation."

Gram Mae raised her chin. "I said *three*, and I meant it. Everyone else go inside and eat. Ribs taste like rubber when their warmed over in the microwave."

Darlene smirked. "How would you know? You use your microwave like a breadbox."

Mae shot her a look that'd scare a buzzard off of road-kill and led Killian toward my house.

Bryson rested his hand on the small of my back and leaned close. "Do you want me to come with you?"

Not trusting my voice, I shook my head.

The frown he'd worn since Killian had arrived deepened. I thanked my lucky stars he didn't argue, but something told me it was coming.

Aaron, on the other hand, had plenty to say. He moved to my other side and didn't bother to whisper. "I'm going with you. None of this adds up. He should have told you he'd talked to Darlene and that he knew Mae when he first drove up."

"I'll be fine." I forced a smile and willed him to listen to reason. "Go eat. This is supposed to be a welcome home party for Tank."

Darlene looped her arm in Aaron's. "Come on handsome. Tessa's a big girl. She can handle herself."

That she'd taken my side surprised me. I opened my mouth to thank her, but she cut me off.

"Besides, we'll be close enough to hear her scream if something goes wrong." She laughed high and shrill.

I suppressed a groan. "Thanks, Momma."

"Darlene, we're not done talking." Stone gave Killian a disgusted look and hurried after my mom and Aaron.

Bryson leaned in and whispered, "I'm with Aaron. Something is off. Be careful."

Great. One of them I could dismiss as overprotective paranoia. Both of them having the same spidey-sense made my pulse race. "I'll listen to what they have to say and send him on his way. Be there before dessert."

His lips curled in a ghost of a grin. "Mind if I check in with you in a bit?"

"That's fine, as long as you bring us some food. I've been smelling barbeque all day. I'm starved."

As if on cue, my Aunt Dottie poked her head out the screen door. "Everything all right out there? Buck Oldham's truck is coming down the road."

"Yes, ma'am. Everything's fine. I'll send Buck in." I prayed she'd take my words for it and go back inside. I didn't think my heart could handle it if I found out she'd been lying to me, too.

"Why are your friend and Mae heading in the wrong direction? Didn't you invite him for dinner?" She made her way down the porch steps.

Killian stopped outside my front door and waved at the elderly lady as if greeting an old friend.

Dottie gasped, pressed her hand to her chest, and darted back inside.

Bryson glanced at me as if expecting an explanation for her strange behavior.

"Maybe she knows him, too." I glanced back toward my brother.

"Maybe." He gave me the same sort of look folks gave grieving family members at funerals. The facial expression equivalent to *I know you're in pain, but I have no idea how to help.* "Go on in, I'll wait for Buck."

"Thanks." I turned and headed across the yard.

Buck Oldham was the Chief of the local Cherokee tribe, and one of my grandfather's closest friends. After I'd come into my powers, Buck hadn't been my biggest fan. He'd come around eventually, and I'd forgiven his shenanigans. After all, had it not been for Buck insisting Bryson become my bodyguard, we never would have met.

It wasn't that I had anything against the guy, but I never knew which Buck we'd get. He could be sweet as Gram Mae's iced tea or as cantankerous as a rattle snake with a toothache.

I stopped and waved to the weathered old man as he stepped out of his equally weathered old truck.

"Is dinner at your place?" Eyes wide and his mouth set in a hard line, Buck stared past me to Killian on the stairs. He seemed to take an instant disliking to my new brother.

Bryson jogged to his side. "We're at Mae's. Tessa had some unexpected company."

Buck shot me a weird look before turning to Bryson.

In no hurry to face my great-grandmother, I watched the men until they disappeared into the little pink house.

Walking through my front door felt like going to the dentist. I knew I'd leave with what I needed, but eventually the numbness would wear off and it'd hurt like hell.

The man who had answers to my life-long questions stood next to the woman who'd been lying to me since birth. Killian was a stranger, but Gram Mae? I thought we'd aired out all of the family secrets after I shifted into the firebird for the first time.

Apparently not.

"This is my nephew?" Killian turned from a newly framed photo of my newborn son. It was one of those horrible baby mug shots they insist on taking in the hospital. Quin resembled a pink raisin in a blue crocheted cap, but I loved it just the same.

"Yep. It was taken a few days ago." I felt like Pandora about to open the box with the secrets of the universe inside.

Let's hope this turns out better for me than it did for her.

"What do you call him?" He motioned to the photo.

Gram Mae's expression brightened. "Quincy Emmet Charles, or Quin for short."

Hearing his name made me miss him. Not to mention, my boobs felt heavy. If I didn't speed things along, I'd have to take a mid-conversation nursing break.

"A strong Celtic name. Quin means an intelligent, wise, leader." He glanced back at the picture.

"Mae named him." I stared at my great-grandmother with a growing sense of suspicion. She'd helped Aaron and Bryson pick out the name. Charles after my grandfather, Emmet after Bryson's father, and Quincy after Aaron's dad. But I couldn't help but wonder if she'd suggested Quin as a nickname for another reason.

"I'd like to meet him," Killian said.

As much as I would have loved to have my son in my arms, my husbands' warnings that something wasn't quite right danced through my head. "You'd have to wrestle him away from his fathers."

Gram Mae shot to her feet. "I'll go get him."

"No." I spoke louder than I'd intended and backtracked. "We have things to discuss first."

"Of course." Killian gave me a wistful smile. "He's a lucky boy to have such a large family. There aren't many O'Roarkes left, I'm afraid."

The weight of his words hit me in the chest. No not his words, his *emotions*. Then again, that didn't seem right either. Something about the way he expressed himself seemed…rehearsed. "I'm sorry to hear that."

He waved me off with a flick of his hand. "Like humans, the Fae have experienced their fair share of war. It's all ancient history."

I had more important things to discuss than the history of the Aos Sí. Unfortunately, I wasn't the only one with questions.

He pointed to a candid shot of Bryson and Aaron with Jolene sandwiched in-between. "And the girl? Who is she?"

"That's Jolene. She's Aaron's biological daughter, but Bryson and I think of her as our own."

He seemed surprised by my declaration. "Is she Fae, too?"

"No." I didn't know him well enough to get into Jojo's past. Not too long ago, she'd witnessed her mother's murder, been haunted by a teenaged spirit, and that was just the start of the girl's troubles. Though she was human, she had the ability to not only speak to ghosts, but to control them.

"Hmm. Her eyes look Fae in this photo."

I had no idea what he was talking about. She had Aaron's Caribbean blue eyes. They were an unusual color, but I'd seen it before, hadn't I?

"Is she with…the woman in the pink house? She's your grandmother?" Killian seemed to choose his words carefully.

"Yes, but I call her Aunt Dottie." I wondered how much, if anything, Killian and our dad knew about the adopted side of my family tree. He'd seemed surprised to learn I called Darlene *Momma*, but he didn't question me referring to Mae as my great-grandmother. It'd broken my heart when I'd found out I wasn't related to Mae and the zillion or so cousins I'd grown up with. But I'd since learned, it took more than genetics to make a family.

"Right. Dottie. The human who married Atsila's father." He nodded to himself. "But you call her your aunt?"

"Tessa grew up believing Charlie was her uncle. She only learned he was her grandfather three years ago." Mae sat on the sofa and seemed to avoid my gaze.

"I grew up believing a lot of things that weren't true." The words fell out of my mouth before I could stop them. What could I say? I was hurt with a side-order of angry.

Gram Mae hung her head.

Killian continued the conversation as if oblivious to the tension between me and Gram Mae. "I don't think I'll ever get used to hearing him referred to as *Charlie*."

I felt like I was attending someone else's family reunion. "You knew him?"

Killian tilted his head and grinned. "Yes, but to me he was Cheasequah of the Red Paint clan, my *seanathair*."

I was fairly certain I'd never heard the word, but it seemed familiar to me somehow. "Your what?"

"My grandfather."

I held up a hand to buy a second or two. When he'd introduced himself as my brother, for some reason, I'd assumed he meant half-brother.

He watched me with a curious expression. "You did not realize we shared a mother as well as a father?"

"No, I didn't. I guess I should have asked, but I jumped to the wrong conclusion when I felt your magic." I found myself envying Killian for knowing both of our parents when I'd grown up without either.

As if she'd read my mind, Mae curled her shoulders forward. Guilty consciences could do that.

Killian glanced between us. "Forgive me. I can see I've made you both uncomfortable."

Rather than outright lying, I shook my head. "It's not your fault we were dealt very different hands."

He turned to me. "Don't envy me, Tessa. I would have preferred to grow up here with our grandfather. He must have been an amazing teacher for you to have both fire and air magic."

"Oh…he…never…" I didn't quite know how to break it to him that Charlie had died before he'd gotten around to telling me I was Fae, let alone teaching me anything about my magic.

Thankfully, Mae had no such problem. "Killian, Charlie bound most of Tessa's magic at birth to keep her safe."

He whipped his head in my direction. His expression morphed to something between shock and horror. "But you aren't bound now."

"No." I felt like I'd woken up in the Twilight Zone. Gram Mae hadn't bothered to tell me my grandfather had locked away my magic. I'd seen spirits my entire life, but the rest had appeared after I'd taken a shotgun blast to the chest, died, and risen as the firebird.

"The spell failed after his death." Mae wrung her hands. "Thank goodness, Bryson came along and helped her learn to control it."

"Bryson?" Killian scoffed. "His abilities are…primitive at best."

I'd heard enough for one day. It was one thing to show up and implode my world—it was another to insult the one man who'd helped me when no one else could. "Excuse me?"

Killian seemed to realize he'd overstepped. "Forgive me. I didn't mean to insult anyone."

"Then what did you mean to do?"

He glanced at Mae as if he thought she could save him. When she didn't, he sighed. "The wards outside and the silencing spell are rudimentary. A child in Tir Na Nog could do more."

I sat too stunned to speak, let alone process what he'd said. Up until a month ago, Bryson and I thought we were the only two Fae on the planet. Maybe we weren't as powerful as folks in Tir-Na-wherever-he-said-he-was-from, but at least we weren't judgmental A-holes.

Killian closed the distance between us and took my hands in his. "I've made a mistake. It was wonderful meeting you, Tessa, but you can't help me. I should go."

He was a stranger, but he'd managed to poke two of my buttons. Hell, he might as well have waved a red cape in front of a bull. First of all, I hated, absolutely positively loathed, when someone underestimated me. Killian Fancy-Pants O'Roarke didn't know squat about me or my magic. He had no way to know what I was, or was not, capable of.

Second, there was no way in hell I was letting him go without telling me what was going on with our father. Sure, I had more baggage than a transatlantic cruise liner, but the thought that he'd leave before I learned anything about my dad paralyzed me.

"Now you just wait a second." I jerked my hands back. "You're not going anywhere until you tell me where our dad is and what kind of trouble he's in."

CHAPTER 4

It might have been a sin, but I enjoyed Killian's shocked expression. Call me an optimist, but I doubted he'd underestimate me again. What I might—or might not have—lacked in magic, I made up for with determination.

Laughing, Gram Mae pushed to her feet. "You might want to do as she says. We might be primitive around here, but we've aren't afraid of kicking some fairy backside."

Killian's shoulders sagged, but he didn't make a run for it. I considered that a win.

Gram Mae squeezed my arm. "I owe you an apology and an explanation, but those will wait until you are done here."

I nodded and waited until she left before turning my attention back to my brother. Motioning to the spot Mae had vacated, I said, "Have a seat and tell me what kind of trouble our father is in."

Killian stared at the worn and slightly lumpy sofa as if it were a steaming pile of poo before perching on the edge of the cushion.

I felt like the country mouse meeting her city cousin for the first time. Or, in my case, fairy brother. However, I refused to make excuses or apologize for the way we lived. Bryson had plenty of money and Aaron and I had respectable jobs. We might not be part of a royal court, but we had a good life.

Holding my head high, I said, "Neither of us will know if I can help until you tell me what's going on."

"You're right." His arrogance seemed to melt away, leaving behind a vulnerability I hadn't seen, except when he'd hugged Gram Mae. "Liam... Dad...is a bit of a gambler, a common habit among the Leipreachán clan." Once again, Killian seemed to choose his words with care.

Outside of the one on the cereal box, I knew absolutely nothing about leprechauns. Rather than asking questions and risk him going off on a tangent, I nodded.

"There was a bet, and it looks like he'll serve one hundred years as the Queen's manservant." His face twisted in disgust. "His only hope of freedom is to escape to the human world."

"Okay..." I don't know what I'd expected him to say, but that wasn't it. "Is this the same queen that you work for?"

"Caoimhe. Yes." He spoke her name as if it were a curse word.

"One hundred years of slavery seems like a ridiculous thing to risk in a bet." Sure, Fae had much longer lifespans than humans, but I'd never really put a number to it.

"You'd be surprised what some people will wager." He sounded as though he spoke from personal experience.

While I would have loved to hear his story, now that I had him talking about our father, I needed to keep him on track. "Where is our dad now?"

"In Tir Na Nog." Killian must have picked up on my confusion because he added, "It's a land in another dimension."

"Like the spirit world?" I had some experience traveling beyond the veil, but it wasn't the kind of place I'd book a summer vacation. It was more of a monster-inhabited rest-stop for wayward spirits on the highway to Heaven or Hell.

He tilted his head. "I'm not familiar with the term, but I believe you're referring to the unseen layer of this world. Tir Na Nog is a separate place."

The explanation did nothing to help me understand. If anything, it created even more questions. *One problem at a time, Tessa.* "If this Kee-wah—"

"Caoimhe."

"Kee-Vah." I stressed each syllable. "If the queen won Liam in a bet, why would she harm him? Wouldn't that be like flushing her winnings down the toilet?"

He cringed, likely at my word choice. "It's complicated."

"Try me."

"Fae rulers have the ultimate authority in Tir Na Nog. They have a say in everything, including who lives and who dies." Once again, he seemed to have cherry picked his words.

I had the feeling he was tap-dancing around the real problem, but I didn't have enough information to read between the lines. "What aren't you telling me?"

"Dad and Caoimhe have a long unpleasant history." Killian lowered his gaze.

I was sick and tired of his evasiveness. Rather than prompting him with another question, I waited for him to continue.

Killian shifted his weight, glanced at me, and sighed. "Let's just say, you don't jilt a monarch and get away with it."

"Sounds like one of Gram Mae's soap operas." While I was certain there was much more to the story, I decided to let it go. For the moment anyway. "Why am I the only one who can help him escape?"

"Only blood relations may enter his chambers without permission from the queen." He leaned forward and rested his elbows on his knees. "I'm too well known at court. Caoimhe's guards watch my every move. They would arrest me the second I opened a portal. I'd hoped you could slip in unnoticed and bring him out."

I hated to disappoint him almost as much as I hated to admit he was right about me not being the right person for the job. "Killian, I'm sorry, but I don't know a thing about opening portals or royal courts, or the Fae for that matter. Other than having the right DNA, I'm no help to you."

"I could teach you the magic and court protocols…" He sighed.

"But I'm afraid it's more complicated than that. Your accent will draw too much attention. The moment you spoke, they would know you were from the human world."

My twang had been the cause of more than one problem. People heard it and automatically made assumptions about me and my intelligence. Still, I had to do something. This was my father we were talking about. If some evil queen had enslaved him, I wanted to help get him out. "What if I pretended to be mute? Or got a voice coach."

"I'm afraid there isn't time for that."

A hint of doubt about him returned. "You've been talking to Darlene. I'm surprised you didn't think I'd have an accent."

"I wasn't sure how close the two of you were. She claimed to be your manager." He flashed me his Hollywood smile. "And I wanted to meet my little sister."

Bryson came through the door, carrying two plates piled high with ribs, potato salad, baked beans, and homemade rolls. "Sorry to interrupt. I thought you two might be hungry."

Aaron followed him in with Quin in his arms. "And someone wants his mommy. Not only does he have your nose, he inherited your *hangry-ness*."

That he'd brought the baby when Killian was still there surprised me. I had no idea what had changed Aaron's attitude, but my money was on Gram Mae.

I stood and took Quin from his arms. The second his sweet baby smell hit me, I knew I had a problem. A big one. There was no way in this world, or Tir Na Nog, I was going to pull a Darlene and leave Quin to go on some adventure. Not to mention, Killian's plan sounded as dangerous as skinny dipping in a hot tub full of water moccasins. I wouldn't risk the little guy growing up without a mother.

Killian kept his distance, but his gaze never left the baby.

"Bryson, would you mind setting the table while I nurse Quin?" I was new to the breast-feeding thing and couldn't help but feel self-conscious.

Killian shot to his feet as if I'd zapped him. "No need. I should be going, but I would be honored if you'd allow me to hold my nephew for a few moments. Babies are rare in Tir Na Nog. Until recently, I believed you were the last Fae born."

My poor overstimulated brain couldn't handle any more new information, nor could I make sense of my jumbled thoughts enough to ask any more questions. "Oh."

Quin's unhappy noises morphed into a full-blown wail.

"Would you mind if we finished this conversation after he has a full belly?" I brought the infant to my shoulder and rocked back and forth in hopes of soothing him.

"Here, let me help." Killian moved to my side and rested his hand on Quin's back.

The baby quieted instantly. The little booger even turned in his new uncle's direction and struggled to hold his head up as if trying to get a better look.

I stood dumbstruck. "Did you bespell him?"

Grinning like an idiot, Killian bent down until he was eye level with Quin. "No, not exactly."

"Then what exactly?" Bryson stepped forward as if to shield his family from the newcomer. Between his size and his touch-him-again-and-I'll-strangle-you-with-your-own-intestines expression, most people would have cowered.

Evidently, Killian wasn't most people.

"Relax." Killian chuckled and made a goofy face at Quin. "He took a little of my magic when I touched him. He's starving for it. Why do you three keep your power under lock and key?"

Starving for magic? Is he kidding?

I moved closer to Bryson to put some distance between Quin and Killian. "We're raising him like any other child."

My brother's eyes widened. "You mean, like any other *human* child."

I didn't care for the way he was staring at us like we were imbeciles. "In case you missed it, we live here, in the human world."

"But he's Fae. He needs magic as much as he needs food, shelter, and love. It's how we learn to use our gifts. Without it, his power will wither and eventually fade."

Bryson and Aaron looked Killian over each in their own way. Bryson with a stoic curiosity, and Aaron with a *just the facts ma'am* detective's eye.

"Is that a bad thing?" My voice came out shakier than I would have liked. I hated the idea of withholding something Quin needed, but more than anything, I wanted him to grow up differently than I had—seeing spirits, never quite fitting in, feeling like a weirdo.

"Maybe it is." Aaron nodded at Quin. "That's the quietest he's been all day."

That he'd even contemplate feeding our son magic shocked me. Aaron was human. The only reason he had any gifts at all was because Bryson had given him a piece of his soul to save his life.

I'd had about enough of the conversation. "Quin is half-Fae, and we'll raise him as we see fit."

"Half?" Killian glanced between my hubbies and pressed his lips together.

What the heck was that about?

"Forgive me. I didn't mean to overstep my bounds. I should go. I have things to attend to at home." Killian gave Quin one last longing look before turning to leave.

"Wait. You're leaving? We haven't had much time to talk, and there's food. Are you hungry?" The idea of him disappearing with no way to contact him gave me a case of verbal diarrhea. "How can I reach you? I need your number? You live in Tir Na Nog right? Do cell phones even work there?"

"I'll be in touch." He made a zigzag pattern with his hand and the room filled with a blueish tinged light. When it dimmed, he was gone.

And Quin started crying.

CHAPTER 5

*A*aron hurried to the window. "Well I'll be damned. He left his car here."

"I'm not sure where to even begin." Bryson sank onto the couch.

At least one of my hubbies seemed more concerned with what had just happened than the Lamborghini.

I plopped down in my easy chair to nurse Quin. "I meant what I said. I want this little guy to have a chance to grow up like a normal kid."

Bryson nodded

Aaron rolled his lips in—a sure sign he disagreed. "As the only human in the room, I'll play the devil's advocate. You see magic as a burden. I see it as an asset. Besides, do we really want to deprive our son of something he needs?"

I opened my mouth to argue, but Bryson set his hand on my thigh and shook his head

"Actually, you're both right, but I'm not sure it's as cut and dry as Killian made it sound." Bryson glanced between us. "I grew up surrounded by magic, but Tessa didn't."

Aaron motioned to me. "She had Charlie, and she's been able to speak to spirits since childhood."

I hated when they talked about me as if I wasn't in the room, especially when they didn't know what the heck they were talking about. "Actually, I was with Darlene and her third husband in Tallahassee until I was two."

"But you never lost your magic." Aaron paced like a lawyer on a bad TV drama.

"Exactly my point. I don't think his magic will fade as quickly as Killian made it seem." Bryson leaned down and kissed the baby's head. "I'd rather find a way to keep his gifts under control until he's old enough to make this decision for himself."

"I can get behind that." Aaron flashed us a grin and turned his attention back to the flashy car in the driveway.

I wanted to point out that I had to take a bullet to the heart for my magic to roar to life, but I didn't want to give Aaron more ammunition. "I need to summon Charlie. I'll ask him about Quin's magic after I get some answers about Killian and my dad."

Bryson took the sleeping baby from my arms. "Eat something first. I'll take care of Quin."

"I won't be able to stomach food until I talk to Charlie." I headed into the office Bryson and I used when members of the tribe would stop by for healings.

We'd put an end to the visits before Quin was born. I'd focused on my work at the police department, and Bryson had opened shop at the tribal house. But we'd kept the office intact for emergencies.

Maddie, our chocolate Lab, and arguably the dumbest dog in the history of dumb dogs, had claimed the room. She was curled up in her dog bed, but hopped to her feet when I walked into the office. Her tongue hanging out one side of her mouth, she tilted her head and burped.

"Excuse you." I wrinkled my nose.

Maddie rolled onto her back. Arms and legs in the air like a dead cockroach, she wiggled around making pig sounds.

I had two choices, toss her into the hall and risk her scratching and whining at the door, or let her stay and risk her distracting me during the summoning.

I let her stay. Worst case scenario, she'd make enough racket to alert Bryson if something, or someone, besides Charlie crossed the veil.

I pulled a jar of salt down from the top shelf and got to work. After drawing a four feet wide circle with the salt, I grabbed Charlie's notebook of spells from the drawer and settled into the center of the circle.

I could have done things the easy way and called out his name in the hopes he'd appear. However, easy didn't come with a guarantee. I didn't have time to sit around and wait. We had things to discuss, and dang it, I didn't want to take a chance on him ignoring me.

Lowering my shields, I let my magic flow through the room and called on the five elements—earth, water, fire, air, and spirit. I felt, rather than saw, the magical circle snap into place. It wouldn't keep my magic contained but it would keep anything that came over from the other side of the veil trapped inside—with me.

I closed my eyes and chanted, "Charles Nokoseka, your blood calls to you. Come into this circle. Charles Nokoseka, hear my plea. Come."

I chanted the summoning a dozen more times but nothing happened.

On the verge of giving up, I raised my hands and formed an image of the thick inky veil that separated the physical and spirit worlds. "Charlie, please. I need to talk to you. Come."

Maddie jumped up from her bed and growled deep in her throat. A ridge of fur stood upright like a shark fin between her shoulder blades, but she hadn't barked.

I took that as a good sign.

"Hell Girl! Long time no see." Gavin Partridge's spirit materialized in front of me. Sitting cross-legged, he floated a few inches off the ground.

"Gavin!" I threw my arms around him, or tried to—they went right through him.

He laughed his stage-performer's laugh, loud and flamboyant. "Easy there, sugar. I'm not tied to this world anymore. It'll take me a smidge to solidify."

I'd met Gavin after he had been murdered by a crazed ex-lover, who just happened to have ties to the Las Vegas mafia. He'd haunted me day and night until I'd agreed to help him. Together with Aaron and Bryson, we'd put the Christmas Killer, and his associates, away for a very long time and freed Gavin's spirit.

Maddie edged closer, sniffed the circle, and returned to her bed.

"Why are you here?" I didn't mean to sound ungrateful, but I'd called Charlie.

"Your grandfather sent me." Gavin motioned to the ceiling. "He's a little busy, but he sends his regards."

Sends his regards? Is he serious?

"It's really good to see you, but I need to speak to Charlie or Atsila." I hated the whine in my voice, but Gavin had a way of bringing out the worst in me.

"I know more than you might think about your predicament." Gavin motioned to my curls. "Do that thing with your hair, and I'll dish."

I didn't have time to put on a dog and flaming pony show. I needed to get some answers before Quin's next feeding. "If you know as much as you say you do, then you *know* I need answers."

He raised his brows and pressed his lips together.

"Fine." I drew the firebird to the surface enough that the tips of my hair and my pupils turned to flames—the trick had earned me the cringe-worthy nickname when we'd first met

Gavin wrapped his arms around his middle and laughed. "Oh, Hell Girl, I've missed you."

Stop calling me that." I swatted him, and this time, I made contact for a split second before my hand slid through him. "Does Charlie know anything about my father?"

"Straight to the point. Some things never change." Gavin sobered. "Liam is in Tir Na Nog. He's not allowed to leave because of a bet."

Killian had told me that much.

I needed to ask better questions. Spirits, even the familiar ones, tended to take things literally—like they lost all sense of nuance after they died. "How do I get him out?"

Gavin's game-show host smile faded. "You can't. Not until the bet is finished."

"That's a hundred years."

He didn't reply.

I threw my hands up and groaned. "I give up. You tell me what I need to know."

"Thought you'd never ask." Gavin tapped a finger to his chin. "Let's see...Charlie said to tell you, things are not always as they seem. You're never truly alone. Last, but not least—lies can be the truth, and the truth can be a lie."

I wanted to strangle him, but that would have been bad for many reasons. First off, I didn't think he was solid enough to choke. Secondly, he'd died by strangulation with a set of Christmas lights. Somehow, I didn't think he'd appreciate a repeat performance.

"That's it?" I shook my head. "Nothing about my dad having a queen for a stalker or why Charlie bound my magic or if we're depriving our child?"

"Nope." Gavin frowned and leaned closer as if to share a secret. "Your grandfather's a great guy, but he's not much of a talker."

"Thanks for coming. It was great seeing you again, but we're done here." I shot to my feet. "Don't be a stranger."

Gavin's mouth fell open and he pressed his hand to his chest in mock indignation. "I've come all this way, and you're not even going to introduce me to your children?"

I hung my head.

He lifted my chin, and when I met his gaze all of the humor had left his expression. "Tessa, you and yours are in a world of trouble. I promised you, I'd come back if you ever needed me. And make no mistake about it, Hell Girl, you need me."

I wasn't buying it.

"What kind of trouble?" I had the spirit trapped inside the circle, and I didn't intend to let him go until he started talking.

"I can't say." Gavin turned to go and slammed against the magical wall keeping him where I wanted him.

"Why?" My gaze fell on Charlie's notebook. I had half a mind to thumb through it for a truth spell, but I doubted I'd find anything that would work on a ghost.

He sighed the sigh parents had been using since children were invented. "I can't tell you that either. There are rules."

"What kind of rules?" I'd been talking to spirits since I was a child and this was the first I'd ever heard of such a thing.

"You're going to have to trust me." He pressed his spectral hands against the barrier like a mime, only this was no imaginary box. "There'll be hell to pay if I break them. Real hell. Not just flaming hair and glowing eyes."

I wanted to pitch a hissy fit, but I doubted it'd do any good. Gavin, for all of his faults, was a good guy and a friend. If he said he couldn't tell me what was going on, he had his reason. "Charlie sent you to help me?"

"Yes." Gavin glanced over his shoulder. "But I can't do much inside this bubble."

I smeared the salt line, breaking the circle. "How do you intend to help me when you can't tell me what's going on?"

He stepped over the salt, smoothed his linen jacket and slacks, and ran a hand through his hair. "Simple. I'll be your Jiminy Cricket."

"My what?" I'd grown up near Orlando. Disney was a part of our culture. I knew the cartoon character, but I didn't understand the reference.

"The angel on your shoulder. Your conscience." Gavin moved his hand in a small circle. "Your dead life-coach. Your ghostest-with-the mostest."

I felt a migraine coming on. Pressing my fingers into my temples, I asked, "And how do you propose to do that?"

"You and I will be joined together like Peter Pan and his shadow."

I wasn't impressed with the notion or his analogy. "Peter had to sew his shadow to himself to keep it from running away."

Gavin tapped his chin as if trying to think of a better example. "Fine. I'll follow you around and make sure you don't do anything to make matters worse."

I could barely manage to get through a day with my sanity as it was. A couple hours of Gavin following me around, and I'd break out in stress hives. Plus, Jolene could see spirits. She'd only recently stopped talking to ghosts in public. Being a preteen was hard enough. She didn't need people thinking she was nuts, too. Then there were the guys to think about, and TJ, and Quin.

"Absolutely not." I shook my head. "Not going to happen."

"Relax. You won't even know I'm here." He batted his lashes.

"Uh huh."

He folded his arms. "I'm not going anywhere, so you may as well get used to the idea of having a houseguest."

"Mom?" Jolene knocked on the office door. "Are you okay in there?"

Maddie raised her head, glanced from me, to the door, and finally to Gavin.

"I'll be right there." My voice came out on the wrong side of hysterical. The last thing I needed was for her to catch me summoning a spirit when we'd forbidden her from doing the same thing.

"I need to talk to you. It's...important." Something in her tone made the hair on the back of my neck stand at attention.

"Be right there." I kicked the salt under the bed and dresser and motioned like a wild-woman for Gavin to disappear.

Jojo turned the door knob. "Why do you sound weird? Are you okay?"

The ghost glanced around the room and did a double take at the chocolate Lab curled up in her dog bed. "I'll be close."

"What do you mean?" I had a feeling I wasn't going to like Gavin's answer.

"Who's in there with you?" She rattled the knob. "I can feel your magic. Are you talking to a spirit?"

Shit.

I gave Gavin one last pleading look, crossed the room, and threw the door open. "Just finishing up a spell."

He vanished.

The dog half-howled and half-yipped before curling up again.

I glanced back at Maddie and opened the door.

Jojo did a quick sweep of the room. "What kind of spell?"

"I was asking for patience and help with the baby." I hadn't lied, not outright.

She rolled her eyes. "That's praying."

"Right, sort of." I drew a breath and reminded myself I was smarter than a ten-year-old. "What did you need to talk to me about?"

"I forgot." She shrugged and walked out of the room.

CHAPTER 6

Three days had gone by and whatever trouble was coming for us had yet to arrive.

Unless Gavin was talking about family drama—*that* I had in spades.

Other than to eat and nap, Quin hadn't stopped crying. Sleep was something that happened to other people. Gram Mae and I had been avoiding each other. Neither of us seemed eager to have that heart-to-heart conversation. In short, running off to Tir Na Nog didn't sound like such a bad idea.

Worst still, I hadn't heard a peep from Killian, or the spirit who'd sworn to stay close. Not that I minded, Aaron and Bryson had mixed feelings about Gavin Partridge standing in for Charlie like a second-string quarterback.

I stared out the kitchen window and went through the motions of doing the breakfast dishes. Lately, I spent most of my time on autopilot, barely aware of the goings on around me. Case in point, I was vaguely aware of Aaron pacing the room while he spoke on the phone.

"…Right, but that's three murders in as many days." Aaron dropped into a kitchen chair.

The word *murders* caught my attention. He had to be talking to Samuels, his partner. Before Quin had been born, we'd agreed Aaron, Bryson, and I would take an extended maternity leave. In my mind, that meant Aaron would have more than a week and a half off work.

"Keep me informed. Any word on the *other* matter?" He went quiet, only replying with the occasional *mm-hmms* and *uh huhs*.

"Mom, I remembered what I was going to tell you the other day." Jolene whisper-shouted from the doorway. "I need cookies for the youth group bake sale."

I assumed she was attempting to be quiet because her father was on a call.

Unlike my daughter, I didn't give a rat's backside about interrupting him. "Homemade or store bought?"

"Homemade please."

Maddie rushed into the room and glanced around as if looking for said cookies. When she realized there were no treats to be had, she made a disgruntled sound and climbed into the chair next to Jojo. Sitting upright with her paws on the table like a person, she flashed me a doggie grin.

"Get down from there." I pointed at the floor.

The dog rolled her eyes, jumped down, and curled up at Jojo's feet.

"I'll be in touch." Aaron slammed his cell phone on the dining room table. "Son of a—" He shot Jojo a guilty look before turning to me. "That shiny red sportscar Killian left in our driveway?"

The soapy plate slipped from my hand, and I hung my head. "Let me guess. It's not registered to a Killian O'Roarke."

The dog growled.

Great. Even Maddie has an issue with my new brother.

"Nope. It belongs to a movie mogul. The last time he saw it was in a garage in Miami." Aaron stood and moved to my side. "That's not the worst part."

I didn't want to ask. I really didn't. I'd had enough *worst parts* to last me a lifetime. "What is?"

"I've spoken to everyone from the FBI to Interpol. Killian O'Roarke doesn't exist." Aaron went on about his law enforcement contacts, and how he had no idea how to explain the stolen car out front, but I tuned him out.

It made sense that a Fae who lived in another dimension wouldn't have a record in the human world. However, it didn't excuse the fact Killian was a thief. A thief who'd left his expensive Italian mess for me to clean up.

Jolene backed out of the kitchen without a word. I'd noticed her tiptoeing around the grown-ups a lot lately. Not that I blamed her. We were all one crisis away from a breakdown.

Thankfully, Maddie followed her.

"I mean it, Tessa. I don't care who he is, his four-leaf-clover-loving ass isn't welcome here." Aaron paced the kitchen. "On second thought, if he ever contacts you again, invite him over so I can arrest him."

Rather than comment, I turned my attention back to the pile of dirty breakfast dishes. This wasn't the first time I'd heard Aaron's opinion about my brother. Bryson, Aaron and I hadn't stopped debating what to do about Killian since he'd vanished from our living room.

Between our arguing and Quin's colic, it was no wonder we'd turned into sleep-deprived zombies.

Aaron's foul mood had as much to do with the stress inside the house as Killian, but I wasn't about to point that out.

I nodded toward the hall where Jolene had slipped away. "Could you spend a little time with Jojo today? I'm worried about her. She's been talking to the dog like Maddie's her only friend."

His scowl melted into a frown. "I'll try, but I need to do some research on a case Samuels is working on. Possible serial killer—"

The thread holding my sanity snapped. "Oh no you don't, mister. We're on maternity leave. The only crazy lunatic you need to focus on is me."

"I know, I know, but this one is—"

I pressed my hands to my ears and sung "Who's Afraid of the Big Bad Wolf." Childish? You bet, but I had no intention of getting sucked into the gory details of a murder investigation.

Aaron folded his arms and waited for me to stop. The second I dropped my hands, he said, "Funny you should mention wolves. One of the victims was allegedly attacked by a wolf."

That got my attention. "Then why does Samuels think it's a serial killer?"

His grin told me he knew he had me. "In each of the cases, witnesses reported seeing the victims speaking to a tall, dark-haired man moments before the animal attacked."

"I'm not following you. What does the dark-haired guy have to do with the wolves?"

He shrugged. "That's what we're trying to figure out. The witnesses saw the animal attacks, but we haven't recovered any remains to verify the causes of death."

"That's…disturbing, but I'm sure Samuels can handle the case." I turned back to the sink. "When were you going to tell me you ran a background check on Killian?"

Aaron sighed and moved behind me. Massaging my shoulders, he whispered, "I didn't want to upset you. I was hoping there wouldn't be anything to report."

As good as his fingers felt pressing into my tight muscles, I jerked away. "So you weren't going to tell me at all? He's my brother. You should have discussed it with me."

"Would you have told me not to look into him?"

I opened my mouth to answer but snapped it shut. I had no idea how to answer. My feelings about Killian ranged from never wanting to see him again to hoping he'd return with a better plan to rescue our father.

Bryson joined us in the kitchen with a crying baby on his shoulder. "Tessa, why aren't you ready to go?"

Dang it.

I'd forgotten about Quin's pediatrician appointment, but I wasn't about to admit it. Instead, I motioned to my clothing with a soapy hand. "I *am* ready to go. You were taking forever, so I decided to do the dishes."

He glanced from my worn-out yoga pants, to the oversized T-shirt I'd practically lived in during the last trimester of my pregnancy, to my frizzy red curls. "Right. We should leave or we're going to hit I-4 traffic."

I could have pointed out that once upon a time before Quin was born, he would have told me I was beautiful no matter what I had on. Or the fact that until that moment, he hadn't as much as looked at me in the past week. Or that despite the fact I'd given birth, died, and risen from the dead as a firebird, I was still hormonal. Instead, I grabbed my purse and marched to the living room.

Quin stopped screaming long enough to spit up all over the front of Bryson's black button-up.

The big guy glanced down, shook his head, and headed for the bedroom—muttering Cherokee curses the entire way.

Aaron trailed behind me. "I mean it, Tessa. He's not welcome here. Grand theft auto is serious business."

"I heard you the first time, Cranky McCrankster." I swung the front door open to find Gram Mae on the doorstep with her hand raised as if to knock. "Sorry, I didn't hear you out there."

She pressed her hand to her chest. "My goodness, child. You scared the daylights out of me."

Aaron rounded the corner. Evidently, he didn't see Gram Mae standing there, or he didn't care, because he continued his mini-tirade. "Since when do we call each other names in this house? And for the record, I am not cranky."

Gram Mae arched an eyebrow. "You sure about that? You're acting like someone licked the red off your candy."

Aaron had the good sense to dip his chin and glance away.

"Mmm hmm. That's what I thought." Shaking her head, she walked into the house, glanced around at the mess and frowned. "Tank called. He's coming by to talk later this afternoon."

"Did he say what about?" My chest tightened. Call it instinct or experience, but I had a feeling Tank planned to dump his son on Gram Mae and leave town. After being released from jail, he'd acted squirrely—the same way Darlene used to before she dropped me at Charlie and Dottie's and disappeared for months on end.

"No, but I'd like for you to be there just the same. Come over after

Quin's doctor appointment." Judging by the tired sag of her shoulders, she had the same concerns over Tank. "It's about time you and I sat down and talked about Killian."

While I hated to add more items to my don't-want-to-do list, I knew I couldn't put it off forever. "Will do."

"Dottie said to give you this." She handed me a mason jar.

I held the glass container of yellowish-brown water to the light. "What the heck is it?"

"Open it." The mischievous glint in her eyes worried me.

I knew I'd regret it, but I unscrewed the lid and inhaled. The pungent odors of onions and something akin to dead opossum filled my nose and throat. "Ugh, gross. What am I supposed to do with this?"

Bryson returned, wearing a clean shirt and carrying a squirming, crying baby. "Good morning, Mae."

She ignored him and went straight for Quin. Her taking him from us was nothing new. He'd spent almost as much time in her arms as ours, but this time...This time she dropped him.

Thankfully, Bryson caught him before he hit the floor.

The baby's wailing hit tornado siren volume, but I didn't think he was injured. More than likely, the short free-fall had scared him. From the looks of it, it'd done the same to my great-grandmother. Her skin had gone two shades past pale, and she was cradling her arm.

Jolene and the dog ran into the room, both with wide eyes. Jojo took in the scene and pressed her back to the wall.

"Gram? Are you okay?" I took her by the shoulders and guided her to the couch. "Sit. You don't look so good."

"I didn't hurt him, did I?" Her voice shook as she glanced at Bryson and the baby.

"No, he's fine." Bryson's expression told me he'd thought the same thing I had. Something was very, very wrong. "Gram Mae, have you checked your blood pressure today?"

She waved her hand in his direction. "Don't worry about me. I'm healthy as a horse."

I didn't believe her. "You don't look it. Did you check your sugar?

How about your heart medication? Did you take it this morning?" I nodded at Aaron. "Call Dottie and have her check."

"The three of you can stop mother-henning me. I pulled a muscle in my shoulder while weeding the garden." She stood a little slower than normal. "I brought onion water for Quin. It helps with colic."

The devil would sell snow cones to polar bears before I fed my child that mess, but I knew better than to argue. "Thanks, Gram."

"Onion water?" Aaron sniffed the jar and made a sour face. "Whoa, this'll clear out your sinuses all right."

Bryson didn't look amused. "Tessa, Aaron and I can handle the appointment. Why don't you stay and help Mae with an ice pack?"

"Aaron can do it. I want to hear what the doctor has to say." I appreciated what he was trying to do, but I wasn't about to stay behind. The second I'd learned I was pregnant, I'd promised myself I wouldn't be like Darlene. I wouldn't drop my child off on Gram Mae and Dottie's doorstep and disappear. I wouldn't miss a single thing in my child's life. Nope, I'd be there for every milestone, good day, and skinned knee. Even if that meant leaving my beloved great-grandmother in Aaron's hands.

"What did I just say?" Gram Mae planted her hands on her hips. "I'm fine. Go to the pediatrician, all three of you. Me and Jolene have plans to plant the fall vegetables this morning."

Jojo nodded and faked a smile. "Yes, ma'am. We do, but if you're sick…"

"Don't you start, too." Gram Mae pointed at the girl. "We'll get to work once you're finished with your math lesson."

Jojo attended virtual school. Her ability to speak to the dead freaked out her classmates and her teachers too much for her to be in a regular classroom. She'd seriously slacked off on her lessons since her baby brother had been born, but I wasn't about to tell Gram Mae that.

Aaron ran his hand over the back of his neck. "I'll skip this one and help out. I'd planned to mend the fence while home on maternity leave."

While I didn't approve of lying, I wanted to hug him. He'd already replaced the rotted planks. My sweet, and sometimes cranky husband had fibbed to save an old-lady's pride.

Gram Mae glanced between us as if she planned to argue but seemed to change her mind. "Good. I could use some help with the wheelbarrow."

"We need to get going." I grabbed the diaper bag and hurried to the porch before anything else could happen.

Gram Mae called after me, "Tessa Marie, make sure you ask that fancy pediatrician about the onion water. It's worked for hundreds of years. It'll work now."

"Yes ma'am." I slid behind the wheel while Bryson strapped Quin into his car seat.

Without a word, he climbed into the SUV and stared straight ahead. He had to be thinking the same thing as me, but neither of us seemed ready to admit our fears.

I waited until we reached the edge of the property before I broke the uneasy silence. "She's sick, isn't she?"

"Her aura is much fainter than it was a month or so ago." He squeezed my thigh. "I believe the only thing keeping her going right now is sheer stubbornness."

My chest tightened at the thought of losing her. "We have to do something. I mean we have all of this magic. There has to be something we can do."

Bryson cleared the emotion from his throat. "Even magic has its limitations. There is a natural order to things that cannot be changed."

"Can't be or shouldn't be changed?"

"Does it matter?" He pressed his lips into a tight line and turned his head, but not before I saw a tear rolling down his cheek.

CHAPTER 7

The visit with the pediatrician was a complete waste of time. After a few questions about Quin's symptoms, drawing blood, obtaining a urine sample, and poking around, he'd diagnosed the baby with colic.

Tell me something I don't already know, like how to fix it.

Aaron met us in the driveway, looking rather peppy with his freshly shaved face and clean clothes. "What'd the doctor say?"

Resisting the urge to bark at him for having the audacity to relax while we were away, I tapped my chin. "Well, let's see. He told me to nurse longer on each breast, but not overfeed."

Aaron wrinkled his brow. "How does that work?"

"Heck if I know." I leaned against the car and inhaled the warm afternoon air. "He also told me to avoid dairy, cabbage, beans, spicy foods, and anything that causes gas. Oh, and onions."

"So much for Gram Mae's miracle cure." He drew me into an embrace.

I sagged against him enjoying his clean-man scent. "I have no intention of feeding our son something that smells like roadkill."

Bryson rounded the car with Quin fussing in his carrier. "She's not supposed to drink caffeine either."

Aaron gasped in mock horror. "Forget colic. Tessa without coffee is a threat to national security."

"Ha ha." I hated to move. In fact, I could have fallen asleep standing in his arms, but I needed to feed Quin. "How's Gram Mae?"

Aaron glanced toward the empty garden. "She decided to take a nap rather than plant veggies."

"Good." I followed the guys up the porch steps. Nothing felt *good* about the situation, but at least she'd taken it easy for a couple of hours.

Aaron opened the front door for us. "Mae's expecting you."

"I know, but I need to feed Quin first." I turned to Bryson and held my arms out for the little one. "Hand him over and go take a nap."

He'd seemed distracted since we'd left the doctor's office. Not surprising, considering we were both worried sick and running on a couple hours of sleep.

Welcome to parenthood.

Maddie padded into the living room, sniffed each of us once, and Aaron twice. I couldn't blame her. He was the only one who'd had a shower.

Bryson lifted Quin from his carrier but hesitated. "This all started after Killian visited."

"Right." I braced myself for another discussion about feeding Quin magic. "But you heard what the doctor said—colic usually starts in babies a week or so old."

He nodded, but his stoic expression told me he didn't agree. "Hear me out, okay?"

"I can't hear anything over his crying. Give him to me." I made grabby hands.

Bryson set the infant in my arms. "I don't know why I didn't think of this before, but could this be a spell?"

Maddie let out a little *woof* and proceeded to circle me and the baby like a freaking shark. She stopped, stared, barked again, and continued to walk around us until Aaron pulled her out of the way.

"You think Killian put a crying spell on our baby?" I settled into the recliner, freed a breast, and started the process of trying to entice Quin to latch on.

"The guy did steal a four-hundred-thousand-dollar car." Aaron glanced out the window at the bright red bane of his existence.

I'd known the car was expensive, but Lord in heaven. "You're kidding? They cost that much?"

Aaron smirked. "It's a wonder a rainbow hasn't appeared in our front yard. It's worth as much as a pot of gold."

Maddie groaned and covered her eyes with her paws.

What the heck is up with that dog?

Bryson made a sound in the back of his throat, impatience mixed with frustration. "I don't know if he did or didn't do something to Quin, but I intend to find out."

"Can you do it after he's finished nursing? It's the only time he's quiet." I ran my fingertips over his fuzzy little head and smiled. Fussy or not, I was completely and totally in love with the little guy.

"Sure. That'll give me time to get a quick shower." He wandered down the hall with the dog following. A few seconds later, Bryson shouted, "Out!"

The Lab rejoined us in the living room.

Enjoying the few moments of bonding time, I closed my eyes. Unfortunately, Aaron's hovering made it impossible for me to relax. I cracked one eye open. "Everything okay?"

"Just watching the two of you thinking, I'm a lucky man." He eased onto the arm of my chair and nudged Quin's hand. The baby wrapped his tiny little fingers around his daddy's and sighed against me.

"Spoken like someone who got a nap." I rested my head back and closed my eyes again.

"I'm sorry I was so…difficult this morning."

"I think we all get a pass on our crabbiness for the next month or so." The only thing keeping me awake was the fear of drooling on the baby or dropping him.

The thought reminded me of my great-grandmother. "I hate it, but I'm worried about Gram Mae holding him unsupervised."

Aaron tensed, but nodded. "I'll let you have *that* conversation with her."

I figured the job would fall on my shoulders—she was my kin after all—but I couldn't help teasing him. "Why me? She likes you better, Detective Blue Eyes."

Jolene shrieked loud enough to startle the baby. "Dad? There's a spider in my room!"

Fumbling to get Quin on my shoulder, I said, "Go. You know she's terrified of them."

Aaron shot into action, and so did the dang dog.

Honestly, the girl could stare down the scariest of spirits without flinching, but the second an eight-legged friend crossed her path, she went into hysterics.

I lowered Quin to my other breast, and I knew I had a problem. His face turned stop sign red, and his little lip quivered. I had to act fast, or I'd never get him calmed down enough to finish his meal. "Shhh...it's okay, sweet pea. Daddy's taking care of Jojo."

His mouth hung open several heartbeats before he let loose a scream that rivalled a banshee.

Try as I might, I couldn't get him to take a nipple. I gave up and burped him. He let loose a huge one but cried right through it.

Patting his hiney didn't work. Rocking him didn't work. Pacing the floor while feeling like the world's worst mother didn't work.

Alone, exhausted, and desperate, I panicked and lowered the imaginary shields that kept my magic contained. I had no idea how Killian had fed him, but I was determined to give Quin anything and everything I could to calm him.

Quin continued to cry. If anything, he grew louder.

I didn't want to hurt him or light him up like the fourth of July, so I pushed a tiny beat of magic through our skin-to-skin contact. Or tried to. It felt like shooting a squirt gun against a brick wall. The magic splattered across his skin and dissipated.

"Tessa? Is he finished?" Bryson called from the hall.

Guilt overwhelmed me. The last thing I wanted was for Bryson to walk into the room and sense my magic. Hell, I'd be lucky if he hadn't felt it already. "Yep! I'll bring him to you."

I walked into the bedroom just as Bryson was pulling on a T-shirt.

He glanced from me to the baby. "Everything okay?"

"Peachy. Let's get this over with." I set Quin on the king-sized bed and settled beside him. My guilt became palpable. So much so, I could barely look at Bryson.

He either didn't notice or didn't push it. "I'm going to focus my attention on rooting out any spells, but I need you to keep an eye on him while I do it."

"Gotcha. It's the same process we use on adults, right?" My voice came out strained.

"Yes, but I need you to relax." He held his hand an inch over the screaming infant's head.

I drew a deep breath and did my best to resist the urge to comfort our child. It killed me to hear Quin cry and know, that even for a few moments, I couldn't touch him.

Quin turned his head toward me and stared as if begging me to pick him up.

I leaned closer so that he could see my face, but I didn't dare speak for fear I'd break Bryson's concentration. Not that I thought the mystical scan would hurt him, but I didn't want to have to start over and prolong Quin's misery.

Hurry up. Please. Hurry up.

By the time he reached Quin's feet, I thought I'd come out of my skin. "Well?"

Shaking his head, Bryson cuddled Quin to his chest. "Nothing, but if I didn't know better, I'd swear he was fighting me."

"Maybe he is." I didn't doubt it for a second. Even at two-weeks old, the child had a strong will. Then again, we'd experienced a similar situation before with an adult woman suffering from a dark curse. "Could this be like what Betty Mathews had?"

He seemed to consider the question. "No. Even with Betty, we felt magic on her."

My mind raced with awful possibilities. "Betty was cursed by a human magic user. What if Fae powers work different? What if we're in so far over our heads we don't even know what to look for?"

"It's possible, but unlikely." He turned for the door.

"I'm serious. We don't know what we don't know about the other Fae. Killian was able to hear through the privacy spell the other day, and he checked out the wards." Be it my lack of sleep, lack of caffeine, or lack of common sense, I blurted out the absolute worst thing possible. "He said our spells were rudimentary and primitive."

I'd said *our* in hopes of softening the blow.

"Is that so?" Bryson's shoulders fell as if I'd broken his heart. Without turning back to me, he said, "I'll reach out to Harrison. Unless, you don't trust him either?"

"I trust you absolutely and completely." I walked to him, took his free hand, and brought it to my lips the same way he did each and every time he apologized to me. "I shouldn't have said anything."

"I'm not an egomaniac. I can admit your brother's magic is far stronger than mine." A ghost of a smile curved his lips. "But that doesn't mean I like it."

"Don't take any of this personally. It's the fear talking."

Cupping my cheek, he said, "And the exhaustion."

I closed my eyes and focused on the warmth of his skin, the unquestionable knowledge he was my mate, one-third of a whole, my world. "I love you."

"I love you, too." He leaned forward and pressed his brow to mine. "We'll get through this. We've faced down much worse than a colicky baby."

"Speaking of worst things, I need to go talk to Gram Mae."

"Remember. Sweet tea has caffeine. Take a box of decaf herbal with you." Bryson winked.

The heck with herbal tea. I'd need a half dozen shots of whiskey to get through this conversation.

CHAPTER 8

I'd majored in Marriage and Family Therapy in grad school, but nothing—and I mean nothing—prepared me to deal with my crazy family. If anything, my education made it worse.

As a kid, I knew we weren't like the folks on television, but I didn't understand how messed up we were. Sitting at my great-grandmother's kitchen table, I realized just how dysfunctional we were. "Could you repeat that?"

Gram Mae curled in on herself. "Charlie swapped you with Darlene's baby and bound your magic to hide you from the other Fae."

I nodded slowly. "Why did I need to be hidden?"

She met my eyes and dropped a bomb. "Because Atsila was murdered before you were born."

Gawking, I sat back to put some distance between us, or maybe distance between me and the truth. "How is that possible?"

"She was attacked while still pregnant. Charlie delivered you after your mother took her last breath." Gram Mae blew out a tired sigh.

I stared into my mug because I couldn't bring myself to meet her gaze. I didn't want her pity or even her understanding. What I wanted was to scream and yell and demand she tell me why she'd lied to me my entire life.

"At the time, he wasn't sure who sent the assassin to kill Atsila…" She kept talking but I'd stopped listening after the word *assassin*.

My mother wasn't just murdered. She was assassinated?

Gram Mae patted my hand. "I know this is a lot to take in."

I bit back an ugly reply. "Did he find out who ordered her killed?"

Her patient smile made me wonder if she'd answered the question, and I'd missed it. "No. Charlie suspected Caoimhe or her father, but Liam convinced him they didn't do it."

"Do you know who Liam suspected?"

She shook her head.

I took a sip of tea to give myself time to sort through my rushing thoughts. "So my dad knows about me?"

She glanced away. "He knew Atsila was expecting his child but assumed the baby died with her."

White spots danced before my eyes. I'm not sure if I set the mug down or dropped it. Either way, it crashed to the floor.

Gram Mae stood, but rather than grabbing the dishtowel, she took my hand and urged me to stand. "Let's sit in the Florida room where it's warm."

I didn't move. It didn't matter where we sat. No amount of sunshine was going to take the chill out of my bones. "Why? Why would Charlie let his son-in-law believe he'd not only lost a mate, but a child?"

"Tessa, I know this is hard, but you have to understand." She eased back into her chair. "Charlie had just lost his daughter. He didn't know who'd ordered her killed. He couldn't risk your safety."

I glanced up at the hitch in her voice. "He thought my father had something to do with it?"

"No. Never. Not directly." She folded and unfolded her hands. "Liam was engaged to the queen when he met your mom."

A flash of a memory crossed my mind. "Killian said something about not being able to get away with jilting a monarch."

Gram Mae pressed her lips into a tight line as if irritated with Killian or the conversation or me. Maybe, all three. Too damned bad.

Great-grandmother or not, she should have told me all of this long ago.

"But that doesn't make sense. You said you hadn't seen Killian in sixty-five years. Why would Charlie think Caoimhe had my mother killed after so long?"

"Sixty-five years seems like a long time to you and me, but time works differently there. Sometimes it stretches, sometimes it contracts."

I didn't want to get into the differences between Tir Na Nog and Earth. "Right, but that doesn't answer my question."

"He suspected Caoimhe because Atsila was about to have a second child." She stood and went to the cupboard for a dishtowel and dustpan. "As far as I know, you and Killian were the last two children born in Tir Na Nog."

Killian had said something similar, but I still didn't understand how that would lead someone to having Atsila killed. Buying myself a few moments to gather my thoughts, I took the rag from her and bent to clean up my mess.

"When Charlie died, I thought your magic would fade." She handed me the dustpan. "Instead, all hell broke loose."

That's putting it mildly.

I'd been attacked by wolf-shifters, taken a bullet to the heart, and almost killed by a power-hungry skin walker. Not to mention, burned down my apartment and accidentally exposed Aaron to so many secrets, the Tribal Elders had called for his death.

"I wish it would have faded." I'd given up the chance to allow the Elders to bind my magic before Bryson and I were mated. However, that didn't mean I hadn't regretted my decision from time to time.

"I can see why you'd feel that way, but think about all of the good you've done." Out of breath, she sat back down.

"I guess." Walking to the trashcan, I did my best to count my blessings. I would never have met Bryson, or stopped a handful of serial killers, or rescued Jolene from foster care and an annoying ghost, or saved a dozen or so lives—but still. "Why didn't Charlie bind all of my magic when I was born?"

"He promised Atsila he would leave enough to allow you to speak to her."

I couldn't begin to imagine what I'd make Aaron and Bryson promise to do if I knew I wouldn't live to see Quin grow up. The very thought made my throat tighten and eyes sting.

"Sweetheart, I know you're disappointed in me, but we all made sacrifices." Gram Mae pulled her sweater tighter around herself.

I hated to put her through this, but I needed to know the truth. "You're cold. Let's finish talking in the Florida room."

"Thank you." She took my arm and half-leaned into me as we made the short trek to the back of her house. After she'd settled into her easy chair, she said, "Charlie brought us here and cut us off from the other Fae."

Including Killian and my father.

I decided to keep that thought to myself. Mostly because I was stuck on the way she'd said *us* and not *himself*. Was there more she wasn't telling me? "Are you Fae, too?"

Laughing, she motioned to her wrinkled face and cotton-puff of gray hair. "Do I look like I don't age to you?"

"Fae age, just not as fast." I grinned despite the seriousness of the conversation. "And you didn't answer my question."

"I'm one-hundred percent human." She shook her head. "Folks that live in Tir Na Nog, and the other fairy lands, are immortal. They only age when in the human world."

"Oh." Once again, my thoughts raced. Had my grandfather given up immortality to be with Dottie? Or had he gone back and forth until I was born? Had he given it up for me? "Charlie made a heck of a sacrifice."

Mae's eyes glistened. "He and Atsila loved you very much, Tessa. They still do."

"I've never doubted that, Gram Mae. I know you *all* love me. I just hate the secrets." I settled onto the little footstool in front of her chair like I had when I was a child. "What's my father like? Did you know him?"

Gram Mae's eyes got that far away look she had when

remembering someone she'd loved. "He was a rascal. Sometimes, he acted like the sun came up just to hear him crow, but I suspected that was all for show."

The more I heard, the more I wanted to know everything about him. "Was he good to Atsila?"

"Your mother was a tough cookie. She didn't take any crap from anyone—especially not him—Liam adored her for it."

It felt like I'd woken up in an alternate universe. Growing up, I'd believed Darlene was my mom and my dad had ran off. After I'd shifted into the firebird, I'd learned the ghost who'd visited me for as long as I could remember was my real mother.

I struggled to keep my bitterness at bay. I loved Mae and Charlie, and I trusted them to have done what they thought was best for me, but the lies...I didn't know if I could ever forgive the lies. "Are you keeping anything else from me?"

"Only my secrets." The mischievous glint returned to her eyes. "I'll tell you, in case Killian mentions something...but it's not something I want anyone else to know."

"Okay." I mimicked turning a key to lock my lips and braced myself for impact.

"My first love was a Fae." Her expression turned as dreamy as Jolene's did when talking about her movie star crush. "His name was Tighe, and he was a real looker. Had eyes even bluer than Aaron's."

"Tessa? Sorry to interrupt, but y'all might want to see this." Aunt Dottie called from the living room. Which might have been a good thing, Mae's cheeks had gone so red, I worried her blood pressure had shot through the roof.

The concern in Dottie's voice had me on my feet and moving. "What's wrong?"

"They interrupted my stories again?" Gram Mae wrinkled her nose. She loved her soap operas. In fact, I was surprised we weren't discussing Astila's death during commercial breaks.

A reporter was interviewing a man that looked like he'd just walked off the set of *Tiger King*. The guy wore a dirty white tank top, jean shorts, and an honest to goodness mullet hairdo—complete with brassy yellow highlights. And that wasn't the strange part. His eyes were bugging out, and he was hopping around like he had springs in his shoes.

I couldn't help but giggle. "Why do they always find the weirdest people in the bunch to talk to?"

"There's been another animal attack. This one was only a few miles away from here." Dottie motioned to the television, her way of telling us to hush.

"I saw it. I saw it with my own two eyes! It weren't nothin' like no animal I ever seen. It had a top half like a gator and the body of a man. It was like something outta a horror movie!" Mullet-guy turned and pointed to the lake behind him. "It grabbed that woman and ripped her in two."

I sent up a prayer for the victim and an apology for making fun of the witness. I would have behaved like a lunatic, too, if I'd seen what he had—or thought he had.

Lord, please let this man be hallucinating.

The camera cut back to a male reporter. "Multiple witnesses have reported seeing the same sort of...creature on the shore. Police on the scene have declined to comment."

Mullet-guy continued to rant, "There ain't nothin' left of her. The gator-man ate every last bit. Even her clothes."

The audio cut out and the images changed to a group of uniformed officers, and a plain-clothes detective standing near yellow crime scene tape. Tiny flashes of light glimmered behind them as if someone had hung Christmas ornaments from the tree branches.

"My word." Dottie pressed her hand to her chest.

Nothing that I'd just heard made sense. I'd seen a lot of horrible things while working with the police department, but I'd also interviewed enough traumatized people to know they didn't always get their facts right. "It was probably a big gator. They like to drag their victims into the water."

"You're right." She shuddered. "But that isn't much better."

"Is that Aaron's partner?" Gram Mae leaned forward to get a better look.

As if he'd heard her question, the camera man zoomed in on Detective Richard Samuels' scowling face.

"It sure is." My stomach churned. Aaron had mentioned a series of fatal animal attacks and something about a possible serial killer. I knew my husband. There was no way he'd miss out on this case willingly.

Dottie seemed to pick up on my unease. "How much longer is Aaron taking off for maternity leave?"

"I'm guessing not very long." I couldn't help but think the trouble Gavin had warned me about had arrived.

The screech of the screen door opening and slamming shut interrupted the conversation.

"Grammy Mae?" TJ called from the kitchen. The boy sniffled and let out a sad little cry. "Aunt Dottie?"

"What in tarnation?" Gram Mae pushed to her feet.

"I'll get him." I reached the kitchen before she'd made it to the hall.

TJ stood beside the table, holding a stuffed rabbit in one hand and a backpack in the other. Tears left clean streaks down his dirty face. "Daddy said me and David Hasselhop were gonna stay here now."

I glanced behind him in hopes of finding his father, but the sound of tires on the gravel driveway told me all I needed to know. I knelt and wrapped my arms around the boy. "It's okay, sweetheart. I've got you. Everything's going to be okay."

CHAPTER 9

After calming TJ down, I made my way across the lawn to tell Aaron and Bryson we'd have a pint-sized house guest for the foreseeable future. While I'd suspected this would happen, I'd hoped against hope that Tank would stick around and raise his son. Afterall, the boy had just lost his mother.

I rounded the big oak tree and caught sight of Aaron pacing on the porch with his phone pressed to his ear. I didn't need psychic abilities to know who was on the other end of the line—or what they wanted.

Glancing at me, Aaron said, "Tessa's here now. I'll talk to her and call you back."

And that, folks, is how maternity leave dies.

He hung up and gave me an apologetic smile. "Remember those wild animal attacks?"

"I saw the news at Mae's. Sounded like a gator to me. I'm sure they'll find the victim's remains when they search the lake." I had other things to discuss. Things that needed our immediate attention. Things that involved family—the Fae and the human sides.

Aaron lowered his voice as if he expected the news media to pop out of the bushes with cameras. "They aren't releasing the details to the public, but CSI has found the same DNA at multiple scenes—human DNA."

I swallowed my hurt for what I knew he'd say next and tried to beat him to the punch. "Call Samuels back and tell him you're cutting your leave short. I know you're itching to be on the case."

Aaron shook his head. "It's not just me they want back. They need you, too. ASAP."

"Me?"

Is he kidding?

I hadn't told him about TJ, but I could hear Quin crying from inside the house. Not to mention, Jojo's schoolwork.

And then there was the situation with my father. Killian could show up anytime with a new plan to break our dad out of Tir Na Nog.

"No." I folded my arms and shook my head. "Absolutely not. Do you hear me? I can't do one more thing. Not. One. More. Thing. Aaron Burns."

He had the good sense to take a step back, but not enough to drop the subject. "Samuels needs you to walk one or two murder scenes. It won't take more than an hour or two tops."

I'd worked for the Orange County Police Department for the last couple of years. Officially, I was a victim's advocate. Unofficially, I helped out on hard cases by reaching out to the dead or by trying to *read* the murder scene.

About fifty percent of the time, I could touch a reflective surface and see images of the crime. Other times, I caught glimpses of the killer or clues, but there was a good chance I wouldn't see anything at all. "There's no guarantee I can do it, and I'm not about to waste my time finding out."

He grinned like he knew something I didn't. "I can guarantee you'll be able to read the scenes."

I lifted a brow but otherwise refused to take the bait.

He sighed. "Someone hung little mirrors around the areas where the killings happened."

I recalled the flashes of light behind Samuels and the other detectives. How in the world had the killer had time to hang mirrors?

Better question, who had hung mirrors without anyone seeing him? It was a weird case, but it still was not my circus and not my monkeys. "That's a *unique* MO, but no. I'm not going back to work. Why don't you try dream-walking and see if you can figure anything out?"

In the weeks before Quin was born, Aaron had developed the ability to walk through the spirit world, visit people's dreams, and at times, see a version of the future. Unfortunately, he'd shredded the veil and a boo-hag had come through the holes.

"I'd rather not risk another monster crossing over." Aaron dragged his hand down his face. "Please, Tessa, I wouldn't ask, but Samuels thinks there's another monster on the loose."

Images of Mullet-guy's terrified expression pushed against my resolve. That, added to what Dottie had said about the latest murder taking place a few miles away, had me second-guessing myself. Lucky for me, Quin's crying amped up, giving me the perfect excuse to end the conversation. "I'll think about it."

"Thank you." He blew out a relieved breath as if he thought it was a done deal.

It wasn't.

Rather than argue, I moved past him and walked into the house. It took me a few seconds to understand what I saw. Quin was in his baby swing, and Bryson was on his phone a couple of feet away. Brow furrowed, head down, he was so engrossed in the conversation he hadn't noticed me.

The telltale tingle of magic hung in the air. He'd done a freaking privacy spell so he could take a call in peace. It was genius, but it felt like cheating. Although, it *would* come in handy when we were taking turns getting up at night with the fussy baby.

"I'll get Quin." Aaron knelt and began the headache of unfastening the straps holding our child in the contraption.

"Thanks. He's probably hungry." Speaking of which, I couldn't remember when I'd eaten last, but the mere thought of food turned my stomach. Stress could do that to a woman, but it'd never done it to me. If anything, stress turned me into a human garbage disposal.

Aaron handed me the baby. "I'll get you some decaf iced tea. Want a snack, too?"

"Nope." I suspected he was trying to butter me up. Petty or not, I didn't want his snack. Not when it had strings hanging off of it.

Bryson turned and met my gaze. His expression reminded me of Aaron's outside. Upset, worried, and needing something from me.

I ignored him and settled into my easy chair with Quin. Unless he was speaking to Tank about reconsidering running off and leaving TJ with us, we had nothing to discuss.

Bryson disconnected and dropped his phone in his pocket. "That was Buck. He called about the animal attacks."

"Not attacks. *Murders.*" Aaron returned from the kitchen without my tea. "Samuels is working the cases. He's convinced it's a serial killer."

I would have put my hands over my ears and sang the "Alphabet Song," but I was holding Quin.

Bryson's frown deepened. "Buck said the same thing. He thinks it's another skin walker."

We'd faced down a skin walker after Charlie died. During the ordeal, I'd been shot—twice, kidnapped, almost lost Aaron, and shifted into the firebird for the first time. Call me selfish, but I had no desire to repeat any of it. "I don't want to hear any more about this. We have three kids to think about now."

"Three?" Aaron turned an odd shade of green.

Bryson's expression grew serious as if counting back to the last time we'd had sex. News flash—it couldn't have resulted in a pregnancy. I was still pregnant with Quin.

I resisted the urge to roll my eyes. "I've been waiting for you two to stop going on about the attacks to talk to you. Tank left TJ with Gram Mae and took off. We all know her and Dottie can't handle that little devil."

Neither man's expression changed. If anything, Aaron looked queasier and Bryson more troubled.

"I know we have a lot on our plates, but he doesn't have anywhere else to go." I glanced between them. When neither spoke, I added, "And he's used to staying here."

Bryson nodded slowly, but avoided my gaze.

To my surprise, Aaron caved first. "You're right. This is the best place for him."

"That was too easy." I didn't trust it. Not that Aaron had a problem with TJ, but committing to taking care of a rambunctious seven- year-old boy indefinitely was a big deal.

"If it had to happen, now is a good time. We're *all* still on leave." He hitched a shoulder. "Bryson and I will step up more around the house. That'll give you more time to yourself. You know, to do Tessa-things."

Like consult on the damned case.

Once again Bryson did a slow nod. It wasn't a yes, but it wasn't a no, more like he was still mulling over the options. When he finally turned to me, I knew I had a problem. "TJ is welcome here as long as he needs a place to stay, but we need to pay Buck a visit soon."

I dropped my head back and groaned loud enough to disturb Quin's meal.

He jolted, all four limbs going rigid.

Cooing softly, I shifted him to the other side in hopes of distracting him with a fresh boob. Thankfully, it worked.

Bryson sat on the side of the couch closest to me. "I understand your reluctance to get involved, but Buck believes the first murder was near the tribal house."

"What?" I turned to Aaron for confirmation, but he seemed as stunned as me.

Aaron tilted his head. "Was it reported?"

"No." Bryson tightened his jaw. "Buck said the victim was Cherokee, and he suspects the perp is a magic user. He doesn't want to involve the police."

"That's bullshit. Not all of the murders have taken place on tribal lands. He could be sitting on evidence that'll help solve the other cases." Aaron's voice rose. "And, if this does involve magic, we need to know what we're dealing with."

As much as I would have loved to ignore anything and everything about this case, I couldn't. Not if Buck was right. Human law enforcement was no match for a murderous magic user.

Until meeting Harris, the Fae root-doctor, and then Killian, Bryson and I had thought we were the only Fae left on the planet, but that didn't mean we were the only people capable of wielding magic. Some humans could use focus objects and spells to do serious amounts of harm. The thought of Aaron putting himself on this killer's radar made my pulse race.

"I'll walk the crime scenes, but that's it. I'm not getting involved any deeper." I shifted Quin to my shoulder and pegged Aaron with a death glare. "And I don't think you should either."

He winced as if I'd thrown a fireball at him. "It's my job."

"Not for another few weeks, it's not." I drew a deep breath. "Now, if the two of you will let me get a word in edgewise…There's another murder I'd like to solve. Gram Mae told me Atsila was assassinated."

CHAPTER 10

I walked along the edge of a patch of charred earth in the middle of the forest. Whoever, or whatever, had burned the ground had managed to create a perfectly round circle. Weirder still, dozens of square mirrors hung from the branches of the surrounding trees at what appeared to be the exact same heights. "Grab the tape measure from my bag and measure the distance from the mirrors to the ground."

Bryson gave me an odd look. "Why are you carrying around tools?"

"I like to be prepared." I kept the basics—screwdrivers, a hammer, wrenches, rope, duct tape, and a Taser—on hand when working. I'd be in serious trouble if I were ever pulled over and the police went through my crime scene bag.

Buck scanned the tree canopy as if expecting to find the murderer perched on a branch. He was never much of a talker, and the stress of one of his own being murdered hadn't changed that.

"Tell me again what Oscar said happened." I would have loved to have spoken to the witness myself, but the young man had left town the day before.

It was partly my fault we'd missed him. I'd insisted on visiting both death scenes on the same day. It'd taken a solid week to coordinate Buck's, Samuels', and my schedules. Not that I'd shared the information about the murder on tribal lands with Samuels. As far as I was concerned, Buck was the person calling the shots on the small reservation. If he didn't want the local police department involved, that was his business.

Aaron disagreed. Loudly and often.

"Oscar and Wyatt were returning from a hike. It was after dark." Without taking his eyes off the trees, Buck drew in a long slow breath. "They heard growling and thought it was a bobcat. Oscar claims he saw a half-man/half-cat walk out of the bushes."

Maybe I was in denial, but as bizarre as the burned circle and mirrors were, I wasn't ready to chalk up the goings-on to magic. "Did he have a flashlight?"

Bryson moved to my side. "Wyatt and Oscar are shifters."

"Oh." Well dang. That changed things considerably. Shifters weren't Fae. They were born human and had been turned into a were-creature by either a bite or a deep scratch. Most had excellent senses of smell and eyesight. They'd be hard pressed to mistake an actual animal for a human or vice-versa.

Buck nodded as if reading my mind. "He tried to get the creature off Wyatt but was knocked unconscious during the fight. He came woke here, in the center of the circle, but Wyatt was gone. Oscar tried to track him, but couldn't find a trail. He said it was like they'd vanished into thin air."

I remembered Aaron mentioning the other victims had been seen with a tall male before the attacks. "Did Oscar say anything about running into a dark-haired man on their hike?"

"No." Buck folded his arms. "If there was anyone else out here, Oscar would have smelled them."

"If he calls, please ask him if they ran into anyone." I turned to Bryson. "Any idea what could have done this?"

He shook his head, but something in his eyes told me he had a few ideas. In fact, he seemed to be warning me with his stare. Against what I didn't know.

Bryson said, "The mirrors are exactly five feet and three-quarters an inch from the ground. Whoever did this had to use magic."

"Yep." I glanced up to where the strings were tied to the branches. Some were easily twenty feet high. "I'll stop trying to convince myself this was a plain-old human and read the mirrors now."

Bryson chuckled.

Buck bristled before walking several feet from the edge of the circle. I don't know what he expected to happen, but I didn't blame him for putting some distance between us.

I focused on the cold magic inside me. Unlike the heat of the firebird, I had no need to call it forward. The icy magic seemed to ebb and flow through my body like a tide. I couldn't help but wonder if the difference between the two was an after-effect of Charlie binding half my magic.

The instant my fingertips brushed against the first mirror, images filled my mind. It was exactly as Buck had described. Two young men walked into the clearing. A half-man/half-panther pounced on them from above. Blood, so much blood. Oscar shifting into a wolf. More fighting. Oscar unconscious. A flash of light so bright and hot it felt as if it'd scorched my brain.

Screaming, I released the mirror and pressed the palms of my hands to my eyes. They weren't physically burnt. The searing pain came from somewhere deep in my skull.

"Tessa!" Bryson wrapped his arms around me and eased me to my knees. "What happened?"

I managed to gasp out, "Light. Burned. Inside."

"Shift into the firebird." His warm, safe magic flowed over my skin but did nothing to ease the pain.

All I had to do was let go and the firebird would burst into existence. The problem was, I couldn't focus on anything except the agony in my head.

Bryson's spirit animal, the Great Hawk, hovered near the surface, but not even the call of her mate could rouse the firebird. His magic changed from coaxing to demanding to violent.

It felt as if he'd reached inside me and pulled the damned bird out.

One second, I was writhing in his arms, the next, I was a blazing ball of fire and feathers flying through the afternoon sky. On the bright side, the pain had vanished.

I'd learned to think of the firebird as a part of myself instead of a separate creature, but after an injury—physical or magical—the bird seemed to have a mind of her own.

She wanted her mate to shift and to go home to her young.

Okay, so maybe I wanted the same thing, but the logical part of me knew I had to return to the charred circle. Eventually.

Using my altitude and heightened eyesight, I scanned the area in hopes of finding broken branches, scraps of clothing, anything that would help to figure out where the killer had taken Wyatt.

There was nothing. Nada. Zilch.

Oscar was right. It was as if they'd vanished.

I returned to Bryson and Buck and shifted back into my human form, or almost human form. I held onto my heightened sight. Though a week had passed since the murder, there should have been traces of blood on the tree trunks or underbrush.

Naked as a newborn and just as oblivious, I wandered the perimeter.

Buck muttered something and turned his back.

Bryson pulled his shirt over his head and handed it to me.

"Thanks." I slid it on and continued the search.

This wasn't the first time I'd experienced an unplanned shift. I'd long since learned to keep a change of clothes in the trunk for such occasions. Unfortunately, the SUV was a couple of miles away.

Bryson watched me with the same curious expression he'd worn when we'd first met. It was nice to know that after three years together, we hadn't lost the mystery. "Are you going to tell us what happened when you touched the mirror, and what you're looking for?"

"I'm looking for blood." Growing frustrated, I gave up my search and turned to him. "I saw everything, just like Buck described. After Oscar was knocked out, there was a flash of light that about melted my brain. It's what burned the circle."

Buck tilted his head. "Could the killer have used the light as a distraction to run off unseen?"

"Maybe, but I didn't see a trail from the air. There would have been something. Broken branches. Blood."

Bryson balled and un-balled his hands into fists, but otherwise remained stoic. I knew him well enough to know he'd figured something out. Something I was obviously missing.

I opened my mouth to ask, but he stopped me with a slight head shake.

Buck motioned between us and settled on Bryson. "What aren't you saying?"

I had no idea what Bryson suspected, but whatever it was, he didn't seem to want Buck to know.

I said the first thing that popped into my brain, "There's no blood splatter anywhere. An attack that violent would have been messy. The killer would have tracked it into the forest."

Buck's gaze went to the ground outside the circle.

Bryson caught my eye and mouthed, "Thank you." He didn't seem the least bit surprised by my discovery—further proof he'd figured something out.

Buck scratched the side of his head. "The attack...what you saw in your vision...was violent?"

"It was." The memory of it made me lightheaded.

He sighed the sigh of an old-man realizing he'd woken up in a new and unfamiliar world. "Do you have any idea who, or what, the killer is?"

"No, I'm sorry." I hated to disappoint him, so I added, "I'm heading to another crime scene now. Maybe I'll pick up on something there that will help all of this make sense."

Buck glanced at my bare feet and legs. "Do you need to borrow some clothes?"

"Thanks, but I have some in the car." Heat flooded my cheeks, and it had nothing to do with the firebird. It's funny how I rarely felt exposed until someone pointed out I was naked, or mostly naked.

We made our way back to the tribal house in relative silence. Of course, it was hard to have a conversation while being carried piggyback style with no underwear. I spent most of the journey tugging on the hem of the shirt to make sure my butt was covered. Not that it mattered, Buck had gotten more than an eyeful when I'd shifted.

The older man seemed lost in thought as we reached the pavilion along the back of the large building. "We will continue with Quin's naming ceremony this weekend as planned."

Bryson set me on my feet before turning his full attention to the chief. "I trust your judgement."

"We should postpone it until we know what we're dealing with." The idea of bringing my newborn anywhere near where a murder had taken place made my palms sweat. Sure, it was tradition to present babies to the Tribal Elders before they were a month old, but I didn't see the rush."

Bryson rested his hand on my shoulder, a sure sign he wanted me to zip it. I understood his desire to keep the peace between us and the Elders, but not when it meant taking unnecessary risks with our family.

Buck glanced back toward the forest. "If the killer was still out there, one of you would sense their magic…would you not?"

"Yes, but who's to say they won't come back?" I turned to my husband for backup. We hadn't discussed it, but most of the magic users we'd dealt with over the years were associated with the tribe. For all we knew, the murderer had an invitation to the ceremony.

Bryson remained quiet.

I motioned to Buck. "Didn't you say you thought this might be a skin walker?"

He nodded.

"Then how do we know the murderer isn't a member of the tribe?" I ignored Bryson's sigh and kept my focus on Buck.

"I don't." He folded his arms. "We will postpone the ceremony one week to make sure there are no other incidents on tribal land."

"Thank you, Buck." Bryson dipped his chin, but not before I caught his grin. "You should get dressed. I'll call Samuels and tell him we're on the way."

Confused by his behavior, I headed to the parking lot and grabbed my spare clothes from the trunk. When I returned, the men were too involved in their conversation to notice me.

Shaking his head, Bryson patted Buck's shoulder.

The older man tilted his head toward the sky and frowned.

I'd have asked if everything was okay, but I knew it wasn't. Buck was grieving. No amount of stupid questions, well wishes, or empty promises would take his pain away.

After I dressed, we said our goodbyes to Buck, and climbed into the SUV.

As soon as Bryson shut the door, I said, "Were you really going to agree to have our son's naming ceremony with a murderer running loose?"

"No." He started the SUV and backed out. "I'd planned to wait until the shock of Wyatt's death wore off before discussing it with Buck."

"Oh." I slumped.

"It's okay." He squeezed my thigh. "All's well that ends well."

I ran back through the events at the murder scene, but nothing made much sense. "You looked like you were chewing iron in the forest. What did I miss?"

"The light in your vision. Was it the same as Killian's when he vanished from the living room?" He spoke without a glance in my direction.

Smart man, because I gave him a dirty look that would make Gram Mae proud.

"Considering Killian didn't burn the carpet, I'm gonna say no." In all fairness, I was overreacting, but I was sick of listening to Aaron moan and groan about my brother. I didn't want Bryson on the Killian-is-trouble bandwagon.

This time he turned his head and met my gaze. "The attacks started the same day Killian showed up at the house."

"Huh." I hadn't done the math, but now that he mentioned it, I could almost see why he'd be suspicious. Almost. "That's an odd coincidence, but do you honestly believe my new brother is running around as a cat-man or gator-guy eating people?"

His lips twitched as if holding back a grin. "Not when you put it like that."

I laughed. It'd been so long, I'd almost forgotten how good it felt.

Bryson entwined his fingers with mine and smiled like he used to back when we had lots of sex and sleep and easy breezy moments together.

I lowered the window. The rush of cool air felt like freedom. Or it did, until my phone rang.

CHAPTER 11

"Tessa! Sorry it's been a few days since we spoke. How are you?" Killian's unmistakable voice filled my ear and worked its way into my heart.

"I'm good, thanks for asking." It seemed strange to me to make small talk with him when we had a lifetime of catching up, of getting to know each other, of memories to make. But we had to start somewhere. "How's Dad? Or should I call him Liam?"

"I'm sure he'd prefer you call him Dad or Da, like I do." His tone reminded me of sunshine breaking through the clouds, full of hope and warmth. "He's a bit more chipper since I told him about meeting you."

"He is?" I felt like Jojo talking to Micah Sterling, her celebrity crush. I wanted to ask what Killian told our father about me, or if he'd mentioned Quin or Bryson and Aaron. But more than anything, I wanted to ask if our father had asked to see me.

Killian lowered his voice to a sly whisper. "He's more determined than ever to break free."

To visit me? Hung on the tip of my tongue, but I couldn't bring myself to ask. One, because I didn't want to sound like a dork, and two, because I'd never smile again if I was wrong. "That's good, right?"

Likely hearing the nervousness in my voice, Bryson squeezed my hand. The small gesture let me know he was there no matter what.

"Yes." Killian cleared his throat. "I have a new plan. Is there somewhere quiet we can meet to discuss it?"

The new mother in me heard the word *quiet* and automatically assumed he didn't want to come to the house because of the colicky baby. The more rational side of me figured he wanted to talk alone. As in without Bryson and Aaron. Neither of those options appealed to me. "I'm handling a work situation, but I'll be home in an hour or so. You can stop by then."

"I see..." Killian went quiet.

I remembered the stolen Lamborghini and Aaron's threats to arrest him. "On second thought, I'm starved. I know a great diner not far from my place."

Bryson's grip tightened to the point of crushing my fingers.

"Great. Text me the time and the address." He disconnected the call.

I fired off a quick text and dropped the phone in my purse. Risking a glance at my hubby, I asked, "Something the matter, Bone Crusher?"

"I'd rather you not go alone."

"Who said I was going alone? I didn't want to risk Aaron cuffing him and reading him his Miranda Rights." I ran my fingertips over the sensitive spot behind his earlobe. "Any chance I can convince you not to mention this to Aaron until after we meet Killian?"

"Keep doing that, and I'll consider it." Bryson leaned into my touch. "Good idea having him meet you at Scarlett's diner. I'll call her while you're working the next crime scene. I'm sure I can talk her into reading him on the down-low."

And just like that, my mood soured.

Scarlett was a seer. She could read a person's past through touch. One hand shake, and the woman had a free-pass to all of your secrets. While I was tempted, I couldn't do it. I'd much rather have Killian share his past with me the old-fashioned way—by building trust over time and good food.

"I picked the place for the food, not the waitress." I pulled my hand away. "I don't like the idea of her getting into his head without permission."

"Since when does Scarlett ask permission?" He gave me side-eye.

"This is different. We're setting Killian up." Technically, every time we took someone to see Scarlett was a set up, but this felt wrong. "I'd like to have an actual relationship with my brother. I'll ask him what I need to know outright."

"You're right. Forget I mentioned it." Bryson took my hand and placed a kiss on each of my fingertips.

I spent the remainder of the drive in a haze of giddy anticipation of seeing Killian again and confusion over what I knew about the attacks. While Aaron liked to refer to them as murders, I wasn't so sure. Without a body or forensic evidence, it was impossible to say what had happened to Wyatt and the others.

Bryson pulled up near the lake shore and helped me out of the SUV. We walked hand-in-hand to the yellow police tape surrounding the death scene. Not long ago, I would never have participated in a public display of affection where my coworkers could see us. Everyone at the station knew Aaron, Bryson, and I were a *throuple*, but I'd gone out of my way not to rub their noses in it. However, at some point in the previous couple of months, I'd gotten over it.

A few of the techs shot us curious looks, but for the most part, no one seemed to care whose hand I held.

Aaron and Samuels stood shoulder to shoulder going over papers on a clipboard.

"What's Aaron doing here? He's supposed to be watching the kids." Mental images of Gram Mae force feeding Quin onion water flashed through my mind.

Bryson said, "He had Darlene help out long enough for him to be here while you walked the scene."

"All the more reason to hurry this up." I understood why Aaron wanted to be on-site while I did my thing, but I hated the idea of leaving Quin with anyone.

Aaron and Samuels smiled as I approached.

Okay, that's different.

I expected Aaron to smile. Samuels? Not so much. The man showed affection through ribbing and bird jokes, not facial expressions and hugs, but boy oh boy, did he hug me.

"Tessa. Good to see you." He set me back on my feet, nodded to Bryson, and leaned close. "What'd you find at the other scene?"

I shot Aaron a glare that could have stopped the glaciers from melting.

He held up both hands and took a step back.

Samuels nudged my side. "Off the record."

"Off the record, I'll tell you if, and when, I find a connection." I pushed past him. "Is the scene clear or do I need the bunny suit?"

I seriously hated wearing booties, gloves, and a Tyvek bodysuit. My mass of red curls never fit into the hood properly, and once my hair went into a ponytail, it was nothing but frizz. It might have been silly, but I wanted to look nice when I met up with Killian.

Samuels tilted his head as if considering his options. I'd be far more cooperative without the full suit, but I'd contaminated a death scene or two in the previous couple of years.

Aaron snapped on a pair of gloves. "Sorry, darlin', you're going to need the works."

"She can't do her woo-woo thing wearing gloves." Samuels handed me a pair of booties. "Put these on. You can reach most of the mirrors if you stick to the stepping plates around the perimeter."

"Thanks." I slipped the paper covers over my spare running shoes and ducked beneath the tape. Careful to stay on the metal plates, I hopscotched my way around the edge to the first mirror.

"Hold up." Bryson jogged to me but remained on the other side of the tape. "I'll stand by, in case you have an issue with the light."

Aaron joined me inside the cordoned off area. "Was there a problem with the other reading?"

"Nothing a little *shift* in attitude couldn't handle." I winked and reached for the first mirror.

Aaron rolled his eyes but stayed within arm's reach.

As with the first scene, images burst through my mind the second I made contact with the glass. Unlike the first scene, I was more interested in what happened before the attack than the attack itself.

The vision started with the half-man/half-gator walking out of the water. As the mullet-wearing witness had said on the news, the creature ripped the woman in two before slinking back into the water with the body. I waited for the flash of light, but it never came.

"Hmmm." I moved to the next mirror and tried again. Like before, the images started with the gator-guy walking out of the water. Nothing before.

"Everything okay?" Aaron followed me to the third mirror.

"I'm not sure." I brushed my fingers across the glass and the same images played through my mind like a GIF on a continuous loop. I moved to the next mirror and sighed when I got the same results.

Bryson gave me a less than patient look. "Anything?"

"No flashes of light, but something's wrong." Dozens of mirrors hung from the trees. It'd take hours to read them all, and I highly doubted I'd see anything different. I glanced back at Aaron. "How far off the ground are the mirrors?"

He arched a brow.

"How many inches?" I waved my hand like a lunatic.

"I don't know." He met my gaze, sighed, and nodded back toward the CSI tent. "I'll go find out."

"Thanks." I surveyed the scene again. The lake was to my left, the parking lot to my right. The creature had come from the water, but in the vision, he'd come directly at the mirror. I nodded to Bryson. "I need to check something. Stay close."

Without a word, he followed me to the opposite side of the perimeter.

I touched the mirror and noted the positions of the lake, the parking lot, and the tree. My pulse picked up steam as the implications of my discovery played through my head.

"This is definitely magic. It defies the laws of physics." My brain churned quicker than my mouth could keep up. "The images. All the same. Same angles. Same everything. It's staged."

Bryson opened his mouth, snapped it shut, and shook his head.

"What's staged?" Aaron's voice startled me.

I jumped half out of my skin, but managed to keep my feet on the dang stepping plates. "Didn't anyone ever tell you not to sneak up on someone at a murder scene?"

"Sorry about that, but you're darned cute when you're flushed." He flashed me a dimpled smile before shifting back into work-mode. "What do you mean, staged?"

"Every vision showed the gator-guy walking out of the water head on, with the parking lot to the right and lake on the left." I motioned to the mirrors nearest to the lake. "From there, I should see him walk by."

Aaron pointed to the one I'd read last. "And this one should show the parking lot on the left."

Nodding, I said, "The weird thing is, I can't see anything before the guy comes out of the water or anything after he goes back into the lake."

Aaron rubbed his jaw. "That's unusual, why?"

"Because the visions are like memories, not movies. There isn't usually a beginning and end when I read an object. If I'm connected to it, I can see hours in the reflection."

Bryson glanced at Aaron. "How high are the mirrors from the ground"

"Five feet and three-quarters."

He growled under his breath. "Tessa, stand directly behind that mirror."

"What? Why?" I glanced back at him.

He wore the same expression he had on the tribal lands when he'd suspected Killian had something to do with the light—hard and uncompromising. "Humor me."

It took some finagling, but I managed to position myself with the mirror hanging in my face without stepping off the plate.

"They're hanging at eye-level." Bryson folded his arms.

"What does that prove? Only at Tessa's eye-level..." Aaron's mouth fell open. "It's like the perp knows how your magic works and laid out the perfect scene for you."

Bryson scowled. "It's not just staged. It's a set up specifically for Tessa."

It took me a couple of heartbeats to catch on, and when I did, I thought I'd vomit. "You think someone's setting me up? For what?"

"That's a very good question, but I suspect this is what Gavin was warning you about." Bryson glanced over the area before nodding back toward the parking lot. "Let's get you home where it's safe."

"But I'm meeting Killian—" Shoot. My mouth had gotten away from me. A quick glance at Aaron told me he'd heard and had some serious opinions about my lunch plans.

CHAPTER 12

It'd taken a half hour, promising to have Scarlett read Killian, and the mention of oral sex, for me to convince Aaron to stay behind while Bryson and I had lunch with my brother. While I still hated the idea of sneaking a peek into Killian's mind, the situation at the crime scene had freaked me out enough that I'd agreed.

Someone had gone through a lot of trouble to create evidence tailor-made for my particular magical skill set. The sooner my hubbies ruled Killian out as a suspect, the sooner we could find the real culprit.

Bryson parked next to a shiny new Aston Martin with a Pinellas County license plate. He nodded to the swanky sportscar. "Looks like Killian beat us here."

"Let's just hope he doesn't leave the car behind." I reached for the doorhandle.

Bryson chuckled. "Let's hope Aaron doesn't drive by and see it."

He had a point.

Rather than commenting, I climbed out and headed for the entrance.

Bryson took my hand and pulled me to his chest before I reached the door. He met my gaze for a half a heartbeat before leaning close. "Keep Killian busy while I speak to Scarlett."

Anyone watching would have assumed we'd shared a private moment. Little would they know that I wanted to stomp on his foot and storm away.

"I still don't like this." My voice came out whinier than I'd intended.

Bryson nuzzled his cheek against mine. "Noted, but we need to know if he has something to do with the animal attacks."

I knew he was right, but I couldn't help second and third-guessing myself. "I know, but what if he figures out what's going on?"

"He won't. Scarlett is pretty good about hiding her talents when she wants to." Bryson pulled back enough to brush his lips across mine.

The tenderness of his kiss warmed me in places that hadn't as much as tingled since before Quin was born. Not ready to let him go, I slid my arms around his waist and rose on tiptoes.

Bryson took the hint. He pulled me closer as he deepened the kiss. We shared more than the press of bodies and tangle of tongues. We were mated in both flesh and spirit. Our magics intermingled, our spirit animals, our lives. Every part of me belonged to this man and vice versa, but we weren't complete without our third, Aaron.

It'd taken me a while to get used to thinking about Aaron while kissing Bryson, or the other way around, but when we were all together…let's just say the real magic happened.

"Ready to go in?" Bryson whispered against my lips.

"I'd rather stay out here kissing you." I felt rather than saw him smile.

Bryson eased away and guided me to the door.

Killian sat in a booth near the window watching the two of us with a curious expression. I didn't know him well enough to judge, but the way he stared made me wonder if he had anyone in his life that loved him the way Bryson and Aaron loved me.

"Hey stranger." I slid into the booth, grinning like I'd unwrapped my chocolate and found a golden ticket. "Were you waiting long?"

Laughing, he hitched his thumb toward the parking lot. "I could wait a little longer if you two need to finish your *conversation*."

My cheeks heated. "We don't usually do that sort of thing in public. It's rare for us to have a few moments alone these days."

Killian draped his arms across the back of the booth. "Don't apologize. I envy you."

"I'm a lucky woman, not one but two great guys." I picked up a menu, though I knew every item on it.

"Most females in Tir Na Nog have many men." He spoke as if he were discussing the weather. "It's…unusual in the human world, isn't it?"

I'd wondered about his nonreaction when I'd introduced my men to him, but it made sense if polygamy was common where he came from. "It is, but we're happy. If someone doesn't approve, that's their problem. Not mine."

Laughing, Killian shook his head. "You might look like our mother, but you sound just like Mae."

A teenaged waitress stopped at the table. "Can I get y'all something to drink? This is Scarlett's table, but she's busy shootin' the bull with another customer."

I couldn't help but grin. "That other customer is probably my husband. Tall, broad, long dark hair?"

"That's the one." The teen popped her gum, unimpressed. "What'll it be?"

To hell with the anti-colic diet. I needed grease and processed sugar.

"I'll have a chocolate malt, cheeseburger, and fries." I offered the menu to Killian.

He took it, glanced at the back page, and set it aside. "Same for me."

The teen rolled her eyes and retreated toward the kitchen.

"Did you spend much time with Mae when you were younger?" I thought back to my discussion with my great-grandmother. She hadn't said much about Killian. Then again, we'd had more pressing matters to discuss.

He sipped his water but kept his eyes trained on me. "I knew her when she was younger than you are now. She was engaged to my best friend."

My mouth fell open. No amount of mental gymnastics would help me understand what it would be like for my bestie to date my grandfather.

He laughed again, rich and full of humor. "I used to tease her by calling her *Mhórai*. I never thought of her as a grandmother. She was the human woman who'd given my grandfather a place to live. She was more of a friend."

"What was she like when she was young?" Gram Mae had been in her sixties when I was born. I'd seen photos of her when she was a young woman. She'd been quite the knock-out.

"The life of the party, but tough. She didn't take grief from anyone." Killian's expression softened. "And she was an accomplished dancer. She would have become a principal ballerina had it not been for her injury."

"Oh?" I had no idea Gram Mae had ever danced, let alone seriously. It broke my heart to think she'd lived an entire life that I knew nothing about. Worst still, I felt like a selfish child for never asking about her past.

He studied me. "She never told you about her relationship with Tighe?"

"She mentioned him yesterday, but that was the first time." It didn't feel right to tell him Mae went all doe-eyed and called Tighe her first love. "What happened to cause her to stop dancing?"

Killian focused on something behind me and pressed his lips together.

Bryson rested his hand on my shoulder. "Sorry about that. I was telling Scarlett about Quin."

The elderly seer flashed me a bright smile and patted Bryson on his shoulder. "He's a proud daddy, that's for sure."

"He sure is." My palm itched to pull out my phone and show her a few dozen pictures of the baby, but I refrained.

Killian glanced between us.

"Where are my manners?" I motioned between him and the seer.

"Scarlett, this is Killian, my brother. And this is Scarlett, the world's best waitress and a good friend."

"Nice to meet you." She offered him her hand.

Killian hesitated, glanced at me as if expecting me to stop him. When I didn't, he wrapped his fingers around Scarlett's.

Magic flared between them and raised the hair on my arms. Scarlett gasped, but Killian didn't seem surprised. If anything, he'd anticipated it.

Mentally, I let loose a series of curses that would have sent Mae running for the Ivory soap. I'd known this was a bad idea, but did Bryson and Aaron listen to me? Nope.

Pale-faced and wide-eyed, Scarlett cradled her hand against her chest.

Bryson stepped closer to her with his arms out as if he thought she might pass out. "Are you okay?"

She nodded, turned on her heel, and hurried to the kitchen.

I turned to Killian and said the only thing I could, "I'm sorry."

He pulled his wallet from his back pocket, tossed enough cash on the table to pay for the entire diner's lunches, and stood. "I would have told you anything you wanted to know. All you had to do was ask."

"Wait." Bryson rested his hand on my brother's arm. "Stay. Please. This was my doing."

Ignoring Bryson, he turned back to me. "Did you know she was going to invade my privacy?"

"I did." The hurt little girl inside me took control of my brain and my tear ducts. "And I'm really sorry. Please don't leave. There's a lot of really bad things going on and... Don't go." My voice cracked. "You never told me your new plan to save our father."

He closed his eyes and drew in a deep breath. When he opened them, the anger had faded from his face. "We'll talk again, but not today. What that *woman* did to me is considered a personal assault in Tir Na Nog."

His words hit me like a sucker-punch to the gut and left me just as breathless. "I didn't know."

Killian bent down and kissed my cheek. "There is a lot you don't know. In some ways, you are like a toddler with a rocket launcher."

Bryson's expression went from remorseful to angry in a millisecond. "That's uncalled for."

"Perhaps, but it is the truth." Killian walked outside, got in his fancy British sportscar, and drove way.

"He left? You're still gonna have to pay for this." The teeny-bopper waitress set two cheeseburger platters on the table. Her gaze landed on the pile of money and her attitude improved dramatically. All smiles and sunshine, she straightened. "Let me go check on your malts."

Bryson slid into the booth beside me and pushed the plates to the side. Hooking his finger under my chin, he lifted my face. "I'm sorry. You were right. It was wrong to read him without his permission."

"Please take me home." I didn't give two hoots about the food or the reading or the annoying waitress. I wanted to wrap myself in a blanket and cry where no one could see me.

"I need to speak to the two of you." Scarlett sat in the seat Killian had abandoned. "It's important."

"Actually, I'd rather not hear what you saw." I nudged Bryson hoping he'd take the hint and let me out. "We never should have done that."

Scarlet grabbed my wrist. Thankfully, I'd worn long sleeves, otherwise she would have gotten a whole lot more information than she'd bargained for, including two gruesome murders.

Bryson didn't move. He did the opposite of *move* and rested his forearms on the table like he planned on being there a while. "I apologize for that. I should have warned you he was *different*."

"Pshh. I knew he wasn't human the second he walked in. He was broadcasting his magic brighter than Times Square." Scarlett watched me as she spoke to Bryson. "He's slipperier than pig snot on a radiator, but he didn't kill anyone."

I whipped my head from her to my husband. I couldn't believe he'd told her he thought Killian was involved in the attacks.

Bryson continued to stare at Scarlett. "He has no ill will toward Tessa?"

She shrugged. "I didn't say that."

"What?" The conversation was giving me a case of whiplash. I was hurt and angry and scared I'd never see Killian again. I didn't need to know he secretly…what? Couldn't stand me? Wanted me dead?

She gave me a patient smile. "Rest easy child. He's a big brother dealing with a new baby sister. He's worried about you, but at the same time, unsure if you're worth the trouble."

I wasn't sure how to respond to her. "Well, that's better than wanting me dead, I guess."

"Dead?" She laughed her two-pack-a-day laugh. "He definitely doesn't want to see you come to harm. He needs you."

"For what?" This from Bryson, who still hadn't bothered to look at me.

"That I couldn't tell you." She frowned, making the lines around her mouth look like accordion pleats. "Some parts of him were wide-open, others were behind a stone wall."

Bryson finally turned to me. "He could be hiding something."

"Or he could have blocked her from seeing his personal life." I wanted to scream. "He knew she was a seer before he took her hand."

"My point exactly. If he knew, he could have—"

Scarlett cut him off. "She's right and you need to let it go. Taking a life leaves a stain on the soul that never fades. He's slippery, but he has a good heart."

Bryson muttered something and plucked a fry from the forgotten plates.

"Scarlett, I was warned we were in some sort of trouble…"

Her expression fell. "I'm afraid that brother of yours wore me out. Come back in a few days if you need me, but I suspect you'll have it all figured out before then."

"Thanks." My stomach growled loud enough for people four tables over to hear it.

"Y'all eat. I'll go see what's taking so long with Tessa's malt." Scarlett slid out of the booth. "Coffee, Bryson?"

"Please." He snatched the greasy burger from one of the plates and bit into it like it'd insulted his mother.

I glanced from him to my food and sighed. "Slide that this way, will you?"

"Are you sure you want to eat this? Quin will be up—"

"Are you sure you want to go there? Now?"

"Absolutely, not. Forget I mentioned it." Bryson moved the plate closer and handed me a rolled-up napkin with silverware inside. "Forgive me?"

"Always." I dunked a few fries in catsup and shoved them into my mouth. "But I'm still mad at you."

He focused on his food. "I know."

CHAPTER 13

Sundays were made for families. Big breakfasts, church, and bigger dinners. In the fall, we'd play croquet or football in the yard, but I always loved the summers. When the weather was hot, Charlie would pull out a long thin piece of Visqueen. He'd put a water hose at one end and a sprinkler at the other. We'd spend all afternoon playing on the homemade slip and slide.

As a child, I'd never given much thought to the amount of work that went into those easy breezy Sundays. Becoming a parent had given me a serious reality-check.

"Hurry up! We're going to be late." I shouted from the bedroom to everyone and no one in particular. Let's be honest, with two husbands, two kids, and a six-week-old, chances were some if not all of them weren't ready to go.

Ignoring the unmade bed and piles of clothes—some clean, some dirty, and some questionable—I swiped on a coat of mascara. It was the first time I'd bothered with makeup since Quin was born, but I couldn't imagine getting through the next couple hours without the warpaint. Not only did I have to attend church with a colicky baby, we were presenting him to the entire congregation.

I kept telling myself it wasn't a big deal. We weren't Catholic, there was no holy water involved, and this wasn't like the naming ceremony with the Tribal Elders—it was a simple acknowledgment of the birth of a new member of the congregation.

Unfortunately, my nerves hadn't gotten the memo.

Bryson strolled into the bedroom with Quin in one hand and a cup of coffee in the other. "You look beautiful."

"I look like ten pounds of crap shoved into a five-pound bag." Frowning at my reflection, I added a third layer of concealer to the world's largest pimple. "Please tell me that's real coffee."

"Decaf." He set the mug on the vanity and turned me to face him. "You're stunning, and I for one, cannot wait until tonight."

Our sex date. How could I forget?

"Me either." I lied. Once upon a time, he could melt me with a look, and boy howdy, the look he gave me was lava level hot. But it hadn't as much as caused a tingle. Let's face it, it was hard to feel sexy while wearing breast pads.

We hadn't fooled around since Quin was born. Which, for the record, wasn't because I needed time to heal. I'd seen to that when I'd shifted into the firebird after a psychopath and a monster had given me a DIY c-section. Nope, the no sex for the first month had been Bryson and Aaron's idea. They'd thought I needed the extra rest.

The no nookie rule had failed on multiple levels. We hadn't gotten any sleep, and we'd taken the world's best stress reliever off the table. Then again, none of us had the energy for sex, and if we had that much quiet time, we'd likely zonk out.

"I'm not sure tonight is going to happen." I faked disappointment. "TJ and Jojo are extra needy lately. Plus, I'm not sure it's a good idea to leave Mr. Fussy-Butt with my mother tonight. She struggled with him the other day, and I was only gone long enough to walk a crime scene."

"Actually, I want to talk to you about Quin's magic." He shifted his weight from one foot to the other as if nervous.

The move was so un-Bryson-like, I put down the makeup and gave him my full attention. "What about it?"

"I spoke to Harris about what Killian said, and how miserable Quin has been—"

"He's not miserable. He's just colicky or something." I knew I came off as defensive, but every time someone mentioned Quin's fussiness, I felt like a failure. What kind of mother couldn't comfort her own child?

Bryson knelt in front of me. "Babe, this isn't any of our faults. We're good parents who want the best for their children."

I hated that we were struggling, and our son was paying the price. However, Harris was a serious miracle worker. He'd helped us repair a tear in the veil and put an end to a boo-hag. The root doctor knew more about the Fae than we could ever hope to. If anyone could help us, he could. "What did he say?"

"Feeding Quin magic is much like getting him to take the breast the first time. All we have to do is allow our magic to flow when we're around him. Harris said, Quin will know what to do naturally."

I laughed an ugly, bitter sort of laugh that only someone who hasn't had a good night sleep in a month and a half could pull off. "Did you forget what a nightmare it was to get him to nurse the first time?"

He took my hand and brushed his thumb over my knuckles. "It wasn't that bad."

"Uh huh." I didn't know who he thought he was fooling, but I'd been there. There was nothing natural about it. It'd taken not one, but two lactation specialists, several attempts, and a hell of a lot of tears to get him to latch on.

Bryson tightened his jaw to the point I thought the bone would snap. "I haven't forgotten, and you're purposely missing the point. I want to try and see what happens."

"I just want him to be a normal kid." My eyes stung, but I forced the tears back by sheer will alone. I didn't have time to redo my make-up. And I'd be damned if I faced the judgmental church ladies with ugly-cry-face.

"I know and so do I." He hooked a finger under my chin and waited until I met his gaze. "But Quin had access to your magic the entire time you were pregnant."

"Did he though? I stopped using magic because we were afraid it'd hurt him." The lie tasted bitter. I was *supposed* to stop using magic but hadn't quite followed orders.

Though he knew I'd stretched the truth, he didn't contradict me. "Aaron thinks this is like stopping smoking cold turkey. It might be better to wean Quin off slowly."

"You and Aaron decided this without me?" I knew that wasn't what he'd said, but I had an inexplicable need to argue. After all, I hadn't bothered to discuss it with them before I'd tried to force-feed the baby magic. Who was I to gripe about them having a freaking conversation? "You know what? Forget I said that. It's the exhaustion talking. Let's try the weaning thing, but it may not be as easy as you think."

He placed a kiss on my brow and stood. "Harris said we needed to give Quin access to magic as much as possible, but I thought I'd try a quick dose before we leave. Do you want to do it together?"

Yes!

One quick glance at the clock told me we'd need to divide and conquer if we ever hoped to make it to church on time. "No, go ahead. I'll round up the troops."

"We have a problem." Aaron stood in the doorway pale and wide-eyed. I'd seen the same expression on the faces of victims at crime scenes—disbelief wrapped up in horror.

My heart didn't know whether to speed up or stop. Instead, it alternated between the two. "What's wrong?"

He drew a slow, steady breath and exhaled on a shudder. "I…uh…I just caught Jolene—" He shook his head as if to clear his thoughts.

Bryson glanced between us before heading for the door.

"Wait." Aaron swallowed hard enough I thought he might sprain his Adam's apple. "She's too young to notice boys, right? I mean, she's only ten."

Bryson widened his stance as if preparing to fight, only the crying baby in his arms made him far less intimidating. "What kind of question is that? She's *way* too young."

The posters of teen-actor, Micah Sterling, on her bedroom walls said otherwise, but I didn't think it wise to point that out to her fathers.

"What happened?" I had half a mind to go see what the girl was up to myself. Lord knew, I wouldn't get a straight answer out of Aaron when he was acting like a shell-shocked soldier.

Aaron dragged his hand down his face. "I caught her stuffing her bra."

Bryson's mouth hung open for a split second before he snapped it shut and turned to me. "That's it. I told you she was too young to go to the tween youth group. I bet this is about that little shit Holden."

"Holden? The kid with the gelled hair? What is he, like thirteen?" Aaron scowled. "I'll break his—"

"Oh, for the love of Pete." I'd had enough of their cave-dad routines. Besides, we didn't have time for this. "You didn't embarrass her, did you?"

Aaron's blush told me all I needed to know.

"Not another word about it." I motioned between them. "Or Holden. I'll talk to her when we get home."

Aaron, God love him, wasn't ready to let it go. He scratched the side of his head. "Since when does she wear a bra?"

"She's too young for a…bra" Bryson's voice hitched on the last word, as if it'd cost him a part of his soul.

"Obviously not. Her body is starting to develop. I also bought some books on puberty. I'm sure she'd let y'all read them if you need a refresher course." I patted Bryson's arm, kissed Aaron's cheek, and headed into the living room.

They followed on my heels, neither seeming ready to drop the subject.

Bryson whispered, "You should have told us."

Aaron nodded, but his queasy expression made me think he could have lived his entire life without knowing his little girl was growing up.

Taking inventory of the diaper bag, I spoke without a glance in their direction. "First off, it's not Victoria's Secret. It's a sports bra.

Secondly, she's getting breasts. What was I supposed to do? Let her nipples—"

Jolene made a strangled sound from the hall. TJ did what any seven-year-old boy would do. He giggled.

Aaron whipped his head in her direction and froze like a deer in front of a speeding locomotive.

Maddie let out a series of woofs that sounded as if she had something to say on the matter.

"TJ, come with me. You too, Maddie." Bryson high-tailed it toward the office with Quin.

Smart man, dumb dog.

I would have run away, too, but I had a freaked-out husband and daughter I had to keep from being scarred for life. "I'm sorry Jojo, that was inappropriate of me."

She folded her arms across the parts of her body that had caused so much fuss. "I thought you said it was our secret."

"No, we don't keep secrets in this house, remember? What I said was I would tell them after we went shopping, but I forgot." I realized how hypocritical I sounded and sighed. Planning to confess something after you did it was basically the same thing as keeping secrets. "Your dad was surprised to see your new bra—"

"Ahhh. Stop saying that word." Jojo looked as close to tears as I felt. "Whatever. It's fine. Just stop talking about it. Okay?" She pegged Aaron with a preteen death glare.

He held up both hands. "Done."

I nodded to her bare feet. "Good. Now that we have that settled, go get your shoes on. We need to go."

She huffed again and stormed down the hall.

TJ ran back into the room. "Why does Jojo need a bra?"

"None of your business," Aaron pointed to the front door. "Go outside and tell Aunt Dottie we're almost ready."

Grinning, he tilted his head. "But she doesn't even have boobs."

Jolene screamed something about brats and peeing the bed from the bedroom.

Laughing, TJ hot-footed it outside.

I leaned against the door jamb to keep myself upright. "I don't know how we're going to handle the terrible twos, a preteen girl, and TJ at the same time."

"Tell me about it." He slid his arms around me and nuzzled my ear. "But I'm looking forward to tonight."

Ugh. When did we become the kind of people who schedule sex?

Rather than whining out loud, I went with honesty. "I'll be happy if the three of us get a solid eight hours of sleep."

Laughing softly, he eased back. "Same here, and I bet the sex will be better once we're all well rested."

Before I could respond, Gram Mae marched through the door. "Where is everybody? We're going to be late."

My eighty-eight-year-old great-grandmother might have been a few inches short of five feet, but she could command armies with nothing more than a raised chin and narrowed eyes. Even in her best Sunday dress, yellow chiffon with orange and pink flowers, she was a force to be reckoned with.

Aaron leaped away from me as if we were two teenagers caught necking on the couch instead of a married couple with every right to fool around. "I'll go start the car."

"You do that, young man." She winked at me, obviously quite pleased with herself.

He turned for the door and his phone rang. Glancing at the screen, Aaron sighed. "It's Samuels."

Gram Mae and I openly eavesdropped on his half of the conversation. What can I say? We were a nosey bunch. Besides, if it was confidential, he would have walked outside.

"Meeting? Today?" Aaron's frown deepened. "We're presenting Quin to the congregation this morning—I understand. I'll be there in fifteen."

Gram Mae gave me a do-something look.

Aaron disconnected the call. "The Chief called a meeting about the murders. I'm sorry, but I need to be there."

"It's okay. Bryson and I can handle it today." I forced a smile for his sake.

He stuffed his wallet, keys, and phone in his pockets. "I hate to miss Quin's debut, but I'll be there for the naming ceremony."

Surprisingly, Gram Mae didn't have anything to say about him missing church. She simply gave him a quick hug. "Will you be home in time for dinner?"

"Yes ma'am. It should only take an hour or so." He winked at me and headed for the door. "Have fun today."

She turned back to me. "Are Bryson and the kids ready?"

"Almost. Bryson's seeing to Quin. He should be done any minute." At least I hoped he'd be finished soon. "I should go check on him."

"He's more than capable of changing a diaper." She glanced around at the messy living room. "I never thought I'd say this, but I'm thankful Bryson's cooking the burgers on the grill today."

The statement was so unlike her it sent me into a tailspin of worry. "Are you feeling better? Did you call your doctor about your shoulder?"

Patting my arm, she gave me a patient smile. "Sweetheart, at my age if I called the doctor every time something went wrong, I'd never get off the phone."

"Still, you should get it checked out." Normally, I admired her stubbornness but not when it came to her health.

"I have an appointment next week." She raised her chin. "Now hurry up or we won't get a good parking spot."

CHAPTER 14

*B*eing trapped in the backseat of the car with a screaming baby was its own special kind of hell. Unfortunately, I'd insisted we all ride together.

Bryson and Gram Mae had taken the front seat, Dottie, Quin, and I were in the middle row, and Jojo and TJ had squeezed into the back. I'd reduced the people I loved most to sardines crammed in a very noisy can.

Over the past few weeks, I'd gotten used to Quin's fussing—well, mostly—but I'd never get used to not being able to hold him while he cried. I'd spent the drive trying to coax him into taking a pacifier or a bottle. I'd become so desperate, I'd stuck my finger in his mouth hoping he'd suck on it and quiet down. It hadn't worked.

I'm a horrible mother.

"Don't worry, Mom. It's not your fault he cries so much." Jolene pulled her earbuds out and stuffed them inside her little pink purse.

That she'd seemed to read my mind surprised me. I turned so I could keep an eye on the baby while speaking to her. "Did *someone* tell you to tell me that?"

And by someone, I mean a ghost.

She finished applying sparkly lip gloss before answering. "Nope. I figured you needed to hear it."

"Thank you, but I'm not worried. Lots of babies get colic."

"Mmm-hmm. Then why do you look the same as you did when you tried to make fried chicken?" Jolene flashed me a glittery, satisfied smile.

I didn't really want the answer, but I had to ask. "How do I look when I fry chicken?"

"Like you can't decide if you want to cry or hit something."

Bryson glanced at me and winked. "She's got you there."

I opened my mouth to argue, but she was right. I was the world's worst chicken fryer and was shaping up to be the world's worst mom. Not only did I have an infant I couldn't soothe, I hadn't spent any quality time with Jolene since Quin was born.

"Jojo, what do you say about you and I having a girls' day? We can go to lunch, get pedicures, and catch the new Micah Sterling movie?"

Her eyes brightened. No big surprise, she loved everything about the massive franchise including the television series, posters, books, and even the creepy dolls. "*Vampires Still Suck*, the sequel? Really?"

"Really." I reached past the car seat and squeezed her hand. "It's a date."

TJ shouted, "Can I come?"

"No." Jojo huffed. "Girls' day is for girls."

Bryson glanced over his shoulder. "We'll have a guys' day when the girls are out."

"But I want to see *Vampires Still Suck*," TJ whined.

Gram Mae gave me side-eye. "When you were their age, you would have had your mouth washed out with soap for using that word."

"Yes, ma'am, and if I live to be one hundred, I'll never forget the taste of Ivory soap."

"It's the name of the movie." Jolene came dangerously close to sass, but I didn't think she'd crossed the line.

"I know what it is, young lady. It's still ugly." Gram Mae glanced out the window and muttered a few ugly words of her own. "Dag gummit. There aren't any spots left. I told you all we'd be late."

Despite her concerns, Bryson found a parking spot near the entrance. He hopped out and rushed to the other side of the vehicle to open her door.

I grabbed for the handle, but Dottie reached across Quin's carrier and squeezed my hand.

Message received. She didn't have to say a word. Her concerned expression said it all. She was worried about Gram Mae.

That makes two of us.

The second I walked into the sanctuary I knew we had a problem.

I'd attended the same church for as long as I could remember. I'd listened to the same preacher, learned from the same Sunday school teachers, sang along with the same choir. Not much had changed over the years—until now.

A cloying magic oozed over me like honey on ice cream.

I held Bryson's hand tighter. "Do you feel that?"

"Yep." He glanced around and frowned. "Killian's sitting with two other Fae in the fourth row."

I counted the pews. Sure enough, my brother was sitting with a dark-haired man and woman. "What are they doing here?"

"No clue, but I intend to find out. Watch the kids." He handed me the baby and marched in their direction.

Jolene speed-walked to me. "Where's Dad going?"

"To talk to some folks. Let's get our seats." I led her and TJ to my family's unofficial pew and motioned for them to slide in.

Gram Mae and Dottie gave me curious looks, but neither commented on the visitors.

TJ's eyes went wide. "You ain't sitting with me?"

"Pastor Miller is going to introduce Quin to everyone this morning, remember?" My heart broke for him. He'd been glued to our sides since Tank had left him on Gram Mae's doorstep.

"But you're coming back?" His voice rose.

"I sure am." I kissed his cheek.

He nodded and crawled in next to Jolene.

Seated in the pew behind Mae and Dottie, Darlene played patty-cake with my baby brother, but her attention was clearly on Bryson and Killian. It didn't take a rocket scientist to figure out she'd invited the Fae.

It might have been a sin to glare in church, but I didn't care.

"Hey, Tessa." Stone stood and hugged me before joining me in the glare-fest.

"Good morning." I decided to take the high-road and not say anything to Darlene. Judging by her husband's icy looks, she'd get an earful after the service. "I'm surprised to see you here. I thought you didn't believe in organized religion."

"I don't, but I…" He glanced at Darlene and frowned. "Your momma likes it when I'm around for family events."

TJ turned backward in the pew and sat on his knees. "Grand-Dude Stone, we're gonna have a guys' day soon. Wanna come? It's a men only family event."

"Sure, little bro." He messed TJ's hair.

It never ceased to amaze me how well my stepdad fit into the family. When Darlene had first introduced us, I'd given him a month tops, but the vegan hippie had proven me wrong.

The choir walked onto the platform and started the welcome hymn. It was our cue to meet the pastor in the back of the sanctuary.

Bryson turned away from the Fae, met my gaze, and nodded toward the exit.

I met him halfway. "Everything okay?"

"Yes." His tense jaw and tight shoulders told me otherwise. "Killian said Darlene invited him."

"Who were those people with him?"

"I'm not sure. He didn't introduce them." Bryson nodded to someone behind me.

Before I could ask any more questions, Pastor Miller rested his hand on my shoulder. "Do we need to wait for Aaron?"

I shook my head. "He was called into work this morning."

It'd taken the pastor and the congregation a little time to get used to our domestic arrangement. While some folks didn't approve, most were content to ignore us or whisper behind our backs.

"Very well. We'll walk to the altar as soon as the choir starts singing, 'Jesus Loves the Little Children.'"

"Thank you." I glanced to the group of Fae, and my pulse sped. They were all so beautiful, I wished I had time to run to the restroom to check my hair and lipstick.

"He's quiet." Bryson ran his fingertips over Quin's head.

I'd been so distracted, I hadn't noticed. Now that I had, I couldn't help but wonder if Quin's good mood had to do with the magic filling the air. "He probably wore himself out in the car."

"Maybe." Bryson didn't say it. He didn't have to. His expression told me he'd thought the same thing.

The choir finished the opening hymn and began the Sunday school favorite.

Pastor Miller stepped in front of us. "Ready?"

"Yes, sir." I shifted Quin to my shoulder, took Bryson's hand, and followed the preacher.

Halfway to the front of the sanctuary, Quin started wiggling and squirming like he wanted to nurse.

"I spoke too soon." Bryson grinned.

"He's hungry." I settled him in my arms and took a step forward, putting me directly in front of Killian and the other Fae.

A burst of magic hit my chest, followed by the sensation of cool air on my back.

Before I could sort out what had happened, Bryson shouted and moved in front of me, and Pastor Miller jumped behind me. At first, I thought we were under attack, but then I felt it—the fabric of their shirts on my *bare* skin.

Praying I was wrong, I glanced down at the same time my four-week-old son latched onto my bare nipple. "What the heck?"

The Fae laughed. At least I assumed the tittering sounds had come from Killian and his guests. A heartbeat later, some of the congregation joined in.

My stressed out, sleep-deprived brain couldn't make sense of what had happened. Part of me wondered if one of the Fae had magicked me naked. I didn't know what they were capable of, or why they'd do such a thing—although, their queen had enslaved my father because he'd lost a bet.

Still hugging me from behind, Pastor Miller asked, "Did your blouse break?"

I had no idea how to answer him, nor did I know how he thought a long-sleeved blouse could *break*. Where he thought the garment had gone. And why on earth I wasn't wearing a bra in church.

"I heard it tear. Quin must have pulled on it." Bryson called to Killian, "I need your shirt."

"I heard it rip, too." Pastor Miller laughed the nervous laughter of a man grasping for an explanation of the impossible. "It's okay. No one saw."

Everyone saw!

I wanted to run away. Better yet, I wanted to shift into the firebird and fly so far from there no one would ever find me. The only thing keeping me in place was the fact I couldn't move without exposing my breasts.

"If I may…" A slender female hand rested on my arm. I didn't need to see her face to know who'd spoken. Her voice had an otherworldly quality to it.

"Step back." Bryson shifted to the side until she had no choice but remove her hand.

She sucked in a sharp breath. "Take this."

Frowning, Bryson eased a few inches away and wrapped me in a pashmina, hiding my boobs and the nursing baby from the crowd.

I stared until he met my gaze. I didn't want to ask aloud, not with the Fae standing so close, but I tried to shout the question with my eyes. *Who did this?*

Bryson grinned. He freaking grinned and nodded down at Quin. The little piglet hadn't stopped nursing throughout the entire ordeal.

"No." I couldn't believe it, or maybe I didn't want to. If he could wish me topless every time he wanted a snack, I was in serious trouble.

Bryson hitched a shoulder.

I glanced back to thank the female Fae, but she was gone.

"We need to proceed." Pastor Miller sighed. "Do you want to wear that or look through the donation bin for a shirt?"

As much as I would have loved to have proper clothing, I wanted to get the heck out of there even more. "Let's get this over with."

Bryson and I followed the dazed and confused preacher to the altar.

Pastor Miller faced the congregation, blinked several times, and shook his head. "Forgive me. That's the first wardrobe malfunction I've seen during a Sunday service."

I'd never wanted to crawl under a pew, and curl into the fetal position, more in my life.

He motioned for Bryson and I to turn around and face the crowd.

I tried not to make eye contact with anyone, but ended up meeting Killian's gaze. I half expected him to flash me his fake-Hollywood smile. Instead, he pressed his hand to his heart and dipped his chin.

"It is my honor to present Quincy Emmet Charles..." Pastor Miller glanced at the baby hidden beneath the pashmina and chuckled. "Who is in the middle of lunch."

Bryson cracked his first grin since we'd arrived.

Finding none of the mess funny, I glanced around and caught Buck Oldham staring. While he belonged to the church, he was more of an Easter and Christmas sort of member.

He nodded and whispered something to the person beside him. It wasn't until the teen boy looked up that I realized Buck was sitting with Holden and his family.

That's odd.

"...together with your parents, dedicate you unto the Lord." Pastor Miller reached forward as if to touch Quin, but seemed to think the better of it, and dropped his hand. "Let us pray."

I hung my head, but a rustling noise drew my attention. Cracking one eye open, I watched Killian and his friends make their way to the side door.

The dark-haired man stopped and stared back at me for half a second, before slipping out with the others.

The moment they left, Quin let out a wail that rattled the stained glass windows.

I wanted to hand the baby to Bryson and chase after them, but there was no way to get Quin out from beneath the soft fabric without flashing everyone. Again.

"At least they used the door this time," Bryson whispered.

CHAPTER 15

The entire morning stunk like last year's Easter eggs, but it'd proven once and for all, Quin's constant crying had nothing to do with colic. Too bad feeding him magic presented its own set of challenges.

Miserable, I sat in the pew with TJ on one side and Jolene on the other. The kids wiggled and squirmed like their undies were made out of steel wool. Although Bryson had taken the fussy baby into the foyer, I could still hear him over the preacher's encouraging words.

The back of my neck itched, a sure sign someone was staring. I turned to find Darlene smirking. Cole, my baby brother, sat in her lap as pretty as he pleased, the perfect picture of a well-behaved toddler. "What the heck happened up there?"

Gram Mae turned and gave my mother a death glare. "We're here to hear the preacher, not you."

Stone covered his mouth, but nothing could hide his grin.

Darlene rolled her eyes and turned her attention to the altar.

Jojo giggled, which set TJ off. The boy snorted out a laugh, covered his mouth, and did it again.

I ground my teeth counting the seconds until the preacher released the kids to Children's Church.

Dottie reached across Jojo and patted my leg. She'd meant it as an encouragement, but it made me want to cry.

I'd done my fair share of embarrassing things, but flashing my boobs in front the congregation, the preacher, and God took the pie and the cake. Heck, it took the whole damned bakery.

"All right." Pastor Miller flashed the congregation a toothpaste commercial smile. "It's time for the little ones to go to Children's Church."

Behind him, the choir broke into a cheerful rendition of "He's Got the Whole World in His Hands."

I sang along, only in my head I imagined the lyrics as: *She's got the whole world on her shoulders.*

Jojo and TJ scrambled out of the pew and hot-footed it out the side doors. I didn't blame them. I'd much rather have spent the rest of the service eating cookies and coloring pictures of Jesus, too.

"Excuse me." Darlene climbed over six people, including Gram Mae and Dottie, and plopped down beside me. "Where's Aaron?"

Gram Mae answered for me. "He's working."

"On maternity leave?" Her voice rose high enough people turned and stared. "Must be an important case... He isn't investigating the Wild Animal Murders, is he? I told Killian what a great detective Aaron was. Wait till he hears this."

Stone leaned forward and tapped Darlene's shoulder. "You said you were going to stop talking to that guy."

"That *guy* is Tessa's brother. That makes me his step-momma, not his girlfriend." Darlene huffed. "What was I supposed to do? Not tell him his nephew was going to be introduced to the church today?"

Stone ground his teeth. "Yes."

"You're not his step-anything. And yes, that's exactly what you're supposed to do." I hated that she'd put herself in the middle of my relationship with my brother. I wanted to be the one to invite him to special days.

Our outbursts earned us several shushes from people around us, and more of Gram Mae's evil eyes.

The rest of the service went by in a blur, probably because I'd zoned out. I gathered my purse and hurried out of there without saying another word to anyone.

Bryson met me in the back of the sanctuary. "Take Quin. I'll go get TJ and Jojo."

"Thanks." I reached for the baby, but before I had the chance, Dottie swooped in and took him from Bryson.

"Dottie, I'd really like to go home." I hated the whine in my voice, but I'd earned the right to moan and groan if I wanted to.

"I'll meet y'all at the SUV." Patting his diapered bottom, she sashayed into a group of older ladies.

Bryson stared after her and took my hand. "If I didn't have to drive everyone home, I'd suggest we run away for a few hours."

"We could drop everyone off and head out to the reservation. It's been ages since we flew together." I couldn't think of anything I wanted more than to shift into our spirit animals and spend the afternoon in the sky—except maybe a good cry and a nap.

He seemed to consider my suggestion before shaking his head. "Maybe tomorrow. I promised Mae I'd grill burgers today."

"Tomorrow then." I guided him through the crowd of parents waiting to retrieve their children. Several people whispered and laughed, but I did my best to ignore them.

TJ leaped from his seat the second we walked into the room. The boy wrapped his arms around my middle and hugged me tight. "I thought you left me."

"The grown-up service ran a few minutes late." Kneeling to embrace him, I shot Bryson a worried look.

He rested his hand on TJ's shoulder. "How about we pull out the Visqueen and make a slip and slide when we get home?"

TJ glanced from him to me. "Can we?"

Looking into his big brown eyes, I would have agreed to buy him a pony if he'd asked. "Sure, it's going to be warm enough this afternoon."

"Yes!" TJ pumped his fist in the air, but his excitement quickly turned to another matter. "What happened to your shirt? Some of the kids saw your boobies, but I didn't."

My mouth fell open.

"It broke." Bryson glanced over the remaining kids. "Where's Jolene?"

"She went to the bathroom." TJ dipped his chin and toed the carpet. "And so did Holden."

In the blink of an eye, Bryson went from annoyed to raging cage fighter. "I'll find them."

"I'll go." I stood, but he stopped me with a quick shake of his head.

He marched out of the room like a man going into battle.

"Don't tell Jojo I tattled." TJ tugged on my hand. "Please. She'll hate me forever."

"I doubt that, but we'll leave your name out of it." I took his hand and headed for the foyer.

Gram Mae sat in a chair near the door. She looked paler than normal, and even from a distance, I could see the shadows beneath her eyes.

My heart sank, but I pasted on a bright smile. "Ready to go?"

"Where is everyone?" She stood painfully slow.

Moving to her side, I hooked my arm in hers. "Bryson went to find Jojo."

Dottie left her friends and walked over with Quin sleeping in her arms. "All set?"

I glanced down the hall. Less people milled about, but I didn't see hide nor hair of Bryson. "Not quite, but we might as well get everyone loaded up."

We'd made it to the SUV when Bryson and a very unhappy preteen girl joined us. Make that a very unhappy preteen girl and a furious father. If he ground his teeth any harder, he'd need dentures within a year.

Jojo glared at TJ, then me, and climbed into the back row.

I turned to Bryson and lifted an eyebrow, but his only reply was a quick shake of the head.

To say the ride home was tense would be like saying Florida summers were a bit warm. No one spoke or fidgeted. Even Quin seemed afraid to make a peep.

We arrived home as Aaron was walking up the porch steps. He circled back and helped Gram Mae out of the vehicle. "How was Quin's big day?"

"You'd know if you'd been there," she snapped.

"Everyone but me saw Tessa's boobies!" TJ shouted.

"That's enough." Bryson's no-nonsense voice left no room for argument, or so I thought.

The boy laughed. "Okay. Only the people in the first couple of rows saw them."

Aaron glanced at me with a what-the-heck look.

"We'll talk later." I hopped out and lifted the seat so the kids could exit, before I unclipped Quin's car seat from the base. Any other time, Bryson would have hurried around the vehicle to help, but he hadn't moved from the driver's seat.

Jolene glared but otherwise didn't acknowledge his presence.

Once again, Aaron turned to me as if expecting an explanation. I had none.

Dottie, likely picking up on the tension, took TJ's hand. "How about you come with me to start the greens?"

"I hate greens." He screwed up his face. "Bryson said we could play on the slip and slide."

Gram Mae stopped walking. "It's too chilly out to play in the water."

I didn't know what the heck was going on with her, or Bryson for that matter, but I wasn't about to ruin what was left of our Sunday with bickering. I pointed to the thermometer hanging on the porch railing. "TJ, when that reads eighty-two degrees, we'll break out the slip and slide."

He ran up the steps and plopped his backside on the swing. I would have bet my right arm he'd stay in that spot until the thermometer hit the right temperature.

Gram Mae shifted her dentures around, a sure sign she was contemplating taking a switch to him. By some miracle, she turned and walked into her house without an argument.

Dottie held her hands out. "Let me take the baby. You three have things to discuss."

"That's an understatement." I gave her the carrier. "Thank you."

"Anytime, sweetheart." She followed Mae into their house.

I rounded the corner of the SUV and caught Aaron and Bryson standing with their heads together whispering. "What's going on with Jolene? And don't say nothing, you about bent the steering wheel in half."

He drew a deep breath as if trying to calm down. It didn't work. The man was as stressed as a mouse in a snake pit. "I caught her with Holden in an empty classroom."

Aaron scowled. "I'll break his—"

"You'll do no such thing." I turned back to Bryson "And?"

I didn't have the patience to play twenty-questions. Jojo was ten years old for crying out loud, I highly doubted she was up to anything too serious with the boy.

"He was going in for a kiss when I walked in." Bryson's tone bordered on deadly.

While I agreed, ten was way too young for kissing, Jojo was a good kid—and from what I'd seen, so was Holden. A call to his parents and a rational conversation with our daughter would likely solve the problem. "Please tell me you didn't do anything to Holden that could get you arrested?"

"I didn't touch him." Bryson deflated like a week-old helium balloon. "I understand the kid is going through a rough time, but this is unacceptable."

Aaron nodded. "Why were they unsupervised? They were at church, for Christ's sake."

"They were excused to use the restroom." I resisted the urge to sigh. "What did you mean, Holden's going through a rough time?"

Bryson glanced at Aaron, frowned, and looked back to me. "Family trouble."

"Right. What kind of family trouble?" I didn't have the patience to play games, nor could I imagine why Bryson hesitated to tell me what was going on with the kid.

He nodded to Aaron. "This is off the record. I don't want to hear about the police showing up at the McAlisters'."

My overactive imagination immediately conjured up images of Holden in the juvenile detention center, or his older brothers on the run from the law.

"Off the record then." Aaron motioned for him to continue.

Bryson drew a deep breath. "I ran into Buck this morning when I was looking for Jojo. Holden had a death in the family."

"Wait. Please tell me Wyatt isn't Holden's brother." I prayed I was wrong. It was awful enough to know something tragic had happened to a stranger, it was unbearable to know something tragic had happened to a young man we quasi-knew.

"Yes, and Oscar is a cousin." Bryson held my gaze as if waiting for me to connect more dots.

Not only did I connect them, they collided in an explosion that rivaled an atomic bomb. "Holden is a shifter?"

Aaron motioned between us. "What do you mean that little shit is a shifter? Is Jojo in danger? And why would I involve the police?"

"Holden won't go through the change for a couple years. Until then, he can't infect Jolene." Bryson clamped a hand on Aaron's shoulder. "Wyatt was the victim at Buck's crime scene."

He jolted and jerked his head in my direction. "These murders are far too close to home."

"I agree." I rubbed my arms to ward off a sudden chill. "But why are you just now telling us this?"

"I didn't know Wyatt was Holden's brother until I ran into Buck this morning," Bryson said.

Aaron raked his hands through his hair. "Young or not, I'd feel better if Jojo didn't have anything to do with the kid."

"Because he's a shifter or because he's too old for her?" I couldn't believe him. Sure, it was scary to think about our little girl hanging out with a boy who would eventually start turning into an animal every full moon, but it seemed wrong to punish Holden for what he was.

"Both," Bryson and Aaron spoke in unison.

"That's wrong on so many levels." I drew a breath and decided to pick my battles. "I'll give Holden's momma a call and have a talk with Jojo, but I'm not going to mention the shifter thing. And for the record, you two are seriously overreacting."

"*We* will have a talk with her." Bryson folded his arms and stared down at me as if daring me to argue.

Aaron let out a nervous laugh. "I'm with Tessa on this one. She can handle it, and we'll back her up if need be."

Bryson shook his head. "We parent as a team."

"We do, but this is a mother-daughter type thing." It wasn't that I didn't trust him to have the talk with Jojo, not exactly. I didn't trust him not to come on too strong when he was so upset. Since, I figured it'd take a couple days for him to calm down, I thought it best for me to address the situation.

I rested my hand on his forearm. "It's perfectly normal for girls her age to have crushes. She needs to know that we honor her feelings, but that touching and kissing are not okay until she's dating age."

"Like forty." Aaron frowned. "And married."

This time I did roll my eyes.

Bryson rubbed his temples. "It's not her I'm worried about. You have no idea what goes on in the mind of a thirteen-year-old boy."

I couldn't help but grin. "I imagine it's not much different than what goes on in the mind of a thirty-year-old man when it comes to sex."

Both men blanched when I said *sex*.

I motioned between them. "If neither of you can hear the S-word without having a physical reaction, you'll never be able to talk to her about it."

"You're right." Bryson dragged his hand down his face.

Aaron blew out a relieved breath. "Dead brother or not, I reserve the right to have a nice chat with Holden."

"You'll only make the situation harder on Jolene. Besides, I'm pretty sure the OCPD frowns on detectives threatening kids." I'd spoken louder than I'd intended, but my patience had run away about the same time Killian had.

Aaron, God love him, didn't seem to notice I was one smart-assed comment away from a meltdown. "What was that about your boobies?"

Bryson chuckled.

Seeing a way to get them both, I smiled my prettiest smile. "It probably had something to do with Killian and the other Fae being there, but I'll let Bryson tell you all about it."

Aaron sucked in a breath and turned the same shade of red as Killian's Lamborghini. Bryson, on the other hand, sighed.

CHAPTER 16

I stood in the hallway with my hand raised, ready to knock.

"He's not even my real dad, Aaron is." Jolene huffed.

My heart stuttered. I knew she'd spoken out of anger, but my emotions needed a few minutes to catch up to my brain.

Bryson, Aaron, and I had forbidden her from speaking to spirits other than Charlie and her mother. While I assumed she was talking to Jenny, it still hurt.

"You're the only one who understands me." Sniffles from inside the room told me she was crying. The *thump, thump, thump* of a dog's tail told me she wasn't alone in her time of need.

"Jojo." I knocked on the purple door and held my breath.

When I'd adopted Jolene, I knew it wouldn't be easy. I could never take her mother's place, but I'd vowed to do the best I could to raise her as if she were my own.

"Go away!"

I drew a deep breath and prayed for the wisdom to say the right things. "Jojo, I know you're upset, but I promised your dads I'd talk to you."

Sure, there was a hint of a threat in my words, but it was better than demanding she open the door. Besides, the parenting experts stressed the importance of giving kids her age options. She could speak to me or the cavemen outside, her choice.

She groaned and peeked out. "They aren't out there, are they?"

"Nope. They're in the yard setting up the slip and slide."

Her eyes widened. "Can I play on it, too?"

"Sure, but we need to talk first."

Nodding, she opened the door wide enough for me to enter.

Maddie stared at me with what looked like a raised eyebrow.

I had more important things to worry with than a judgmental dog.

Jolene sat on the floor and rubbed Maddie's belly. "Am I grounded?"

"Nope." I plopped down beside her. "But you will be if you sneak out of Children's Church again."

She hung her head and I regretted my words.

Smooth, Tessa. Shut her down before you even get started.

"Will you tell me what happened?" I nudged her shoulder with mine.

"Nothing." Her expression was somewhere between embarrassed and horrified. "Holden and I were talking. Dad came in and freaked out."

Bryson did not, as a general rule, *freak out*. He was the most even-tempered man I'd ever met.

"Freaked out how?"

She shrugged. "He yelled at Holden to get away from me, then told me to *come* like he does Maddie when she gets into the garbage."

The dog snorted—a sound that reminded me a little of Gavin Partridge.

I could picture the entire thing, but her story and Bryson's were quite different. "He was surprised to find you alone with a boy when you were supposed to be in class."

"I know, but we didn't do anything wrong I swear it." She turned to me, her eyes filling with tears. "All of the boys were talking about seeing your... Seeing you without your shirt on."

"Oh." I'd often wished boys didn't hit puberty until their thirties. "I'm sorry you had to hear that. It was an accident."

"Quin's too young to know better."

I opened my mouth to ask how she'd figured out her baby brother had magicked my shirt off, but she waved her hand to change the subject.

"Then TJ started teasing me about being in love with Holden and wearing a bra. He's not even old enough to be in our class." Her cheeks pinkened more with each word.

I could picture that, too. "I'll have a talk with TJ when we're done."

"Holden said we should tell the youth pastor we needed to pee and meet in the classroom." She sighed. "I knew it was wrong to lie, but TJ is like a gnat buzzing around. Only I'm not allowed to squash him."

"TJ's acting like a little brother. Chances are he felt left out and wanted your attention." I'd never had a brother while growing up. It struck me as funny that as an adult, I had two. One who was angry with me, and one who wasn't potty-trained.

"That's what Charlie said." She sighed and my throat tightened.

I hadn't heard a peep from Charlie since Quin was born and I missed him more every day. While it made me happy that he was still around, I would have loved to pick his brain about Killian and the things Mae had told me about Atsila.

"Charlie said, TJ's gonna be living with us for a really long time. Maybe until we're both grown." Jojo glanced at me as if for confirmation.

While I hoped Tank would come to his senses and return home, who was I to argue with a spirit? Especially a spirit who likely had inside information.

"Charlie's probably right. Which means, it's important that you two get along." I slung my arm around her and she sagged against me. "You like Holden?"

"Noooo." She pulled away as if I'd burned her. "He's just a friend."

Nodding, I said, "So there was no kissing going on?"

She wrinkled her nose as if the very thought were disgusting, but the blush on her cheeks made me wonder.

Rather than pressuring her outright, I waited for her to reply.

Jojo shook her head. "No kissing, but he did hold my hand."

Inside, I blew out a breath of relief. Outside, I played it cool. "Good. It's okay to like a boy but kissing and touching are for when you're older and dating."

She sighed. "I know. Gavin already told me that."

Maddie nodded and yipped.

"You talk to Gavin, too?" I hadn't heard a peep out of the guy since the day I'd tried to summon Charlie.

"All the time." Jojo grinned. "He says he's here to protect us, but the only thing I need protecting from is TJ."

"Next time you speak to Gavin, please tell him I really need to talk to him."

Maddie whined.

Staring at the dog, I thought back to the last time I'd seen Gavin. That was the same day Maddie had stumbled around. He wouldn't have possessed the dog. Would he?

That's it. I'm losing my mind.

"How old do I have to be to date?" Her question came out in a rush as if she were nervous.

"Your dads say forty, but I think sixteen is about right. We'll know for sure when you're older. Everyone's ready to start dating at different ages." I poked her side. "But not ten, or even thirteen."

She knitted her brow. "Holden is thirteen."

And now for the hard part.

Choosing my words carefully, I said, "I know and thirteen is too old to be holding hands with a ten-year-old. I know Holden is going through a really hard time, but I'd rather you not be alone with him again."

"Oh." Jolene frowned.

I braced myself for an argument.

"Promise you won't be mad?" She nuzzled Maddie, likely to avoid meeting my gaze.

I had no idea what she had to tell me, but with an opening like that, it couldn't be good. "I promise to listen to what you have to say and to be fair."

She hesitated so long, I thought she'd decided not to share.

"Jojo?"

She glanced up and blew me away. "Wyatt isn't dead."

I don't know what she saw in my expression, but whatever it was, she panicked.

"I was only trying to help. Holden was so upset about his brother last week. I thought maybe he'd feel better if he could talk to him again." Her words came out so fast I had a hard time following her. "But I couldn't reach Wyatt. I keep asking my mommy, but she can't find him in Heaven. He's not dead, Mom. I know it."

"I believe you." I drew her into my arms to calm her down and to give myself a chance to think. I'd suspected the same thing. It was impossible for someone to be eaten alive without leaving blood behind, but I hadn't ruled it out. Magic had a way of making even the most unlikely scenarios possible.

I needed to talk to Bryson, but first, I had to set some boundaries while being reassuring. After that, I needed to call a mother, who was grieving for a son that wasn't dead, about another son who'd tried to kiss a girl.

I eased Jojo back until I could look her in the eye. "I thought we'd agreed that you wouldn't use your powers around other people?"

She hung her head and nodded. "I was only trying to help."

"I understand…" I'd been in her shoes more times than I could count. The last thing I wanted was to shame her for having a big heart. "How about we compromise? Next time, you talk to your dads and I first?" I lifted her chin. "If it's really important to you, we'll figure out a way for you to help them without scaring them."

She sighed. "That's just it. Holden wasn't scared. He was happy."

"That's good, but you still need to ask first. Okay?" I ached for her. She reminded me so much of myself at her age. All she wanted to do was help folks, but she seldom stopped to consider the repercussions.

"Okay." Jojo bit her lower lip. "Can I go play on the slip and slide now?"

"Yes, but I have to call and speak to Holden's mom. Do you want to hear what I tell her?"

"Nope." She rushed to her dresser and pulled out her bathing suit.

Feeling quite pleased with myself, I walked into the kitchen and pulled the church directory from the drawer. I glanced out the window. TJ sprayed Bryson and Aaron with the hose. The men laughed like they didn't have a care in the world. I would have loved to forget all about our problems and join them. Instead, I dialed the number.

"McAlister residence." The woman sounded stressed. I would be too if my oldest son was missing and presumed dead.

"Hi, Mrs. McAlister, this is Tessa, Jolene's mother—"

"Oh, Tessa. I was planning to call you later tonight. One second." A rustling sound filled the line and the background noise grew louder. A second later, the line went quiet. "Sorry about that, I needed to go someplace private."

"No problem." I hoped to goodness Holden hadn't told his mom what Jolene had said about Wyatt, but I needed to test the waters. "I'm sorry for your... To hear about Wyatt."

"Thank you. Buck told me you were helping find him. Thank you." She sniffled through her words.

"We're doing our best." I hated to change the subject, but there wasn't much I could do about Wyatt. The situation with Jojo was another story. "I'm calling about Holden—"

"Exactly how old is Jolene? I know she's small for her age, but she has such poise, I thought maybe she was Holden's age."

What the heck? "She's ten."

Mrs. McAlister sucked in a breath. "Oh my."

"I'm confused. What is it you wanted to talk to me about?"

She hesitated. "Holden has quite the crush on your daughter. It's inappropriate, I know, and completely out of the blue...but..."

I wasn't sure I wanted to hear what came after *but*.

"He's been walking around the house singing that old Dolly Parton song, 'Jolene,' since last Sunday." She laughed, but it came out high and shrill. "And he's doodling her name and hearts like a...well, like a girl."

"I see." I bit back a comment about toxic masculinity. I had bigger things to worry about than Mrs. McAlister shaming her son's doodles. "I know your family is going through a very difficult time, but my husband found them alone together in an empty Sunday school classroom. Jolene said it was Holden's idea to lie to the youth pastor and sneak off."

She made a choking sound.

"I'm not placing the blame solely on him. I've already set some boundaries with Jolene. I would appreciate it if you'd have a talk with Holden. There's a world of difference in maturity between ten and thirteen."

"Of course." She sighed. "I apologize for this. It won't be a problem anymore. We're going to find a new church."

"Not because of this business with the kids?" I bit my tongue to keep from telling her she was overreacting. The last thing they needed to do was lose their support system in their time of need.

"No. Holden is... He's taking Wyatt's disappearance hard. We're going to homeschool him and limit his exposure to other children for a while." Her words came out slow and measured. Almost like she was trying to tell me something without actually telling me.

"I understand." I hoped I'd read her wrong, but I worried their decisions had to do with the boys being shifters. Whatever their reasons, it was none of my business as long as Jolene was safe. "I have to run. Enjoy the rest of your weekend." I hung up before she replied.

Deep down my reaction was the same as Aaron's, and I hated it. Much like my family, the McAlisters were good people who happened to be different. But I'd be lying if I said I wasn't relieved we wouldn't have to run interference between Jolene and a boy who turned furry once a month.

I glanced back out the window in time to see Jojo dive onto the slip and slide. TJ cheered and squirted her with the hose. She bent down, scooped up two handfuls of mud and threw it at him.

Yep, she's definitely still a little girl.

Dottie and Aaron sat in lawn chairs watching the kids. He rocked Quin while she made silly faces at the baby. Mae was busy supervising

Bryson at the grill. Part of me wanted to go outside and join them, but I couldn't get what Jolene had said out of my head.

She'd spoken to Charlie, and from the sound of it, it wasn't unusual. She'd mentioned it so casually, it seemed like an everyday occurrence. If that were the case, his spirit had to be close.

And it's high time he gave me some answers.

CHAPTER 17

I glanced from the half-circle on the floor to the empty salt container in my hand. "Son of a bit—"

Aaron opened the door and ducked when the cardboard cylinder smashed into the wall inches from his head. "Whoa!"

"Sorry." Desperate to contact my grandfather, I dropped to my knees to make the circle smaller, the line thinner, anything to get the two ends to touch.

"What's going on?" Aaron eased into the office as if afraid he'd fall through the floor.

"Well, let's see..." I took a piece of paper from the desk and used it like a dustpan to catch every stray crystal. "Mae's sick. TJ might as well be an orphan. Jojo is lonely and using magic. I'm starving my own baby, but even if I could figure out how to feed him, he'd magic me naked every time he got hungry."

Once upon a time, that sort of outburst would have made Aaron nervous. Thankfully, he'd spent enough time with me to know exactly what I needed to calm down. He stepped across the salt line and drew me to my feet.

Looking into my eyes, he whispered, "Breathe."

"Everything is a mess. I don't know what else can go wrong." I inhaled and exhaled three times before throwing myself into his arms.

Aaron held me until I relaxed against him. "Darlene and Killian are here."

"Seriously? What the heck is he doing with her?" I jerked away from him. "What are they? BFFs?"

"I don't like the two of them together any more than you do, but you need to check on Darlene. She was crying when they pulled up." He took a step back as if afraid I'd throw something else. "They have another Fae with them."

"Did Bryson say if it was one of the people Killian brought to church?"

Aaron shook his head. "Different guy."

The news surprised me. I couldn't help but feel like an animal in Killian's private zoo. "Are they outside?"

"No, they went straight to Gram Mae's."

"Let's go." I marched out of the house.

Bryson glanced up from the grill and frowned.

Even the kids seemed on edge, Jojo and TJ stopped making mud pies as I passed by, and Quin cried louder.

I felt bad for leaving Bryson alone with a screaming baby and two hungry kids, or I did until Aaron and I walked through Gram Mae's kitchen door.

I would have traded places with Bryson in a heartbeat, but I couldn't.

Not with my great-grandmother on the floor.

"Gram Mae!" I pushed past Dottie, Darlene, and Killian and knelt beside a male with long dark hair.

I knew beyond a shadow of a doubt the man cradling Gram Mae wasn't human. Magic crackled and popped around him like electricity from a downed powerline. What I didn't know was who he was or what had happened or why the others were just standing there watching him rock my great-grandmother as if she were a scared child.

"What's wrong? Did she fall? Is it her heart?" Resting my hand on her arm, I blew out a breath when her aura flashed brighter than I'd seen it in months.

The dark-haired Fae met my gaze. "She fainted. I caught her before she fell."

"Why did she fall? It could be something serious. Has anyone called 911?" I glanced from my mother, who had her butt in a chair, to Dottie glaring at the Fae men.

"It is not her heart." His voice washed over me like cool rain on a sticky summer day. The tension in my body eased, and I exhaled a long slow breath. A long slow breath that wasn't natural.

"Did you really just bespell me?" I would have smacked his overly handsome face if he weren't holding Gram Mae.

The guy glanced to someone behind me.

Killian stepped forward and rested his hand on my shoulder. "Tessa, this is Tighe. He didn't bespell you. He's working to bring Mae around, and you... Well, you got in the way."

Although he spoke in a soft tone, his words needled my last nerve. I opened my mouth to tell him as much, but Gram Mae chose that moment to speak.

"Stars in heaven. Am I dead?" Blinking, she raised a trembling hand to Tighe's face. "Is it really you?"

The Fae leaned into her touch and drew in a deep breath. "It's me and you are very much alive."

In all my years, I'd never known Mae to have a beau. My very human great-grandfather had died before I was born, and she'd never dated. I wasn't sure how to respond to the tender scene playing out before me. One thing I did know was that I was absolutely in the way.

I eased back from the couple and stood.

Aaron gave me a what-the-heck look.

I shrugged. What else could I do? It's not like I could explain what Mae had told me in front of an audience. Besides, she'd asked me to keep her relationship with Tighe between us.

Darlene glared, but that was nothing new. I was her favorite target when she was having a bad day. And from the looks of it, she was having a doozy.

I offered her what I hoped was a sympathetic smile.

She smirked and turned her attention back to Mae and Tighe.

Dottie hadn't stopped frowning since Aaron and I had come in. I'd chalked it up to concern for Gram Mae, but I had a feeling there was something else going on. She marched to the cupboard, pulled out the coffee filters, and closed the door hard enough to rattle the mugs inside. My normally mild-mannered aunt didn't as much as murmur an apology.

I moved to her side and took the coffee canister from her before she threw it at someone. Leaning close, I whispered, "Are you okay?"

She shook her head a fraction of an inch but spoke loud enough for the others in the kitchen to hear her. "I thought our guests would appreciate some coffee."

"As long as it has caffeine, count me in." Her behavior puzzled me. I'd all but dismissed her reaction the day Killian had shown up out of the blue. However, this was twice now she'd acted weird around him.

Dottie narrowed her eyes. "Decaf for you, young lady. Doctor's orders."

Killian tilted his head. "Are you ill?"

"I'm fine." I didn't want to get into Quin's colic with my brother, especially not in front of a stranger. "Just a little jittery lately."

Tighe helped Gram Mae to her feet.

She glanced around the room as if she didn't recognize her home of nearly thirty years. She met my gaze, and her hand flew to her face. Wide-eyed, she patted her glasses, her sunken cheeks, the lose skin on her neck.

I had no idea what was wrong, but I'd never seen her so alarmed. "Gram Mae?"

My great-grandmother turned back to Tighe, cried out, and all but ran for her room with him on her heels.

I started after them, but Killian took my arm. "Wait. Let him speak to her."

I jerked free. "The heck with that. She either bumped her head, developed dementia overnight, or the magic he used on her is playing with her memories."

He dipped his chin, but not before he gave me the same look Jolene gave TJ when he said something childish.

Aaron moved to my side. "What exactly did he do to her? And why are you here?"

Killian squared his shoulders, but before he could respond, Darlene jumped into the mix.

"I called Killian for moral support." She turned her tear-stained face toward me and Aaron.

I had no idea what she'd meant by that. "Why did you need moral support?"

"Stone and I had a big fight after church. He left. Said he needed some time." Her voice dripped with accusation. "Honestly, would it have killed you to stand up for me today?"

Killed me? no. Gone against everything I believed in? Yep.

"Momma…" I couldn't exactly get into my frustration with her and Killian's relationship with the Fae standing right there. "You could have called me. I would have come over."

Darlene's expression reminded me of a ticked off chihuahua. Narrowed eyes, barred teeth, nasty little snarl.

"I'm sorry." I'd apologized out of habit. For as long as I could remember, it was my job to diffuse her anger when no one else was around. Sure, we were in a kitchen full of people, but every last one of them seemed ready to explode.

Every one of them except Killian.

Half expecting to find him flooding the room with anxiety-producing magic, I turned my attention back to him.

He arched a brow and shook his head as if saying, *this isn't my fault.*

Aaron sat in the chair beside Darlene and took her hand. "I'm sure he'll come home. Do you need anything in the meantime?"

Shaking her head, she crumpled against him.

I made a mental note to tell Aaron to stop reinforcing my mother's dramatics. Coddling her was like feeding a stray cat. Sure, he meant well, but if he kept it up, we'd never get rid of her.

Aaron held my mother. Dottie had her back to me, but her spine was ramrod straight. Killian busied himself staring at the family photos on the wall.

"I'm going to check on Gram Mae," I said to everyone and no one.

I eased the door open and peeked into my great-grandmother's room.

Tighe sat on the edge of the bed, holding her hand while she slept. The magic hanging in the air told me her slumber wasn't natural. Given her reaction when she'd come to in the kitchen, rest was probably the best thing for her.

I walked farther into the room and drew a deep breath. The sweet floral scent of her powder took me back to my childhood. Gram Mae wrapping me in her quilt when I was cold. Rocking me when I was sick. Drying my tears when I was sad.

Tighe lifted his head and offered me an apologetic smile. "Her blood pressure rose quite high."

"Not surprising. She's had quite a shock today." My words came out nastier than I'd intended. They obviously cared for one another, and I doubted he'd hurt her on purpose, but I needed some answers. "Why did she react the way she did when she came to?"

"I suspect it was a defense mechanism. Some part of her recognized my magic and tried to protect her from heartache." His shoulders slumped as if admitting his concerns had cost him dearly. "I've waited too long."

"To come back?" I sank into a chair near the foot of the bed.

"Yes. She is the love of my life." He brought her hand to his lips, kissed it, and set it down again before turning to me. "I came back once, but she was married with young children."

I couldn't imagine what it must have been like to find out the woman you loved was committed to someone else. Then again, Mae had married in her early thirties, much later than other women of that time. From what Gram Mae had told me about him, I guessed he'd been gone for years before she moved on.

"Why did you leave her in the first place?" It was none of my business, but I told myself I wasn't being nosy. The more I understood the situation, the more I'd be able to help.

His eyes went wide before he could smooth his expression. "She never told you about me? About us?"

"She mentioned you the other day, but we were interrupted before we finished our conversation."

"Relationships between *our* kind and humans are forbidden." He paused as if to make sure I'd caught his meaning.

My immediate thought was of Aaron. He had magic thanks to Bryson sharing a piece of his soul with him, but he was technically human.

"When the queen found out I'd not only fallen in love with a human, but pledged myself to her..." He sighed the kind of sigh that old people did when recounting their regrets. "I was forbidden from leaving Tir Na Nog for ten years."

"Did Mae know?" The more I heard about this queen, the more I wanted to throttle her.

"Yes. I wrote everything in a letter and had Killian give it to her." He turned back to Gram Mae's sleeping form and sighed. "I promised to return to her the day I was released, but the queen found every reason to extend my punishment. Mae married before I could come for her."

"That's awful." I glanced anywhere except at him and my great-grandmother. Bryson and I had no idea if Aaron would age as a human or a Fae. It killed me to think he'd grow old and die while we remained young. "Killian said she was a ballerina until she was injured."

"Broken ankle." Tighe balled his hands into fists. "That was her punishment for loving me."

My heart shattered like porcelain falling onto a tile floor.

He brushed a kiss on Gram Mae's weathered cheek and whispered something to her in another language. When he stood and turned to me, his entire demeanor had changed. "She is not long for this world."

He might as well have stomped on the broken pieces of my heart with steel-toed boots. I could barely get enough air into my lungs to keep from passing out, let alone reply.

"You should know, I'm going to ask her to come with me to my home." He folded his arms and stared down at me.

The idea of him, or anyone, taking her away from me had me on my feet and ready to fight. "She's not going anywhere any time soon. Her family is here, not in Tir Na Nog."

"I have not set foot in that wretched place since I was released." He glanced back at Mae. "I understand your desire to keep her here, but her time is short. Once she no longer has breath, she will not be able to travel to the Summerlands."

"The Summerlands?" I'd heard the term before, but I'd always thought of it as another word for Heaven. Not someplace folks could buy a house and settle down.

"It is a place made from magic." He turned back to my great-grandmother. "When a Fae escorts a human to the Summerlands, they become as they were in their youth. Mae will dance again."

"It sounds a little like Heaven."

"The creator and untethered souls inhabit Heaven. The Summerlands is for the living." Tighe gave me the same condescending look Killian had in the kitchen. "You have a lot to learn and time is running out."

Although his delivery sucked, his message was eerily similar to something Gavin Partridge had said. "What do you mean? How is time running out? Is my family in danger?"

He opened his mouth and closed it three times before he growled under his breath. "Your path is much like mine. Learn from my mistakes, Tessa."

I freaking hated the way magic-folk spoke in riddles. Talking to the older ones was like reading Shakespeare in Old English, only there were no study guides to explain their meaning. "I don't understand. Is it Aaron? Am I going to have to leave him for ten years?"

Tighe tilted his head. "Why would you think the changeling has anything to do with the—" His words cut off like someone hit the mute button mid-sentence. "I can't say more. It is forbidden."

I'd had it up to my eyebrows with people telling me I needed help, but they weren't allowed to tell me what sort of trouble I was in. "What the heck is a changeling? And forbidden by who? Caoimhe?"

He grabbed my upper arms hard enough to leave bruises. "You must never speak her name. Do you hear me?"

His reaction sent my anger and frustration running for the hills. In their place, a cold, hard nugget of fear grew. "Yes."

Tighe glanced around the room as if expecting her royal highness to pop out of the closet or crawl out from beneath the bed. "I have to go. Please, tell Mae I will return when it is safe."

I opened my mouth to ask him when he'd come back and what he was afraid of and what kind of things I needed to learn. Before I had the chance, he vanished in a ball of white light.

Gram Mae lifted her hand from the bed. "Tessa Marie?"

"I'm here." I wrapped my fingers around hers.

"Lies can be the truth, and the truth can be a lie." As soon as the last word left her lips, she fell back to sleep.

CHAPTER 18

I had no idea what was coming for us. When it would arrive. How we'd defeat it. What I did know was who could tell me what in blazes was going on.

I stormed into the kitchen, pointed at Killian, and motioned to the door. "You. Outside. Now."

Aaron shot to his feet so fast he knocked his chair over in the process.

Darlene gaped like a guppy at feeding time, but I ignored her.

"Is Mae all right?" Wringing her hands, Dottie glanced between me and the hallway.

"She's resting." I spoke without taking my eyes off of Killian. No way would I risk blinking and having him vanish into a ball of freaking light.

My brother did a sort of bow and waved his arm toward the door. "After you."

"Uh-uh. Nope." I glared hard enough to tell him I meant business. "You first, and don't even think about accessing your magic."

"Tessa?" Aaron's voice cut through my angry haze, but I couldn't look at him. Not until I had a come to Jesus talk with Killian.

Flames danced along the tips of my curls, and the firebird pushed against the walls of her cage—my skin—to get out. I'd underestimated how emotional the conversation with Tighe had left me. If I didn't rein in my emotions, I'd lose control and shift before I had my answers.

Killian looked me over and strode to the door.

Aaron followed him. "Dottie, would you mind sitting with the kids? I have a feeling Bryson and I need to hear this."

"Sure, sweetheart." She dried her hands on a dishtowel.

I walked outside into the bright Florida sunshine, but nothing could warm the bone deep chill inside me. Not the weather and not the firebird threatening to burst out of my body and ignite everything in her path.

Killian plopped down in the wrought iron chairs where we'd talked for the first time. "I take it Tighe left quite an impression on you."

"This isn't about him." I drew a deep breath and imagined my power reaching into the earth like tree roots. On the exhale, I imagined it reaching skyward like branches. The centering helped, but not enough.

"Shall we wait for your husbands to join us?" He seemed bored.

Rather than respond with an insult, I nodded. Questions slammed around in my brain, but for once, I managed to sort my thoughts. The magic coursing through me made me feel powerful, more sure of myself, and less like a lost child looking for a family.

I had a family, an amazing one. Killian was the outsider, not me.

Holding Quin, Dottie ushered the older kids inside Mae's.

Bryson and Aaron joined us at the table, but neither spoke.

I waited until they'd settled before turning to my brother. "Why can you say the queen's name, but Tighe acted like I'd summoned Beetlejuice?"

With my magic running loose, I was more in tune with Bryson and Aaron's emotions. Their tension jostled me like people on a crowded subway, but I continued to stare at Killian.

He arched a brow.

"Answer me." I refused to play the facial expression game. My hubbies gave me odd looks all the time, and I'd never lost any sleep over it. I was sick of backpedaling and explaining myself to Killian. He'd accept me or he wouldn't—but it was high time he saw the real me.

"Names have power, Tessa." He studied me. "Some are so powerful, they can summon their owners."

I'd never heard of such a thing, but it seemed that I hadn't heard of a lot of Fae things. "You used her name the first time we spoke."

"Did I?" His left eye twitched. Had I not been staring, I would have missed it.

"Stop playing games and answer me..." The bit about lies being true and vice versa came back to me. "You did, and you're going to tell me why it's okay for you to use the C-word."

"C-word. That's an oddly fitting way to refer to her." He chuckled. "I work for her, spend a lot of time in her presence. She's not going to notice if I utter her precious name."

I believed him, but something told me there was much more he wasn't saying. "But she wouldn't have known you were here, right?"

Killian frowned at his hands and shook his head.

Bryson and Aaron exchanged unhappy glances.

"Not a yes, but not a no." I stood and paced a rut in the yard beside the table. "I'll take that to mean the queen knew exactly what you were up to."

He stared with a neutral expression. Again, neither confirming nor denying.

I stopped moving and pegged him with a glare. "So the bullshit you fed me about our father being in trouble was a lie?"

He stiffened his spine. "Fae do not lie."

"Right." I had news for him, I was Fae and I routinely bent the truth like warm taffy. Lord knows, Charlie had lied about our parents. But had he lied? Outright? Rather than debate a moot point, I shifted gears. "What's a changeling?"

This time, Killian made no effort to hide his surprise. "A changeling is a Fae baby that was switched with a human child."

"Like me?" The little voice inside my head screamed not to tell him that Tighe had called Aaron a changeling, but I had no idea why. First off, I doubted Aaron was any such thing. Secondly, if Tighe had guessed it so easily, Killian would have, too. Wouldn't he?

"Technically, yes. You were switched with a human child, but you are not a changeling." He seemed to struggle to explain, or maybe, he struggled to find a non-answer. "Changelings are raised by humans. Because they have no access to magic, their powers fade until they are essentially human."

My thoughts immediately went to Aaron's new found ability to dream walk. It'd surprised the daylights out of Bryson, because we'd assumed any supernatural power Aaron possessed had come from Bryson—but *he* couldn't walk the spirit world.

And then there was Jolene…Aaron's biological daughter. She had more spirit magic in her little finger than I had in my entire being. Could she have inherited that from her father, like she had his startling blue eyes?

The men at the table watched me as if waiting for me to come to some sort of conclusion.

I sank into the chair and did my best to give him an explanation that didn't involve Aaron. "I understand now why you were so worried about Quin's magic."

"It would be a shame if the little one's powers were starved to death." He rested his hand on mine. "Tessa, you can trust me. Tell me what's really troubling you."

Stiffening his spine, Bryson glared at Killian's hand.

I didn't mind the physical touch. In fact, I wanted to believe him. To believe he cared. To believe he could help me figure out what sort of trouble I was in. But I couldn't. "For starters, meeting my great-grandmother's former beau had me on edge."

Killian sighed as if I'd disappointed him. Maybe I had, but I wasn't about to spill my guts.

"Then there's the situation with our father." It struck me as odd that he hadn't mentioned anything about Liam since he'd called to invite me to lunch. Sure, he was angry with me about the Scarlett situation, but still. "Is he still alive?"

"He's very much alive." Killian glanced toward the wooded area beyond the lawn. "The queen seems to have softened where he is concerned."

"Who killed our mother?" The question came straight from my subconscious without hitting my brain. I covered my mouth.

Killian gasped. Bryson stood, and Aaron went wide-eyed. I wasn't sure which of us was more surprised.

Hanging his head, Killian said, "I don't know, but I'm fairly certain it was a human."

I'd expected him to give me a cryptic answer or dodge the question. "What makes you think that?"

"Atsila's death caused quite the commotion in Tir Na Nog. Many believed the Queen was responsible. Our mother's assassination nearly caused a civil war." He glanced away, cleared his throat, and turned back to me. "Many Fae were interrogated, but none who were questioned knew anything about her murder."

I sat back and let his words sink in. "Was the queen questioned?"

"Yes." He made a sour face. "Publicly."

Aaron folded his arms. "Am I right in assuming Fae interrogation techniques involve torture?"

Killian stared at Aaron as if he'd kicked a puppy. "No. We are not barbarians. We use magic."

Since he'd been so candid about our mother's death, I decided to go for broke. "Are the Fae involved in the animal attacks in this world?"

"Tessa, there are things I *cannot* speak of."

Bryson broke his silence. "Can't or won't?"

"Can't." Killian answered him, without taking his eyes off me. He wore such a pained expression, it was my turn to gasp. "The rulers in Fae, they have absolute control over their subjects…"

"Right. Like who dies and who lives. You told me that before, but —" A piece of the puzzle snapped into place, or I hoped it had. "They can forbid folks from talking about certain things?"

Nodding, he smiled and motioned for me to continue.

My husbands' confusion swirled around me, but I didn't dare take the time to explain. Not when I'd finally asked Killian the right question.

I remembered my conversations with Gavin and Tighe. Both had alluded to wanting to help but insisted there were rules. "And from helping someone in trouble?"

His smile faltered, but he nodded again.

I had no idea what he was trying to tell me without telling me. "I'm in trouble, aren't I?"

"Yes and no." He pressed his lips into a tight line.

It didn't take a rocket scientist to realize I was tap-dancing around a subject he wasn't allowed to talk about. The problem was I didn't know enough about what was going on to play word games. "Are mine or my family's lives in danger?"

"No one will *physically* harm you." He hesitated before adding, "Unless you force their hands."

Aaron opened his mouth as if to say something, but I silenced him with a quick shake of my head. He nodded and pressed his thigh against mine. Bryson moved behind me and rested his hands on my shoulders. Their physical touch gave me the strength to press forward with the hardest question of all.

"Does the queen have the authority to force me to go to Tir Na Nog?" My voice came out wobbly.

"No, not by force." Killian sighed and made a show of looking at his watch. "I've already been away too long. I should go."

"Why are you befriending Darlene?" Once again, my mouth got away from me. If I were honest, it bugged the ever-loving-crap out of me he was spending time with her instead of me.

"She needed someone to talk to." He gave me a pointed look and stood.

"Talk to about Stone?" I had a sinking feeling he'd come when Darlene had called for other reasons, like keeping tabs on me.

"That and other things." Once again, he seemed to be waiting for me to say the right thing or ask the right question.

Panicked, I ran back through our conversation. Then it hit me.

He'd given me a veiled warning. "How can I avoid forcing someone's hand?"

He blew out a breath and flashed me a genuine smile. "Don't break the rules."

I wanted to scream, or better yet, tie him down until he told me everything I needed to know. I stood and met his gaze. "How can I follow rules when I have no idea what they are?"

"Finally, you asked the right question." Killian drew me into an embrace. "Little sister, the golden rule of Fae is both simple and complicated. Humanity must never know we exist."

My blood turned to a cherry slushie. Not only did I live with humans who knew Fae existed, I used magic at work on a regular basis.

Aaron muttered under his breath, and Bryson closed his eyes.

I took a quick step back from all of them. "What about the ones who already know? What if I used magic in front of humans to save a life? Or to stop a killer? Is this rule retroactive? I mean, is ignorance a defense?"

Killian mimed locking his lips and throwing away the key. A split second later, he vanished in a ball of light.

Aaron shot to his feet and let loose a string of curses. "Is he kidding? How can you be expected to live in this world and never slip up and use your magic?"

"Before they died, my parents stressed the importance of keeping my magic a secret." Bryson glanced between us.

And he'd done the same with me. Unfortunately, we'd encountered one crisis after another that demanded we use everything at our disposal to stay alive.

I ran through everything that had happened since Killian had first arrived. "I don't think I've done anything too obvious since Quin was born."

Bryson's expression fell. "It's safe to assume we are being watched."

"We'll need to be careful." Aaron glanced to the driveway and threw his hands up. "But we aren't the only ones breaking the golden rule. That son of a bitch left another car here!"

CHAPTER 19

Aaron, Bryson, and I had decided to postpone our sex date.

Actually, we hadn't *decided* anything. We'd fallen into bed exhausted and forgotten all about our plans. Not that I was complaining, I would have traded a dozen orgasms for a solid eight hours of sleep.

Unfortunately, I hadn't gotten either.

Any other night, Aaron's body heat and steady breathing would have soothed me, but I'd sailed past exhaustion and landed in too-tired-to-sleep land. To make matters worse, my brain spun like a carnival ride. I couldn't focus on anything long enough to solve any of our growing list of problems. Instead, I stared at the ceiling debating on waking Bryson and asking him to knock me out with a spell.

Aaron rolled over and slung his arm across me. His face in my hair, he went as still as the grave—as in not breathing.

The sane part of me knew he was perfectly fine, dream-walking to Lord knows where. The irrational, completely in love, terrified-to-lose-him part of me freaked out.

"Bryson." I shook his shoulder. "Wake up. Aaron's dream-walking."

"Not surprising, considering everything that's going on." Bryson's sleep roughened tone sent a tingle through me. I'd always been a sucker for his sexy morning voice.

"You don't think he'll tear the veil again, do you?" The last thing we needed was for Aaron to open the door for every big-nasty in the spirit world.

"He'll be fine. He's been working with Harris remotely." Bryson caressed my cheek. "Want to talk about what's keeping you up?"

"Sure." I doubted I'd make much sense, but speaking to another human being was better than arguing with myself. "Let's go in the other room. I hate it when he feels like he's dead."

"I'm here." Aaron tightened his grip and pulled my back to his chest. "You're not going anywhere."

I relaxed against him and allowed the magic to flow between us. Under normal circumstances, skin to skin contact with my mates worked better than a good night's sleep and a pot of coffee. Too bad for me, I couldn't remember what normal looked like. "Where'd you go?"

He tensed. "I checked in on TJ and Jojo's dreams... You know, to make sure they weren't having nightmares."

A little warning bell rang in the back of my mind. His explanation didn't match his body language, but we had more important things to discuss.

I wasn't sure where to start, so I went with the most urgent matter. "Jojo reached out to Wyatt, Holden's brother. She's certain he's not dead."

"That explains a lot. I sensed Jojo's magic on Holden." Bryson draped his arm around Aaron and me.

"That's news to me."

Aaron nipped my earlobe. "It wouldn't be if you'd stuck around a little longer after you guys got home from church."

Bryson must have sensed my confusion, because he added, "I didn't have the chance to tell you before you dropped the bomb about Killian being at church and left me to explain it."

"Oh, right. Sorry-not-sorry." Rather than grill him until he told me everything I'd missed, I forced myself to focus on the matter at hand.

"Jojo tried to reach Wyatt's spirit last week, but I suppose she could have tried again today."

Bryson pressed closer, sandwiching me tighter between them. "I'm not thrilled she disobeyed us."

"I agree, but her heart was in the right place. I told her she needed to ask permission before trying to contact anyone else's dead relatives." I felt safe in their arms—safe enough to bring up the one topic I'd been avoiding. "Today in church proved to me that Quin needs access to our magic, but we have to make sure he doesn't zap me topless again."

Both men tightened their grips.

Aaron chuckled. "Of all the days to miss."

I reached back and swatted his butt. "It wasn't funny."

"Maybe not then, but I can see the humor in it now." Bryson laughed. "But you're right. I'll see if Harris has any advice about controlling Quin's magic."

"I hate to bring it up..." Aaron went still behind me. "I'm worried about Mae."

I nodded because I couldn't get the words past the lump in my throat.

Bryson swallowed hard, but otherwise remained quiet.

We'd talked about Gram Mae's age and health many times over the years. Any reasonable person would agree she wouldn't live forever, but I wasn't exactly reasonable when it came to my great-grandmother. What was the point in having magic if we couldn't use it to save the people we loved?

Aaron cleared his throat. "The murders are too close to home. We need to catch this guy."

I loved him for changing the subject, but sooner or later, that wouldn't be an option.

"I agree," Bryson said.

I'd been running a hundred miles an hour since the killings had started, but it was past time for me to slow down and think things through. "I'll walk the crime scenes again and check out the evidence at the station. I feel like we're missing something obvious."

"I've been thinking the same thing." Aaron drew slow circles on my belly. "The scenes seem tailor-made for you, but why?"

I'd asked myself the same question too many times to count. "I thought the perp was testing me and my magic, but I'm not sure that's it."

Bryson brushed my hair back and cupped my face. "Why do you say that?"

"The scenes all have common elements, but they're different." I found myself caressing Bryson's chest. What can I say? Touching them helped me think.

"Do you still believe the images are staged?" Bryson inched close enough to slip his thigh between mine.

"Absolutely. They start right before the attacks and end right after, but they're…" I struggled to find a way to explain what I'd seen. "They're obviously fake, but in different ways."

Aaron propped himself up on his elbow. "It's not uncommon for serial killers to toy with law enforcement."

"I know. I've seen the Hannibal Lecter movies, but this is different." I closed my eyes and thought back to the first murder scene. "The images of Wyatt were clean, but at the time, they seemed real. I knew right away something was off with the gator-man attack."

"Because the angles didn't change?" Bryson dipped his head and kissed a line from my shoulder to my jaw.

"Right. It was like watching a television show instead of actual events." I brushed my lips across his out of habit, but I was too distracted to pay much mind to the kiss.

Aaron sucked in a breath. "He wants you to know he's responsible for all of the deaths."

Is that it? Does the perp want me to know he can change into multiple animals?

I rolled to my back and met his gaze. "I'm not sure, but he's definitely sending me a message."

"He's not hiding the fact that the images in the mirrors are fake. If anything, he's making it more obvious." Bryson took advantage of my change in positions to lick his way across my collarbone.

My skin broke out in goosebumps, but his warm breath on my bare breasts chased them away. "Why? Why would the killer want me to know he's planting false evidence?"

Aaron cupped my cheek and turned my face toward his. "He's trying to get into your head."

"It's working." I stared into his Caribbean blue eyes and lost my train of thought. Between his I-want-you expression, and Bryson working his way down my body one kiss at a time, the blood had left my brain. "Oh God, that's working, too."

Bryson laughed against my inner thigh.

I froze, unable to reconcile the chaos in my head with the desire in my body. "Is it weird I'm getting hot and bothered while discussing potential murders?"

"As long as it's us, not the conversation, turning you on, I'm good with it." Aaron snickered.

Bryson lifted his head. "Should I stop?"

"No." I curled my fingers in his long hair. "Don't stop. We need this. *I* need this."

Aaron claimed my mouth with a kiss that stole my breath and my worries. Between the two of them, any thought of murders and kids and fairy-brothers melted away.

Those few stolen moments were about more than pleasure, although there was plenty of that to go around—they were a chance to reconnect. We'd talked, shared a table, a bed, and even a shower, but we hadn't slowed down enough to enjoy each other's company.

Naked in the early morning hours, we shut out the world and focused on what mattered most. Each other.

For a while, anyway.

"Cut it out, Bryson." Aaron's laughter bordered on a giggle. Not exactly the sound I wanted to hear while straddling a man.

Evidently, laughter was contagious because Bryson joined in. "I'm not doing anything."

I disagreed. He was doing marvelous things to my body, or he was.

Wiggling and kicking his feet, Aaron raised his head and shoulders and peered past me. "Maddie! Down!"

I glanced behind me and caught the dog with her tongue out mid-lick. Waffling between joining their giggle-fest and being completely grossed-out, I eased off Aaron. "How did she get in here?"

"Better question, what was she doing?" Still snickering, Bryson took the dog by the collar and pulled her off the bed.

Aaron shuddered. "She was licking the inside of my knee."

"Could be worse." Bryson pushed the dog into the hall and took a step toward the bed.

I hated to bring it up, but Maddie's behavior had gone from strange to disturbing. "I really think we need to do an exorcism on the dog. I think Gavin's in there."

Bryson frowned.

Aaron gave me the same you-can't-be-serious look Bryson had when I'd first mentioned the possibility of Gavin possessing Maddie. "That would explain why she's been watching me in the shower."

"See?" Pointing at Aaron, I turned to Bryson. Playing Peeping Tom wasn't proof, but it was a start.

He grinned. "Do you really think we need to do a dog exorcism?"

Quin's whimpers came through the baby monitor. Half a heartbeat later, he'd worked himself into a tizzy.

Bryson glanced from us to the door as if considering his next move. He was closer, but technically, it was Aaron's turn to see to the baby.

As much as I would have loved to keep fooling around, the sunlight seeping through the cracks in the curtains told me we didn't have time. I hopped up and snatched my robe from the floor. "I'll get him."

"Three more minutes. Tops." Aaron reached for me, but I sidestepped him.

Motioning toward his man parts, I shook my head. "I hate to *deflate* your high hopes, but it looks like playtime's over."

He covered the area in question. "Nothing a kiss won't fix."

The pitter patter of little feet filled the hallway.

"TJ and Jojo are up. They're going to want breakfast." I flashed him an evil grin. "But I suppose I could call Maddie to—"

"Don't you dare finish that sentence." Aaron's mouth fell open.

"That's just…wrong, Tessa." Bryson pulled on a pair of PJ pants. "Teasing a guy when he's…*down*."

"Out." Aaron tossed a pillow at us. "Both of you."

Cackling like a couple of old ladies, Bryson and I walked into the hall. He headed toward the nursery, and I went straight to the kitchen. The kids could wait, but the adults in the house would need coffee—and I wasn't talking about the decaf crap.

CHAPTER 20

Mondays were never my favorite day of the week, but this one promised to be a good one. I had plans to spend the afternoon with Jolene. The girl had been through so much, she deserved a few hours outside the house to forget her troubles.

Lord knows I did, too.

"Mom?" Jojo knocked on the bedroom door. "Are you ready?"

"Almost. Come in." I frowned at my frizzy red curls and got to work on a French braid. Despite everything going wrong, I wanted to look nice for our girls' day out.

"Will you help me with my hair?" She gave me a tired smile. "I'm pooped. Dad made me catch up in math class."

"How'd you do?"

"Okay, I think. But he says my social studies essay needs work."

I loved that Bryson had taken the lead with her education. While I'd taken math and science in college, I'd forgotten most of the information after final exams.

I pulled her into an embrace. "Are you sure you're up for this today?"

"I'm up for it. This is Micah Sterling we're talking about." Jojo wiggled out of my arms. "But maybe just the movie. No pedicures or lunch?"

"Sure, as long as we can stuff ourselves on movie snacks." I would have bought her a theater, loaded it with ponies, and kidnapped Micah Sterling to do a live reenactment if it meant she kept talking to me instead of glaring.

"Popcorn and chocolate…and two hot dogs." She flashed me a grin that gave me hope she'd be okay. Maybe we all would, with time and love and ridiculous amounts of junk food.

"You got it." I glanced at the clock. "We can catch the earlier showing."

Aaron came into the room, pulled his shirt over his head and kicked off his shoes. "Give me five minutes."

"For what?" The view of his abs and toned back short-circuited my brain. Aaron had one of those tall lean bodies that looked good in everything, from a suit to jeans and a T-shirt to nothing at all.

He motioned between me and Jojo. "I'm going with you."

"On girls' day?" She groaned.

Still shirtless, he knelt in front of her and flashed his dimples. "What's wrong with me wanting to spend time with my two favorite girls?"

Between the beautiful child and ridiculously handsome man, my ovaries sat up and took notice.

Whoa Nelly. No more baby thoughts.

"Nothing, but you can't come." She turned to me for backup.

"We've scaled back out plans. We'll be okay on our own for a two-hour movie." I understood where he was coming from. The whack-a-doo staging murder scenes was still out there, but I highly doubted we'd run into the guy at a teen vampire movie.

Aaron's expression told me he disagreed.

I sighed. "Fine. You have five minutes. If you're not ready, we're leaving without you."

Jolene whispered, "And TJ can't come."

"I'll go warm up the car." He grabbed a clean shirt from the closet and left the room.

I grabbed a brush and motioned for her to sit on the wrought iron vanity stool. "Ponytail or braids?"

"One French braid like yours." She sat straighter.

Brushing her long blonde hair, I forgot about my troubles and allowed myself a few minutes to be a mom. It wouldn't be long before she hit her teen years and thought everything I said, did, or wore was awful.

"All set." I tied the braid off with an elastic band and gave her a hand mirror.

She turned and inspected her reflection. "Pretty. Thank you."

"You're welcome." I smiled what felt like my first smile in years. "Ready for *Vampires Still Suck?*"

"Yes!" Jojo took my hand and pulled me toward the living room.

Aaron and Bryson stood shoulder to shoulder in the kitchen door. Aaron was shaking his head, but Bryson had his arms folded.

I hated to ask, but I had to. "What's wrong?"

Aaron turned to me. "We aren't going anywhere until one of you figures out how to get that ghost out of Maddie."

A headache bloomed behind my eyes. With everything else going on, we'd forgotten all about the dang dog. "What did she do?"

They motioned into the kitchen.

I peeked around the corner and my world stopped spinning.

It looked like the refrigerator had exploded. Food, some still in its container but most not, littered the floor. The bread was mauled. All that was left of the lunch meat was a plastic bag. The only clean thing in the entire room was the platter that once held the left-over pot roast I'd planned to serve for dinner.

I glanced from the mess to the dog.

Maddie sat upright in a chair with a container of left-over beef stew in front of her—and that wasn't the weird part. Judging from the brown goo dripping down the front of the cabinet, she'd reheated it in the microwave.

She looked up at me, flashed a doggie grin, and let out a belch that put teen boys everywhere to shame.

"Gavin?" I took a tentative step forward.

Maddie, or should I say Gavin, nodded.

"Get out of there this instant!" I stomped my foot. Like that would help. The absolute last thing I wanted to deal with was a ghost in a dog with an upset stomach. The second to the last thing was cleaning the kitchen.

The dog howled.

Jolene pushed past me. "What did you do? I told you I'd bring you a hotdog from the movie theater."

Maddie/Gavin, hung his head.

Bryson, Aaron, and I exchanged surprised glances.

Bryson cleared his throat. "Jojo, how long have you known Maddie was possessed?"

"Since last Sunday." Her guilty expression reminded me of the dog, big eyes, dipped chin, and a healthy dose of sorry-not-sorry. "I didn't want to tell you. It's nice to have someone to talk to whenever I want."

Once again, the parents in the room exchanged glances. Only this time, we were the ones with the guilty expressions.

Aaron rested his hand on her shoulder. "We've been pretty busy lately, but you know you can talk to us about anything."

"Any time." Bryson knelt in a puddle of brown goo and didn't seem to care. I had no doubt he'd swim through an alligator infested septic tank for her. "I'm sorry I haven't had time for you. Let's plan on getting back to the studio and sculpting this week."

"Sure, but I don't mind that y'all are busy." She hitched a shoulder. "You guys are my parents. Gavin's cool and makes me laugh."

Aaron's brows rose. "Hey, we're cool."

Jolene rolled her eyes. "Yeah, but Gavin doesn't tell dad jokes."

The possessed dog snorted.

As much as I enjoyed watching her teasing them, Gavin had been in the chocolate lab long enough, and I missed the real Maddie. She might not have been the crunchiest bone in the box, but she was our goofball. "Come out, Gavin."

"He can't. He's stuck." Jolene dipped her chin.

"Stuck?" Bryson turned to me as if I had the answers.

I hated myself for having to ask, but her expression worried me. "Stuck on his own, or stuck because you wanted a friend?"

"On his own…" She continued to avoid my gaze.

While I believed Gavin had gotten in over his head, I had a feeling she'd kept him trapped on purpose. "Can you get him out?"

"Yep." Jojo sighed and placed one hand on each side of the dog's face. "This might make you puke."

Aaron's eyebrows climbed into his hairline.

I didn't know why he was so worried. It wasn't like a little dog vomit could make more of a mess.

Jolene's magic worked its way across my skin like ice crystals on a window. A cool wind blew through the kitchen, sending wrappers and bits of food flying. The dog whimpered and shook her head, but Jojo refused to let go. Glasses crashed to the floor, dishes rattled in the cabinets, and the cupboard doors flew open.

And then it stopped.

At some point during the commotion, Maddie had collapsed.

Jojo knelt beside the dog and ran her hand over her brown fur. "Good girl. You're okay now."

The poor thing lifted her head and glanced from the mess to us and barked like the boogeyman had walked into the room.

"Did it work?" I didn't sense the spirit nearby.

"Yep. Gavin says he'll be close, but he needs to do ghost stuff." Jojo stood.

I had a feeling ghost-stuff meant he needed time to recoup.

Surveying the mess, Aaron blew out a breath. "And she didn't puke."

Maddie's racket stopped, but she continued to move as if barking. It looked as if someone had hit the mute button.

Quin squealed from his swing.

I turned to Bryson. "We have to do something about his magic. This is getting ridiculous."

"I'll call Harris today." Bryson walked to the sink, scraped chunks of food off his arms, and turned on the disposal.

"Quin is like Baby Yoda, only cuter." Jojo frowned down at her clothing. "But we can't fix him now or we'll miss the movie."

The four of us looked like we'd been on the losing end of a middle school cafeteria food fight.

I glanced at the clock. It hung at an odd angle, but it'd withstood hurricane Jolene. "Your dads can deal with Quin and this mess. Go clean up and be ready to go in ten minutes."

"Wet ghost-dog-hair, don't care!" Laughing, Jolene bolted for the bathroom.

Aaron and Bryson stared with you-can't-be-serious expressions.

"I'm still going with you." Aaron squared his shoulders and raised his chin. But the tough guy impression would have worked much better if he didn't have macaroni noodles in his hair.

"No need. Now that Gavin's free, he can be our bodyguard." Heading for the master, I waved over my shoulder. "Gotta run. Have fun."

"Shouldn't we talk about what just happened?" Bryson trailed after me with Aaron on his heels.

"Which part?" I played dumb, but they weren't buying it.

"Please tell me she didn't keep the ghost in the dog to have someone to talk to," Aaron said.

"Maybe. I doubt Gavin would have stayed in the dog willingly." I started the shower, stripped, and stepped in. "As for what just happened—she's been lonely and feeling neglected. The best thing for her is to spend an afternoon with her non-dad-joke-telling parent. We can have a family meeting after the movie."

"Ha-ha." Aaron poked his head in the shower. "Are you sure you'll be okay without me?"

Bryson laughed, "Are *you* sure you don't have ulterior motives?"

Aaron winced. "Who me?"

Ignoring them, I sang the theme song to *Vampires Suck* while I washed the food scraps from my hair.

Aaron grumbled under his breath. "Go, but promise me you'll be careful."

CHAPTER 21

Jolene and I made it to the theater snack bar with five minutes to spare. We loaded up on goodies, including the world's largest bucket of popcorn. After handing over the equivalent of most folks' monthly mortgage payments, we headed to our movie.

Or tried to.

"Hi, Holden!" Jolene waved a pack of chocolate covered raisins in his direction.

The boy's entire face went ooey-gooey before he broke out in song. "Jolene, Jolene, Jolene, Joleeeeene."

I hadn't dealt with teen boys since I was in high school, but I seemed to recall they went out of their way not to embarrass themselves.

Jojo glanced from him to me with a look of pure horror.

Holden took a step in our direction and froze. I'm talking so still, I wondered if he'd stopped breathing. The color drained from his face and his eyes went so wide if someone tapped his shoulder, they would have popped out.

"Holden?" Jojo took a step in his direction.

He shook his head, flashed her a lovesick smile, and seemed to *try* to move forward. It was like his feet were made of concrete.

"What's wrong with him?" Jojo whispered.

"I'm not sure."

Rubbing his temples, he muttered something about loving her and monsters and death.

Something was seriously wrong. I glanced around but didn't see his parents. "Are you okay?"

Stupid question, but my mouth–to-brain filter didn't always work when faced with bizarre situations.

A dark spot formed on the front of his pants, but he didn't as much as flinch. In fact, he'd gone still again.

"Mom?" Jolene's voice sounded like a squeaky toy.

I had no clue what was going on. My first thought was that he'd gotten in trouble for the shenanigans at children's church, but his mother hadn't seemed angry. If anything, she'd seemed nervous. Had his father punished him?

I took a step forward and held out my free hand as if I thought he were a frightened puppy. "Holden, sweetie, are you okay?"

He stared, tears forming in his eyes.

Jojo moved closer, and the boy screamed high and shrill. It was the sound of pure unadulterated terror.

And then it changed into something more primal, more...wolf-like.

Oh crap!

I was a licensed mental health professional, but none of my training had prepared me for a teenaged shifter.

It's broad daylight and the full moon is a week away. He can't shift now. Can he?

I took a slow step back. "Where are your parents?"

Holden either didn't hear me or had other things on his mind. Other things like my daughter. He raised his hand and pointed a finger at her. "You...you stay away from me!"

Jojo backed away so fast she tripped and spilled the enormous bucket of popcorn. She covered her face, but not before I saw her broken-hearted expression.

People stopped walking to their theaters and crowded around us, but I didn't see Holden's family. A young man in a uniform polo studied us for a couple of seconds and darted off. I needed to deescalate the situation before someone called the police.

"I've really missed you. You're so pretty." Holden's voice had deepened and developed a gravelly quality. He backed up, tripped over his feet, and scrambled on all fours to get away from her. "Don't tell your dad I talked to you."

"We won't tell anyone. Please…it's okay. Just calm down." I was torn between helping the boy, comforting Jojo, and driving home to strangle Aaron. As sure as the sun would rise, Aaron Burns had paid Holden a visit in his dreams. Lord only knew what he'd said to the poor kid.

Growling and shaking his head, Holden bent at the waist and tangled his fingers in his hair.

It was my turn to be scared motionless. The sounds coming out of his mouth transported me to another time and place—me afraid for my life, stuck in a tree, with werewolves circling below.

The longer the boy yanked at his hair, the longer and more misshapen his fingers became.

Murmurs rose up in the crowd. They had to be seeing the same thing.

Brushing popcorn off herself, Jojo stood.

"Jolene, stay back." I took a step to the side, putting my body between the kids.

"I'm here, Hell Girl, and so is Charlie." Gavin Partridge's spirit appeared beside me. "Do as I say."

As much as I appreciated the moral support, I wasn't sure what a couple of spirits could do against a baby shifter. "Get Jojo out of here."

"Will do, but no sudden movements." Gavin disappeared from my peripheral vision. "Jolene, listen to me. You can't run. No matter what."

"Okay," she whispered.

"Hell Girl, Charlie says to burn him if he charges, but don't let anyone see the fire." Gavin made an exasperated sound. "Does that make sense to you?"

Nodding, I drew my magic to the surface, but stopped short of creating actual flames. Charlie was right—the last thing I needed was to light up like a roman candle in front of an audience.

"Don't hurt him." Jojo's voice cracked. "He can't help it he's different."

Holden's head snapped in her direction. Raising his elongated chin as if scenting the air, he curled his lips back and flashed us a rather impressive set of teeth.

"She won't but you have to be quiet," Gavin said.

It might have been better for all concerned if Holden had fully shifted. The partial change was downright terrifying. A couple of bystanders screamed, others ran, but most continued to stare at the poor kid.

The young werewolf kept his eyes trained on my daughter.

In ultra-slow motion, I took another step backward.

Fast approaching footsteps echoed to my left, but I didn't dare turn my head.

"Damn it all." Gavin's voice rose. "Tessa, be ready. Charlie says he'll likely come claws first. Use Bryson's training."

Easier said than done. All I had to do was make contact without getting mauled to death. I widened my stance and pooled the heat of the firebird in my palms. Early on, Bryson had spent countless hours teaching me to fight, but we'd stopped practicing when I became pregnant.

A large man in a theater polo shirt pushed his way through the bystanders. "Is there a problem here?"

Holden let out a growl that anyone with half a brain would have taken as a warning.

Evidently, movie-guy didn't have much in the way of common sense. He reached for the kid.

"No!" I lurched forward out of instinct. Stupid move. One scratch and I ran the risk of turning furry on the next full moon, but I couldn't let an innocent human get hurt. Worse still, I couldn't let the boy ruin his life on what was likely the first time he'd shifted.

Holden launched himself at me.

Avoiding his claws, I dropped my arms to waist level and shoved my hands up at an angle toward his chest. Grabbing his forearms, I released the magic from my palms and shoved him to the side.

Holden let out an ear-piercing yowl and lost his balance. Unfortunately, he dragged me down with him. My shoulder took the brunt of the fall, but as far as I knew, he hadn't scratched or bitten me. I scrambled back to put some distance between myself and a life-long subscription to the Hair Removal Club for Women.

The boy's whimpers reminded me of the sound Maddie had made in the kitchen. He kicked and floundered but managed to get to his feet. The second he stood, he bolted for the emergency exit.

The mother in me hoped I hadn't burned him too seriously, but I had my own child to worry about. Cradling my arm, I stood and turned to Jolene.

Gavin's spirit crowded around her. "It's okay, sweet girl. It's going to be okay."

Jolene sat curled into a tight ball. Rocking back and forth the way she had in the weeks after her mother's murder.

I reached for her, but stopped short.

Blood dripped from a gash on her arm.

CHAPTER 22

"What the hell happened?" Bryson took the crying girl from my arms and headed for the house.

"We had an *incident* at the movie theater. We need to bandage her arm and have an adult chat." I struggled to keep up with his long-legged strides.

I'd called from the car but hadn't gone into the specifics. For starters, I was driving with one good arm while on the verge of a panic attack. Not to mention, I didn't want to get into the werewolf thing and scare Jolene even more.

Aaron met us at the door with Quin in his arms. He took one look at Jojo's blood-soaked bandage and gripped the wall to remain upright. "That looks bad. We should take her to the hospital."

"This isn't the kind of thing *regular* medicine can handle." I spoke loud enough for Bryson to hear me, and hopefully, catch my meaning.

"You never should have taken her alone." Anger deepened Aaron's voice.

While I understood it was the fear talking, his reaction was so un-Aaron-like I didn't know how to respond. "You're right, but none of us could have seen this coming."

As soon as the words left my mouth, I knew I was wrong. Aaron *should* have seen it coming, all right. He'd known Holden was a shifter, and unless I completely missed my mark, he'd used his dream-walking abilities to scare the kid senseless.

Bryson glanced back at me with an expression that promised pain, and a slow death, to whoever had hurt his little girl. "Tell me it wasn't an animal."

"We'll talk once Jojo is patched up." I prayed he'd take the hint and drop it until we were alone.

He didn't. "I need to know what we're dealing with."

"Lupine." I hoped Jolene didn't know the meaning of the word. Sure, she'd seen her friend transform into a monster, but he hadn't gone full wolf yet. It was unlikely she knew what a scratch from a shifter could lead to.

Aaron made a strangled sound in his throat.

Bryson's expression softened as he whispered to the girl, "I'm sorry this happened to you. Let's get your cut cleaned up."

She didn't respond.

My chest tightened. We'd fostered her shortly after she'd witnessed her mother's murder. It'd taken weeks for her to trust us enough to speak. Seeing her go from our smart, vibrant daughter to traumatized and nonverbal was more than I could bear.

Aaron pulled me to his side but stopped when I cried out. "Are you injured?"

"I went down hard on my shoulder, but I'll be fine." My words came out frosty, but I didn't care. He'd caused this. He should have left well enough alone where Holden was concerned.

Aaron threw up his hands. "What the hell did I do now?"

I marched into the office without another word.

Jojo sat on the twin bed with Maddie's head in her lap. Standing beside her, Gavin whispered words of encouragement.

Bryson's power rushed over me as he chanted a calming spell. He held his hands a few inches from Jolene's body. Starting at her head, he searched her tiny frame for malignant magic and wounds. I doubted Bryson knew the ghost was there, but I didn't want to tell him and risk breaking his concentration.

Bryson frowned and took a step back. "Jojo, I'm going to help you rest for a while. Okay?"

She looked up at him, her big blue eyes welling with tears.

He brushed her curls from her forehead. "It won't hurt. I promise. I'll sing you a type of lullaby, and you'll drift off to sleep."

She nodded and stretched out on the bed.

I turned my back to them, so she couldn't see my face. We'd dealt with a were-attack once before, but I'd forgotten about that part of the healing process. With adults, it was best to put them under a healing spell for two full moons. It took that long to tell if they were going to shift. But I wasn't sure how it worked with kids who hadn't reached puberty.

"Tessa, I need you to get the salt and make a protection circle." Bryson began chanting the spell.

"Salt?" Gavin moved away from the bed. "I'll, uh...step out."

Jojo made a sad little sound and reached for him.

The spirit smiled and retook his place by her side. "Don't you worry, little one. I'm not going to leave you until your daddy fixes you up."

Jojo nodded and closed her eyes.

I hurried to the shelves for the salt. It took my muddled brain a few seconds to understand why the cardboard container wasn't in its usual place. "We're out."

"What do you mean, we're out?" He growled and any doubt I had about who he blamed for Jojo's situation vanished.

"I'll get the shaker from the kitchen," Aaron said from the hall.

"Table salt is less potent." Bryson gave me the same look he had Maddie when she'd chewed his favorite boots.

"Get the fancy pink stuff from the cupboard," I called after Aaron.

Starting the chant from the beginning, Bryson met my gaze. I'd seen him at his best and absolute worst, but I'd never seen such pain—or such anger—in his brown eyes.

I hugged my midsection to keep from flying into a million pieces.

Aaron returned with the Himalayan Sea salt. "Got it."

Bryson motioned to the container in Aaron's hand and continued to chant the sleeping spell.

"Oh right." I took it from him. Leaving a trail as I went, I circled the bed.

Bryson finished the verse before turning to me. "Are we out of anything else?"

"Nope." I bit the inside of my cheek to keep from saying something ugly.

I got it. I did. They were angry and scared and needed someone to blame. I'd taken Jojo out by myself. I was an easy target. However, Bryson hadn't seemed all that concerned with us going alone before we'd left. And Aaron had no room to point fingers, only he didn't know it yet.

"I detected a high concentration of were-venom in her." Bryson raked his hands through his hair.

"What now?" Aaron rocked back and forth on the balls of his feet without taking his eyes off Jolene.

"Now, I'm going to stitch the gash in Jojo's arm, and Tessa's going to tell us what the hell happened." Bryson pegged me with a stare before grabbing a bottle of cleansing herbs, a huge needle, and special thread from the shelves.

I sank into the chair far enough away from the bed that I couldn't see him sewing our daughter up like a ripped rag doll. "Holden did this, and before you say anything, it wasn't his fault."

"Holden? I thought you said he was too young to shift." Aaron gaped and went two shades past pale, but I couldn't tell if he'd reacted to the news or the first stitch.

Bryson winced but kept his gaze on his work. "Usually they don't go through their first change until sixteen or so."

"Let me guess, severe stress or trauma can bring it on early?" I shot Aaron a dirty look.

He whipped his head in Bryson's direction.

"From what I understand, yes." He furrowed his brow and hyper-focused on Jojo's arm.

"You knew?" My anger worked better than anesthesia to dull the pain in my shoulder. I stood and motioned between them. "You knew about the dream walking, and you didn't stop him?"

Aaron started to speak, but I held my hand up.

"Tessa, neither of us thought it would go this far." Bryson glanced at me for a split second.

"Is she going to…" Staring at the girl, Aaron waved his hand. "You know."

"We won't know for a couple of months." I couldn't look at them. Sure, part of me knew they'd never do anything to hurt Jojo, but that's exactly what had happened.

"Not months. Years." Bryson's crestfallen expression about did me in, but I wasn't ready to forgive him. Not yet. "We won't know until she's older. Girls usually go through their first shift around thirteen."

Gavin sighed. "Oh, Tessa…"

I nodded, but otherwise kept my focus on Bryson. I didn't want sympathy. I wanted to scream.

He tossed the dirty hemostats, needle, and bandages in a bowl. "I'll keep her asleep for two full moon cycles to slow the venom, but given the amount of time it took to get her here… It may be too late."

"Dear God." I needed to get out of there before I said something we'd all regret. "I need to call Holden's parents. Then I'm going to shift and spend some time in the sky. Alone."

"I don't think that's a good idea." Bryson gave me a pleading look. "Buck called. The Elders want to see us tonight."

"Buck can kiss my lily-white fanny."

"It could be about Holden." He rubbed the twin lines between his eyebrows. "If anyone puts two and two together about Aaron's dream-walking, there could be repercussions. It's not safe for you to be out there alone."

"Yeah?" I rounded on him. "Well, it's not safe for me to be in here with the two of you. What the hell were you thinking, terrorizing a kid?"

The men stared with their mouths hanging open.

"That was a little harsh, Hell Girl." Gavin shook his head. "They were foolish and overprotective, but what father isn't?"

He was right, and I knew it. But I wasn't ready to hear it. "Don't call me that!"

Bryson raised a brow, likely wondering who I was speaking too. Most of the time, he wasn't able to see or hear spirits.

"Gavin's here," I said.

Aaron glanced over his shoulder to the ghost. "She's right. We royally screwed up."

"Oh, I never said you didn't." Gavin shook his head.

"Jojo is paying the price for our mistake." Aaron motioned to me. "And so are you. Shift so you'll heal, but he's right, please stay on the ground."

Bryson seemed to have caught the gist of the conversation from listening to Aaron's half. "You were hurt? Did he break your skin?"

It ticked me off that he'd changed his tune, and stopped blaming me for what happened, the second he thought I might turn furry once a month. "Not that I'm aware of, and I'm not about to get naked so you could search for scratches."

Bryson stood. "If you're—"

"I'm fine." I walked out the door and headed for the master bedroom.

"Tessa, will you listen to me? Even a small scratch can lead to the change." He reached for me but seemed to think the better of it and dropped his hand. "If he scratched you, the sleeping spell slows the venom and diminishes the chances of infection."

"Even if I were bleeding to death, I wouldn't let you put me under." I jabbed my finger against his chest. "In case you forgot, Quin needs to eat. TJ can't stay at Dottie and Mae's forever. He's going to flip out when he finds out Jojo is sick. He's barely okay as it is."

"You aren't walking this path alone." Bryson tucked a frizzy curl behind my ear.

"I know, but I can't dream my way through the next month or two. People are counting on me." The weight of my words made my shoulders sag and the not-so-dull ache return.

To my surprise, he nodded. "No sleeping spells, but we'll need to be prepared. If you're infected, it takes time to learn to control the beast."

My hands flew to my mouth. "Oh my God. You're afraid I'll hurt someone."

"Not you... the wolf." He paused until I met his gaze. "This is different than the firebird. Our spirit animals are part of us. Shifters are dual-natured. When the beast is in control, the human ceases to exist."

"Funny, half the time when I shift, I still feel like the bird is in control."

"Don't sell yourself short. You've come a long way since we first met." His expression softened. "Will you let me check you for scratches?"

"Sure, but I need to call Holden's parents first."

"First, you need to get a shower and change out of those bloody clothes." He took my hand and pulled me toward the master bath.

My eyes stung as if I might cry. I would have welcomed the tears, anything to relieve some of my stress, but they wouldn't come. "I'm scared, Bryson."

"Me, too." He eased his arms around me. "After we clean up, I'll call the McAlisters."

While I appreciated the offer, I felt like I should be the one to reach out. "I was there. I'm sure they'll have questions."

He pulled back and met my gaze. "Yes, but this is also a matter for the Elders. The McAlisters are tribe members."

"This is going to turn into a mess, isn't it?"

"Not if I can help it." He kissed my brow. "When we're finished in the shower, I need you to reach out to Killian. See if he knows of a cure for shifter venom."

"I'll try..." That he'd even contemplate asking my brother for help told me just how much the situation frightened him—and that shook me to my core. Bryson was the strong one. Aaron and I leaned on him more than either of us cared to admit. If he broke, we were all doomed.

It occurred to me that Gavin was in contact with Charlie. I bolted for the office. "Forget Killian, I have a better idea."

"Tessa?" Bryson followed me.

Aaron and the ghost startled when I burst into the room.

"Gavin, is Charlie still close?" Under any other circumstances, it would have ticked me off that I had to go through a third party to reach my grandfather, but I would have walked through Hell to speak to him if it meant helping Jojo.

Gavin nodded to the foot of the bed.

I turned and met Killian's gaze.

CHAPTER 23

"I didn't know our parents, but I'd like to think they taught you it was polite to knock before barging into someone's house." I'd come off rude, but I didn't give a crap.

My brother crossing our wards whenever he pleased was one thing. Him zapping his way into Jojo's room was another.

He glanced from the girl to me and shrugged. "I was under the impression you needed my help."

While he was right, there was only room for one smart-ass in my house. Me. "Let me guess...You heard me say your name and you came?"

"Something like that." Killian continued to stare as if daring me to tell him to leave.

"Tessa." Aaron stood and turned from the bed. "I never thought I'd say this, but if he can help Jojo, what does it matter how he got here?"

He had a point, but I disagreed with the how he got here part. It mattered a great deal when we suspected someone was watching us.

Was that it? Was Killian the one watching our every move?

Gavin huffed. "You mean to tell me a good Southern girl like yourself has never heard the expression about flies and honey?"

"You're right, but it would have been nice to know he was here." I smirked at the spirit.

"He popped in right before you walked in the door." Aaron spoke too loud and too fast. He had to know I was talking to Gavin, but he'd answered anyway.

I glanced from him, to the spirit, and finally to my brother. Was it possible Killian couldn't see Gavin?

Interesting.

"Would you like for me to go?" Wearing a smug smile, Killian tilted his head.

I dipped my chin and sucked it up for Jojo's sake. "Sorry I was rude. You took me by surprise. Can you help her?"

"I'm not sure. May I?" He motioned to Jolene.

"Please."

Aaron moved to my side to give him room to work.

Killian sat on the edge of the bed. Much like Bryson had done, he held his hands a few inches from her body. Unlike Bryson, Killian poured so much magic over the girl the temperature dropped and a couple of the glass jars cracked.

"Holy smokes. You're going to freeze her to death." Rubbing my forearms, I hurried to the linen closet and returned with a couple blankets.

"You do healings differently?" The confusion in Killian's expression surprised me. In the short time I'd known him, he'd seemed like a know-it-all.

"You could say that." I spread a quilt over Jojo.

"Why does she not wake?"

I glanced to Aaron, but he seemed as shocked as I was with Killian's question. "Bryson put a sleeping spell on her to slow the spread of the venom."

He touched her forehead as if checking for a fever. "But she's not *sleeping…not in the traditional sense.*"

"It's a type of stasis. Her bodily functions are slowed to the bare minimum to prevent movement, rises in heartrate, and brain activity. Think of it as the ultimate form of meditation."

"Bryson did this?" He covered the girl in magic again.

"Yes, but I've done similar spells." I felt like I was in the Twilight Zone, or maybe I had another brother—Killian's less self-confident twin.

"I see." He raised his chin.

I had a feeling that was as close as Bryson was going to get to an apology. Petty or not, I enjoyed seeing my brother knocked off his high horse.

Killian leaned down and sniffed Jojo. "Dare I ask how she came in contact with a werewolf?"

Gavin waved his arms over his head. "Share as little detail as possible. And for the love of God, don't let on about me."

"Oh...um...we had an incident with a teen going through his first shift." I would have loved to ask Gavin if the advice had come from him or Charlie, but I didn't want to tip my hand.

Killian curled his upper lip. "Filthy creatures. They are none in Tir Na Nog."

Nothing other than the high and mighty Fae were welcome there, but I kept that thought to myself. "Can you help her?"

"Young shifters are like baby snakes. They do not know how to control their venom. That coupled with her young age..." Killian brushed his fingertips over Jolene's hand and stood. "But you have nothing to worry about."

Aaron glanced between us. "I don't understand."

Killian looked him square in the eye and delivered a verbal sucker punch. "Fae are usually immune to were-venom, but we should take her to Tir Na Nog before she shifts for the first time...to be sure."

Gavin coughed into his hand. "Bullshit."

"No." I shook my head. No way was I going to allow him to take her anywhere. For starters, Jojo was human. Second, I agreed with Gavin. It sounded like BS. And finally, when Killian had said *we*, he likely didn't include the lowly human in the room. "We'll figure something else out."

"We should get Bryson, and listen to what Killian has to say." Aaron glanced between us.

I put my face in his line of vision. "We can table this for now, but it's never going to happen. Do you hear me? Never."

"Regardless, he should be here." Aaron turned for the door.

"He's on the phone with the McAlisters."

Killian's spine stiffened before he could stop himself. While I couldn't be sure if his reaction came from my snarky tone or if he'd recognized the name, my money was on the latter.

"There's no need to rush a decision." Gavin floated closer to Aaron. "He said she needed to be in fairy-land before she shifts."

Aaron nodded. "You're right."

Gavin sighed. "You just have to keep her calm between now and the full moon."

Aaron's expression soured. "And how do you suggest we do that?"

"Who are you talking to?" Killian's magic brushed against me, cold and demanding. "Is there someone else here?"

"Careful, Tessa." The spirit eased behind me.

I needed to do something to throw him off Gavin's trail. "How do you know the McAlisters?"

Killian didn't react to the name. Not outright anyway, but the more he stared me down, the more I was convinced he was hiding something. "Who is Gavin?"

I shot Aaron a warning look before turning back to my brother. "A friend, and you can put your magic away."

"You were shouting at someone called Gavin when you came into this room." He narrowed his eyes but eased back on the deep freeze routine.

"I don't shout." I knew I sounded like a complete idiot, but for some unknown reason, I needed to keep quiet about my ghostest-with-the-mostest. "And you can't take Jojo to Tir Na Nog. She's a halfling."

Aaron gave me side-eye but remained quiet. Thank God.

I'd lied. As far as I knew, she was a human with some pretty spectacular supernatural powers, but I didn't want to rub Killian's nose in Aaron's mortality.

"Her mother was human?" Killian eyed us.

Aaron didn't miss a beat. "As far as I know."

Why does everyone keep assuming Aaron's Fae, or in Tighe's case, a changeling?

"Halflings are considered a lesser Fae, and that is all the more reason to take her to Tir Na Nog. She may not have full immunity" Killian seemed to realize I'd pulled a bait and switch on him and waved his hand. "Enough about the girl. Why did you ask if Cheasequah was close?"

"Because I wanted to speak to him." I couldn't figure Killian out. Either he was playing some serious games, or he had no idea about my abilities.

"Stop talking, Hell Girl." Gavin appeared a half an inch from me. "You're digging yourself a hole you can't climb out of."

Eyes wide and mouth open, he took a step back and stumbled over the corner of the bed. "But he's dead."

"Tessa!" The spirit covered my mouth, a useless gesture, but I got the point.

Besides, I'd had about all I could take of Killian's weird behavior. Something was wrong in fairy-brother-land. The poor guy was acting like he couldn't find his butt with both hands in his back pockets.

Gavin mimed praying. "Play down your gifts, deny them—hell, throw him out of here if that's what it takes."

"You can speak to the dead?" Killian waited for me to reply. When I didn't, he said, "And you are able to read objects, heal the sick, call forth a mythical creature, and conjure fire…"

I didn't care for the tone of his voice, like he didn't know if he should be horrified or impressed, but I could ignore it. What I couldn't ignore was the fact he knew so much about me. "Did Darlene tell you those things?"

"Yes, but I assumed she was exaggerating. Birth mother or not, she is very proud of you."

"Oh, she's definitely exaggerating." I hadn't lied, but hopefully I'd said enough to appease my brother and the anxious ghost.

"Tessa, it's rare to have all five elemental magics. When we first met, I was surprised you had two, given—" He motioned to the room or the house or my childhood in general. "How you grew up. But this…this is…"

I stared at my brother unsure if I wanted to thank him for the compliment, ask a dozen questions, or punch him in the nose.

"Elemental magic?" Bryson stood in the doorway with his arms folded.

Gavin let out an exasperated sigh. "Any chance you can keep Mr. Tall Dark and Gorgeous quiet?"

I had an idea. A potentially terrible awful idea, but if it worked, it'd make Bryson feel a heck of a lot better about his gifts. "Killian's come to understand we aren't as rudimentary and primitive as he first thought."

Bryson raised a brow. "Is that so?"

My brother, on the other hand, turned his head and cursed under his breath.

Aaron took in the situation, cracked a grin, and threw gasoline on the embers. "*Grand Theft Auto* over there didn't realize Tessa could speak to spirits."

Gavin groaned.

Bryson snickered.

And Killian? Killian stared at me as if I'd cured cancer, solved world hunger, and risen from the dead before breakfast. "So, it's true."

I shot Aaron a look that'd scare a buzzard off a pile of guts. He'd heard Gavin tell me to keep quiet. Either he wasn't thinking, or he'd let his dislike of Killian get in the way of common sense.

Aaron shoved his hands in his pockets and glanced away.

Bryson turned to Killian. "Jojo will sleep until I release her from the spell. Let's go sit in the living room and talk."

Still a little green around the edges, Killian gave Bryson a curt nod and followed the guys out of Jojo's room.

"I'll be right there. I need to check on Quin." I hurried into the nursery, turned to Gavin, and whispered, "Talk."

"Before I get into it…is it possible for a spirit to have a stress induced aneurysm?" He pretended to sag against the wall, but half his backside slipped through.

I tapped my toes.

"I'll take that as a no." He motioned to the ceiling, or more likely, the spirit world. "It's Charlie. He's pacing a hole in the veil."

Keeping my voice as low as possible, I asked, "Why isn't he here?"

"He would be, if he could be, but he can't." Gavin made a face that told me he was thinking, or constipated. "I was there when Bryson gave Jojo a math lesson."

I nodded, unsure what that had to do with my situation.

"I know it killed Bryson to watch her struggle with the problems, but he had to let her figure them out by herself—"

I mimed strangling someone.

"I'm trying here. There are rules!" He rolled his eyes. "If Bryson did the problems for her it'd be cheating, right?"

Nodding, I motioned for him to continue.

"And if her virtual teacher found out, she'd fail the class…and maybe have other, more serious, consequences."

The room spun and what little food I had in my belly threatened to make a return appearance. "He can't help because someone is keeping tabs on him?"

"And…"

"And me." I pressed my hand to my churning stomach. "That's why Charlie didn't want Killian to know about my abilities?"

"Yes, but there's more to it." Gavin's expression grew serious. "Only one other living Fae has control of all five elements."

"The queen?"

Gavin frowned. "I can't say."

I sank into the antique wood rocker and put my head in my hands. I'd known someone was toying with me or setting me up or testing me since visiting the murder scenes. But now…now I had a possible motive. "Is she testing me to find out what I'm capable of?"

"No. That's not it." The spirit went wide-eyed, and he began to fade. "Sorry, Hell Girl. I may have said too much."

Adrenaline flooded my bloodstream. I couldn't lose him. Not when he was my only lifeline to Charlie, the one person who seemed to know what the hell was going on. "Are you in trouble?"

"I'll be back…if I can." Gavin vanished.

Bryson came into the room, peeked into the crib at the sleeping baby, and turned to me. "Killian's gone."

"We need to talk." I glanced down at my ruined blouse. "But first I need to get out of these bloody clothes."

He pulled me from the rocker and guided me into the bathroom. "I apologize for being gruff with you earlier."

"We were all worried about Jojo." I stripped while he started the water.

"I guess we don't have to worry about checking you for scratches."

"Aaron told you what Killian said?" I stepped into the shower and let the water soothe me.

"But what was that business about Jojo being a halfling?"

"Killian and Tighe both think Aaron is Fae. I haven't bothered to correct them." I reached for the shampoo, but stopped when the door slid open.

He looked as tired as I felt, maybe more so. "Mind if I join you?"

"Not at all. Did Killian explain elemental magic?" I stepped to the side to give him access to the water.

"Not much. From what I could gather, there are five types of magic, the four elements and spirit. Most Fae have one type." He grabbed my shampoo and motioned for me to turn around.

"Gavin said only one other living Fae has all five—" My brain stuttered. "But when I asked him if it was the queen, he couldn't answer. I don't think it's her."

He worked the shampoo into a lather. "I'm not sure what to think, Tessa. All of this is new to me."

"Me too." I rinsed my hair and applied the useless anti-frizz conditioner. "How did your talk go with Mr. McAlister?"

"As good as can be expected. He assumed Holden shifted because of the stress the family is under." Bryson soaped up a pouf. "I didn't mention Aaron visiting Holden's dreams."

"But Holden is okay?"

"Yes. His parents found his wolf in the woods behind the theater." He took his time scrubbing me clean.

We slipped into a comfortable silence, each of us seemingly lost in our thoughts. I believed the Elders would be understanding of Holden's situation, but Aaron would be another matter. *If* they found out.

After the shower, we dressed in our PJs and headed into the living room.

Aaron took one look at me and held his arm out. "Come here."

I rushed to him and buried my face in his chest. Bryson moved behind me and drew us both into an embrace.

Sandwiched between them, I thought back to our wedding day. We'd promised to love, cherish, and stand beside each other till death we parted. After the talk with Gavin, I wondered if our vows would be fulfilled sooner than any of us could have imagined.

Bryson guided us to the couch. "Talk to us."

I didn't know where to begin, but once I got started, I didn't stop until I'd told him every detail of my conversation with Gavin.

CHAPTER 24

Another Sunday had rolled around, and like everything else in our lives, this one was different. Aaron had taken the ladies and TJ to church, but Bryson and I had stayed home to keep an eye on Jojo.

In a last-ditch effort to save the day, I'd sent Bryson to the store to buy a fresh turkey. I figured he could put it in the fryer while the ladies and I prepared the sides and dessert. It wouldn't be the same without Jojo at the table, but hopefully, we'd have years and years of Sunday dinners together once Bryson lifted the spell.

I covered the sweet potato casserole with foil and set it in the fridge. I'd already snapped the beans, fried the salt pork, and set the pot on the stove to simmer until the turkey was ready. The mashed potatoes could wait, but I needed to get started on the cherry pie.

"Mom?" Jojo's sweet voice startled me.

Whirling around, I pressed my hand to my chest. "You're awake!"

I had absolutely no idea why Bryson's spell had failed, but I needed to find out fast. More importantly, I needed to keep her calm.

"I'm starved and my arm hurts." She shambled to the fridge, opened the door and stared inside.

"Have a seat, and I'll whip you up some pancakes." Placing my hands on her shoulders, I eased her to the breakfast table. "Did a spirit wake you?"

She yawned wide enough for me to see her molars. "I don't think so."

I lowered my shields and allowed my magic to flow through the house just in case. If there was something or someone lurking about, I would likely sense them.

Jojo gave me an odd look. "Where is everyone?"

"At church." Once I was certain we were alone, I pulled the flour, baking soda, and salt from the pantry.

She wrinkled her brow. "But it's Monday."

"You've been asleep for a while." I didn't dare turn around for fear she'd see the concern in my eyes. "Blueberry or chocolate chips?"

"Both." She scratched her head. "How long was I sleeping?"

Bryson came through the front door with both arms full of groceries. He rounded the corner and froze. "Jojo?"

"She just woke up." I forced a smile into my voice. With the werewolf venom in her system, the last thing we needed was to scare her and send her heart racing. "We're alone. No one's come to visit."

Bryson nodded, set the bags on the counter.

"Why are you guys acting so weird?" She glanced between us.

"We're parents. I thought we were born weird." He knelt in front of Jojo. "How do you feel?"

"Hungry and my arm's sore." She made a sour face. "I think I forgot to brush my teeth. My mouth tastes gross."

He shot a worried look over his shoulder before turning back to her. "Jojo, I need to use magic to check you for infections. "Okay?"

She glanced down at her bandages and furrowed her brow. "Because of my arm?"

It worried me she hadn't asked any questions about Holden. Part of me hoped she'd blocked it from her memory, but I knew sooner or later it'd bubble to the surface.

"Yes." Bryson pressed his hand to her forehead. "No fever. That's good."

"You can check me." Jojo grinned. "But only if Mom gets going on my pancakes."

"Whoops. I got distracted." I turned my back to them and focused on mixing the batter.

Bryson's magic caressed me, but I couldn't turn around. One look at my face and she'd know something was more wrong than a simple cut on her arm.

I'd pulled the first pancakes off the griddle when his magic finally receded. Holding the plate in one hand and the syrup in the other, I turned to face them.

Bryson sat on the kitchen floor at the girl's feet. His expression confused me. His mouth hung open as if stunned, but he had tears running down his cheeks.

"Dad?" She touched his face. "Am I going to be a werewolf?"

My heart stopped as if waiting for his answer.

He cleared his throat and pressed a kiss on her palm. "No, baby. You're not. . You're healed."

"Healed?" I didn't know if I'd heard him wrong or if we'd experienced a miracle…or if Killian was right.

Is Jojo part Fae? And Aaron? Is he a changeling?

Jolene blew out a breath. "Good."

Good? That's it?

I wanted to ask what she remembered about the attack but didn't have the mental energy to word the question in a way that wouldn't potentially freak her out. "Do you have any questions?"

"Nope." She motioned to the pancakes. "Can I have those?"

Bryson stood, took the plate from me, and set it on the table in front of the girl. When he turned back to me, he mouthed, "Outside."

Playing it cool, I put the turkey and cold items in the fridge. "Jojo, Dad and I need to set up the turkey fryer. Will you be okay here by yourself for a few minutes?"

She shoved half a pancake in her mouth and nodded.

"We'll be right back. Holler if you need us." Bryson hovered around her like a worried mama duck.

"I'll be fine. I'm not a baby." She rolled her eyes and made kissy sounds.

The dog barreled into the kitchen, skidded to a stop, and proceeded to watch the movements of Jojo's fork like it was the ball at a tennis match.

Bryson and I walked onto the porch, exchanged glances, and shook our heads. Neither of us seemed to know what to say, so we kept quiet as we crossed the yard to the shed.

He opened the rolling door and paused. "I'll talk to her about Holden later."

Nodding, I said, "Thanks. I wanted to but I couldn't figure out what to say."

"You and me both." He met my gaze. "The other day with Killian, you asked him about changelings. You were referring to Aaron, weren't you?"

"Tighe said something about Aaron and changeling, but I didn't believe it. I thought he'd felt your magic in Aaron and jumped to the wrong conclusion." The more I thought about it, the more I wondered if Tighe was on to something. "Now, I'm not so sure."

"I think Tighe was right." A slow smile split Bryson's face. "Aaron's always felt like the outsider with us. He'll be thrilled."

"And if it's true, we don't have to worry about him getting old while we're still young."

Bryson chuckled. "Speak for yourself. I'm already old."

"Yeah well, you look pretty good for a hundred- and sixty-eight-year-old." I slid my arms around his waist. "But he may not be as happy as you think."

He pressed his brow to mine. "Why is that?"

"You heard what Killian said about changelings. Do you really think it's a good time to tell Aaron the people who loved and raised him were not his real parents?"

"Is there ever a good time to learn something like that?" He glanced toward the house. "It explains a lot. I've always wondered why Dottie doesn't have magic, but Aaron does."

I'd never stopped to consider the differences. Like Bryson had done with Aaron, Charlie had gifted Dottie a piece of his soul in order to bring her back to life. Now that I thought about it, I had questions.

A lot of them.

I pulled back and met his gaze. "While we're on the subject…why is it okay to play God with Aaron, but not with Gram Mae?"

"I didn't play God. Aaron was in the prime of his life when he was attacked by the conjurer. Mae has lived a long time." He made a sour face as if realizing how hypocritical he sounded.

"Uh huh." I nudged his side. "That sounds a lot like deciding who lives and who dies."

"Tessa, I know you don't want to hear this, but Mae may not want to live forever. She wakes up every morning in pain, puts on a brave face, and does what she can. But she's tired."

I regretted starting a conversation I wasn't ready to finish. I knew he was right, but I hated it. I didn't want her to suffer, and maybe it was selfish, but I didn't want to suffer either.

"I'm sorry. This isn't the right time for this conversation." He pulled me close.

I held onto him for dear life. "I don't want to talk about this. We should focus on the bigger problem first."

"Which one is that?"

"I don't know." Hiding my face in his chest, I mumbled. "I'm beginning to think we should write them all out on cards and drop them into a hat."

The sound of tires on gravel interrupted our private moment.

"What are they doing back already? Church isn't over for another half-hour."

"That wasn't the SUV." Bryson took my hand and half-dragged me to the front yard.

Buck Oldham and two Tribal Elders climbed out of the old truck. The men glanced around the property, but Buck stared at us.

I pasted on a smile and spoke without moving my lips. "What the heck are they doing here?"

"Don't know but follow my lead." He released my hand and strode to the men. "Good morning. We weren't expecting you."

Buck stared down his nose at Bryson. Quite the feat considering he was a foot shorter than my husband. "I'd hoped to catch you at church this morning."

Bryson's shoulders tensed. "Jolene wasn't feeling well."

"So I heard." Buck nodded to the house. "Is there somewhere private we can talk?"

I didn't like the sound of that one bit. Bryson had said the Elders wanted to speak with us, but with everything else going on, I'd forgotten. "We can talk here. Everyone except Jolene is at church."

"This doesn't involve you." Buck seemed to realize he'd come across as a jerk, and backpedaled. "What I mean to say is, this won't take long. Bryson can speak for the both of you."

My husband, God love him, set the other man straight. "If this is in reference to what happened to our daughter, Tessa will be present."

Buck motioned to me and smiled, but there was no mistaking the anger in his expression. "Lead the way."

"Let's sit outside. I'd rather Jojo not overhear us." Bryson motioned to the wrought iron table and chairs beneath the oak tree.

"The girl isn't under a sleeping spell?" He glanced at the house as if debating going in and seeing for himself.

"No," Bryson said.

The Elders who'd come with Buck whispered back and forth.

I bit the inside of my mouth to keep from giving the men an explanation.

Once we'd settled at the table, Buck got straight to business. "Holden McAlister is not to blame for the attack on Jolene."

My heart beat hard enough to crack a rib.

Bryson nodded. "Glad to hear it. Despite Jojo's injuries, we didn't want the boy to be punished."

Once again, the Elders seemed surprised by his response.

Buck, however, gave us a mean little smile. "Holden was acting under the influence of *foreign* magic."

My mouth fell open. "A spell caused him to shift?"

Bryson glanced at me, likely to tell me to hush.

"I've had him examined by two magic-users. Both say the boy was afflicted by a spell." Buck met my gaze. "Did he say anything before he lost control?"

What kind of spell? He had been acting love sick, but who in their right mind would put a love spell on a teen boy?

I immediately thought of Jojo, but that didn't make sense. As far as I knew, her only gift was speaking to the dead.

"Tessa?" Bryson's voice brought me back to the moment at hand.

I glanced between Buck and the other Elders. "Holden did seem quite smitten with Jolene."

The more I thought about it, the more I could see how a love spell, coupled with Aaron threatening him in his dreams, would have caused the teen to react the way he had.

Bryson nodded to Buck. "You said foreign magic. Did you mean Fae?"

"My people weren't sure of the origin." The old man curled his upper lip as if he smelled something foul. "But considering there were three *Fae* in our house of worship the day you presented your son to the congregation, I would say it's a safe bet."

I didn't care for the way he said "Fae" like it was another F-word. "One of them was my brother."

Buck's eyes widened. "I see."

"Yes, and you realize the Nunnehi are also Fae?"

Bryson reached beneath the table and squeezed my thigh. Hard.

"I do." Buck narrowed his eyes. "But the Nunnehi have been friends of the Cherokee since before the resettlement. Unless that has changed…"

"Me and my family remain loyal to the Tribe." Bryson bit out his words.

The Elders exchanged glances and shifted in their chairs. They seemed uncomfortable with the conversation, but I couldn't tell which part had upset them.

"How long have you known the other Fae were back?" Buck motioned between us.

His word choices puzzled me. Then again, he'd known my grandfather. It was entirely possible Charlie had told him about the Fae, but that didn't make sense either. Buck had done his best to manipulate Bryson and me into getting married. At that time, he'd insisted we were the last of our kind. While we were the last of the Nunnehi, I couldn't shake the feeling he'd lied to us.

Bryson sat back and folded his arms. "We learned other Fae existed shortly before Quin was born, and of Tessa's brother a week later."

"And you're just now telling me?" Buck scoffed and turned to me. "What do you know about these creatures?"

"Not much." I glanced at Bryson for help.

"They are not Nunnehi." He spoke as if that little fact explained everything.

It didn't.

If anything, pointing out they had nothing to do with the Cherokee Nation, or Buck's tiny part of it, made things worse. Buck Oldham and the other Elders thrived on control.

"These *creatures* are trouble. You *will* report any additional Fae activity directly to me." Buck stood as if the meeting were over.

I would have loved to tell Buck Oldham he could stick his bossy attitude where the sun didn't shine, but he was the chief of the local Tribe. Bryson and Charlie had dedicated their lives to serving the Cherokee.

Bryson stood, but remained silent.

"Hi, Mr. Oldham!" Jolene waved from the front porch.

"Hello, there Jojo. How are you feeling?" He walked toward her without as much as a glance in our direction. "I understand you were hurt the other day."

Bryson muttered under his breath and jogged toward the house. "Jojo, you shouldn't be out here. You're sick."

I wanted to order her back inside, or to zap Buck with a tiny fireball, but all I could do was watch the on-coming train wreck in slow motion.

She gave her father a what-are-you-stupid look. "But you said I was healed."

The Elders went wide-eyed, and one of them gasped out, "How is that possible?"

Bryson muttered under his breath.

Buck Oldham marched up our front steps. "Where were you hurt?"

Likely picking up on the adult's tension, Jojo took a step toward the door. She glanced from her dad, to me, to the jerk in front of her. "My arm."

Buck reached out as if to grab her, but seemed to think the better of it. "May I see it?"

"We were shocked. It was like a miracle!" I'd be damned if I was going to stand there and let him scare a defenseless child. However, I knew better than to bite the hand that could smack us into next week. "She woke up this morning healed."

Bryson shot me a WTF look before turning back to Buck. "There is no trace of venom."

Jojo took advantage of the old man's momentary distraction and darted back into the house.

As if in a daze, Buck stood and closed the distance between him and Bryson. "The child is…"

"Half-human, half…Nunnehi." He folded his arms and stared down at Buck as if daring him to contradict him.

"She's Fae?" He nodded to the Elders before turning back to Bryson. "And capable of bespelling Holden."

Flashbacks of the hell we'd gone through when the Elders discovered Aaron had magic stole my breath. I didn't want to believe Buck would hurt a child, but I wasn't so sure.

"No." Bryson shook his head. "Her only gift is speaking to the dead."

"Well then, she has nothing to worry about." Buck turned and marched to his truck.

I didn't like the sound of that. "I'll let the McAlisters know the girl wasn't infected."

The two Elders followed him, but they seemed unsettled.

Forcing a smile, I waved. "Enjoy the rest of your weekends."

Bryson waited until they'd driven away before shaking his head. "We need to tread lightly with him or this will end badly for Jojo."

"You mean for all of us."

Bryson nodded.

CHAPTER 25

"No. Absolutely not." I turned from the kitchen sink and gave Gavin my best Gram Mae evil eye impression.

When he'd returned from the other side, I'd been thrilled to see him. Silly me, I'd hoped he had news or advice or something useful.

Nope.

Gavin Partridge had lost his ever-loving-ghost mind.

"Think about it." He came close to whining. "The dog is the perfect cover for me. I can keep an eye on everything without having to worry about anyone catching on that I'm here."

I glanced at the chocolate Lab, who was sleeping on her back with her legs in the air like a stunned baby goat. "It's not good for her."

"But it's great for me." This time he did whine. "I've missed food and physical touch and breathing. Please, Tessa."

"What if you get stuck again?"

He blew out an exaggerated sigh. "I won't. Now that I know how to do it, I should be able to come and go as I please."

I turned back to the window and watched the kids playing croquet in the yard. I'd worried about Jojo's arm, but she seemed fine. Bryson was keeping an eye on the turkey fryer, and the ladies were sitting in lawn chairs chatting. It took me a second to find Aaron. He'd stepped away from the others to take a call, and judging by his pacing, it was work.

While I hated the idea of traumatizing poor Maddie, I could see the benefits of having Gavin in a physical form—even if it was a dog.

I turned back to him and folded my arms. "You'll behave yourself this time?"

His smile brightened the room. "Absolutely."

"No sniffing my husbands, interrupting sexy-time, or making a mess in the kitchen?"

"Fine. I'll respect your privacy." He held up his hands and wiggled his fingers. "And for the record, the mess wasn't my fault. You'd be surprised how much we take opposable thumbs for granted."

"I'll make sure you get human food." A mental picture of the dog at the table filled my mind. "But you'll be eating alone. I can't have hair in the mashed potatoes."

"Done." Gavin leaned in, cupped his mouth, and did a stage whisper. "And I'll bite anyone who threatens you or this family."

"Okay, you have my permission, but do it in the other room. It breaks my heart every time Maddie makes that sad howling sound." I walked to the stove to check on the potatoes.

"Yes!" Gavin floated out of the kitchen. "Maddie, come. Who's a good girl? Who is?"

Aaron came through the front door and headed straight for the kitchen. "Something smells amazing in here."

"Thanks, but why do I get the feeling you didn't come in here to compliment my cooking?" I dipped a clean spoon in the stuffing and held it up to his mouth.

He took a bite and hummed his appreciation. "I'll deny saying this, but that's even better than Gram Mae's."

"Now I know you're buttering me up." I shoulder checked him. "Was that Samuels on the phone?"

"Yeah." He ran his hand over the back of his neck.

Maddie/Gavin padded into the room and sat at my side.

I dropped the spoon in the sink and glanced out the window to an empty yard. "Where is everyone?"

"The farmer who owns the land behind us called 911." Aaron turned me to face him. "He claims he saw a monster-sized gator eating a man down by our lake."

My hands flew to my mouth. "Please tell me it isn't anyone we know."

My thoughts drifted back to what Charlie had said to Jolene. TJ would be with us for a long time. Could it be Tank out there? No one except blood relatives could trespass on our land. The new and improved wards saw to that. If it wasn't Tank, it had to be a cousin of some sort.

"I don't know yet. The first responders are there now, but I haven't heard anything." He sighed. "Samuels and CSI will be here soon."

My brain seized up like an overheated engine. "How did the killer get on our property?"

Aaron swallowed hard and dipped his chin. "Bryson's checking the wards, but if they're still up, we need to consider—"

"No." I shook my head. "I know what you're about to say and you're wrong. Killian doesn't have anything to do with this. I told you what Scarlett said. He's not a murderer."

"I'm sorry, Tessa, but I'm not ruling *Lucky Charms* out just yet."

Maddie/Gavin snorted.

"Don't call him that. It's not funny." My lips twitched despite myself.

"It's a little funny." He pulled me back into his arms and kissed my brow. "Samuels is going to need me at the lake, but I want you to stay here with Bryson and the kids."

"Sure, but if this is like the other scenes, there might not be a murder."

Aaron glanced away. "This time, there are remains."

"Oh God. Jolene." My thoughts raced almost as fast as my pulse. "Newly dead spirits can be scary. Is she okay? Has the victim reached out to her?"

"Take another breath, sweetheart." He pressed his forehead to mine.

I tried to do as I was told, but my lungs had gone on strike. "What if the killer is still there? I could shift and fly down there to make sure it's safe."

"I'd feel better with you here ready to incinerate anything that gets close to our kids."

I could get behind that idea. "Okay."

Maddie/Gavin barked.

"By the way, I gave Gavin permission to possess Maddie again. He said it was easier for him to keep an eye on things in a physical body." I braced myself for Aaron's reaction.

He glanced between me and the dog several times and settled on me. "Did you set boundaries?"

"I did." I narrowed my eyes at the Lab.

Maddie/Gavin licked her lips.

He threw up his hands. "What's done is done, but that's not funny."

I shot Maddie/Gavin a warning look before packing the hot casserole dishes into a carrying bag. "Do you have time to help me get this stuff to Mae's?"

"Sure." He balanced the remaining food in his hands and headed for the door.

By the time we'd delivered the side dishes and desserts to Gram Mae's, the first of several marked OCPD cars, a CSI van, and two plain gray sedans had pulled into the yard. I couldn't help but stare at the abandoned lawn chairs and kid's toys.

The people I loved most in the world had been outside, exposed and vulnerable, while a murder had taken place less than a half a mile away.

"Keep everyone inside. I'll be back as soon as I can." Aaron pressed a kiss to my temple before bounding off the porch to meet Samuels.

So much had happened since Charlie had died. Some good things like Bryson and Aaron and the kids, and some bad. I'd had about all I could take of murders and monsters and loss.

Maddie/Gavin glanced up at me. Tail still, tongue inside her mouth, she stared as if waiting for me to say something.

I scratched the soft spot behind her ear. "Remember. You promised to behave yourself."

She made a happy grunting sound that I swear sounded like she'd asked for more.

"Come on." I patted the side of my leg and made kissy sounds.

The dog huffed and followed me inside Gram Mae's.

The smell of fresh baked bread and something sweet made my stomach growl. The kids were busy setting the table, while Mae and Dottie put the food into serving bowls. Quin's cries and Bryson's humming drifted from the front room.

Dottie brought the mashed potatoes to the table. "Is Aaron with the officers?"

"He says he'll be back as soon as he can, but these things can take hours."

TJ gave me a toothless grin. "Can we go see the body?"

My mouth fell open. He'd come face-to-face with his mother's skinless ghost a few weeks before. I'd expected him to be scared, not acting like the circus had come to town.

"Absolutely not." I went to the sink to wash my hands.

Jojo joined me. "I think it would be cool to see Dad working a case."

"I'll take you into the station one day." While I agreed with her in theory, I doubted homicide detectives participated in *Bring Your Child to Work Day*.

TJ groaned. "That's no fun. We wanna see the blood and guts and the white body drawing."

Jolene rolled her eyes. "It's called a chalk outline."

"Somebody's been watching too much grown-up TV." Mae motioned to the table. "Finish setting out the napkins, TJ."

Bryson poked his head around the corner. "Tessa, can I borrow you a minute?"

"Sure." It occurred to me that Quin had stopped crying. Taking extra care not to wake him, I eased into the living room.

The baby wasn't sleeping—he was in his carrier, staring at the dog.

"That's odd. I didn't think he could see that far." I ran my hand over his peach-fuzz head. "Fair warning, I gave Gavin permission to possess the dog again."

"Ah, so that's what he's staring at. Another thing he got from you."

I couldn't help but sigh. "Poor kid."

Bryson lowered his voice. "Someone tampered with the wards earlier."

"Oh thank God." I pressed my hands to my cheeks and shook my head. "It's awful someone died, but I was worried we'd lost another family member."

"I had the same thought." He squeezed my shoulder. "Did you sense any changes in the wards earlier?"

"I don't think so."

He ran his hand over the back of his neck. "This killer seems to know a lot about you. How you read the scenes. Your exact height. Where you live, and how to break through our wards."

My appetite shriveled more with each word.

He stared directly into my eyes. "I think it's time we load everyone up in the SUV and head for the mountains."

I wanted to argue, but he was right. We had two elderly women and three kids to think about, but there was a problem with running away. Several actually. "Aaron can't go. He's working the case. Plus, who's to say the killer won't follow us? He or she obviously has strong magic."

"I don't know how to keep you and our family safe." His voice grew hoarse, and the lost look in his eyes broke my heart.

I knew Bryson inside and out. Protecting his family was as much a part of him as breathing or his magic. To him, not being able to keep us out of harm's way was a failure as a husband, a father—as a man.

I slipped my arms around him and rested my head on his chest. "The best way to keep us safe is to stop the killer. I have every faith in you and Aaron and myself to do just that."

"Dinner is on the table." Gram Mae called from the kitchen.

"We'll finish this conversation later, with Aaron." He picked up Quin's carrier with one hand and slid the other to the back of my neck. The skin-to-skin contact with my mate made the tension drain from my shoulders.

Or it did until Quin started crying the second we walked into the kitchen.

Bryson took the baby back into the room with the dog. Quin stopped fussing like someone had flipped a switch. Bryson brought him back into the kitchen, and he cried again. It would have been comical if it wasn't so dang weird.

Not wanting to miss my chance at a peaceful, dinner, I turned to my great-grandmother and pressed my hands together. "Can Maddie come in the kitchen if she stays away from the food? Quin seems enamored with her."

"Maddie, come." Gram Mae narrowed her eyes at the poor dog. "You'd better stay in that corner and not even think about this food."

The dog groaned and hung her head, but the drool hanging from her jowls told me she was thinking about it all right.

We settled in for what I hoped would be a quiet meal.

Jojo glanced over the food and wrinkled her nose. "Why are we having turkey? Thanksgiving isn't for another couple of weeks."

TJ snorted out a laugh. "They're all messed up around here. Dead bodies, turkey any old day, *and* they forgot Halloween."

The adults at the table froze. Even Gram Mae, who always had something to say about his sass, went wide-eyed.

I wasn't going to earn the mother of the year award anytime soon.

Halloween had come and gone sometime between Killian showing up in our driveway and the *Mom's Gone Wild* dedication ceremony. With the million things going wrong in our world, we'd all forgotten. Still, there was no excuse.

I caught Jolene's eye. "I'm so sorry. Can we have a late Halloween? I'll buy lots of candy and we can watch a Micah Sterling marathon."

"Yes! That's even better than trick-or-treating." She hopped up and threw her arms around my neck.

"*And* we can go down to the lake and look for blood." TJ wiggled his brows.

CHAPTER 26

Bryson and I tucked the kids into bed and settled on the couch for some quiet time before Quin woke for his nine o'clock feeding. After the disaster of a day, I wanted nothing more than to watch a cheesy romance movie and put my feet up.

Bryson glanced around. "Where's the remote?"

I bit back a groan. One of the things I loved about being pregnant was how he and Aaron had waited on me hand and foot. I hadn't poured my own tea during my entire last trimester, and they'd stopped asking me where everything was.

Why did men think women were walking inventory sheets?

Bryson lifted the couch cushion. "Check your side."

"Or we could use the buttons on the TV." I stood, grumbling the entire time.

"You can't access your girlie station without the special remote."

Maddie/Gavin lifted her head and yawned. She'd settled her furry butt into my easy chair. Not that I was fundamentally opposed to animals on the furniture—I'd happily share the couch with her. However, I had a problem with dog hair all over the brand-new microfiber rocker-recliner where I nursed Quin.

Snapping my fingers, I said, "Get down from there."

The dang dog gave me a dirty look but didn't move.

A split second later, the television powered up and switched to the romance station.

Bryson glanced from the TV, to my empty hands, and back. "Did you butt dial the channel?"

"How could I butt dial anything when I'm standing up?" I turned my attention to the dog. "Did you do that?"

She snorted and nosed the remote onto the floor.

"Uh." Bryson scratched his jaw. "This is going to take some getting used to."

"Tell me about it."

"It's been a long day." Bryson sat and pulled my feet into his lap. "Let's watch the movie."

My phone went off with Aaron's ringtone.

"Dang it." I hated to miss out on my first foot massage since giving birth, but I couldn't ignore him when he was calling from a crime scene. I snatched the cell from the coffee table. "Hey. How's it going down there?"

"I hate to ask, but I need you to come to the lake." His tone sent a chill skittering down my spine. "There are mirrors here, but otherwise it's different. Can you come?"

I loathed the idea of trudging to the other side of the property, at night, alone, with a magic-wielding homicidal maniac on the loose. "Sure. I'll be right there, but could you send someone to walk with me?"

"Samuels is on the way." Aaron sighed. "Thanks, Tessa."

I disconnected the call and turned to an unhappy Bryson. To my surprise, he didn't argue or list the reasons why it was a bad idea for me to go. He simply stood and grabbed my hoodie from the coat rack.

I couldn't wrap my brain around his reaction. I mean, part of me was impressed that he trusted me enough to handle the situation, but another part wondered what had changed. Bryson was never one to let me run headlong into trouble without a lecture. "Aaron's sending Samuels to walk with me."

"I heard." He plopped back down on the couch. "Be careful."

"Will do." Tilting my head, I waited for him to say more. The longer he remained silent, the more I worried. "What's wrong?"

"I had every intention of using the movie as foreplay, but it's probably a good thing Aaron called." He yawned, the sort of yawn that seemed to come from the bottom of his soul. "I'd likely fall asleep in the middle of sex."

I couldn't help but laugh. "You say the sweetest things."

"I try." Bryson rested his head against the couch cushion and closed his eyes.

I wanted nothing more than to use his shoulder as a pillow, but I had a freaking murder investigation to get to. "I'll be back as soon as I can."

"I'll be here." Bryson patted the couch and Maddie/Gavin hopped up beside him. "With my possessed dog."

Samuels met me on the front porch. The man was a decade older than me, but he looked closer to Dottie's age in the harsh flood light —gruesome murder scenes could do that to even the hardest detectives.

I took in his emotionless expression. "Is it that bad?"

"Worse." He ran his hand over his closely cropped hair. "This time the guy left the body behind…or parts of it anyway."

Great. Just what I want to see in the middle of the night on my family's land.

"The neighbor might have spooked him." I forced a smile to lighten the mood.

Samuels nodded, but otherwise didn't say a word as we walked to the crime scene.

I'd worked plenty of nighttime investigations, but this was different. The yellow tape surrounded the small beach where I used to play as a child. The flood lights illuminated the rope swing where TJ pretended to be Tarzan. Technicians sorted through sand mere feet from where Jolene built castles.

Aaron met us at the top of the common approach path. He looked exhausted, but more than that, he looked…haunted. "I hated to ask you to come down here. This is a rough one."

The sinking feeling I'd had after first learning about the murder returned. "The victim… Is it?"

"It's hard to say." He shook his head. "Stick to the perimeter. There's no reason for you to see the remains."

I didn't like the sound of that.

Aaron and Samuels went back to work while I suited up in the paper jumpsuit, complete with booties and gloves. At first glance, the scene looked identical to the others. It wasn't until I crossed the tape that I noticed the charred earth sticking out from beneath the white tarp covering the remains. Or what I assumed were the remains. Whatever rested beneath the plastic wasn't bumpy enough to be a body.

Pushing those thoughts from my mind, I walked to the first of a dozen or so mirrors. I lowered my shields and let my magic flow from my fingertips as I touched the piece of glass.

Images flashed through my mind so quickly, I had a hard time making sense of them. A man fishing. A wolf the size of a pony behind him. Blood spraying. Flesh tearing. So much gore.

Every fiber of my being screamed for me to pull my hand away, but I couldn't. The victim went limp, but the wolf kept ripping, gnawing, eating the body. Something must have caught its attention, because its head shot up. The animal scented the air, turned, and ran.

A wolf, not a gator?

Maddie/Gavin came barreling down the path from the house like she had the devil on her tail. She stopped, sniffed, and darted off to the side into the bushes. Her movements reminded me of the damned wolf—so much so, that a shot of adrenaline sped my pulse.

"Aaron? Could you come over here?" I squinted to where the dog had disappeared, but the bright flood lights made it impossible to see outside of their glow.

And easier for something to hide.

"What's up?" He hurried to my side.

"Maddie's out here. I saw her run into the bushes." I nodded toward the place she'd disappeared. "Are you sure the responding officers cleared the scene?"

He winced and glanced back toward the house. "We've been here for hours. If the perp was still around, we'd have seen or heard something by now."

"Right." I chewed my lower lip. "What exactly did the neighbor say he saw?"

"He said the gator had to be twenty feet long, but it had a human torso and arms." Aaron tilted his head. "What did you see in the mirrors?"

"I've only read one, but I saw a wolf."

His eyes widened. "Hard to mistake a gator for a wolf."

"Yeah." I walked to the next mirror. "I'll keep going. See if I can make sense of this."

He shoved his hands in his pockets and followed me.

"Let's get this over with."

The next reading started the same as the first. A man fishing on the shore. From behind, he didn't look familiar, but it was hard to tell. My family's dress code consisted of jeans, T-shirts, flannels in winter, and ball caps. Heck, some of my female relatives dressed the same way unless they were going to the bar.

The wolf stalked up behind the victim, but before it reached him, the image blinked in and out like a television with a wire antenna. When it came back into focus, a gator was eating the man. It blinked out again, and the animal changed into a wolf. Another blink and the animal was a panther.

"What the unholy hell?" I dropped my hand. "Did forensics identify what kind of animal did this?"

Aaron frowned and shook his head. "Not yet."

"I need to see the body." I turned from the mirror and made it to the edge of the tarp before Aaron took my arm.

"Tessa, wait." His expression told me there was more going on beneath the plastic than he'd let on.

"Show me." My voice came out strong and commanding—a miracle as far as I was concerned. Nothing, and I mean nothing inside me felt strong. I knew beyond a shadow of a doubt that Aaron had identified the victim.

Maddie/Gavin raised Cain from somewhere in the bushes. I opened my mouth to silence her, but she wandered into the light before I had the chance. She did her best Lassie imitation, staring at the bush, barking, looking back to me, and barking again. Whatever she was going on about must not have been too serious or she would have growled.

"Give me a second!" I glared at the dog and turned back to the victim's remains.

Aaron stepped in front of me blocking my path. "Come with me."

"No. I want to see—" I motioned to the tarp.

Samuels moved to my right, hooked his arm in mine, and half dragged me away from the remains. "We found scraps of clothing."

"Samuels..." Aaron followed us, and judging by the edge in his voice, he was not happy with his partner.

I stopped walking and jerked my arm free. "For the love of Pete. Someone tell me who it is!"

Several officers and techs turned and stared, but none would meet my gaze. It was like everyone knew except me.

Aaron took my hands in his and swallowed hard. "We recovered part of a Grateful Dead T-shirt."

My knees buckled and I couldn't seem to get enough oxygen to my brain to think straight. Stone was the only person I knew who would wear such a thing.

Stone. My stepdad. The father of my baby brother. The one man on the planet who knew Darlene through-and-through and loved her anyway.

"No." I shook my head hard enough to crack a few vertebrae. "You're wrong. What in the world would he be doing out here? Fishing?"

Aaron moved in for a hug, but I sidestepped him.

Laughing and waving my arms as if drowning on dry land, I said, "He doesn't fish. He doesn't even kill bugs. He's a vegan, for crying out loud."

Aaron and Samuels exchanged surprised glances, but I didn't know if they were shocked at my hysteria or my line of reason.

To drive my point home, I pulled my phone from my pocket. "I'll prove it. I'll call him. There's no way that's Stone under that tarp!"

Rustling sounds from the bush where Maddie had disappeared drew our attention.

Jolene and TJ walked into the glow of the flood lights.

My already frazzled nerves heaved their last breath and keeled over dead. Jojo and TJ loved Stone. He was her step-grandfather and his cool uncle.

Wide-eyed, Jojo asked, "Daddy, is that Grand-Dude Stone?"

CHAPTER 27

Aaron made it to the kids before I remembered that walking involved putting one foot in front of the other. He knelt to their eye level and took them into his arms. "We aren't sure who it is yet."

TJ sobbed and babbled incoherently against Aaron's shoulder.

"I can ask the ghosts. They'd know." Jojo pulled away from her dad, held her arms out at her sides, and closed her eyes. Her power rushed over me.

"Jolene, no!" It was one thing for me to use magic in front of the officers and techs. Mine was subtle, and they'd seen me do it hundreds of times. Jojo's gifts were an entirely different matter. Desperation and grief made her power wild, uncontrollable, and hard to ignore.

A gale blew across the water, causing leaves and small branches to rain down over the area. The officers and techs shouted and scrambled for cover. A flash of white material caught my attention as the tarp flew past me and tangled in a tree.

Maddie/Gavin bolted for Jojo. Eight pounds of chocolate-colored determination barreled into Jolene.

Aaron shouted. I screamed. But we were too late. Girl and dog hit the ground with a meaty thud.

"Get off!" Jolene shoved at the Lab, but Maddie was having no part of it.

Sitting on Jojo's chest, she barked like a lunatic at something behind me.

Aaron grabbed the dog's collar and pulled her off Jolene.

Maddie/Gavin continued to bark, only she'd added a whiney quality to the racket. She flailed and jumped, twisting her body like a dolphin performing until she broke free of Aaron's grip.

The dog darted directly into the crime scene—straight toward TJ.

His little face frozen in a silent scream, he stared down at chunks of meat and bone, all that was left of the victim.

My feet suddenly remembered how to function. I made it to his side, swept him into my arms, and had him halfway back to the house before I slowed enough to realize TJ wasn't moving or crying or screaming. He hung limp in my arms staring into space.

Cradling him close, I whispered, "I've got you. It's okay, sweet boy. I've got you."

Aaron caught up to us with Jolene in his arms. He gave me a hard look and nodded toward the house.

Covered with mud and crying, Jojo glared at me over Aaron's shoulder. Intellectually, I understood she handled her grief differently than her younger cousin, but it was still grief. On an emotional level, I took her dirty looks as condemnation. Condemnation for stopping her from reaching out to the ghosts and for Stone's death.

Aaron opened the front door and ushered us inside.

Bryson stood in the kitchen trying to get Quin to take a bottle of breast milk. The man looked as shell-shocked as I felt. Rather than asking stupid questions, like I would have, he assessed the scene, nodded, and took TJ from my arms.

"They snuck down to the death scene." Aaron stated the obvious.

"I need to… I have something I need to do." I hurried to the bedroom and closed the door before anyone could stop me.

Once I was alone, I sank to my knees and let the events of the previous ten minutes wash over me. Make that the events of the previous three weeks since Killian had shown up at my doorstep. I didn't want to admit it, but deep down, I knew there was a connection between him and everything that had happened.

Aaron knocked on the door. "Tessa, have you called Stone or Darlene?"

"Not yet." I wiped my eyes, surprised to find them dry. Maybe I'd used up all of my tears, or more likely, they were lurking below the surface waiting to drown me once things quieted.

A deep exhaustion, the kind that came after hours of sobbing, settled over me.

Aaron slipped into the room and sat on the floor beside me. "We're going to need a DNA sample to ID the remains."

I couldn't ask my mother for her husband's hairbrush without explaining there wasn't enough left of the body to identify the victim. The thought made me break out in a cold sweat. "There has to be another way."

"Maybe we should let Jojo do her thing. You're right. Why would Stone be fishing?"

"I don't think that's a good idea. You saw what happened back there. Besides, I just gave her the lecture on using her magic." Needing to anchor myself to something good and pure, I snuggled against him. "I'll try to reach out to the spirit of the victim. He or she may still be close."

"Thanks." He stared off as if in thought. "What's going to happen to her if she flies off the handle like that, and we're not around to stop her?"

"Nothing good, that's for sure." I drew in a deep breath in hopes his scent would soothe me, but ended up with a nose-full of sweat and crime scene stench. "Her magic is getting stronger every day. I'm worried what will happen when all of that power gets mixed up with teenaged hormones."

He ground his teeth.

"And poor TJ. That kid is going to be in therapy for the rest of his life." I only saw a flash of the victim's remains and would have nightmares. God knows how long he'd stared at them before we'd realized he'd slipped past us.

"I think a forgetting spell is in order." He spoke as if the words tasted sour.

I understood how he felt. The idea of messing around in someone's head made me queasy. After the debacle with Killian and Scarlett, I'd sworn I'd never use magic on someone without their permission—or in cases of life and death. TJ possibly seeing someone he loved reduced to pieces of meat wouldn't kill him, but it would impact him for the rest of his life.

"I agree. We'll do the spell after I call Stone." I pulled my phone out. "If he picks up, problem solved."

"If all else fails, you'll need to speak to Darlene."

"I'll go talk to Bryson about the spell." He pushed to his feet.

"Don't you have to get back to the crime scene?"

He winced. "Samuels called. They're wrapping it up for the night."

"I don't suppose having a little boy, a dog, and me messing up the evidence has anything to do with it?" Lord in heaven, I did *not* want to think about what the gossips at the station would have to say about it.

"Why would you think that?" He laughed the sort of laugh usually reserved for funerals and unemployment lines.

I waited until he closed the door behind him before dialing Stone's number. The phone rang several times and went to voice mail. I redialed twice more before giving up and trying him on the otherside.

Closing my eyes, I focused on the icy magic flowing through my veins. I could sense spirits nearby, but only one seemed familiar. "Gavin? Can you hear me?"

He didn't respond.

I hopped up and went into Jojo's room and found the dog sleeping in her bed. "I need to speak to you." I felt a little foolish talking to the dog. "I'm sorry. I should have listened to you when you first started barking. "Please come out of there."

He still didn't respond.

I pushed my magic in the dog's direction but didn't sense the spirit.

Great.

Either Gavin was ignoring me, or he'd found something else to occupy his time. Judging from past experience, I placed my money on spying on my husbands.

"Don't make me get the salt and force you to come."

I waited for him to reply a few minutes before reaching out to the other ghosts I'd sensed nearby. One by one, I brushed my magic against their essence. Most were old souls who'd been dead longer than I'd been alive. Only one felt like a new arrival to the Spirit World, but they seemed at peace. Murder victims, especially those who'd suffered violent deaths, were anything but peaceful.

Rather than continuing the ghostly goose-chase, I gave up and called my mom.

"Tessa Marie, do you know what time—" She went quiet. "Is everything okay? Mae?"

"Mae's fine, Momma." My voice quivered. "Is Stone home? I tried to call him, but he didn't answer."

"No. He hasn't come home since that day at church." She sounded as if she'd smirked. "He didn't answer because he's out of town with his band for a few days. They have gigs up in the panhandle, remember?"

I most certainly didn't remember her mentioning gigs or a road trip. "When did he leave?"

"This morning." She sighed. "It's after midnight. What is going on?"

I had no idea how to answer her question without worrying her, so I went with the truth. "Momma, there was a murder out by the lake tonight. The police think… They asked me to get in touch with him."

"Stone is not a killer!" She laughed too loud and too long. "Honestly, Tessa, what are you thinking?"

"Momma, the victim was wearing a Grateful Dead T-shirt."

The line went as quiet as the grave.

"Do you have any of his band member's contact info?" I hated that I hadn't driven over there to speak to her face-to-face, almost as much as I hated how impatient I sounded. No one deserved this kind of news over the phone, even if it wasn't true.

God, please don't let it be true.

She huffed out a breath. "Of course I do, but they're probably on stage."

"It might be nothing, but keep trying to call them." Every muscle in my body begged for rest, but I didn't want her to be alone. "I'm coming over."

"You don't need to do that." She let out a shaky breath.

"I know, but I'd rather be there…just in case."

Darlene laughed again, but this time it came out choked. "You're overreacting. There's no way in the world it's him. He was too excited about the gig to miss it. He's been practicing every afternoon for weeks."

I didn't know if she was trying to convince me or herself, maybe both. "You're probably right, but go ahead and call the band members."

"I'll let you know when I reach someone, but I don't want you to come over. I'm still not speaking to you, young lady." She hung up and I hung my head.

Turning to the digital clock on the nightstand, I gave myself two minutes of alone time. Alone time I needed to clear my thoughts and center myself enough to help Bryson and Aaron with a forgetting spell.

After my brief mental health break, I made my way into the living room. TJ was passed out on the sofa, and Quin was fast asleep in his port-a-crib.

Surprised by Jolene's absence, I checked her room and found Maddie sleeping in her bed.

Pulse racing, I rushed through the house, checking each room and closet. "Jojo? Are you here?"

Assuming she was outside with her dads, I opened the front door.

Bryson and Aaron stood on the porch, each with a beer dangling from their fingers. They turned to me with surprised expressions.

"Where's Jojo?"

CHAPTER 28

"What do you mean? She's in the living room. Bryson and I knocked all three kids out with a spell." Aaron pushed past me. He glanced around and spun to face us. "She's not here."

Thank you, Captain Obvious.

"That's what I just said." I could barely speak past the fear rising in my throat.

Bryson cursed under his breath. "Did you check her bedroom?"

"Yes and the rest of the house." I pressed my hand to my chest and forced myself to take a deep breath. "You two used a spell to get the kids to sleep?"

Bryson's eyes widened. "Shit."

"What's going on?" Aaron shouted.

Tightening the grip on his beer, Bryson met Aaron's gaze. "Jojo seems to have developed the ability to resist spells."

He shook his head. "No, she fell asleep. You saw her."

Worrying Bryson would shatter the bottle and end up in the emergency room, I took it from him. "But she broke the sleeping spell Bryson cast after the incident with Holden."

"I thought you lifted it?" Aaron glanced between us. "What am I missing?"

Crap on a cracker. This isn't the time to tell Aaron he might be Fae.

Bryson said, "We aren't sure why she woke up, but—"

"But we need to find her." I panicked. We didn't have time to explain the very real possibility Aaron's entire life had been a lie—or his parents' identities anyway.

"I'll check the studio, you two check the yard." Bryson headed for the back door.

Aaron turned for the kitchen. "I'll get a couple of flashlights."

"I don't need one." Hurrying out front, I pulled the firebird to the surface. More specifically, I called her sight forward. "Jojo!"

Even in the dead of night, I could see the heat signatures of small animals scurrying around the yard. A young deer lifted its head and stared from the tree line. If Jolene was out there, I'd find her.

Aaron called her name from the far side of the yard.

A loud screech echoed through the night air. Bryson had shifted into his spirit animal, the Great Hawk. While his night vision wasn't as good as mine, his overhead view made up for it.

"Jojo!" I couldn't help but curse Gavin. Of all the times for our Jiminy Cricket to disappear, this was the worst.

Cold magic wafted over me.

I spun in a slow circle in hopes of figuring out which direction it'd come from. "Jojo!"

A faint heat signature drew my attention. It was too pale to be a human, but then again the girl was using a serious amount of magic.

I ran toward Gram Mae's unplanted vegetable garden. The closer I came, the more oppressive the magic. It felt like running through vertical layers of frozen quicksand. I'd make it a foot or two just fine, push against a barrier, break through, and repeat the process.

The Great Hawk swooped lower, likely trying to reach the girl from above. He slammed against the magic. The giant bird cried out and fell backward toward the ground.

"Bryson!" I fought to reach him but couldn't get through the sheets of magic in time.

He landed with a hollow thud.

"Jojo! Stop this!" I drew flames into my hands and burned my way through the icy barriers.

By the time I reached Bryson, he'd shifted back to human form. He was lying on his side with his arm bent at an unnatural angle beneath him. Even more troubling, the fall had knocked him unconscious.

Sending up a silent prayer, I pressed my fingers to his neck. The steady thump of his pulse brought tears to my eyes.

Aaron ran to us and dropped to his knees. "What the hell happened? And what is that?" He pointed to the magic bubble surrounding our daughter.

"It's Jojo. She's doing some sort of summoning. I've never seen anything like it."

He glanced between Bryson and the barrier. "Can you heal him?"

"Yes, but you might have a hard time getting through that magic." I hated the doubt in my voice, but Aaron's gifts had surfaced weeks before.

He tilted his head. "Maybe, but it feels a lot like the veil."

I couldn't wrap my brain around what he'd said. Did it *feel* like the veil or *was* it the veil? What would that mean if a ten-year-old girl could pull the freaking veil down and use it like a security blanket?

Aaron stood and walked to the barrier, and much to my surprise, he passed straight through.

I turned my attention back to Bryson. Placing my palms on his back, I pulsed magic into his body with one goal in mind—to draw out his spirit animal.

I could feel the Great Hawk inside him, but the energy was faint. Part of me panicked, but the saner part remembered injuries sustained while in our spirit animals took longer to heal. Plus, he'd fallen from a considerable height. I feared it could take weeks for him to recover—longer if I couldn't coax the bird out

"Come on Bryson. I need you to shift." I closed my eyes and visualized reaching inside him, cupping the hawk in my hands, and lifting it out of Bryson's body.

The mythical creature nipped and cawed before shying away from me.

"Come on, baby. You can do this." I lowered my shields and allowed the firebird to come to the surface. The tips of my hair cast a yellowish-orange glow around us as I tried again.

This time, the hawk seemed to recognize me as his mate and eased its way forward. Bryson shifted so suddenly, a wing caught me in the solar plexus and knocked me to my back.

The Great Hawk dipped its head, cried out once, and sank to the ground beside me.

Struggling to get air back into my lungs, I pushed myself upright. I trailed my hand down the ridge of his wing, but stopped when he made a pained sound. "Okay, let's get you shifted back now."

I used the same process as before, only in reverse, but nothing happened. I tried using more magic, less magic, shoving the firebird back behind the shields. Nothing worked.

My chest tightened, but it had nothing to do with the blow I'd taken. Aaron and I needed him to keep us sane, to stop us from doing dumb things, to help make sense of the tornado our lives had become.

"Jolene. Enough!" Aaron's voice cut through my thoughts.

I turned and gasped.

He'd managed to reach Jolene, but she appeared to be in some sort of trance.

She sat cross-legged in the center of the loose soil. Her long blonde hair and nightgown swirled around her, along with what appeared to be every ghost in the tri-county area.

Aaron grabbed her shoulders and shook the girl like Maddie with her favorite toy.

I wanted to yell at him to stop and march in there and pull her away from him, but I couldn't. I doubted I could cross the barriers again with what little magic I had left. Not to mention, I wasn't sure what removing Jolene from her circle would do to the spirits she'd summoned. They needed to be returned to wherever they'd come from, not let loose to wander central Florida.

Jojo opened her eyes, glanced around, and screamed.

The sound made the hair on the back of my neck jump up and try to run away. I'd heard that sort of scream too many times, it was the pure unadulterated horror of someone who thought they were going to die.

And then all hell broke loose.

I leaped to my feet.

Bryson shifted back to his human form and rose to his knees.

Aaron dropped the girl, raised his hands over his head, and shouted a spell in a language I'd never heard before, let alone understood.

The spirits and magics spun faster and faster until the vortex slimmed to the width of a telephone pole. Aaron balled his hands into fists and slammed his arms toward the ground. The Earth shook beneath our feet and everything went still.

CHAPTER 29

"But I had to know if Grand-Dude Stone was alive! And he is." Jolene looked from me, to Aaron, to Bryson resting on the couch. When none of us as much as blinked, she threw her hands up and let out the same frustrated sound teenagers have made since the dawn of time.

"That's enough." Aaron clamped his hand on her shoulder. "That temper tantrum earned you another week of grounding."

She narrowed her eyes, but remained blessedly quiet.

Every parenting book I'd read discouraged disciplining a child while angry, but I highly doubted any of them had ever raised an out-of-control Fae child who could summon a freaking *ghostnado*.

I inhaled through my nose to the count of three, and exhaled through my mouth. "Jojo, we understand why you tried to summon Stone's spirit. That isn't the problem."

She hung her head.

"We were planning to do the same spell—"

"But I'm stronger than—" She glanced at Aaron's hardened expression and clamped her mouth shut.

I'd heard this sort of thing from her before, and I was tired of it. "You may be stronger in spirit magic than I am, but you're not stronger than him." I nodded to Aaron. "And your certainly not stronger than the three of us combined."

Her cheeks turned bright red. "Yes, ma'am."

Cradling his broken arm, Bryson shifted to the edge of the couch. "Jojo, the strength of your magic doesn't matter if you don't know how to control it. You disobeyed our rules and put our lives in danger."

"I didn't mean to." She squeaked out her words.

"Which is why we have rules." Aaron knelt to her eye-level. "Our job is to protect you, even if that means we have to protect you from yourself."

"I think we've talked enough for tonight. We can finish this conversation in the morning." My heart broke for her. She hadn't as much as glanced at Bryson's bruised face since we'd called the family meeting.

"Good night." Jojo nodded and turned for the hall.

Aaron grabbed her hand. "Hey. We love you very much."

"I love you guys, too." She wrapped her arms around his neck. "I'm sorry."

"Apology accepted, but don't even think about sneaking out again.

She released him and turned to me. "Mom, I never said it, but thank you for not hurting Holden too bad."

The change in subject took me off guard. I opened and closed my mouth several times before I could finally form a thought. "I wasn't sure how much you remembered."

"I do." She hurried to Bryson and moved as if to hug him, but stopped short. "And thanks for helping me. It would have been cool to be a wolf, but I'd want to be like you and Mom."

He pulled her close with his good arm. "Like me and Mom?"

"You guys poof into birds. Holden had to go through a whole disgusting process." She wrinkled her nose.

Chuckling, Bryson kissed her forehead. "Goodnight, Jojo."

Aaron followed the girl down the hall to tuck her in.

Bryson grimaced and settled against the cushions. "You should call Darlene."

I lowered my voice. "Are you sure Jojo's right about Stone?"

"After that display tonight, I'm surprised you have to ask." He gave me a crooked smile. "Thanks for healing me. I thought I was a goner when I hit that forcefield."

The memory of it sent a shiver down my spine. "Me too."

Aaron returned and plopped into my easy chair. "I'm all for positive parenting, but sometimes I can see the merits of military school."

"Speaking of positive parenting..." I motioned between them. "No more knocking the kids out with spells."

"Agreed, but tonight was an emergency. We have to decide what to do about TJ. He's seen too much in his short life." Bryson didn't seem particularly happy about the situation we found ourselves in. "Aaron and I can do a forgetting spell on him, but Jojo is going to be a problem."

"Why?" I glanced between them.

"She's liable to say something to him that will trigger his memories." Bryson's frown deepened. "We could tell her what we're doing and why, but she's been..."

"Unpredictable," Aaron added.

"That's an understatement." I stared at the ceiling trying to figure out what to do. Forgetting spells were tricky. The memories weren't pulled out like weeds. They were covered up. "Our best bet is to make TJ forget the gore and deal with the rest if and when we have to."

Bryson stared at me like I'd suddenly sprouted wings and a halo. "Good idea."

"Agreed." Aaron rested his elbows on his knees and clasped his hands. "I've been thinking about something Killian said."

Bryson and I exchanged glances. We needed to tell Aaron the truth, but we needed more than five drama-free minutes to do it.

"He thinks I'm Fae." He met my gaze. "And the other day with Tighe... I think I might be one of those change-things."

So much for waiting for the right time.

"Changeling, and so do I." I stood and seated myself on the floor beside him.

Bryson nodded. "I do, too."

Resting my hand on his, I asked, "Are you okay with the idea you were switched at birth?"

He hitched a shoulder. "I think we've proven that parents don't have to be blood to love you."

"Yes, we have." I'd never thought about it like that, but I could say the same for Charlie and Dottie and Mae, and even Darlene—to a point.

"And that makes Jojo a halfling." He sat back and did the absolute last thing I would have expected. He grinned. "And she's a strong one considering she was able to heal the venom, and the little devil is resistant to our spells."

"It does." Bryson raised a brow.

Aaron's grin morphed into a full-blown smile. "So unless Jenny was secretly Fae, that means we don't have to worry about Quin's magic fading anytime soon."

Before I could answer, my phone rang.

One glance at the screen and my pulse was off to the races. "It's Darlene."

"Answer it." Aaron motioned to the cell.

"Hi, Momma. We have some good news"

"So do I! That SOB is a lying, cheating, sack of dog shit." She continued to cuss Stone up one side and down the other. Once she'd worn herself out, her shouting morphed into gut wrenching sobs. "There was never a gig. He lied better than a no-legged dog getting a suntan."

I couldn't keep up with her mood swings, let alone figure out what the heck was going on. "Did you talk to Stone?"

"Noooo!" She wailed into the phone. "Bobby-Ray told me everything. Stone's been working at a music store in the afternoons."

"Who's Bobby-Ray?"

"The lead singer. Honestly, Tessa. Keep up." She huffed.

I counted to ten, and then ten more. "Okay, where is he?"

"He's on some kind of walk-around-thingy to find himself." She hiccupped and burst into fresh tears.

"Stone's on a walk-about?" I glanced between Bryson and Aaron. Both men stared at me slack-jawed. "Do you know where?"

"In the panhandle." She blew her nose. "You know what this means, right? He's cheating on me."

"You don't know that." I resisted the urge to bang my head against the coffee table. "Momma, we don't think it was Stone down by the lake. Something funky is going on, but I don't think he's dead."

"Oh, something funky is definitely going on." She laughed as cold and bitter as last week's coffee. "But he's gonna wish he was dead when I get my hands on him!"

I knew her particular form of crazy as well as I knew my own. She was one crying spell away from a total meltdown. "I'm coming over."

"No. I don't want your company." Darlene groaned. "Great. Now the baby is crying. I have to go."

"Momma, wait."

"I'll talk to you tomorrow." She disconnected the call.

I stared at the phone for a few seconds, shook my head, and dropped it on the table.

"Wow." Aaron raked his hands through his hair.

"How much of that did you hear?"

"Enough to know she's a mess." Bryson sighed.

"She says she doesn't want me there, but I should go." I pushed to my feet.

Aaron took my hand and pulled me into his lap. "Give her some time. Besides, you're not going anywhere alone."

"Aaron's right. Until we catch this guy, it's too dangerous." Bryson shifted as if to stand, winced, and let his head fall back.

For once in my life, I didn't mind their overprotectiveness. Whoever, or whatever, was killing people wanted my attention.

And they had it.

CHAPTER 30

"How are you feeling TJ?" I set a plate of Gram Mae's famous brownies on the coffee table.

Earlier that morning we'd cast a forgetting spell and woken him. Only time would tell if his memories of the body by the lake would return, but the sleeping spell had been a success. Judging by the wild look in the boy's eyes, he wouldn't fall asleep again for a week.

TJ stuffed half a treat in his mouth and gave me two chocolate-covered thumbs up.

Jolene turned to me. "Mom, are we still going to the movies today?"

"Sure, but this time it's a family outing." The idea of going back to the theater made me break out in a cold sweat.

TJ pumped his fist over his head. "Best day ever!"

Jolene rolled her eyes and turned her attention back to the television and the dog at her side.

Unfortunately, Maddie was just Maddie. Gavin had disappeared yet again.

After their ordeal, the kids deserved the belated Halloween celebration—sugary treats and a *Vampires Suck the TV Show* marathon.

I walked back into the kitchen and checked on Quin in his carrier.

Unlike TJ, the little guy seemed groggy from the sleeping spell the night before. His constant napping made me nervous.

After making sure the baby was still breathing—for the hundredth time—I glanced at the mess Aaron had made on the table and felt a headache coming on. He'd taken the cork bulletin board from the office and set up an investigation board, otherwise known as a crazy wall. Red yarn connected sticky notes containing clues, locations, details, and suspects. Make that one suspect—Killian.

Bryson came in through the back door barefooted and wearing a pair of low-slung PJ pants.

Normally, I would have admired the view, but the bruises and abrasions on his chest and back made me queasy. "Where's your splint and sling?"

He rotated his shoulder several times. "I don't need it. I was able to fly a bit this morning. I think the third shift was the charm."

"I'd feel better if you weren't still bruised like an overripe banana." I poured myself a fresh cup of full-octane java. "How are your ribs?"

"Sore." He eyed the mug in my hand. "But now that the more serious injuries are healed, another shift or two should take care of the superficial ones."

I didn't consider cracked ribs superficial but refrained from commenting.

"I have a working theory." Folding his arms, Aaron stared at his crazy wall. "The fake-murders are all an elaborate plan to force Tessa to break some bullshit Fae rules that she didn't even know existed."

Once again, I found myself biting back a comment. Only this time, I failed. "We stayed up all night, raided Jojo's school supplies, and made a mess to come to the same conclusion we started with?"

"I'm a visual person. I needed to see it all laid out." Aaron motioned to his craft project. "Now that I have, it's obvious the animal attacks are tests."

"Suffice to say, we failed everything they threw at us last night." Bryson stared into his coffee.

"We've been over this." I rested my hand on Bryson's arm. "Other than Jojo's outburst at the crime scene, there weren't any human witnesses."

"I'd like to know how much longer this is going to go on." He glanced between us. "Eventually, we're going to fail and face some sort of consequences."

"You mean punishment?" Aaron sat straighter.

Bryson nodded. "The question is what kind."

Careful to keep my voice low in case the kids were listening, I whispered, "I'm guessing it'll involve being forced to spend time in Tir Na Nog."

The color drained from Aaron's face. "Can they do that?"

"I don't know." Bryson rested his head in his hands.

I didn't have the heart to tell them what Killian had said about Fae being welcome in Tir Na Nog, or that he thought I needed to go there. The inhabitants of Hell would need snow parkas before I left my family.

"We're almost certain Wyatt and Stone are alive, but where are they? And what about the *other* cases?" Aaron glanced toward the living room and lowered his voice. "And if that wasn't Stone down there, who the hell was it? Are the Fae killing people to *test* you?"

Bryson winced as if Aaron had struck him.

I had the same reaction, only mine centered in my gut. I couldn't breathe through the sudden nausea.

"It's a very real possibility." Bryson's words came out in a low growl.

Why would the freaking Fae do such things? Why not drag me to Tir Na Nog and give me the magic equivalent of the SAT? Why kill or kidnap innocent people?

The house phone rang and startled Quin.

The second ring ended mid-way through.

Bryson cast a thoughtful look in the baby's direction.

My brows rose. "Did he do that?"

"Good job, Quin." Aaron puffed out his chest, ever the proud papa.

I resisted the urge to roll my eyes. "It's all fun and games until you miss work calls."

He smirked. "He's smart enough to know the only people who call the house line are solicitors and wrong numbers."

My cell rang a few seconds later. Once again, it went silent mid-ring.

"What did I tell you?" I opened my mouth to ask Bryson if he had any idea how to stop baby magic from ruining our lives, and my phone rang again.

"That's Dottie's ringtone." I scrambled to get to my purse in the living room but missed the call.

Bryson's phone rang next. "Dottie? Everything okay?"

He glanced at Aaron first, then at me.

The second I met his gaze, I knew something was wrong. Very wrong.

The worst possible scenario settled into my heart and wouldn't let go. "It's Gram Mae, isn't it?"

"We're on our way." He disconnected. "Mae's not feeling well. Dottie called an ambulance."

I hit the front porch in a blind panic. I hadn't stopped to put on shoes or to make sure the kids were okay or even to ask one of the guys to keep an eye on them. My one, and only, thought was to get to my great-grandmother and *magic* her until she was healthy.

Bryson caught up with me halfway between the two houses. "Tessa, wait."

I didn't want to wait or talk or listen to what he had to say. We'd been over it a million times before. He didn't agree with interfering with the natural order of things. Death was as natural as birth to him.

I disagreed.

"No! I know what you're going to say." I hadn't meant to shout. He didn't deserve it, but I couldn't stop myself. Nor could I stop myself from darting toward the little pink house.

"Damn it. Will you listen?" Bryson ran up behind me, grabbed my waist and spun me to face him. "You need to take a breath and calm down before you go in there. For Mae's sake."

He was right, but I had as much of a chance of calming down as I had convincing Darlene women her age shouldn't wear hot pants and halter tops.

Sirens wailed in the distance, and I took advantage of the situation to get Bryson off my back. "Stay here and make sure EMS goes to the right house."

He gave me a look somewhere between worried and frustrated, but didn't argue.

Doing my best to swallow my panic, I walked through the screen door. No one was in the kitchen, but the soft murmur of voices drew me toward the back of the house.

The sirens grew louder and red and white lights flashed outside the windows.

I had to hurry and do what I could before the paramedics burst into the room.

Dottie on one side, Darlene on the other, Gram Mae sat upright in her easy chair. Despite the sheen of sweat on her face, a thick quilt covered her lower half. She glanced at me and forced a tight-lipped smile.

I gave her a quick kiss on her brow. "Can I have a minute alone with her?"

Dottie stood. "I'll go let the EMS folks in."

Darlene squeezed my arm. "Take care of her, Tessa."

My mother seldom made sense, but I knew exactly what she meant.

"I will." I sat on the little footstool in front of my great-grandmother and took her hands in mine. Lowering my shields, I allowed my magic to flow between us. Her frail body absorbed the power like a dry sponge.

Gram Mae moved her legs as if she couldn't quite get comfortable. "Tessa Marie, I'm an old woman. I've had a better life than most."

"And you'll have many more years." Ignoring the sounds of the screen door opening, and the voices of strangers, I continued to push my energy into her.

Gram Mae pulled her hands back and cupped my face. "When it's my time to go, I'll go. You're not to try to stop me, do you hear me?"

I met her eyes and my vision blurred. I couldn't stand the thought of losing her. Nor could I admit to her, or myself, I could let her go. It'd be a lie.

"Summon Tighe. I'd like to see him one more time." Her words came out breathy as if it hurt her to speak.

"I will. I promise." For the first time since I'd walked in, I took a good look at her. Her skin had gone so pale, I could see the bluish veins beneath the surface. Her eyes had lost their twinkle and seemed deeper set than normal. But that wasn't the horrible part.

Not by a long shot.

Her normally bright purple aura had faded to a dusty gray. My magic reflected back at me in bits of shimmering gold, but even that was wrong. The healing energy should have boosted hers, not sat on top of it like shells on a beach.

A paramedic said something to me as he pulled me away from her, but I didn't hear him. Two others swarmed around her, taking her vitals, asking questions. Someone else wheeled in a gurney.

"I'm going with you." I glanced around for my purse or shoes or cell. I had none. Not that it mattered. The only thing I cared about was Gram Mae.

"Miss, you'll have to follow in your vehicle. We'll need room to work—"

"I'll drive you." Bryson followed us out to the ambulance.

Gram Mae flexed her fingers as if trying to reach for me.

I hurried to her side. "I'm here."

She stared as if to remind me of her wishes or that she'd had a good life or to say goodbye.

I chose not to believe any of that. "I'll call Tighe. He'll take you to the Summerlands, Gram. You're going with him. You hear me? You're going. You'll be young again and dance. You'll dance like you used to."

She squeezed my fingers.

The paramedic shot me an odd look. "Ma'am. We have to go."

I released her hand and collapsed against Dottie.

CHAPTER 31

"Damn it." I let my head fall back against the seat. I'd spent the previous fifteen minutes attempting a summoning spell inside a moving SUV. To say I was carsick was an understatement.

"Did you reach him?" Bryson squeezed my thigh.

"Maybe?" I kept my eyes trained on the ambulance in front of us, or more specifically, the woman on the gurney. As long as no one was pounding on her chest or shocking her, I figured she was holding her own. "It's not like I have a magical cell phone. It's more like wishing his name into the universe and hoping he hears me."

Bryson, being Bryson, didn't react to my outburst. Instead he lifted my hand to his mouth and kissed my knuckles. "If he doesn't show, try reaching out to Killian or your father."

"Okay." I doubted I could reach anyone in my current state.

"Worst case scenario, I'll have Aaron bring salt to the hospital, and we'll do a proper spell in a supply closet." He gave me a half-hearted grin.

We followed the ambulance to the emergency entrance of the hospital and parked. I knew better than to try to go in through the back with Gram Mae, but I was sorely tempted to try.

The moment Bryson and I walked into the main door of the ER, we were approached by one seriously freaked out Fae.

"Tessa." Tighe drew me into a rib-cracking embrace and didn't let me go until I made a pained sound. "Thank you for calling me. Where is she?"

"They took her in through the ambulance entrance." I took a step back and a deep breath.

"Is she..."

I appreciated him not finishing the question. Somehow, saying the words out loud makes the possibility, that the person you love most in the world might not survive, more tangible. "Her aura was faint, but she's too stubborn to..."

Tighe gave me the same half-smile Bryson had, a robotic gesture without warmth or feeling. "I need to see her."

"It'll probably be a while before they allow visitors."

"We'll see about that." He winked and headed to the check-in desk.

The woman working reception and several nurses openly stared at the dark-haired Fae. Not that I could blame them—the guy was easy on the eyes. I half expected the women to roll out the welcome mat and escort him to Gram Mae's bedside, but to my surprise, they turned him away.

Bryson sighed and led me to a seat in the corner of the room. "I should call Aaron while it's quiet."

"You mean before Darlene gets here."

"You said it, not me." He had the good manners to dip his chin. "I'm glad she's bringing Dottie instead of Aaron. I would have hated to leave the kids with your mother under these circumstances."

"Me too." I watched as Tighe ducked into the restroom. A few seconds later the door opened, but no one stepped out. "I think Tighe is up to something."

With his phone to his ear, Bryson nodded.

A faint ripple of energy shimmered near the windows. The double doors leading to the exam rooms opened. Once again, no one went in or out. No one I could see anyway.

I nudged Bryson and pointed to the doors, but he was too busy giving Aaron the run down on Gram Mae's condition—the little we knew anyway.

He disconnected the call and glanced in my direction. "Everything's good at home, but the kids are disappointed about the movie."

"They'll have to wait. We don't even know what's going on. What if Gram Mae's... I won't leave her to go to a stupid movie." My pulse went into hyper-speed. I pressed my hand to my chest as if to slow my heart or stop it from breaking.

Bryson slipped his arm around my shoulders and kissed my temple. "Tessa, they understand. They're worried about Mae, too."

Mom guilt crashed over me and sent my already racing pulse even higher. TJ needed all the stability he could get. And Jojo... Other than our failed girls' day, I'd all but ignored her since Quin was born. Heck, I'd forgotten Halloween.

"I'm a horrible mother." I burst into tears. I'm talking big fat soap opera tears. Only, I didn't have the benefit of professional hair and makeup people to make it a pretty cry. My meltdown was closer to something Quin would do, complete with snot and slobber.

Wide-eyed, Bryson pulled me close. "You're doing better than anyone could expect given the circumstances."

The weight of everything that had happened rested on my chest. My mind pinballed from Gram Mae's heart to Stone to Quin's colic to thinking my newfound brother was setting me up to the realization I might never meet my dad. I hadn't stopped to think or breathe, let alone grieve or process any of it.

Poor Bryson alternated between patting my back, stroking my hair, and rocking me, but nothing helped. If anything, he made it worse. He was a man teetering on the edge of the same cliff I'd fallen from.

I eased away from him and wiped my eyes. "Sorry. You've been beside me during every horrible thing that's happened. The last thing you need is for me to fall apart."

He took my face in his hands and stared into my eyes. "Tessa, I vowed to walk with you through good times and bad."

I couldn't speak past the lump in my throat.

"It's not good to hold everything in. If you need to cry. Cry. If you need to scream, we'll lock ourselves in the SUV and scream." He crushed me to his chest. "Just please...let me be there for you. Lately, it's all I have to offer."

Another chunk of my heart broke off. Bryson was used to being the strong one. The one who had the answers, who knew magic, who protected us. Since Killian had shown up, he'd taken one blow to his confidence after another.

"You're the only reason I'm still standing. You and Aaron are my rocks." I did my best to convey how much I loved him by throwing my arms around him and sobbing all over his shoulder.

"Oh no! Are we too late?" Darlene stood a few feet from us with her hand covering her mouth.

Dottie glanced from me to Bryson and swayed.

He shot to his feet and steadied her. "As far as we know, she's okay. We haven't heard anything or been able to see her."

Both women blew out a breath.

"Honestly, Tessa, you scared the daylights out of me." Darlene gave me the same annoyed expression she'd given me since birth, but it melted away as quickly as it came. She sat on the other side of me and took my hand. "I'm sorry, I snapped. It's been a rough few days."

"Yes, it has." I squared my shoulders and wiped my face. Again. My heart might have been shattered, but I needed to hold the pieces together for Dottie and Darlene's sakes. "But Gram Mae is going to be okay, and Stone's going to come home. You'll see. Everything will work out."

Bryson glanced at me and pressed his lips into a tight line. "I'll go ask the nurses if there's any news."

If I had to guess, I'd say he disagreed with my need to take care of them, or maybe I'd gone overboard. Either way, I stuffed down my worries and put on a happy-freaking-face.

Bryson had made it halfway to the reception desk when his phone rang. He gave me a quick nod, and stepped outside to take it.

"Any word from Stone?" I hated to poke a skunk, but the sooner he came back, the sooner the police could rule him out and find the real victim.

"Nope." Darlene dipped her chin and wiped her eyes.

Although Bryson, Aaron and I believed Stone was alive, we couldn't exactly tell the Chief of Police our ten-year-old daughter had conjured up every spirit this side of Interstate Four and hadn't found Stone. The murder investigation had continued as usual, including the awful process of identifying the remains.

We sat for what felt like forever before Bryson came back inside and walked to the reception desk. I wasn't sure who'd called, but his expression told me it hadn't been a good conversation.

By the time he rejoined us, I thought I'd come out of my skin. "Well?"

"They're still running tests. The doctor will come out when they know something." He glanced out the window and got a faraway look in his eye. I didn't need to ask to know what he was thinking. When things went sideways the sky called to us, but we couldn't fly our cares away this time.

Dottie perked up a bit. "Can we see her?"

Bryson snapped his head toward her as if she'd startled him. "Only one visitor at a time, and she has someone with her now."

"Who?" Darlene scoffed. "The only people she'd want to see are sitting right here. Except Aaron, of course."

"She asked me to call Tighe before they put her in the ambulance." I hated to mention it and make things worse for Dottie. I didn't know why, but she had a problem with Fae—especially Mae's former beau.

Darlene glanced between us. "You know they used to date, back when dinosaurs roamed the earth."

"We are all aware." Dottie snapped her mouth shut and folded her arms.

I wanted to ask her what was troubling her, but I figured it was none of my business.

Darlene, on the other hand, had no such reservations. "What's the deal with you and Tighe? You've had a bee in your bonnet since he showed up."

Dottie glared. "I do not."

Ignoring the arguing women, Bryson leaned close and lowered his voice. "Buck scheduled the naming ceremony for Saturday."

"Did you tell him about Gram Mae?" I couldn't deal with another thing. Especially not one that could easily be put off until things settled. Or at least until my great-grandmother was out of the hospital.

"I did, but he already sent out invitations." Bryson didn't seem any happier about the situation than I did.

"But Quin's our son. Shouldn't we be the one's inviting people?" I knew I sounded like a nut-cake, but I didn't care. Buck Oldham was a serious pain in my butt.

"Normally, yes, but Quin is Cheasequah's grandson. Welcoming him into the Tribe is also about honoring Charlie's memory." Dottie patted my hand. "Sorry to interrupt."

Bryson winked at her. "Thank you."

"Lamar family?" A woman in light blue scrubs called from the check-in desk.

"That's us!" Waving her arm over her head, Darlene hot-footed it to the woman.

The rest of us moved slower.

I studied the doctor's expression, but couldn't tell if she had good or bad news.

Her gaze darted between us and her mouth moved as if she had something to say, but no words came out. The doctor gave herself a visible shake and forced a smile. "I'm Doctor Payton, the head of cardiology. Come with me to the family conference room. Please."

"Nice to meet you." My mother pointed to herself. "I'm Darlene, Mae's granddaughter. And this is—"

"Please. It's best if we speak in private." Dr. Payton turned and walked toward a door near the check-in desk.

My poor heart couldn't take anymore. I understood why she wouldn't want to do introductions in the middle of a crowded emergency room, but surely, she could have given us some encouragement. If nothing else, it would have been nice to know Gram Mae was still alive.

Please, God. Let her still be alive.

Bryson took my hand, but I nudged him and nodded toward Dottie. She'd gone pale and was clutching a tissue like it was a life preserver.

He stepped away from me and slipped his arm around her shoulders.

Dottie glanced up, smiled a miserable little smile, and followed the doctor.

Once we were seated, Dr. Payton let out a nervous laugh. "I have to tell you, in thirty years of practicing medicine, I have never seen anything like this case."

I closed my eyes, tilted my face toward the ceiling, and sent up a silent thank-you.

"That's our Gram Mae." Darlene spoke louder than necessary, a sure sign she was as stressed out as the rest of us. "But we'd really like to hear what's wrong with her."

As if she realized she'd behaved unprofessionally, the doctor sat straighter and raised her chin. When she spoke again, she sounded more like a television reporter, and less like an awestruck normal person. "The tests are contradictory. The readings EMS took showed a major cardiac event, but all of the tests we've run here show her heart is performing like a twenty-year-old's."

Tighe. It has to be.

I made a mental note to give him a huge hug, bake him a cake, and name my next child after him. And then I scratched all of that off my imaginary to-do list. If he had the power to heal her, why hadn't he done it the day she'd collapsed instead of waiting for her to almost die? Was he playing games, or was he buying himself time to convince her to go away with him?

Dottie hung her head and muttered under her breath.

"Are you sure the second tests are accurate?" Bryson furrowed his brow. "Mae hasn't been feeling well lately, and she's been on blood pressure medication for years. Not to mention she's diabetic."

Darlene nodded. "Did you mix up my grandmother's tests with someone else's? I saw a TV program where that happened."

I sat on my hands to keep from smacking her.

"It's highly unlikely the lab work, ECG, and imaging were all wrong. We are rerunning the tests now. If they come back the same, we'll discharge her tomorrow." Dr. Payton stood and clasped her hands behind her back as if she wanted to smack Darlene, too. "If you don't have any more questions…"

"Thank you, Dr. Payton." I offered her a smile.

"You're welcome." She glanced to each of us, except Darlene. "I'm not a religious woman, but I believe I've witnessed a miracle today."

We watched her walk out of the room before the four of us turned to each other. Bryson grinned, Darlene wore a smug expression, and Dottie just shook her head.

I followed my family out of the conference room in a state of shock. Shock with a bit of confusion mixed in. I hated to kick a gift horse in the teeth, but I worried Gram Mae would pay for Tighe breaking the rules. Bryson always said magic came with a price. Healing years of diabetes, high blood pressure, and fried foods would likely cost a fortune.

However, the Fae in question strolled into the waiting room like he didn't have a care in this world, Tir Na Nog, or the Summerlands.

Despite my nagging questions, I couldn't stop myself from hugging him. "Thank you for saving her."

His expression turned serious. "It is temporary. The magic will fade sooner rather than later."

Talk about a sucker punch!

"How long does she have?" My voice came out squeaky.

Dottie marched over and poked a bony finger in his chest. "You aren't welcome here."

Bryson and I exchanged worried glances, but neither of us moved.

"Dottie! What are you saying?" Darlene looked around and lowered her voice to a whisper-shout. "He just saved—"

"Let's have this conversation someplace private." Tighe turned to me, likely looking for backup.

It took me a half-second to get over my shock. I'd only seen my Aunt Dottie speak to one other person that way, and he'd done unspeakable things. Sure, Tighe's magic might be temporary, but he'd given us a gift. "I could use some fresh air."

"No, Tessa." Dottie shook her head. "No. I'm not going anywhere with him."

Tighe's resigned expression told me he knew why Dottie couldn't stand him.

I moved to her side and nodded back to the conference room. "I think it's time we sit down and talk. Alone."

"You're right, but Bryson should join us." She sighed and trudged back the way we'd come.

"Of course." He followed her.

Darlene turned toward the room, but Tighe whispered something in her ear and guided her away.

I couldn't figure him out. He obviously cared about Mae, but something about him bugged me. He was like the guy at the party who blurted out the punchline before you'd finished telling the joke.

I walked into the conference room and closed the door behind me.

Dottie didn't waste any time diving in. "You were too young to remember, but Mae had a heart attack about twenty years ago."

"I remember hearing about it." I sank into the chair beside Bryson. "It was bad, right? Everyone was surprised she survived."

"Everyone but Charlie. He knew she would live." She drew a deep breath and met my gaze. "He said I'd know when it was her time when a *young* man from her past came calling."

While that absolutely sounded like something my grandfather would say, I was puzzled. "How could Charlie possibly know when and if Tighe would return?"

"I asked him that very question." Dottie let out an exasperated sigh. "You know your grandfather... He just smiled and patted my cheek."

"At least I'm not the only one he talks to in riddles." I laughed despite myself.

Bryson wore the same expression as the day Gram Mae dropped Quin. He knew what was coming and dreaded it.

I knew the feeling, but I wasn't ready to give up. There had to be a way to save her.

Dottie grinned through her tears. "I'm not ready to lose her, Tessa."

"Me either." I wrapped her in my arms more determined than ever to magic another ten years out of Gram Mae.

CHAPTER 32

The remainder of the week passed without drama—make that external drama. I still had a broken-hearted mother, a fussy baby, a seriously ill great-grandmother, a moody daughter, and a devil of a seven-year-old to deal with. However, the fake-killer had taken a few days off.

I chose to remain positive. Or as positive as I could with Gram Mae still in the hospital and Darlene currently crashing on my couch and having to face Buck and the Elders in a couple of hours.

I'd changed my dress four times in as many minutes. I wanted to look my best for Quin's naming ceremony. Not that I cared what Buck and the others thought. I wanted to look nice in the photos. Special days came and went, but bad pictures were like bad pennies. They turned up again and again.

I walked into the living room to model my latest outfit. "How about this?"

Cole, my baby brother clapped his chubby hands. Having him under my roof was the silver lining that made putting up with Darlene around the clock almost bearable. Almost.

Darlene pursed her lips and motioned for me to turn.

Smiling, I did a slow spin. The dark green pantsuit was perfect. It was dressy but practical when wrangling children. And yet, I knew I had a problem when she frowned.

"The jacket makes you look short." She waved her hand as if dismissing me.

I planted my hands on my hips. "I am short."

She tapped her lips. "Try the white blouse with those pants."

I sank onto the couch and put my head in my hands. "Gram Mae should be here. I don't want to do this without her."

My great-grandmother's condition had deteriorated to the point we weren't sure she'd make it home. And to make matters worse, she'd forbidden Tighe from healing her again.

"I know, sweet-pea. I know." She patted my shoulder. "But the show must go on."

I should have known better than to expect warm-fuzzies from Darlene. Rather than fall through the cracks in my broken heart, I mentally pulled up my big girl britches. "You're right."

"Of course I am." She motioned to my chest. "And for crying out loud, would it kill you to show a little of what the good Lord gave you?"

"I'm not going to walk down the aisle in front of the Elders with my cleavage showing." I had my doubts about relying on Darlene for fashion advice, but the guys were no help.

"It wouldn't be the first time. I thought Stone was going to faint when your blouse fell apart in church." Her lower lip quivered like Quin's did before he cried. Holding her eyes open wide, she fanned her face. "Dang it. I can't tear up now. I'll ruin my makeup."

I sat beside her and slung my arm around her shoulder. We'd come to an unspoken understanding over the previous few days. She didn't want to be alone, but that didn't mean she wanted to talk about her run-away husband.

"Why is the lab taking so long to get the DNA results?" Darlene pulled a worn-out tissue from her bra and blew her nose.

I gave her shoulder a little squeeze. "We should get word Monday, but it's not him."

"I know, but the longer he's gone, the more I wonder." She shook me off and stood. "They get results back in an hour on the Maury Povich show."

I didn't have the heart to point out most television shows were fiction, and the ones who weren't tested their guests long before the episodes aired. "There was a problem with the first set of tests. We should hear something by Monday."

"It's the hair. It's not as reliable as body fluids." She shook her head. "What did I tell you? Aaron should have taken the rubber out of the trash can."

I loved her. I did. But she'd scarred my poor husband for life when she'd tried to hand him a used condom. "The techs test hairbrushes all the time."

She pursed her lips. "I put the rubber in the freezer just in case."

"I'll be sure to let Aaron know." I made a mental note to never drink iced anything at Darlene's place.

Bryson poked his head into the room. "Are you ladies ready? We need to go."

A quick glance at the clock sent my pulse racing. "I need five minutes."

Darlene's phone chimed and she gasped.

"What's wrong?" I peeked at the name on the screen and froze. Stone had texted her. "Call him. Right now."

Darlene continued to stare at the cell.

What the heck is she waiting for?

"Momma, call him. We need to hear his voice to know he's okay."

She dropped the phone into her purse. "I have nothing to say to that lying bastard."

I snapped my mouth shut. For the life of me, I would never understand her. She'd moped and cried and prayed to the heavens for Stone to be all right. Now that he'd finally reached out, she didn't want to talk to him?

Rather than arguing, I plucked my phone from the coffee table and dialed Stone. The call went straight to voicemail. "Hi, it's Tessa. Please call me when you get this message."

"Tessa Marie, I told you I didn't want to talk to him. Besides, we need to get ready." She tugged the hem of her skintight minidress down to mid-thigh. "Without Gram Mae and Dottie here, it's up to me to make sure everything runs smoothly."

The pain in the center of my chest made it easier for me to resist rolling my eyes at her comment. No one, not even Dottie, could take Gram Mae's place—and certainly not Darlene.

She continued yammering on. "That is if I make it through a day with all of those puffed-up Elders and the extended family," she whispered the last two words as if they were a dirty little secret.

Actually, the words were a secret to me. "I thought we agreed to only invite the immediate family?"

"Right. That's what I said." She rolled her lips in, frowned, and glanced away. "I don't suppose you've heard any more from Killian?"

"Not a word." The fact that my brother had blown in, blown up, and blown out—again—hurt more than I cared to think about. Still, I wasn't about to admit it out loud. I squared my shoulders and stiffened my spine. "I say good riddance. He left another stolen car in the driveway."

"Fae folk aren't like the rest of us. They're flightier than a bunch of parakeets in a thunderstorm."

"I've noticed." I ditched the jacket, changed blouses, and slipped on a pair of flats.

Darlene tilted her head and stared at my chest. "Tessa Marie, did you use Kleenex instead of the nursing pads? Your boobs look…square."

I didn't have the confidence or the patience for this conversation. "I tried a different brand. They're awful, but they're all I've got. If I don't wear them, I'll soak my shirt."

"I'm sorry, sweetheart." She bit back a smile. "But your bosom barely fits in your brassiere as it is. All that extra padding isn't helping."

Bryson walked into the room in time to catch the last bit of our conversation. He laughed, and miracle of miracles, Quin stopped fussing.

While I was over the moon that the baby seemed happy, I was about to say something ugly enough to ruin my hubby's good mood. I was used to Darlene teasing me, but I didn't appreciate him getting in on the action.

"Bryson Declay, I'm not sure what you think is so funny." Darlene raised her chin as if imitating Gram Mae.

His eyes widened as if he realized he'd stepped into a giant pile of poo. "I apologize. I wasn't laughing at you."

"Mmm hmm. What *were* you laughing at?" I grinned. It might be a sin, but part of me enjoyed watching him squirm.

"It explains what Jojo was doing in the bathroom last Sunday before church." He motioned to my chest then mimicked shoving tissues down the front of his shirt.

"Daaad!" Jolene had yelled from the doorway, but her glare was all for me. She groaned one more time for good measure and marched out the door.

Bryson watched her go with a guilty expression. "I should stop speaking or get used to the taste of shoe leather."

"Yep." I moved to him and lifted Quin from his arms. "But at least this little guy seems better."

Bryson stood straighter. "He's ready for his big day."

Darlene tilted her head. "Did you give him the boiled onion water Gram Mae gave you?"

Before I could reply, Quin let out a wail that shook the rafters.

She patted my shoulder. "Next time try pickle juice. My momma gave it to me when I was his age, and I still drink it every time I get an upset stomach."

Well, that explains a lot.

CHAPTER 33

The tribal house was fairly large. It contained a dozen dorm rooms, offices, and a massive reception hall. Outside was a sizable pavilion and an open area with a firepit where the Elders conducted sacred ceremonies. Normally, there was ample enough parking for a couple of hundred guests, yet cars filled every square inch of the parking lot and overflowed onto both sides of the road. I'd never seen the place so crowded.

I leaned forward to get a better look at a white convertible Mercedes. "I have a bad feeling about this."

Bryson reached back and took my hand.

Darlene either hadn't heard me, or she'd chosen to ignore my concern. "I knew we were going to be late."

Aaron hitched a shoulder. "It's not like they can start without us."

"Being new parents is no excuse to keep everyone waiting." She mimicked Gram Mae's voice.

"Good one, Aunt Darlene." TJ giggled.

She turned and shook her finger in his face. "Watch your sass, young man."

"Momma, stop it." I wasn't sure if she thought she was being funny or was taking her self-assigned authority too seriously. Either way, the constant reminders that my great-grandmother wasn't there hurt.

Aaron met my gaze in the rearview and furrowed his brow. It seemed I wasn't the only one she was irritating.

"Looks like everyone beat us here. We need to get inside." The moment the vehicle came to a stop, Darlene hopped out.

I climbed out, handed Bryson the baby, and moved the seat to allow TJ and Jojo to exit the back row.

Buck Oldham joined us beside the SUV. The older Cherokee wore his ceremonial robes, and for a brief moment, all I saw was my grandfather. The men had the same coloring and height.

Special days, family gathering, and holidays were the absolute worst reminders that he was gone. Until then, the only way I'd managed to survive them was Gram Mae's constant presence. I couldn't imagine my life without her—*wouldn't* imagine it.

Buck's gruff voice pulled me back to the matter at hand. "We'll start as soon as everyone is seated. You have quite the *unusual* crowd."

I opened my mouth to ask about said crowd, but Darlene cut me off.

"Honestly, Tessa, get a move on. We have a ton of people waiting for the ceremony to end so they can eat."

"Glad to know they're only here for the food." I narrowed my eyes. "And we wouldn't have had a full house if you hadn't invited so many people."

She huffed and hurried TJ and Jojo inside.

Aaron joined me. "What's up with her?"

"No idea, but it can't be good."

"I'll go see who's in there."

Bryson looped his free arm with mine and guided me to the entrance. He'd drawn his magic to the surface and then some. It spilled out of him and engulfed me in its warm embrace.

Something was wrong. More wrong than Darlene inviting every cousin on the planet. The second I lowered my shields, an unfamiliar magic hit me. It was strong, like walking into someone's secondhand smoke, only less smelly. "Is that…?"

"Fae." He ground out the word.

"Darlene did this." My already frazzled nerves frayed into millions of tiny pieces. I would have marched in there and given her a piece of my mind, but what was the point? I couldn't put the milk back into the glass.

Bryson nodded. "When this is over, we're going to set some boundaries with that woman. She's crossed the line one too many times."

I didn't envy Darlene.

Walking through the door, I whispered, "They could be here to see Quin. Killian said Fae babies are rare."

"Maybe." He stopped long enough to meet my gaze. "It's more than likely another test."

The entire situation made me queasy. "Let's call it off and go home."

"It's not that simple. Every medicine man on the east coast is here to honor Cheasequah's great-grandson." Bryson sighed like a man choosing pistols or blades at dawn.

I didn't want to duel at all. I wanted to wave the white flag and get the heck out of there. "I don't give a damn about them. Our kids are here."

"I doubt anything will happen until after the ceremony."

"And if it does?" My voice came out on the wrong side of hysterical.

Bryson lifted my chin and stared into my eyes. "Stay between Aaron and me. As soon as it's over, we'll slip out the back door."

I nodded but I didn't like it.

Harris, the root doctor who'd helped us with the boo-hag and taught Aaron to control his magic, strode toward us. "Had I known what sort of trouble was brewin' I would have hung around a little longer."

Bryson shook Harris's hand. "Had we known, we might have gone to Georgia with you."

The root doctor turned to me. "The skies are dark now, but the sun will return sooner than you think."

I didn't have it in me to fake optimism. "If you say so."

"I'm here to help. When you need me." Harris winked and walked back outside.

I prayed he meant it. More so, I prayed he wouldn't vanish on me like Charlie and Gavin had.

We walked inside Buck's office and found him standing with a handful of Tribal Elders. The men had their heads together but stopped talking when Bryson and I approached. No one smiled or acknowledged our presence.

Aaron came in a few seconds after us. He glanced around and ran his hand down his face. "There are at least two dozen...*people* from the O'Roarke side of the family out there."

I wouldn't have thought it possible, but the Elders' faces hardened even more.

"They are not people." Buck spoke with such hatred I turned my upper body from him to shield Quin.

"Some of them are family." Aaron took a step away from him.

"I don't care what they are or who they're related to. Those *things* are not welcome here."

His tone caused a familiar pit to form in my stomach. The same black hole of rage that opened every time someone told a Native American joke or treated the brown-skinned members of my family different.

Aaron squared his shoulders. "And why exactly is that?"

Buck rounded on him. "A member of this tribe was murdered on this land by a magic-user."

I stepped closer to Buck and the other Elders. "I apologize. We had no idea they were going to show up here today."

Ignoring me altogether, he glared at Bryson. "I ordered you to tell me if anything else happened with the Fae."

Bryson said, "I don't take orders—"

"You are here on this land because I invited you to help Cheasequah's granddaughter learn to control her magic." His expression told me exactly what he thought of the job Bryson had done.

Bryson balled his hands and took a step forward, but stopped, drew a deep breath, and exhaled slowly. "We suspected the Fae have something to do with the animal attacks, but have good reason to believe Wyatt and the others are alive."

One of the Elders in the room gasped. The other glared.

Buck turned an unhealthy shade of red. "What makes you think that?"

Bryson didn't as much as flinch at the shouting. "As you well know, Tessa is able to speak to spirits."

Buck scoffed. "Why would anyone go to such lengths to create an elaborate scene and not commit murder?"

The way he'd arranged his words sent a chill down my spine that had nothing to do with the cold Fae magic in the air. It sounded as though he'd spoken from personal experience.

Aaron eased to my side and rested his hand on the small of my back.

"We believe someone is testing Tessa or trying to force her to break Fae law." Bryson glanced at me before turning back to Buck. "The fact that there are so many Fae here today could mean they have something planned."

Buck looked me over as if weighing my worth. Judging by his sneer, I'd come up wanting.

Bryson made a growly sound in the back of his throat. "We're calling the ceremony off."

Buck scoffed. "Like hell. My people may be *simple* humans, but many of them are skilled in magic. No one's going to cause problems on my watch."

Aaron's voice brought me back to the moment. "Just the same, I'd rather avoid a confrontation."

A knock on the door stopped the conversation.

"Come in." Buck glanced from Aaron to me. The mean little glint in his eyes sent a shiver down my spine.

Holden McAlister walked in. The boy took one look at Aaron and paled. "The uh…cook sent me to tell you…um the food is ready."

"Thank you, Holden." Buck motioned to us. "You know Jolene's parents from church. Why don't you say hello?"

He licked his lips several times and shifted his weight from one foot to the other as if debating making a break for it. "Hi."

Buck and the Elders had watched our every move.

I stood and gave Holden a quick hug. "It's good to see you. I'm glad you're okay."

"Good to see you, too. I'm um…glad you're okay, too." He hurried for the door.

Bryson and Aaron seemed to hold their breaths until the teen left the room.

One of the Elders stepped forward. The guy was human, but magic coiled around him like a rattlesnake ready to strike. "We should give them time to discuss what they wish to do about the naming ceremony in private."

I had a feeling what he really meant was he had something to say that he didn't want us to hear.

Buck nodded and followed the others out of the room.

Bryson blew out a breath and glanced between us. "That was…"

"Unexpected." Aaron frowned. "Was that a test?"

"I believe so. They likely wanted to see how we would react to Holden being here." Bryson stood and paced.

Aaron winced. "Why *is* he here?"

"A dozen or so shifters live in the dorms. They're keeping an eye on him until he learns to control his beast." Bryson closed his eyes and rubbed his brow. "I think we handled that okay, but we can't let our guards down."

I'd had it up to my eyeballs with people testing us. "All the more reason for us to call the ceremony off and go home."

Bryson sighed. "I understand you two want to leave, but I'm not sure that's a good idea."

Aaron motioned for him to continue. Me? I stood there dumbstruck by seeing Holden, the Fae outside, and Buck's racist behavior.

By all accounts, Buck had loved Charlie, but he'd given me more than my fair share of grief since learning I was a Nunnehi. Heck, at one point he'd tried to have another medicine man bind my magic. It wasn't until we'd reached an agreement on how Bryson and I would function in the tribe that he'd backed off—or so I'd thought.

"We know we're in danger, but we don't know enough about it to protect ourselves or the kids." Bryson glanced away and swallowed hard.

"Which is why we should go." For the life of me, I didn't understand why he was so hell bent on going through with the ceremony.

Bryson wouldn't look at either of us. "Once Quin is a member of the Tribe and of Tessa's clan, he will have the sworn protection of every medicine man and woman out there."

"So?" Aaron pointed at me. "Tessa has all of that so-called protection, and it hasn't helped her."

I shook my head. "No, Bryson's right. He and I aren't technically part of the tribe. We renounced our status when we stopped them from executing you."

Aaron threw his hands up. "And these are the people you want our son involved with?"

Bryson closed the distance between us and placed both his hands on Aaron's shoulders. "Buck and the Elders, no. People like Harris? Yes. Short of allowing Killian to take him to Tir Na Nog, the human magic-users are the only ones who can protect him..."

"If we're dead." Aaron pulled away from him and cursed under his breath. "Let's get the blessing and get the hell out of here."

"Do I get a vote in this?" I raised my hand like a schoolchild.

Before they could respond, Buck Oldham came back into the office and smiled. Not a mean smile, or even a forced one. He seemed like a different man than the racist A-hole that had walked out. "What did you decide?"

The guys turned to me, but I was still trying to decide if Buck was a sociopath or one hell of an actor.

"Tessa?" Bryson raised a brow.

"Majority rules." I held Quin tighter.

Bryson nodded toward me and the baby. "I'm taking Tessa and this little guy home as soon as the ceremony is over."

"I understand." Buck stared at the baby.

The conversation had left me exhausted. All I wanted to do was go home. "If we're going to do this, let's do it now."

"I agree." Buck walked to me and traced a line from Quin's forehead to the tip of his tiny nose. "You're one handsome boy."

Quin's eyes widened and he cooed.

Buck chuckled. "I understand Mae gifted him with his English name?"

"Yes, we call him Quin." Bryson stood taller. "His tribal name is not yet known, but I suspect Cheasequah will gift it when the time is right."

Once again, emotion clogged my throat. Charlie had taken the traditions of his people very seriously, and so did Bryson. Potentially, Quin would have many tribal names over the course of his life. The first would be a gift from a medicine man, or his grandfather's spirit, the others would come as a result of his accomplishments.

"Very well." Buck took a step back. "Normally, I'd ask the three of you to take the child to the water for cleansing before the ceremony, but today is not *normal*."

Bryson and Aaron nodded. Me? I was still stuck on the idea of calling it off.

Quin let out a peel of laughter. I'm talking a full-on squealed baby-giggle.

"I guess he didn't want a bath in the river." Aaron laughed along with the little guy.

Bryson and I exchanged worried glances.

CHAPTER 34

Aaron, Bryson, and I followed Buck out the double doors that led to the ceremonial gathering place. The second my eyes adjusted to the sunlight, my stomach fell to the floor and tried to crawl away.

We had a crowd all right. A crowd whose collective energy threatened to choke off the oxygen to the ceremonial fire. Humans on the right. Fae on the left. Both sides armed with magic. I felt like the bride at a Hatfield and McCoy wedding.

Sandwiched between Aaron and Bryson, I made my way down the long path toward the redwood altar. My men seemed almost as tense as I was, but the baby hadn't stopped squealing and giggling since we'd stepped outside.

I brought Quin to my shoulder and kept my eyes straight ahead, or tried to. The Fae in attendance were hard to ignore, each was more beautiful than the last.

The tension in my shoulders seeped away with each step. I highly doubted any of the Fae were there to hurt us.

Then it hit me.

I'd experienced the same sensation at Gram Mae's when I'd gotten in the way of Tighe's magic.

They're projecting calm, but why?

I turned to tell Bryson, but stopped when I caught sight of Killian.

My brother met my gaze and frowned. Hard. I thought he was upset with me until he gave the woman standing beside him side-eye and shook his head a fraction of an inch.

I glanced at the female. She looked a lot like the woman who'd accompanied Killian to church, but that woman had been pretty. The woman watching my son was…what?

A single word lodged in my brain. *Regal.*

I didn't need introductions to know I was staring at Caoimhe, Queen of the Aos Sí. Everything about the raven-haired woman was classy, from her perfectly arranged curls to the tailored fit of her black silk pantsuit.

Quin turned his head toward her and lifted his entire upper body. I'd been so distracted by the queen I almost lost my grip on him. The rush of adrenaline at nearly dropping my child in front of an audience left my heart racing.

Bryson stopped walking and whispered, "Everything okay?"

"I'm not sure." I smiled, although it probably looked more manic than reassuring. "The magic in the air… It has a calming effect."

"Not on me," he half-whispered and half-growled.

I wasn't sure he was right. Any other time, Bryson would have whisked us away at the first whiff of trouble, but he'd marched us into the middle of it.

By the time we laid Quin on the redwood altar, Buck looked like he could spit fire.

I took Bryson's hand and wished I hadn't. The man was a ball of magic and tension. He gave me a tight smile without taking his eyes off the baby. Maybe the Fae magic wasn't working on him as much as I'd thought.

"Quin, great-grandson of Cheasequah." Buck dipped his finger in a fragrant mixture of green goo and smeared the mess on the baby's tummy. "I see you and welcome you among my people."

A few of the Elders behind him muttered in disbelief, but the others looked on with hard expressions.

I'd been to enough of these ceremonies to know Buck hadn't followed the script, but not enough to understand all of the implications.

Bryson's entire body went rigid. "Not into the tribe?"

"No." He raised his chin.

The blood whooshed behind my ears. Buck had marked our child an outsider, welcome on these lands as a guest, not as a member. He'd insulted us, but more shocking, he'd insulted Charlie's memory.

Bryson rested his hand on Quin's chest. Likely perceiving a threat, Aaron moved closer to me.

Buck raised his chin. "Who of the Red Paint clan will speak for this child?"

A soft murmur ran through the crowd. My human family likely had no idea Buck had put us in an untenable situation. I doubted the Fae recognized the significance of what was happening, but the members of the tribe most certainly did. If no one spoke for Quin, he would have no clan, no protection, and could never follow in Charlie's footsteps and serve as a medicine man.

Seconds ticked by and no one came forward.

A male voice, with a heavy brogue, rose up over the whispering crowd. "I will."

I turned and watched the dark-haired man, who'd come to church with Killian, step away from Caoimhe. He gave me a quick smile and strode to the front of the gathering like he'd done it a thousand times.

Buck looked like he'd swallowed a wasp. "You have no standing here."

"Since when?" The other man's eyes twinkled with mischief. "It's been nearly three decades since I was here last, but surely, you know who I am."

Aaron's brows rose as he glanced between me and the guy.

Having no clue who he was or what he had to do with Charlie's clan, I shrugged.

Bryson looked the man over from head to toe and shot me a surprised glance.

"I know who you are. You and your *kind* are not welcome on these lands." Buck Oldham slammed his ceremonial staff on the ground hard enough it scared Quin.

Bryson lifted the baby into his arms.

The proclamation caused tribe members and Fae alike to speak out of turn. I had no idea what was going on, but I knew one thing—it was time to get the heck out of there.

The man shook his head at Buck. "Cheasequah would be appalled that you have abandoned sacred traditions. First you deny his great-grandson a place in your tribe. Then you refuse to allow the eldest member of the Red Paint Clan to bless him?"

Bryson handed the baby to me, but otherwise remained in place.

Cradling Quin to my chest, I swiveled my head back and forth between them like a spectator at Wimbledon. I'd met several members of my clan over the years, and none of them looked like him. Besides my deceased mother, I was the only pale skinned member.

Rage contorted Buck's face. . "You will leave these lands!"

Several of the visiting medicine men and women moved between Buck and the dark-haired man.

Human magic pressed against us from one side, Fae from the other.

Aaron's hand went to his side as if to grab his weapon. Unfortunately for us, he'd left it at home in the safe.

"I am Liam, son-in-law of Cheasequah. Husband to Atsila." He met my gaze. "Father to the Firebird, and grandfather of Quin. I am the eldest surviving member of the Red Paint Clan. I have every right to be here, and it is my duty to bless that child with his birthright."

My entire world tilted. Had it not been for Aaron at my side, I would have toppled over. Forgetting Buck and the Elders and my stunned family members, I took a shaky step toward the man I'd waited my entire life to meet. "Dad?"

His brow wrinkled and his eyes glistened. He glanced away and wiped his cheeks, before staring at me again. He opened his mouth as if to speak, but instead, he nodded and gave me a lopsided smile.

There was no self-help book to prepare someone to meet their parent for the first time as an adult. I didn't know what to say or do or think. My heart lurched as if it wanted to get to him before the rest of me.

Liam closed the distance and wrapped me in his arms. Kissing first my cheek, then Quin's head, he wept into my hair. "It's you…I can't believe it's you."

CHAPTER 35

*L*iam pulled back, glanced, around and hugged me again. This time, he put his lips close to my ear and exhaled. "Whatever happens today, no magic."

Darlene tugged on my sleeve. "Tessa, we should go."

I glanced from her to the commotion going on around us. Buck's people were shouting at the Fae. The Fae were doing their best to ignore them, but the magic in the air had taken on an oppressive quality that left me breathless.

She was right. The crap was about to hit the industrial sized fan, and no one was getting out clean.

Aaron hurried to my side and offered Liam his hand. "I'm Aaron, Tessa's husband. It's a pleasure to meet you sir, but I need to get my family out of here."

My father's expression softened. "I would expect nothing less."

Aaron wrapped his arm around my mother. "Let's get you and Quin to the SUV." He spoke in a calm tone, but the wrinkles around his eyes told me he was worried.

I glanced around for my other hubby. "Where's Bryson?"

"He's looking for Jolene and TJ."

"What do you mean looking for them?" Since learning about my father, I'd dreamed of the day I could introduce him to my family. I'd never imagined it would be in the middle of a nightmare.

Aaron lowered his voice. "We're not sure."

"They were right there." Darlene turned and pointed to two empty chairs.

Patting Quin's bottom, I scanned the crowd for the kids. "They're probably hiding under the dessert table eating brownies."

Please God, let them be stealing sweets.

Caoimhe joined us. Trailing her hand down my father's arm, she said, "Liam, we must be off."

"Of course." He didn't pull away from her—if anything, he leaned into her touch. "Tessa, it was an absolute pleasure to meet you. I hope we can see each other again under less...stressful circumstances."

I blinked to restart my brain. "You're leaving?"

Caoimhe dipped her chin and gave me a shy smile. "We couldn't miss the chance to see the child again, but this is our honeymoon."

"Honeymoon?" I dropped my gaze to her hand on his arm and his hand on her hip. My stomach wrung like a wet dishtowel, and the contents threatened to spill out my mouth.

"We were married a few days ago." The queen reached for Quin's hand, but I twisted away from her.

Married? What the heck? What happened to a hundred-years-a-fae-slave?

"It was a private ceremony." Liam smiled, but something told me he didn't mean it. "But we are planning a larger celebration in a few weeks. I'd be honored if you and your family were there."

"Of course she will be there." Laughing softly, Caoimhe patted his chest. "You're welcome to visit us in Tir Na Nog, anytime. Lucky for you, your brother is an air elemental and can see you safely through the portal."

The way she'd spoken about his powers made me wonder if he'd kept quiet about mine.

"Thank you...but I'd rather y'all visit us here. From what I've heard, Tir Na Nog isn't my cup of tea." I plastered on a wide smile. "I've never been much of a fan of slavery or gambling."

Caoimhe released my father, squared her shoulders, and raised her chin. "How dare you."

Liam ran his hand over the back of his neck and looked away, but not before I caught the gleam in his eye. I didn't know him well enough to know for sure, but it looked a lot like pride.

The queen said something to me, but her sticky sweet voice was swallowed up by the noise around us.

I didn't bother to ask her to repeat it.

Sensing rather than seeing Bryson's approach, I scanned the tree line. One glance at his grief-stricken face, and I knew something was wrong. Really wrong.

Bryson met my gaze, lifted Jojo's little pink purse, and shook his head.

"Aaron." I reached for him without taking my eyes off Bryson.

"I see him." He angled Darlene away from the forest. "Let's get you out of here."

For once in her life, she did as she was told without questions or arguments.

"Wait. Take Quin with you." I handed him our son. "Don't let him out of your sight, and for the love of everything good and holy, don't let anyone touch him."

"I'm not leaving." Aaron juggled the baby but eventually got him settled on his shoulder. "I'll have Darlene take him home."

I didn't have time to argue. He was a smart guy—a homicide detective. He had to realize we were in too much danger to send our child off with Darlene. I pressed my hand to his cheek and turned his face toward mine. "I'll find the kids, but I need to know Quin is safe. Now go. Please."

"She's my daughter."

"She's *our* daughter. I swear to you, we'll do whatever it takes to bring her home."

He nodded, but the hard look he gave me told me he'd have quite a bit to say about it later.

I turned back to where my father and the queen had stood moments before, but they were gone.

Freaking great.

What good was having a bunch of Fae in the family if they didn't stick around long enough to help?

Bryson surprised me by pulling me into his arms. Like Liam had done before, he used the embrace to whisper into my ear. "I found Jojo's purse near the river."

He pressed something against my belly. I glanced down and my world screeched to a halt. "Is that blood?"

He nodded.

"This can't be happening." I sagged against him for a split second before pulling myself together. There'd be time enough to fall apart once everyone was safe.

"Did Aaron get Quin and Darlene out of here?" Bryson glanced over the thinning crowd.

"They're on their way home." At least I hoped they'd managed to get to the car safely.

Bryson nodded. "We need to shift and search for the kids from the air."

My father's words hit me like a battering ram. "I was warned not to use magic."

He snapped his head back. "By who?"

Keeping my voice low, I said, "Liam. He said no matter what happens, no magic."

"So help me God, if they had something to do with this—"

I pulled him to the side of the gathering space. "We'll worry about that after we find the kids. Go in the woods and shift, just make sure no one sees you. I'll join you in the air as soon as I can."

"Are you sure that's a good idea?"

I couldn't believe he'd asked. "What choice do we have? They've forced our hands."

"Be careful." He pressed a kiss to my brow.

"Tessa. Bryson. I need to speak with you." Buck stormed over to us. "What happened here today will not stand. Until the Elders decide what to do with the Fae—"

"Whatever you're about to say. Don't." Bryson held his hand up to the older man.

Buck's eyes widened. I'd smarted off to him more times than I could count, but Bryson had always spoken to him with respect.

Bryson shoved Jolene's bloody purse into Buck's hands. "Our daughter and Tessa's seven-year-old cousin are missing. I found this in a pool of blood beside the river."

"What did you think would happen with those…creatures here?" He spat on the ground and tossed the purse at me. "I'll send out search parties, but once those kids are found, you and yours will not set foot on these lands again."

Bryson dipped his chin in acceptance or gratitude or what-the hell-ever.

I was having no part of it. "This isn't our fault. You're the one that said you have enough magic users here to stop trouble, but you damned sure started it with denying Quin!"

Bryson rested his hand on my shoulder. "There will be time for talk once the kids are safe."

Buck gave us a once over, sneered, and walked away.

I motioned to the retreating Elder. "One day he loves us, the next he treats us like something he stepped in. We've come every time he's needed us and never asked a thing in return."

Bryson turned me to face him. "Forget about Buck. Round up any of the Fae who are still here and ask them to help us find Jojo and TJ. I'll meet you in the air."

I watched him disappear into the woods before heading back into what remained of the crowd. At first glance, it appeared the Fae had all gone. I told myself that they'd left with the queen. That they didn't know children were missing. But I sucked at lying. Even to myself.

Lost in thought, I jogged down the path leading to the river. With any luck, Buck was still pissing vinegar about the Fae and hadn't gotten around to sending out the search parties. If I hurried, I could stash my clothes and shift before anyone else made it to the water.

As luck would have it, I found a Fae straggler standing on the bank staring off into space. "I'm surprised you're still here."

Killian glanced back at me and sighed. "I'm in no hurry to return to the palace."

Part of me wanted to lay into him for not telling me about Liam and Caoimhe, but I had more important things to do. "Jolene and my little cousin are missing. Will you help me find them?"

"They probably wandered off during the excitement back there. I'm sure they're fine." He shoved his hands into his pockets.

His lack of concern ticked me off, but it made sense if he had something to do with their disappearance. "Did you do this? Are you the one behind all of these freaking tests?"

He held up his hands. "No. I didn't do this. I swear on our mother's spirit."

"Did the queen? Who's doing this to me and my family?"

"I'm sorry." Killian raked his hands over his head. "I can't say. I'm so sorry."

I swallowed my anger, and my pride.

"Please, Killian. I'm begging you." The tears I'd held back since learning the kids were missing finally fell. "Bryson found Jojo's bloody purse near here, and there was a murder not far away. Please. I have to find them."

He hung his head. "We aren't permitted to use magic around humans."

"That's crap. Every Fae here was loaded with it."

Nodding, he said, "Because we were trying to prevent a scene. How did you and your men not realize the humans in the crowd wished you ill?"

"You could sense their intentions?" The words fell out before I'd thought the better of them. Once again, he'd proven just how ignorant we were when it came to our magic. But he'd missed something important. "If that's true, how did you miss the fact Buck and half the Elders were ready to toss you and the other Fae out of there?"

He gave me a less than patient smile. "Tessa, this is ridiculous. What you *don't* know is going to get you killed. It's time that you come to Tir Na Nog."

I found myself at a loss for words, and a loss for time. I needed to find the kids, not discuss my failings as a freaking fairy. "I'm not going anywhere. My family is here."

"All Fae are welcome in Tir Na Nog."

"And there's the rub." I shook my head. "Fae are welcome, but humans are not."

Killian turned away.

"Family isn't just about sharing DNA. It's about love and history and acceptance no matter what. That may not mean much to you, Killian O'Roarke, but it's everything to me." I ducked behind a live oak and stripped.

"You don't understand." He followed me, but turned when he caught sight of my bare skin. "Everything I've done is for you and your *family*."

"If that were true, you'd help me find the kids." Moving as quickly as possible, I hid my clothes. "We have a saying around here. Talk's cheap."

He threw his head back and groaned. "Things aren't always as they seem."

I'd heard the same thing from Gavin, or from Charlie through Gavin, but I was sick to death of the games. "How are two missing kids and a bloody purse not as they seem? Unless…they aren't really in danger? Is that it? Do you know where they are?"

"I can't say for certain…"

I wanted to scream or throw something or beat the truth out of my brother. "Then tell me what you know or what you think or anything that can help me."

He pinched the bridge of his nose. "I *can't*, damn it."

"Right. Just like you couldn't tell me our father married the queen who was supposedly holding him hostage?"

"I couldn't tell you what I didn't know and will never understand." Disgust thickened his voice.

I almost felt sorry for him, but not quite. "The only thing I'm worried about right now is finding Jojo and TJ. I'll take whatever punishment is coming to me, but dead or alive, I'm bringing them home where they belong."

Storm clouds roiled overhead and fat rain drops fell around us. Weird weather wasn't unusual in Florida, but that was the second time a storm had popped up out of nowhere when Killian was around.

"Knock it off with the rain." I waved at the sky. "The clouds will make it harder to find the kids."

Killian muttered under his breath, and the rain slowed. "I'm providing cover. Remember what I told you about exposing your magic to humans?"

I remembered all right. It was hard to forget when my newfound-father had pretty much told me the same thing. I understood the reasoning behind the rule, but reasoning went out the window when children's lives were on the line.

Voices carried from farther up the path.

I had to make a decision. Trust him and search on foot, or use my magic and break Fae law.

I chose the latter.

Dropping my shields, I held my arms wide and let the firebird consume me. One moment I stood on two legs, the next I soared through the afternoon sky in a ball of fire. My vision sharpened until I could count the whiskers on a mouse from ten stories up. Spectrums of colors I couldn't name danced before my eyes.

Searching for any signs of the children, I flew over the area in ever widening circles. Heat signatures of the people, and creatures, below drew my attention. Men shouted and pointed, but they weren't the ones I sought. The firebird mistook my heightened emotions for danger and wanted to roast them alive. My control faltered, and for a terrifying moment, I worried the predator in me would take over.

The only thing that stopped her, and saved the men below, was the unquestionable knowledge that Bryson was close. Though he was a good half-mile away, his magic drew me to him like a homing beacon. The firebird's natural instinct was to go to her mate. Her split focus allowed me to maintain control.

I doubled back and flew over the muddy river bank where I'd left Killian. A blast of magic sent shockwaves into the sky. The air currents around me shifted with such violence I had no hope of escape. As if caught in a rogue wave, I tumbled end over end through the air, not daring to stretch my wings for fear they'd snap.

A millisecond later, a creature the size of an elephant blew past me and disappeared into the clouds.

One word lodged in my brain.

Dragon.

CHAPTER 36

Don't panic. Dragons are giant lizards. Birds eat lizards. What the heck am I thinking? To that monster, I'm fun-sized!

I caught movement from the corner of my eye, but the dragon's white and silver scales blended with the clouds. Normally, the firebird could see heat signatures, but the creature had none. Then again, reptiles were cold blooded.

A shadow passed above me.

Fear made it difficult to breathe, let alone fly.

The dragon snaked its long neck down until its head was close enough to strike. There were plenty of horrible ways to die, but being a dragon's hors d'oeuvre had to be the worst. I prayed the damned thing would swallow me whole.

Using my only defense, I blazed brighter. The heat turning my flames from oranges and yellows to white. If I was going to be a snack, I intended to cause some serious heartburn.

The creature jerked its head back, and a familiar magic caressed me. The icy power reminded me of snowflakes—cold and delicate.

Killian?

I met the dragon's emerald green eyes and my heart lurched. Not only could my brother shift into a freaking dragon, but he'd broken Fae law—*for me*.

Had I been in human form, I would have hugged him or cried or both. Instead, I flew in spirals around his long neck and let out a short series of chirps.

Someone screamed, high and shrill, below. I recognized the pitch immediately—Jolene's spider shriek.

Cursing my weird bird hearing, I scanned the ground, but it was no use. I couldn't make out lower tones enough to get a sense of where the sound was coming from.

Killian nodded to the north, away from the tribal house and river.

Message received.

I dove below the clouds and headed in the direction he'd indicated. Jolene and TJ were down there somewhere.

Bryson's magic brushed against mine. He was close. Maybe too close. I didn't know what he'd do if he saw the dragon after hearing the girl scream, but I doubted it'd be good.

As if Killian had read my mind, he veered into a heavy cloud bank. Of course, just when I thought we were on the same wave-length, my brother let out a roar that shook the trees below.

The Great Hawk cut through the sky like a bullet, far faster than a natural bird could fly.

I had no way to warn him about Killian's spirit animal other than to calm my nerves and project a sense of peace. Easier said than done given my situation.

Killian dove toward the ground.

Bryson screeched, tucked his wings, and barrel rolled after him.

I followed, praying they'd recognize each other before one or the other did something I'd regret.

A flash of light blinded me. At first, I thought I was under attack. It wasn't until another, smaller, beam hit my eyes that I realized where the light was coming from.

Mirrors. Dozens of tiny mirrors.

Once again, fear robbed me of my innate ability to fly. Free-falling, I struggled to regain control of my magic. Mere inches from the tops of the trees, I spread my wings in hopes of catching an updraft.

Another roar filled the air and a gust of frigid wind sent me soaring. The sensation was a bit like being fired out of an ice cannon —exhilarating with a heavy dose of oh-shit.

Below me, Killian and Bryson shouted, but I couldn't tell if they were going at each other, or something else. The only thing I knew for certain was that I needed to get down there.

Zigzagging my way through the branches, I tried to make sense of the scene. Killian looked on as Bryson crouched inside a charred circle. From my position, I couldn't tell what—or who—he was looking at.

The moment my feet hit the ground, I shifted to human form and ran to them.

Bryson stood with TJ's little lifeless body in his arms. He turned, met my gaze, and pressed his lips into a tight line.

"Oh God, no!" I ran toward him, but Killian grabbed my arm before I reached my husband and the boy.

Jerking me back, he turned me to face him. "The child is bespelled, but alive. We should leave him and find the girl."

"Are you crazy? We can't *leave* him out here!" I jerked free and hurried to Bryson. "Is he okay? Can we break the spell?"

"I believe so, but we shouldn't do it here. I'll take him back to the tribal house." His pained expression stole my breath. "You two keep searching for Jojo."

I brushed my fingertips over TJ's damp forehead and nodded.

"You'll need clothing." Killian's magic crackled around us.

I looked at him for the first time since shifting and was surprised to find him wearing the suit he'd worn earlier. "How did you—"

The weight of fabric on my skin stunned me speechless. I had no clue how Killian had conjured jeans, T-shirts, and boots out of thin air, but I wasn't about to complain.

I motioned between us. "You can just make stuff appear?"

"Only if it already exists, and I am familiar with it." Killian shrugged as if it were no big deal. "It's much like choosing which mythical beast to shift into. Imagine it in your mind's eye and call it into reality."

I had absolutely no idea what he was talking about. I'd never even considered I could shift into anything other than the firebird. "You had a choice? You could have picked something small and nondescript like a wasp, but you chose to turn into a freaking dragon the size of a rhino?"

"What Tessa means is, *thank you*." Bryson's shoulders sagged, but I doubted it had anything to do with my outburst. Once again, my brother had proven we were outclassed in the magic department.

Killian's expression softened. "Bryson, what I said about your magic... I was an ass. Your healing skills are extraordinary. And you're a better man than I can ever hope to be. I couldn't have asked for a better husband for my sister."

"Thank you." Bryson stood a little straighter and headed for the path with TJ in his arms.

I'd lost count of the number of times Killian had shocked me in the previous couple of hours. That he'd given Bryson a compliment, when he'd needed it most, impressed me even more than his ability to turn into a dragon. "Thank you for that, and for helping me...but you broke the Fairy Golden Rule."

"Terrorizing children is a new low...even for the Fae," Killian muttered under his breath.

I reached for one of the mirrors hanging above the charred circle.

"Wait!" Killian grabbed my wrist. "We don't have time for that. We need to find Jolene."

"You're hurting me." I jerked my arm back and stared down at the red fingerprints on my pale skin.

"That wasn't my intention." He paced away, turned, and paced back. "We need to talk before you read the mirrors."

"But you just said..." It dawned on me a few seconds too late that he likely didn't want me to see *him* in the visions. "You did this?"

"No...not this time." Killian motioned to the area around us. "Don't you recognize where you are? You've been here before. This is the first circle."

I glanced around and nodded. "Right. Where Wyatt disappeared. Did you hurt him?"

"No one was hurt. It was all manufactured." Killian hung his head. "Wyatt's been having the time of his life in Miami. When the time comes, he'll wake up in this forest with no memory of what happened to him."

I wanted to argue that losing weeks of your life and waking up not knowing what happened to you was harmful, but I had too many questions and a missing girl to worry about first. "Where's Stone and the other victims?"

"Stone was never involved in this. He left Darlene because he's a jealous fool." Killian shook his head. "After the first time and the mess with Wyatt, there were no victims. It was all Fae magic."

"You magicked a dead body?" I couldn't believe the lengths he'd gone to and for what?

Killian hung his head. "Yes, and for the record, I didn't think the children would see the remains."

"Yeah, well, you should have thought about that before you decided to fake a murder so close to my house." While I was glad Wyatt was on a vacation and Stone was out there somewhere finding himself, the entire situation ticked me off. "How is it you can tell me this now, but couldn't before?"

"I broke Fae law. Unlike you, I am bound to the queen, or I was." He held his arms out wide. "Now I'm an outlaw."

"Why now? Why would you put yourself in this situation?" I hated everything he'd done to me and my family, but I still had hope that somewhere under the piles and piles of crap, was the brother I'd always wanted.

"Something you said about family rang true for me." He cleared the emotion from his throat and scrubbed his hands over his face. "Enough talk. We have to hurry. We have to find the girl before the queen's men find me."

Questions buzzed around in my head like bees in a hive, but I forced myself to focus. "Where do we start?"

He motioned to the circle where we'd found TJ. "Jolene should have been here, under the same spell as the boy."

"Jolene's been...resistant to magic lately." As much as I wanted to let my guard down and trust him, I couldn't. Not yet, maybe not ever. "You said you didn't take her, but how do you know so much about this?"

"I was ordered to take her from this circle to Tir Na Nog." Killian knelt and pressed his palm to the ground. "Resistant how?"

"For starters, she woke from the healing spell on her own."

"That would explain why she's not here, but not where she is now." He pulled his hand back and furrowed his brow. "I don't sense any malevolent magic. Read the mirrors."

"I will, but..." I couldn't help but wonder if he wanted to find Jojo because he cared, or because he intended to save his own hide by taking her to Tir Na Nog. "Why were you ordered to take her in the first place?"

"After that summoning the other night, do you really have to ask?" His tone grew more desperate. "We can talk more about this later, but she's in serious danger. Either she's lost in this forest or someone else took her."

I'd never felt so unsure of what or who to believe. My indecision not only paralyzed me, but was costing time Jolene didn't have. "How can I trust you?"

Killian winced as if my doubt had physically hurt him "I just gave up my life for you."

Spots danced before my eyes. "You're life? You mean years of your life, right?"

He turned away. "Right."

"He's twisting the truth, Hell Girl." Gavin's spirit shimmered beside me. "His level of disobedience is punishable by death."

"No. That's...no." I hurried to my brother. "I'm not going to let them take you back to that wretched place. Do you hear me? I'm not going to allow it."

A hint of a smile ghosted across his lips. "I have no intention of going, but the sooner you read the mirrors and we can get out of here, the better my chances of survival."

I gave Gavin a we-need-to-talk look on my way to the first mirror. As with the others, images filled my mind on contact. Unlike the others, there were no creatures. No half-man half-gators or wolves or big cats. Only the kids in the distance.

TJ and Jojo seemed to be playing a game of tag. She'd touch him and run away. He'd give chase and touch her. At first, their path seemed random. They ran in circles around each other or zigzagged between the trees, but somehow, they moved closer and closer to the burned circle.

I moved to the next mirror. The angle of the images was consistent with the angle of the mirror. At times, the picture would shift to the sky or twirl and twist as if caught in the breeze. "These don't seem staged."

"What do you mean staged?" Killian asked.

"The images from the other scenes were fake." I touched the third mirror and caught an odd ripple to the left of the children. Focusing my magic, I replayed the vision several times. I couldn't be sure, but my instinct told me the shifting energy was a Fae.

"Fake how?" His voice rose. Evidently, my brother didn't know everything about the situation.

"Hold that thought. I saw something." I jogged to the far side of the circle and tried another mirror. As with the first three, the images were natural. They came to me as if I were standing near the tree watching the children play. And then I saw them. Two ripples, one on either side of the kids. Each time Jojo ran close to the strange energy, she'd dart back in the other direction.

"I see *shimmers* near the kids. They look like ripples in water flowing over a stone." I moved to the next mirror.

"They're Fae guiding the kids to the circle. Keep watching. We need to know what happened after they fell asleep."

I touched the next mirror and focused on the moment the children reached the circle.

TJ collapsed instantly. A few feet behind him, Jojo threw her head back and laughed like she thought he was still playing. She ran into the circle and froze. Eyes wide, she glanced around her, not at TJ. She lurched forward as if pushed or startled by a touch. A split second later, she fell unconscious.

I continued to read the images, but nothing changed. The only movement came from the light breeze.

"Hurry. Someone's coming." Killian whispered, but there was no mistaking the urgency in his voice.

"It's Bryson. I can sense his magic." I reached for another mirror.

Killian made a comment about mates and love and our father's sham of a marriage.

I tuned him out and concentrated on the mirror. Pulsing a hint of magic into the glass, I imagined pushing a fast-forward button.

In the vision, Jolene bolted upright. She glanced down at herself and her mouth fell open. I couldn't hear her, but it looked like she'd screamed. The girl jumped to her feet and swatted her arms and legs.

"She woke up and screamed because there were insects on her." Continuing to read the mirror, I watched in horror as Jolene tried to wake TJ. She cried out, glanced around, and lunged toward the forest...

And the breeze caught the mirror. When it settled, she was gone.

My heart lurched as if to chase her. I released the mirror and turned in a half-circle searching for any indication of the direction she'd gone. The pine trees all looked the same. No leaves to tear off. No branches to break. Nothing.

"Tessa?" Bryson's voice pulled me back from the brink of an anxiety attack.

What's he doing here? Where's TJ?

I swiveled my head back and forth between him and Killian. "She ran. She woke up and she ran, but I can't tell which direction."

Gavin whispered, "Read another mirror."

"Right." I hurried to the mirrors closest to the trees, but Bryson stopped me.

He took me by the shoulders. "The SUV is still in the parking lot, but there's no sign of—"

"No." I jerked away from him. "No, please. I can't..."

Bryson pulled me into an embrace. "I'm sorry. They're all missing."

CHAPTER 37

Every doubt, insecurity, and fear about my ability to be a good mother roared to life. I hadn't wanted to work with kids or adopt Jolene or get pregnant with Quin because deep down, I knew I'd fail them.

And boy was I right. But never, and I mean never, had I thought my inability to parent could cost them their lives.

Killian rested his hand on my back. "I'll find Jolene, but I need you to read the mirror."

"And I'll find Aaron and Quin and your mom." Gavin's spirit hovered to my right.

Bryson tightened his grip on me and said the one thing I needed to hear, but wasn't ready to accept. "None of this is your fault."

Easing away from Bryson, I grabbed the mirror hard enough to crack the glass. Pain bloomed in my palm, but I didn't care. The vision hit me like a semi-truck on rocket fuel.

Not only could I see Jolene waking from the spell, I could feel the insects crawling on her, her terror when TJ wouldn't wake. I could smell the sharp, but sweet, scent of pine mingled with the damp musty smell of mud and old leaves. I could feel her heart pounding, her lungs expanding, the rattle of a scream escaping her mouth, and the wind on her face when she ran.

Something slammed into my side and knocked me to the ground. I opened my eyes to find Killian looming over me.

"Are you crazy?" Killian shouted. "Never use blood in a reading. You'll get lost in the vision."

Bryson shot him a hard look and eased me upright. "Are you okay?"

Nodding, I pointed in the direction Jojo had gone. "She went that way."

He opened his mouth as if he had more to say, but shook his head and took off. A heartbeat later, a wave of magic crashed over us, followed by the whooshing of air beneath massive wings.

Bit by bit, my brain made the transition from the vision to reality. I stared at Bryson trying to remember why I'd been surprised to see him. "Where's TJ?"

"He's safe with Harris." He brushed my hair from my face. "Are you sure you're okay?"

"I'm getting there." I turned to Gavin. "Where have you been?"

"Stuck on the other side. Until you learned the truth. If I had slipped up and said any more, the entire bet would have been forfeit, and you would have been forced to go to Tir Na Nog."

"What bet?"

Bryson swore under his breath.

Gavin frowned. "That you'd break Fae law."

"All of this is because of a *bet*?" Pushing myself to my feet, I shouted louder than I'd intended.

Gavin's eyes bugged. "On that note, I'm going to find Aaron."

"Not until you answer my questions."

The spirit vanished.

"I can't believe this." I needed to punch someone, but Bryson was one of the few beings I didn't want to strangle.

"When it comes to the Fae, nothing surprises me."

Voices carried from somewhere to my left. Whoever they were, they were close.

Bryson's magic washed over me like a warm bath.

"We need to go." He stood close enough that his breath tickled my cheek. "Now."

"It's too late. We need to shift and get out of here."

He pulled me to the far side of the oak tree. Pressing his lips to my ear, he whispered, "I'll distract them. Go, but don't light up."

The voices came closer still.

"I'm not leaving you." I took in my surroundings. Either I'd lost track of time during the blood reading, or he'd cast a spell to darken the area around us.

"Damn it." Bryson pressed my back against the rough bark, and covered me with his body.

For the life of me, I would never understand why he insisted on using himself as my not-so-human shield. I was the one who could die and rise as the firebird. Last time I checked, Bryson wasn't bulletproof.

"She called forth the firebird at the first sign of trouble." The female laughed, but it did little to hide the exasperation in her voice—a voice I recognized instantly.

What the hell is Caoimhe doing here?

Bryson set his index finger on my lips.

I nodded, but everything in me wanted to jump out from behind the tree and go ten rounds with the prissy-queen and whoever-the-hell was with her. Better yet, burn her toes off one at a time until she told me where Quin and Aaron were.

Male laughter filled the air. "Don't nitpick. Tessa didn't use magic in front of the humans. She passed the test."

My heart thump, thump, thumped and came to a stop like a flat tire on a highway. I'd only spoken to him once, but I knew his voice. My dad was with the queen. Worse still, he'd known about the tests.

"You haven't won yet." Caoimhe chided him. "You are her biggest fan, and yet, you conceded the changeling should be—"

"The changeling is…an anomaly." He went quiet for so long, I worried he'd sensed us or Bryson's magic. "He's not part of the bet."

He's in on the bet?

I'd wanted a dad my entire life. Just my luck, I finally had one and he turned out to be a monster. And Killian? He obviously knew about it. So much for the whole *Fae don't lie* routine. My spinning thoughts left me feeling like I'd spent an hour on the teacup ride at Disney.

Bryson tensed to the point I struggled to get air into my lungs.

"True, but we may have to renegotiate after that stunt your son pulled." The *pouty* tone in her voice made me want to puke. She probably thought it made her seem cute and innocent.

Imprisoning a man for a hundred years and forcing him to marry you isn't cute or innocent. I gasped, out loud. *It's all a lie. Every last word of it.*

Bryson ground his teeth together so hard I heard them grinding.

"I'll have a talk with him." Liam sighed.

"Talk?" She scoffed. "There will be no talking involved. His fate is sealed."

Liam murmured, "Yes, my queen."

He agreed? To Killian's execution?

"Now, tell me who took the girl." Caoimhe's delicate footsteps retreated.

I felt as though I'd come out of my skin. What they heck were we doing hiding behind a freaking tree while two of the people responsible for traumatizing our kids, murdering innocent humans, and lying about everything except the color of the sky were feet away? We needed to confront them and demand they return our son and Aaron.

Liam hummed a tune that took me back to lazy days with Charlie, Dottie sitting in the sun, and Mae tending to her roses. The haunting melody unlocked the box holding my grief and allowed it to consume me.

Bryson relaxed and dropped his cheek to mine.

Liam's cold magic raised goosebumps as it tickled across my skin. The tune he hummed changed to an old Celtic folk-song. Mirrors clanked together, and I fought not to peek from behind the tree to see if he read them the same way I did.

As if he'd read my mind, Bryson shook his head.

Liam's humming changed to full-fledged singing. *"The little red lark, like a spark of sunburst fly. It's time you've risen, earth is a prison, full of my lonesome sighs. Out of thy hiding, silently gliding, go now, take to the skies."*

Bryson took my hand and eased me away from the tree.

My father sang the song again, louder and bolder, but this time the lyrics were as I remembered.

He's telling us to go.

"Liam! If you insist on singing while you work, pick a better song." Caoimhe's laughter made my pulse race.

Bryson led us a safe distance away from Liam and the queen. Crouched behind a fallen log, we stared at one another. I didn't know what to say. I'd gone from hating my father to confusion to a guarded optimism in the span of a few minutes.

Bryson pulled me into his arms. "We need a plan."

"I don't know where to start." I slipped my arms around his waist and buried my face in his chest. "When do you think Liam realized we were there?"

"I'm not sure. The spell I cast was meant to keep us in shadows and muffle any sound we made." Bryson dragged his hand down his face. "But my guess is Liam sensed your residual magic when he walked into the circle. If the queen picked up on it, she might have thought it was his."

"He was reading the mirrors. Now we know where I get it from." The tiny ember of hope in my belly glowed brighter, but I doused it with distrust. "Not that it matters. I don't want a father who uses me like a poker chip…"

He took my face in his hands. "Tessa, no matter what his part is in all of this, he's still your father. You have every right to know him. Just promise me you'll be careful."

"I'm not sure I want to know a man who places bets on my abilities." I pulled away. "I don't want to talk about this anymore. We need to find Aaron and…"

"They're still alive. We would have felt it if Aaron had…"

That neither of us were capable of finishing a sentence worried me. We were too emotional to think straight, which could lead to mistakes that got people killed.

A scream tore through the forest.

A woman's scream.

CHAPTER 38

I shot to my feet, but Bryson grabbed my hand and pulled me back down.

"As far as we know, Caoimhe is the only woman out here." He searched my eyes as if asking a question so horrible he couldn't verbalize it.

I cupped his cheek and brushed my lips across his. "We wouldn't be us if we didn't help, even if it is my evil stepmother."

Bryson gave me a quick nod. "We're not running into this with guns blazing. We'll get close enough to see what's going on first."

"Don't you mean *wings* blazing?" I winked and eased out from behind the fallen log.

Following me, Bryson mumbled, "And Jojo says I tell dad-jokes."

Men shouting, followed by another gut-wrenching scream came from the direction of the charred circle where we'd left Liam and Caoimhe.

Careful to stay as concealed as possible, I picked up my pace.

Cloyingly sweet Fae magic, along with the coppery scent of blood, filled my nose and clung to the back of my throat.

Bryson pushed past me and slipped behind the live oak where we'd hidden before.

I moved beside him, crouched, and peeked around the tree.

Caoimhe was on all-fours struggling to stand. Blood had soaked through her silk jacket and formed a puddle beneath her.

Two women and three men surrounded her. Their clothing marked them as medicine people, but their actions were the opposite.

Her face twisted in agony, Caoimhe reached her hand out for help, or maybe to blast them with magic.

The woman closest to the queen's head raised her hands and chanted a spell. Though I only caught every few words, there was no mistaking her intent.

Without looking away, I whispered, "They're going to kill her."

"I need you to focus on the queen. Don't take your eyes off of her." Bryson slid his hand under my T-shirt and pressed his palm flat against my back. In the past when he'd done this sort of thing, he pulled energy from me. This time, he pushed his power through my body.

Caoimhe jolted and a column of magic burst from her fingertips.

The chanting woman collapsed, but so did Caoimhe.

The other four magic-users shouted and glanced at each other. Whatever Bryson had done seemed to have worked; they assumed the magic had come from the Fae queen.

The humans tightened their circle around the queen. Chanting in unison, they raised their hands toward the sky. Power rose in their palms. All they had to do was lower their arms and Caoimhe would be a goner.

"Focus, Tessa," Bryson whispered.

My heart raced and I struggled to keep my gaze on the queen. "She's unconscious. How can she—"

Bryson pushed another torrent of power through me.

Once again Caoimhe's body jolted, only this time our collective energy burst from her torso in an arc.

Two of the humans fell to the ground.

One of the remaining men shouted, "It's not coming from her!"

Bryson whispered the same spell he'd used to conceal us from my father and the queen, but I doubted it would be strong enough to protect us from those actively searching for us.

He pulled me to my feet and wrapped his big body around mine. "Don't move."

An icy breeze ruffled the hair on the top of my head and familiar magic encased me and Bryson. I had no idea if Killian had returned or if he'd been there all along, but I was happy for the help.

Shouts came from the direction of the Tribal House, along with howls. From the sound of it, there were a half dozen wolves headed in our direction. Shadows were fine and dandy to trick human eyes, but they wouldn't do squat to obscure our scents.

Bryson tightened his grip on me, but otherwise remained silent.

The human who'd first caught on that we were helping the queen passed feet from us without as much as turning his head.

A tugging sensation in my chest stole my breath. At first, I thought it was fear or a heart attack, but it came from outside of my body. More confusing, it didn't feel like a spell or malevolent magic.

I needed to alert Bryson, but I didn't dare move, let alone speak.

The tugging grew stronger. A yearning, so deep and all-encompassing I could barely remain upright, filled me. I needed to go, to find the source of the...of the what? The feeling? The person or object on the other end of the rope tied around my heart?

My body moved before my brain caught up.

Bryson's arms felt like a vise grip, hard and unyielding and keeping me from doing what I knew in my soul I needed to do.

To go.

And then I heard it. The source of my need.

Quin's cries.

Bryson whipped his head toward the sound, but otherwise remained still, holding me so tightly against the tree the bark cut into my skin.

The baby's cries where high and shrill and devastating. These weren't hunger cries or even colic—these were the same as when Gram Mae had dropped him. He was terrified.

Tears ran down my cheeks and I thought my heart would explode if I couldn't hold him.

More icy magic rained down on us, but did nothing to quell the war going on inside me.

"I know you're there. Show yourselves!" Buck Oldham shouted from the clearing where Caoimhe had fallen.

Oh God. Oh God. Oh God.

Droplets of water fell onto my face. Not water. Tears. Bryson's tears. His entire body shook as if he fought the same battle as me.

The sound of animals circling sent my already racing heart into palpitations. Our only advantage was Buck and his men didn't know where we were. If we had any hope of saving Quin, we had to do something before they found us, and they *would* find us.

"We have your son. Can you not hear him?" Buck must have done something to Quin because his cries became shriller. "We have the dream-walker, too. Did you really think Holden didn't tell me what he did to him?"

Bryson sucked in a breath. "Damn it."

I whispered against his chest, "I can't do this. I can't hide while Quin is in pain or scared."

"Neither can I." Bryson raised my chin, met my gaze, and whispered, "You've given me more than you will ever know."

"Don't you dare say goodbye." I barely got the words out around the emotion clogging my throat. I didn't know where he was going with this, but I didn't like it.

"It's never goodbye." Bryson pressed a kiss against my temple. "I love you."

Unable to speak, I shook my head and clung tighter to him. It was an impossible choice—

him or our son—but I had to believe that together we could escape. Without him, Quin and I were both doomed. And Jolene and Aaron and all of the other people counting on us.

Bryson released me so quickly, I stumbled forward.

"Wait for my signal." He gave me one last longing look, and shifted into a creature I had no name for. The Great Hawk was triple the size of a natural redtail, but this...this bird was massive. It took me a moment to realize his feathers weren't copper colored—they were metal.

Charlie's voice whispered inside my head. *"Tla'nuwa."*

I'd grown up with a Cherokee medicine man for a grandfather. I knew the legends. The Tla'nuwa were mythical birds of prey, with impenetrable wings, who killed the evil serpent, Uktena. Buck had called Bryson *Tla'nuwa* when we'd first met, and Bryson had used the name when we'd renounced our memberships in the Tribe.

Shouts rose up from the clearing, followed by the whoosh of wings and screams. I pressed my back against the tree and rubbed the middle of my chest where I felt Quin.

Where I felt Quin's *magic*.

He's calling for me to help him.

Gunshots and the high-pitched clink of bullets on metal sounded from overhead. The earth rumbled and men and wolf alike cried out in agony.

I couldn't stand it. I had to look. To see what was going on behind me. To make sure Quin was okay.

Moving slowly, I peeked from behind the tree.

It took my brain a beat to make sense of what I was seeing. Pieces of men and wolves were strewn throughout the clearing, and Buck Oldham stood in the center of it all, holding Quin by the back of his neck.

The baby kicked and squirmed and screamed, but I couldn't hear him over the chaos.

A blast of magic screeched through the sky like a firework, but hovered when it came closer to the Tla'nuwa. Bryson lifted his wing in flight, and the magic shot forward, striking him in the chest.

He fell.

Unable to watch, I curled in on myself and closed my eyes until the ground shook beneath my feet.

Gasping for breath, I reached out through the mystical connection that bound me to my mates. Aaron's essence came through first, weak and far from here. Bryson's flashed once and blinked out like a candle deprived of oxygen.

"Show yourself, firebird!" Buck laughed the laugh of a man who thought he'd won. "Your mates are dead. Will you bury your son, too?"

Bryson isn't dead. He can't be. He wouldn't leave us.

An anger rose up inside me, but it died as quickly as it'd come.

Please, God no. Charlie, where are you? Atsila? Mom? You'd be here if he were gone. Please. Tell me he isn't gone.

A black hole opened in my chest and threatened to consume me.

"Tessa...my daughter...things are not always as they seem." My mother's voice came to me on the breeze. *"You are never alone, little flame."*

Not always as they seem. I'd heard it over and over since this nightmare had begun. But I still couldn't quite understand how it applied to my current situation. Was she telling me Bryson was alive? That wasn't my child dangling from a madman's grasp? Was I imagining her freaking voice?

Buck's taunting pulled me back to reality. "You have until the count of three to show yourself, Tessa. I killed your mates. Do you think I'll hesitate to kill your son?"

Tired of hiding like a coward, I stepped out into the open. "Here I am. What do you want, Buck?"

Quin went quiet at the sound of my voice. At least I hoped he'd stopped crying because he knew I was close and not...

An evil smile stretched across Buck's face. "Your life for the child's."

"How do I know you won't hurt him anyway?" I couldn't bring myself to look at the bodies littering the ground. Not when one of them was Bryson.

My knees threatened to buckle at the thought, but I had to be the strong one now. I had to stand on my own, without Charlie or Bryson and Aaron or Gram Mae.

"Bring the woman." Buck nodded to someone to his left.

Until that moment, I thought he was the only one left alive. How many others were hiding in the trees? Would he order one of them to kill me or would he do it himself?

Magic trickled through the connection I shared with Bryson. He was alive, but I didn't dare look for him. Not when it could mean tipping Buck off.

Is that his signal?

One of the Elders, who'd been in the office that morning, walked into the clearing dragging Darlene behind him. She turned her bruised and swollen face toward me and stumbled.

I'd cycled through the stages of grief twice already, but this time I skipped straight to anger. There was no call for hurting an innocent baby and a defenseless middle-aged woman. "You can have me after you let them go. Give the baby to his grandmother."

"Defy me and you'll watch them both die." He gave Quin a little shake.

Quin's screams ripped my heart from my chest, but all I could do for him was to convince Buck to hand him to Darlene.

Holding my hands out at my sides, I said, "I'll do what you want once Quin and Darlene are safe."

Darlene fainted.

So much for that idea.

"Do it!" Buck drew a blade from his belt and held it to Quin's tummy. A trickle of blood stained his little ceremonial gown.

Be it the blood, good old-fashioned anger, or the sudden flare of magic between mine and Bryson's connection, I lost control of the firebird.

CHAPTER 39

The firebird burst to life, but she wasn't alone. The moment my feet left the ground, a second flaming bird barreled into me. But rather than going on the attack, it locked its talons with mine and rolled us end over end across the grassy clearing. When we slowed, it released me, nodded toward the sky, and took flight.

Confused, I followed.

The other firebird flew toward the tree line and unleashed a column of flames. A half dozen or so men made the wrong decision to run into the clearing, and the bird incinerated them one at a time.

The cries of my young drew my attention. I circled above Buck and the baby. Movement below caught my eye, along with the pull of my mate. He was there, injured but alive and reaching out.

Gunshots rang out and bullets whizzed by me. I tucked my wings, dove for Bryson and covered him in flames. Not to burn, but to heal.

The other firebird called to me.

Its magic felt so familiar, and yet foreign. It bobbed its head toward Buck and Quin, circled and barreled toward them. I thought it intended to attack the man, but it turned away a few feet from Buck's head.

More gunshots barked from below.

The human part of me realized what was happening. The second firebird was drawing the attention, and the bullets, away from me.

Shouting orders, Buck dropped the knife but held Quin tighter to his chest.

The other firebird dove again, but this time it released a ball of flames about the size of an orange. The fireball grazed Buck's back, but missed the baby entirely.

Screaming, Buck dropped to the ground and rolled to put out the fire.

Seeing my chance, I dove for Quin. I shifted two feet from the ground, darted to the child and scooped him into my arms. Before I could run, something hard and heavy smashed into the space between my shoulder blades.

I rolled into the fall in hopes of protecting Quin. Landing half on my side and half on my back, I felt the dagger hit bone.

Buck Oldham's weathered face filled my line of vision. He smiled as he leaned in and whispered, "I used this very blade to kill your mother. She was just as disobedient as you."

I didn't move or blink or take a breath.

Buck had seen me go through this process once before. Heck, he and I had discussed it at length. He knew exactly what to expect. I'd die, but my spirit would remain in my body. I could see and hear, but I couldn't feel a thing. Seconds, or minutes or hours would pass, but eventually, I would rise as the firebird—and when I did, he'd be waiting to kill me for keeps.

Only this time, I wasn't dead.

"Don't you worry about Quin. I'm going to raise him as my own. He'll become what Bryson and Charlie were before you came along— loyal Nunnehi slaves." He pulled Quin from my arms.

I bolted upright, slapped a hand on each side of his face and shoved the heat of the firebird into his flesh.

The acrid odor of burning meat threatened to gag me, but I refused to let go. Buck Oldham was the worst kind of evil. He was the sort that lured you in with guidance and friendship and trust. I'd be damned if I allowed him to take another loved one from me or anyone else. "This is for my mom and Charlie and for hurting my baby!"

Buck screamed and dropped Quin the short distance to the ground.

It killed me to leave my child there, but we would never be safe as long as Buck Oldham lived. Determined to make him pay for every lie, every betrayal, every ounce of heartache he'd caused, I pulled more fire magic into my palms.

Slender female hands reached for Quin.

"No!" I turned, ready to fry her, and met Caoimhe's gaze.

"Please, let me heal him." She nodded down to the baby.

"It's okay, Tessa. It's over." Bryson eased me away from Buck.

I stared at the charred bits of flesh and yuck on my palms and gasped. In the heat of the moment, I'd wanted nothing more than to kill the man, but the thought I might have succeeded left me horrified. "Is he? Did I?"

He shook his head. "No."

"Death is too good for him." Caoimhe spoke while smiling at the baby. "He will spend the rest of his days in my dungeon."

I glanced from her to Bryson and back. "I thought the humans killed you."

The queen breathed out a sigh, and her magic swirled around us. But it wasn't her magic. It was my fire and Bryson's warmth intermingled with her cool-sweet essence. "I believe I was close to the end, but you two saved my life. I owe you many favors."

The brush of silky fabric on my skin made my breath catch. I glanced down to find myself not only clothed in a flowy dress, but clean.

Bryson said, "Thank you."

"Hell Girl, sorry to interrupt." Gavin's spirit hovered a few feet away. He motioned to the queen. "Can she hear me?"

I glanced at Caoimhe and made a how-the-heck-do-I-know face at the ghost. After all, he was the one who'd told me only one living Fae had all five types of magic. Surely, Gavin had someone more informed to ask than me.

He went quiet for a sec, then shook his head. "She can't. Okay, here's the deal. In theory, Aaron found Jojo."

"Aaron's alive." The words fell out before I could stop them. To cover my tracks, I forced a smile. "I mean, I can sense him. He's alive."

Bryson gave me an odd look but seemed to catch on. "Do you know where he is?"

"He's safe. Some of Bryson's friends have him hidden in a room at the Tribal House." Gavin glanced behind me at something and looked away just as quickly. "Be careful not to let on about me. You're not out of trouble just yet."

"He's safe." I stared, hoping against hope he knew what was going on.

"Aaron has a good idea where Jojo is, but Killian needs your help," Gavin said.

Killian was still searching for Jolene? How was that possible? He'd shown up as a decoy firebird, but I hadn't seen him since Bryson had peeled my hands off of Buck's face. Then again, it made sense Killian would leave since Caoimhe was there.

The spirit sighed. "Something's wrong. I can feel Jojo calling for me, but Killian and I can't find her. She's scared, but I don't think she's hurt."

My poor battered heart couldn't take much more, and my bruised brain struggled to come up with a way to communicate with the spirit that wouldn't tip the queen off. "I have to go to him."

"We have no idea what we'll face there. We should both go." Bryson stood and helped me to my feet.

"I'll summon reinforcements and someone to clean up this… mess." Still holding Quin, Caoimhe moved to my side. "But surely, you don't intend to take this sweet child with you while you search?"

I had no intention of leaving our son with the woman responsible for the mess we found ourselves in, but I couldn't kick her Fae butt back to Tir Na Nog. I had to handle the situation carefully—and diplomacy was never my strong point.

"Tessa Marie!" Darlene stumbled toward us like a drunk at closing time. "My God, what happened here?" Darlene tripped over a detached leg and fainted again.

"Go. I'll get her and Quin to safety." Bryson's long-legged strides ate up the distance between him and my mother.

"Hurry, Hell Girl." Gavin paced a few inches from the ground. "Jojo's becoming more desperate."

I turned back to the queen. "I'd like to call in one of the favors you owe me."

She raised a perfectly shaped eyebrow.

"Promise me, under no circumstances, that you will not take Quin to Tir Na Nog without my express permission." I'd tried to cover my bases and leave no loopholes, but just to be sure I added, "Mine or one of his fathers' permission. I mean Bryson or Aaron. Grandfathers don't count."

Caoimhe winced and turned her head. "I swear it."

I didn't have time to sort out her reaction. Part of me wondered if I'd hurt her feelings, but I doubted that was possible.

"Find our girl, Tessa." Bryson gave me a heartbreaking smile.

I loved that he trusted me to find Jojo, but the thought of disappointing him scared the dickens out of me. Rather than responding, I shifted into the firebird and followed Gavin's spirit away from the clearing.

CHAPTER 40

I found Killian beside a dilapidated hunting cabin near the western bend of the river. My normally calm, cool, and collected brother looked almost as ramshackle as the building. Mud had dried on his clothes, and small scratches dotted his face and forearms.

I wasn't all that surprised he looked like hell. He'd put up quite a fight against Buck's men. "Are you okay?"

"I'm fine." He motioned to the area around him. "I'm not so sure about Jolene."

Adrenaline flooded my bloodstream. "Gavin said she's scared but not hurt."

"That doesn't mean she's alone. Someone could have taken her." He raked his hands through his hair.

My knees threatened to buckle. "Oh God...I didn't think—"

"Do you sense her presence?"

"Sense her? You mean her magic?" I'd never thought to search for her power. Why would I? The only way it would work is if she happened to be communing with ghosts.

He gave me an odd look. "It's more a matter of..." His brow furrowed as if he struggled to put it in terms I would understand.

"Think of it as sniffing out her scent, only instead of using your nose, you'll use your magic."

"That makes sense." It *didn't* make a lick of sense. "But you're obviously stronger than I am. Can't you do it?"

Gavin piped in, "Hell Girl, we've been searching for her for hours. Don't you think one of us would have done it by now if we could?"

"Hours?" I glanced between the spirit and Killian.

"I haven't been around her enough to recognize her essence." Killian glanced around the dense forest. "I'm just as likely to lead us to another Fae."

"There are other Fae out here? You think one of them took her, don't you?" My voice bordered on hysteria. The only Fae I could imagine being this far out in the forest were the ones looking for Killian.

I thought back to the promise Caoimhe made and pressed my hand to my chest. I'd made her swear she wouldn't take Quin, but that wouldn't stop her from having someone else take him.

"I'll try." I walked a few yards from them and closed my eyes. Planting my feet, I imagined my power as vines spreading and covering the forest floor. I felt the gentle slope of the land near the river, fallen logs, the root systems of countless trees.

Rather than calling out with my voice, I spoke through my spirit. *"Jojo, are you there?"*

I felt her essence, small and shivering. Forcing more energy through the web, I wrapped my magic around her in hopes she'd feel it and recognize me.

"Mommy!" Jolene's spirit vanished.

Refusing to think of what her disappearance could mean, I bolted in her direction.

"Jojo!" Branches bit into my arms and face, but I couldn't stop. Not until I found her. *"Jojo! Where are you?"*

"Here. Please find me. Please." She sobbed loud enough for me to follow the sounds with my ears instead of my magic.

Or so I thought. It seemed as if I were running in circles. "Jojo? Where are you?"

"No, this way!" Gavin flew in a different direction only to stop and cry out in frustration. "I swear I heard her."

Killian caught up with me and grabbed my shoulders. Bending to meet my gaze, he said, "This is what I've encountered all day. I hear her, but can never find her."

"I don't understand. I felt her *spirit*."

His eyes widened. "Her spirit? You sensed her spirit?"

"But something was off. It seemed smaller than it should be, and then it vanished. But I could hear her calling me." I hoped I hadn't screwed up and admitted something I wasn't supposed to, but I couldn't bring myself to care. I'd face whatever came my way as long as my family was safe.

Killian laughed and pulled me into an embrace. When he released me, he wore the same expression Bryson had when I'd left the clearing —complete trust in my ability to find Jolene.

If only I was so sure of myself. "What? What did you figure out?"

"Tessa, listen to me. She's not hiding. I would have found her by now. I think someone put an *obscufication* spell on her. Don't search for her this time. Search for the magic."

Obscufication? Right. Whatever that is.

Closing my eyes, I pushed my power out over the area. Rather than using it to find Jolene, I imagined searching for an unfamiliar magic. I found something. Something similar to mine but bigger and bolder and more deadly.

"It's the same magic that was at the fake crime scenes." I glared at Killian. He'd all but admitted he'd set up the burned circles and mirrors.

Holding up his hands, he took several steps back. "I didn't do this."

Ignoring him, I turned my attention back to the magic. This time when I brushed against it, it tugged my heart the same way Quin's had earlier in the day.

My feet moved before my brain caught up. "This way."

"Focus on her. I'll make sure you are safe." Staying close, Killian worked like a Fae machete to clear branches and underbrush from my path.

The strange but familiar magic grew stronger, but faded as I passed an old oak tree.

I circled back. My magic told me she was close, but the part of me that still thought of myself as human didn't believe anything it couldn't see. "Jojo?"

"Mommy!" She wrapped her arms around my waist. "TJ's hurt. He wouldn't wake up. He needs help."

Fear overwhelmed me, leaving me breathless, shivering, and mute. I could *feel* her, but couldn't *see* her.

Is she dead? Is this her spirit?

"Bryson has TJ. He's safe." My words came out in a gush.

Killian stepped closer and patted the space in front of me where the girl—or the ghost—stood. His hand made contact and he blew out a breath. "She's been bespelled."

I glanced at him and wished I hadn't. His expression reminded me of Bryson's when Buck had denied Quin. Shock mixed with rage. "You know who did this."

He opened his mouth, snapped it shut, and turned his head.

"Mommy?" Jojo's voice cracked, but her body flickered into view for a split second. "What's wrong with me?"

"It's okay, Jojo. Uncle Killian is going to help you."

"Tell me what's wrong." She screamed loud enough to disturb the birds perched above us.

"We can't see you." I met Killian's gaze and silently pleaded for him to do something.

He drew a ragged breath and glanced down to where the invisible girl stood. "I'm going to help you, but I need you to not touch me or your mom. Okay?"

"No!" Clinging to me, she flickered in and out of sight like the images in the damned mirrors. "Why can't you see me? Am I dead? I screamed and screamed but no one could hear me! Am I dead?"

Kneeling again, I pulled her close. "Jojo, listen to me. You're very much alive. We're going to take the spell away, but I need you to calm down, sweetie. Can you do that for me?"

She sagged against me.

Killian took a step back and dragged his hand over his face. "Her fear is breaking the spell. This is exactly like something our father would do."

It took me a heartbeat to catch on to what he'd said. "Our dad?"

He refused to meet my gaze. "I recognized his magic."

"Great. Whatever. I don't care who did this or why. Just how to break it." As far as I was concerned, I was way too old to need a daddy. I'd done just fine without one since birth.

Killian motioned to the seemingly empty space in front of me. "She's stopped flickering since she's calmed down."

I had an idea, a horrible awful idea that would likely make Jolene hate me for the rest of her life, but if it worked...*when* it worked, I'd be able to see her sweet little glaring face.

Kneeling to where I guessed was her eye-level, I wrapped my arms around her. "Killian and I are going to do something, but you can't move from this spot."

"I'm scared." She held tighter.

"I know, baby, but we're not going to leave you. I promise." It shattered me to lower my arms and take a step back. "Don't move."

Killian arched a brow.

I leaned closer to him and lowered my voice. "She has arachnophobia."

His eyes widened but he nodded. "That could work."

"Jojo. No matter what, don't run away." My mind reeled with horrific *what-ifs*. What if she's invisible forever? What if she passes out or runs? What if we can't find her?

"Mom?" Uncertainty thinned her voice.

Killian waved his hand in her direction.

Spiders. Thousands of them. Appeared out of thin air.

They covered Jolene in a layer, so thick they resembled a black wiggling fuzzy blanket wrapped around a girl.

CHAPTER 41

As I'd predicted, Jolene hadn't stopped glaring since she'd broken the spell, or more specifically, since I'd ordered Killian to scar her for life. The dirty looks I could handle. Heck, I could even deal with her giving me the silent treatment. What I couldn't handle were the questions still zinging around in my skull.

Killian and I trudged through the river and made our way up the path to the Tribal House. Each step closer to the building sent my pulse up a notch. I glanced at Gavin.

I don't know what the spirit saw in my expression, but he sighed. "Relax. It's safe. Buck, and anyone who sided with him, are either dead or on their way to a dungeon in Tir Na Nog."

The ceremonial space came into view and Killian stopped walking. He set Jojo on her feet and turned to me. "This is where I leave you."

The thought of never seeing him again left me breathless. I had questions and doubts about him, but he was my brother. Despite his shortcomings and questionable behavior, he'd put his life on the line for me. Twice.

I took his hand. "Please don't go. The queen owes you favors, too. Bryson and I may have saved her the first time, but if it wasn't for your firebird, Buck would have won and we'd all be—"

Jojo stood between us. The last thing she needed was to hear the gory details of what had happened while she'd been lost.

Killian furrowed his brow. "Tessa…I don't know what you're talking about. I do not have fire magic. I can't shift into the firebird."

"You weren't in the tree protecting me and Bryson? You didn't…?" My hands flew to my mouth. "The magic was so like ours. It had to be our father."

I'd assumed Killian had flown away after the fight to find Jojo, but I didn't remember seeing Liam anywhere on the battlefield. Had he fled the queen?

"That's possible. He has fire magic, as well as the other four."

Like with my brother, I had mixed feelings about my dad, but knowing I'd inherited something from him made me smile.

Killian stared off into the distance. When he turned back, he knelt in front of Jojo. "I'll see you again soon. I promise."

Jolene threw her arms around him. "Please stay. I don't have any uncles."

"After everything the queen has put us through, she owes me a brother." Emotions thinned my voice.

Killian drew me into an embrace. "Dad was never her servant, Tessa. I was. I'm sorry I bent the truth, but I was under her orders to get you to Tir Na Nog no matter the cost." He glanced down at Jojo. "I'm not proud of the things I did before I knew who you were, but please know, I had your best interests at heart."

I wanted to ask what he'd done. To tell him I could forgive anything. To beg him to stay, but I couldn't. "Then let me return the favor. Go. I'd rather know you're free than keep you with me and risk your happiness."

"Remember, little sister, names have power. I'm a whisper away." He winked and vanished in a ball of light.

Jolene sighed and took my hand. "Everyone we love leaves us."

"Not everyone." I led her the rest of the way up the path.

Aaron and Bryson sat on a bench near the ceremonial space. They turned, smiled, and met us halfway.

The bruises on Aaron's face were awful, but I didn't notice a limp or other obvious injuries.

Bryson swept Jojo into his arms. Holding her tight, he whispered, "There's my brave girl."

"God, it's good to see you." Aaron drew me into an embrace.

I choked back a sob and buried my face in his neck. "Are you okay?"

"I'm better now." As if afraid to let me go, he held me close long after Bryson took Jolene into the Tribal House. "Thank you for bringing her home...and for saving Quin."

"We never would have found her if not for your dream-walking." I eased back enough to meet his gaze. "Is TJ here? Have you seen him? Is he okay?"

Aaron chuckled. "Harris just brought him back. He's fine, but anxious to see you and Jojo."

"He's a rascal, but I'm glad he's ours—for now or forever." Now that things had settled and the adrenaline had worn off, I was exhausted. "Can we go home now?"

A frown tugged the corners of his lips. "We need to speak to Caoimhe first...and..."

"Let's get it over with." I pulled away from him and took a few steps forward.

Aaron stared as if he had something to say, but sighed and followed me.

We joined Bryson and the queen in a small conference room near Buck's office. The three of us on one side of the table, Caoimhe and a Fae I didn't know on the other. It reminded me of a scene from a movie where the wealthy couple meets to discuss a divorce. In a way, that's exactly what I intended to do. Get her out of our lives.

Caoimhe rested her forearms on the table and clasped her hands. "I cannot thank you enough for saving my life."

Bryson, Aaron, and I nodded, but otherwise remained silent.

"I owe you an explanation for the events that brought us to this point." She lowered her gaze and studied the table.

I got the distinct impression she wasn't used to apologizing or answering for her actions, but I wanted her to do both.

She drew a deep breath. "I sent several Fae here to find the person responsible for the tears in the veil."

Aaron winced and leaned forward as if to speak.

I put my hand on his thigh to stop him.

Caoimhe gave us a knowing look. "It wasn't until they found the source of the tear that they discovered the website and that you were Atsila and Liam's daughter."

I'd never get used to hearing myself referred to by my parents' names. Though I hadn't spent time with my mother while she was alive, her spirit had always been there for me. As for Liam, I hoped to speak to him, to hear his side of the story, and perhaps to get to know him.

To speed things along, I asked, "Killian told me you ordered him to bring me to Tir Na Nog."

"Yes, but your father had other ideas." Her expression turned wistful, as if the memory was bittersweet. "He believed in you even then. He bet me you could handle whatever I threw at you."

That my dad had thought so highly of me made my stomach flutter.

Bryson stood and paced. "Including kidnapping our kids?"

The Fae beside Caoimhe tensed and pulled his magic to the surface, but she turned and shook her head at him.

"They have every right to know the truth." She met Bryson's gaze. "The girl, Jolene, cast a very dangerous spell. My intention today was to bring her to Tir Na Nog. I thought I could solve two problems at once. Educate the girl and give you three the incentive to follow her."

I sat back to put some distance between us. "What was the purpose of the invisibility spell Liam cast?"

Caoimhe's eyes widened before she shook her head. "I can't say why he chose to use an *obscufication* spell, but it was likely to keep her hidden until he could get her to safety. Your father has cheated since day one of this infernal bet. He went behind Killian and tampered with the visions in the mirrors."

Aaron ran his hand over the back of his neck. "No wonder the visions were so bizarre. He was trying to help."

"Yes, well, there have been many mistakes during this ordeal, and we have all paid dearly." Caoimhe stared at her hands. "I apologize for that business with the wolf-boy. Killian had no idea he was a shifter when he put the love spell on him." She motioned to Aaron. "Or you were a dream walker."

"That was Killian?" My voice rose in pitch and in volume.

Bryson rested his hands on my shoulders, likely to keep me in the chair. "I assume he was acting under your orders?"

"Yes. I understand your anger. I should never have involved children. Your father was none too pleased with me when he found out." Caoimhe dipped her chin, but not before I noticed the tears in her eyes.

I'd heard enough and wanted nothing more than to check in on Gram Mae at the hospital and go home. "I think we're done here, but before we go, I'm going to cash in another of those favors you owe us."

She raised a brow. "Yes?"

"A couple actually." I hesitated long enough to get the wording right. "I wish for you to give Killian a full pardon, and I wish for you to stop trying to force me, my men, and our children to go to Tir Na Nog."

Caoimhe Tapped her lips, glanced to the Fae beside her, and turned back to me. "Done, with one minor change. Killian will remain in this realm as your servant. You will need a way to travel back and forth to see to your duties."

"Duties?" I didn't like the sound of that any more than I liked her treating Killian like my personal Uber driver.

"Yes, I will not force you, but I hope you will agree to step into your father's shoes. As the first of the *Leipreachán* clan, you will be needed to attend privy council meetings. And I would like it very much if your children attended school in Tir Na Nog. You can commute, of course."

I couldn't believe her. Sure, she was a queen, but the woman had some nerve. "I'll agree to keeping Killian here as a member of my family. After what you've put us through, I don't want anything to do with Fae. Besides, Liam should be in charge of the leprechauns."

Caoimhe glanced between Bryson and Aaron. "She doesn't know he's gone?"

"Gone?" I wanted to believe her tears were because he'd left her, but my husbands' grim expressions told me otherwise. Was this what Aaron had tried to tell me outside? Why Liam wasn't with Caoimhe after the fight? Why he wasn't at the table?

"Where is he?" I stood and glanced between them.

Bryson hugged me. "He sacrificed himself to save you and Quin."

"No. Let me go." I pushed him away and scrambled back from the table. "I need to see him."

He hung his head, but motioned to the door.

Bryson led me into a small room in the back of the building. Aaron and the queen followed, but remained in the hall.

Several small wooden chairs had been shoved against the walls, and a low table sat in the center of the space. It looked like a classroom except for the flag draped body resting on top of the table.

As if in a trance, I stepped forward and ran my fingertips over the silky fabric. The rich blue, emerald green, and gold emblem was beautiful, but the name written across the bottom made my knees buckle.

O'Roarke.

Bryson held me until I could stand on my own.

I turned and lifted the flag. My vision blurred. I'd only seen his face a couple of times, only spoken a handful of words, only embraced him once.

But he'd given his life for me.

"How do I do it?" I spoke to Bryson without taking my eyes off of my father's face. "How do I give him a piece of my soul?"

Bryson moved closer and whispered, "This is a precious gift. It can only be given once. Are you certain this is what you want to do?"

I caught the message beneath the message. If I did this. If I brought my father back from beyond the veil, I couldn't do it again for Gram Mae.

While it broke my heart to admit it, even to myself, Bryson had been right when he'd said Gram Mae had lived her life. Mae had told me the same thing in her own way, *"When it's my time to go, I'll go. You're not to try to stop me."*

I nodded. "I'm sure. It seems only fair. He gave me life. I'd like to do the same for him."

The sounds of Caoimhe weeping and Aaron consoling her echoed from the hall.

Bryson rested his hand on my shoulder. "Reach past the self you project to the world to the part of you that you hide from everyone."

Not understanding, I glanced at him. "The darkness?"

"Your soul isn't dark, but it isn't all light either." He seemed to struggle to find the words.

I caressed his cheek. "I think I understand. Then what do I do?"

"You must offer that part of yourself to his spirit. He will choose whether to accept the gift or not." Bryson kissed my cheek. "I'll be in the hall if you need me."

"Okay." I stared at my father's body, wondering what it would have been like if he'd raised me. For his strong arms to be my safe haven. For his jokes to make me cringe and laugh at the same time. For him to cry at my wedding and when holding my newborn children.

The sad lonely little girl inside me wept for all of the moments we'd never had with him and for those that we never would.

I closed my eyes and reached out to my father. "Liam O'Roarke…"

I felt him turn, a heartbeat later his spirit revealed itself to me. I could see bits of myself reflected in his face. The curve of my nose, the shape of my eyes, the slightly crooked way he smiled. "Tessa."

The little girl inside me hid, only to peek out a moment later. She reached a tentative hand out toward him and whispered, "Will you be my daddy?"

CHAPTER 42

When I took to the sky as the firebird, I was free. All I needed was an updraft and my mates to be happy. Nothing could touch me, not even death. But no matter how high I soared, the human part of me knew it was an illusion.

Light and darkness, freedom and captivity, joy and heartache, love and loss…

The previous few years had taught me they weren't two sides of the same coin—they were two children on a see-saw. The highs made the lows bearable and the lows made the highs sweeter—but the best things of all happened while balanced in the middle.

Case in point. Holding my great-grandmother's hand during the last hours of her life. The only thing that made the agony bearable was the unquestionable knowledge that she knew I was there. That she knew I loved her. That despite my pain and grief, I would stay by her side until the end.

I wanted to show her it was okay to let go. That we'd be okay. That maybe, just maybe, I'd finally become the woman she'd raised me to be.

Bryson squeezed my shoulder. "How about some coffee?"

Ignoring three mostly full cups of cold hospital muck, I turned my face up to his and nodded. "That'd be great. Thank you."

"I'll be right back." He kissed my forehead and headed for the door.

I leaned closer to the bed and rested my head on my arm. I'd intended to catch a cat-nap, but when I woke, a fourth cup of coffee sat on the bedside table and a blanket rested on my shoulders.

Darlene knocked lightly and peeked inside.

"Come on in." I rolled my head from side to side to relieve the tension.

"I brought company." She smiled and opened the door wider.

Stone stood in the hall, looking rather uncomfortable in a dark suit and tie. He had his hair pulled back in a ponytail and had shaved his goatee.

I rushed to him. "My goodness. I hardly recognized you."

He hugged me tight. "I finally decided to put my PhD to good use. You're looking at the newest professor of anthropology at the University of Maryland."

PhD? Is he serious? Wait, Maryland?

Had he not been squeezing the daylights out of me, I would have fallen over. "You're moving?"

"We'll talk about this later." Darlene eased into the chair I'd abandoned and took Gram Mae's hand. "How is she?"

"The hospice nurse says it won't be long now." That I'd managed to get the words out without my voice cracking was a miracle that rivalled Stone's transformation.

She nodded and turned her attention to Mae.

I could only imagine what my great-grandmother would say if she opened her eyes and got a look at him. Either she'd tell him he looked spiffy, or she'd ask if he'd finally found Jesus.

Thinking of what she would or wouldn't do, instead of her sitting up and being her usual mischievous self, made my throat tighten.

That Darlene, Doctor Stone, and my baby brother were moving away didn't bother me as much as I thought it would. I'd miss them, but I understood. Of course, those folks up in Maryland had no idea what they were in for.

We'd made small talk or sat in silence for fifteen minutes or so, when Darlene stood, wiped her eyes and shook her head. "I...I'll be back later tonight. Tell her I was here if...if she wakes up."

"She knows, Momma, but I'll tell her." I hugged her and Stone goodbye and returned to my chair.

Aaron came in sometime later. He kissed my cheek. "How are you holding up?"

"I'm okay."

He moved to the other side of the bed, kissed Gram Mae's brow, and sat in the hospital version of a recliner. "I saw Stone and Darlene in the lobby."

"That must have been one heck of a walkabout." I laughed despite the situation, or maybe because of it. She wouldn't want us moping around. She'd want laughter and family and good food.

Gram Mae made a pained sound and shifted her leg an inch or two.

Humming her favorite song, "Some Enchanted Evening," I ran my fingers through her cotton puff hair until she settled. At some point over the previous forty-nine hours we'd developed the little routine, or actually, I'd borrowed it from her. She'd done the same for me when I was little and didn't feel well.

"Would you like for me to bring the kids to say goodbye?" That he'd asked made me love him a little more. That his eyes misted and brow wrinkled with emotion nearly broke my heart.

"Sure, but let them know it's their choice." I glanced from the crayon drawings of our patchwork family TJ had sent to the lifelike sketches of Gram Mae's roses Jolene had drawn. "Tell them she knows they love her."

"Will do." He kissed me quick and speed walked from the room.

Gram Mae opened her eyes and drew a shallow breath.

I leaned close enough for her to see me without her glasses. "I'm here."

"Have you been here all night?" She squeezed my hand.

Her sudden burst of energy gave me hope that the doctors were wrong, but I knew better. The hospice nurses had warned me she would have lucid moments, but her organs were slowly shutting down.

"Nope. I went home, showered, ate dinner, and played with the kids." I pressed my lips to the back of her hand to hide my lie. I hadn't left her side since she'd been moved to hospice.

"Good." She glanced around. "I can't see a dog-gone thing."

I slid her glasses on. "How's that?"

"Better." She patted my face. "I'd like to see Tighe."

"All right." I pulled my cell from my purse and fired off a text. The Fae hadn't left the human world since Mae had first been admitted to the hospital. Heck, he'd barely left the building. "I think he's downstairs with Bryson."

"I don't know what he wants with an old lady like me." The uncertainty in her voice broke my heart.

"If I had to guess, I'd say he still loves you, but maybe you should ask him?"

"I intend to." She tried to push herself upright, but the effort was too much for her.

"Let me help you." I fumbled for the button to lift the head of the bed.

She patted her hair and went wide-eyed. "Mirror and brush."

It was my turn to bug my eyes. Little bursts of energy were one thing, wanting to primp while on your deathbed was another. Pulling a compact and brush from my purse, I said, "You should rest."

"There'll be time enough for that." She took the mirror and studied her reflection while I put her hair in some semblance of order.

Tighe came through the door and glanced from Mae to me and back, before exhaling a relieved breath.

Mae squeezed my hand, raised her chin and blew my mind. "I'm ready to go to the Summerlands, but I have some questions first."

Tighe jolted and lit up as if he had jumper cables hooked to his ears. "Ask away."

"I'll um..." I stood and hitched my thumb toward the door.

Mae shook her head and dropped her head back to the pillow. "Stay."

I all but collapsed back into my chair.

Tight sat on the edge of her bed and sandwiched her hand in hers.

"Can I come...back?" She struggled to catch her breath.

"No, but Tessa and other Fae can visit us." He glanced at the monitors behind her head and shot me an alarmed look.

I had no idea what the numbers meant, nor did I need to. I could feel her spirit growing restless inside her body. The part of me that still believed I was human panicked. Her time had come. She was dying before my eyes, but somewhere deep inside me, a bright burning ball of hope formed.

Tighe pressed her hand to his face and covered it with his. Rocking back and forth, he hummed, "Some Enchanted Evening."

I shot to my feet. "Take her! What are you waiting for?"

Gram Mae gave me one last loving look.

"That." He swept her into his arms and vanished in a light so bright, so pure, I wondered if the Fae was truly an angel.

CHAPTER 43

Sundays were still my favorite day of the week, but this one was bittersweet.

I stood beside the hole in the ground as the gleaming white casket slowly descended. Although I knew beyond a shadow of a doubt Gram Mae was with the love of her life in a wonderful place, I felt as empty as the pretty box disappearing into the Earth.

Bryson slid his arm around my shoulders, and Aaron pressed a hand to the small of my back. Though they hadn't said a word, it was past time to go. The rest of the mourners had left the graveside service and were likely waiting on us to get home.

"I'm ready." I wasn't ready. Not by a long shot.

Bryson tugged me to his side. "You'll see her in a few hours."

Not trusting my voice, I nodded.

"It's not the same." Aaron shoved his hands in his pockets. "I swear every time I walk into her house, I expect to see her at the stove frying chicken."

"Or watching soap operas in her easy chair." I rolled my lips in and willed myself not to cry. Again.

Bryson sighed from deep in his soul. "I'm worried about Dottie. She's taking this hard."

"Me, too." I rested my head on his shoulder. "But this isn't like when Charlie died. She's gone out with her friends once and has been spending a lot of time on the phone with her beau."

We walked the rest of the way to the SUV in silence.

I eyed the sleek black sportscar parked behind us. "Is that…?"

"Looks like it." Bryson chuckled. "I was wondering if he'd come."

"That better not be stolen," Aaron said under his breath.

Killian climbed out of the driver's seat and gave me a nervous smile. "I thought we'd follow you to the house."

I ran to him as fast as my heels would allow and threw my arms around his neck. Laughing through my tears, I said, "I wasn't sure I'd see you today."

Technically, Caoimhe hadn't agreed, or disagreed, with my stipulation that I'd treat Killian like any other member of my family and not like a servant—and I didn't plan to call and ask for clarification. I figured, as long as he stayed out of trouble, he had every right to come and go as he pleased.

"If it's okay with you, I thought we'd go to the Summerlands with you." He eased away from me and nodded to someone in the car.

I squinted but couldn't see a darned thing through the tinted glass.

The door opened and my heart stopped.

Liam pulled the dark glasses from his face and flashed me a smile that chased every last shadow away. "Hi, Tessa."

"You're…you're…here?" The ground tilted beneath my feet, but Killian caught me before I made a complete fool of myself.

Liam closed the distance between us, but stopped a couple of feet away as if unsure of himself. "I'm sorry it took me so long to come to you. I needed to heal and to get the Fae equivalent of an annulment."

Killian rolled his eyes.

"It's okay. Bryson explained it could take time, and Gram Mae once told me the days weren't the same in Tir Na Nog." I babbled like an idiot, but I was so dang happy to see him, I couldn't stop myself. "Besides, knowing you were alive and carrying a piece of me with you was enough."

"You gave me quite a gift." My dad pulled me into a tight embrace. "If it's all right with you, I would very much like to see Mae again."

"Absolutely, but we have a going away party to go to first. Then I've arranged a special surprise for the kids."

Liam and Killian stared as if I'd told them I had to dance on a pole before we could leave.

"The party is for Gram Mae. It didn't feel right to… I mean, she's not really… It shouldn't be a sad day." I bit the inside of my cheek to keep from saying anything else.

Liam scratched the stubble on his jaw. "Do all of your hundred or so cousins know where Mae is?"

"Dottie and our daughter are the only family who know the truth about Mae." Bryson stepped in and saved me. "We're raising Tessa's seven-year-old cousin. He lost his mother a couple of months ago. We decided to call the wake a going away party for his sake."

Killian looked as if he'd swallowed a bug. "Thank the stars you didn't tell Darlene."

Laughing, I said, "She suspects something's up, but we're neither confirming nor denying Mae ran off with a handsome Fae."

"Keep it that way." Killian smirked. "That woman told me everything from your bra size to how to get under your skin."

"And yet you kept going back for more." I jabbed my finger into his side. "One day you and I are going to sit down and have a long chat to set the record straight."

"I hate to cut this short, but we need to get home." Bryson rested his hand on the small of my back.

Liam nodded. "I'd love to spend some time with my grandchildren."

Aaron motioned to the car. "Is this one legal?"

Jangling the keys, Killian said, "Yep. Would you like to see my license and registration?"

Aaron seemed to consider taking my brother up on his offer.

I looped my arm with his and pulled him to the SUV.

We drove the short distance to the house, me bouncing with

excitement and my men gently reminding me my family believed we were hosting a wake.

The moment we turned onto the gravel road on the edge of our property, I knew something was wrong. I unbuckled and leaned between the two front seats. "Why are there no cars out front?"

Aaron shrugged. "Did we forget to lower the wards?"

"I took them down before the funeral." Bryson parked between our house and Gram Mae's little pink cottage.

Killian pulled in behind us and cut the engine. "Doesn't look like much of a party."

My heart hammered against my rib cage. "Where are the kids? And Darlene should be here."

Dottie stepped onto the front porch with a little suitcase in her hand. "There y'all are. I thought you'd gotten lost."

Bryson, Aaron, and I stared slack-jawed.

Liam glanced between us and Dottie. "Is everything all right?"

"That's what I'd like to know." I strode to my aunt.

She wore her date outfit, sensible brown walking shoes, her favorite green slacks, and a twinset that brought out the color in her cheeks. Only the suitcase seemed out of place.

Dottie shifted her weight from one foot to the other and avoided my gaze—a first for her. She'd always been a straight shooter.

I lowered my voice to give us a little privacy. "Are you going on a trip?"

"I'm going with you to the Summerlands." Her words came out in a rush.

"But you won't even take an airplane." Silly thing to say, but it was all my overloaded brain could manage.

She set the suitcase beside her, took my hand, and pulled me farther away from the men. "Tessa, now that Mae's gone, I'd like to be with Charlie again."

Holy Moses skiing down the mountain. I was not expecting that.

"Does Charlie know?" I glanced around, half-expecting my grandfather's spirit to pop out of the bushes.

"Of course he knows. It was always our plan." She gave me a sly smile. "Why do you think I had lunch with my friends and spent so much time talking to Malcolm this week? I was saying goodbye. They all think I'm moving to North Carolina."

"No." I folded my arms. I'd already lost Mae. Sure, she wasn't dead, but she wasn't a short walk away either. And Darlene was moving, but that was probably a good thing. "You can't leave me, too. You're all the family I have left."

She caressed my cheek. "Sweetheart, turn around."

I turned and took in the four men. All four loved me enough to give their lives for me and the kids. My heart swelled, along with a little bubble of shame. How could I ask her to stay when all she wanted was what I had twice over?

Crying big fat soap opera tears, I hugged her tight. "You're right and I'm sorry."

The men talked amongst themselves. Bryson must have drawn the short straw because he stepped away from the others and walked toward us. "Where is everyone?"

Dottie let out an honest to goodness giggle. "I sent them all home with the sympathy casseroles the ladies from church dropped off."

"Good riddance on both counts." I laughed along with her.

Poor Bryson looked like he didn't know if he should call 911 and have us admitted or run away.

I decided to put him out of his misery. "Dottie's coming with us to the Summerlands."

"Oh." He nodded. "Oh!" He turned to me. "And you're okay?"

"More than okay." I squeezed Dottie's hand. "But where are the kids?"

"Quin's sleeping in his crib and Darlene is getting TJ and Jojo dressed for their big day." Dottie glanced back at the little pink house. "I've packed up the sentimental stuff and set it aside for you."

I had a feeling it'd be a while before I was ready to go inside, but I nodded. "Thank you."

"Come with me. There's someone I'd like for you to meet." I looped my arm with hers and walked to the cars.

Dottie gasped when Liam smiled. "That has to be your dad. I always thought you looked like Atsila, but you have his eyes."

I didn't think I'd ever get tired of hearing that. I introduced the two and for once, Dottie didn't freak out about meeting a Fae. "Dottie's going with us to the Summerlands. She has a date with Charlie."

Aaron's eyes about fell out of his skull. "You're leaving us, too?"

"We'll talk about this later." She gave him a quick hug. "Why don't we go inside while we wait for the limousine?"

"Limo?" Killian tilted his head.

"I planned a special day for the kids while we're away." I winked, took my father's hand, and walked inside my front door. "I grew up here, back then this was Charlie and Dottie's house—"

TJ and Jojo came barreling into the room dressed in their best Sunday clothes.

"Tessa!" TJ shouted and headed straight for me. He had a mason jar in his hand that looked suspiciously like Gram Mae's onion water. "Is this moonshine?"

"Trust me. It's nothing you want to drink." I scooped him into my arms and breathed in his little boy smell, gummy bears and puppy.

"Uncle Killian!" Jolene beelined for her new favorite person. "Guess what? We're going to a private screening of *Vampires Suck the Sequel* at Micah Sterling's mansion!"

My brother nodded and smiled and nodded some more, but I would have bet my right arm he had no idea what she was talking about.

The noise woke the baby.

Jolene pulled something from her pocket, leaned closer, and half-whispered, "Look. I'm not afraid of spiders anymore."

TJ shrieked and wiggled out of my arms. In the process, he dropped the jar and the stench of onion covered roadkill filled the room.

Aaron grabbed the boy, and Bryson headed for the kitchen and returned with a dish towel.

Darlene rushed into the room with Quin and came to a screeching halt. "My word, I didn't know you were bringing company!"

The noise level had ratcheted up so high so fast, I was terrified to sneak a peek at my father for fear I'd see disappointment in his eyes. I couldn't imagine anything at the Fae court had prepared him for my particular brand of chaos.

Liam slung his arm around my shoulder, pulled me close, and kissed my cheek. "Thank you. I thought gifting me a piece of your soul was amazing…but this? This is perfect."

My mouth fell open. "This circus?"

"This family."

~

THANK you for reading **Spirit Dancer**. I hope you enjoyed meeting Tessa and her crazy family. Continue reading for a sneak peek of The Immortal Reign series **Blood Vows**.

BLOOD VOWS CHAPTER 1

NEW ORLEANS, 1995

For all living things—animal, human, or immortal—beginnings and endings involve pain, suffering, and blood. Serena intended to make Nicholai King experience all three. The man had spent his last night partying on Bourbon Street.

Serena molded her frown into a smile and turned to the five-year-old child trailing behind her. "It's all right, Nick. We're going to find your dad."

Unlike other females, she had no interest in motherhood, but as with most things, Nicholai had made the decision for her when he'd brought the boy home.

Nick stared with big green eyes that reminded her of Nicholai's and a lost expression she fought to resist. "Okay, Mommy."

Serena cringed and tightened her grip on his hand. *Mommy* hadn't been part of the deal when Nicholai had compelled the kid to forget his birth parents.

Immortal assassins did *not* answer to "Mommy" outside of the bedroom, and *that* was saved for special occasions.

The beeper on her hip buzzed. Over the previous hour, Lochlain, her commander, had paged her repeatedly. This time, 911 followed the number. "Damn it."

Serena hurried to the closest payphone, just inside the door of the Irish pub at the corner of Toulouse and Burgundy Streets. Keeping a hold on Nick, she lifted the receiver with two fingers. The stench of stale beer and sweat from previous callers turned her stomach. "Lochlain, it's Serena."

"Where the hell are you and Nicholai? I've been trying to reach you for over an hour."

"The house phone's still giving us problems. I'm on my way to Nicholai now. What's going on?" She released the boy's hand.

"The councilmember from Rome will arrive tomorrow to interview Heather. I've called a meeting to discuss protocol."

Not much could rattle Lochlain, but a high-ranking member of the Order in the city would put him on alert. Although several members of the Sinistra Dei, including Lochlain, predated Christianity, the secret organization—also known as the Left Hand of God—was a part of the Catholic Church. Long ago, members had been closely monitored and controlled by the High Council, but in modern times, the councilmen tended to stay inside the Vatican City.

A ball of ice formed in her gut and thinned her voice. "That's unusual, isn't it?"

"Yes. Which is why I called a meeting. Shall I expect your company soon?"

In the rare instances when members broke their laws, the High Council had a nasty habit of punishing first and asking questions later. Whatever the reason for the visit, Lochlain would want everything to be perfect. "We'll be there as soon as possible."

"Good. About your phone. Was it cut off again?"

"No." She laughed, higher pitched than she'd intended. "It's an old house. You know how temperamental they can be."

"I see." A scraping sound came over the line, followed by muffled conversation. "I'll start without you, but I expect to see you and Nicholai here within the hour."

"Yes, sir." Serena hung up and stared at the sky. The High Council normally interviewed initiates in Rome. A visit to New Orleans had to mean someone had stepped out of line or the Order wanted something. Either way, this wasn't the time to have a human child in tow. Her decision to leave Nicholai became easier by the minute.

Determined to do what she had to do, Serena turned and found Nick squatting on the curb, inspecting a dead rat. Tears sprang to the child's eyes as he picked it up and cradled the bloated corpse.

"Drop it!" The bubonic plague happened long before her mortal birth, but she recalled the entire ordeal had something to do with rats.

"Is he dead?" The child's voice shook.

"Yes, and it's full of germs." She grabbed his arm and shook until he dropped it.

Nick's lower lip quivered, and his slow tears gave way to hiccupped-gasps.

"None of that. We have to hurry." Serena held the child's wrist the same way she'd held the phone, with as little contact as possible.

"Why's it dead?" Nick turned back to the rat. "What happened to it?"

"I don't know."

The boy wiped his snot with the same hand he'd used to touch the carcass. "He needs a funeral. When my friend's dog died, he had a funeral. It's how stuff goes to Heaven."

Nick stopped and tried to go back, but Serena tugged him forward. "I'll have Nicholai come and get him later, with gloves."

Appeased, Nick walked alongside her. She'd chosen to take Royal Street to their destination to avoid the lewd storefronts and strip clubs on Bourbon, yet the humans cast disapproving stares at her and the boy as if they were covered in filth.

A young child shouldn't be out at this hour, but there was nothing she could do about it. Despite the rodent incident, he *looked* clean. She'd overlooked something, but what? Serena noted the adults wore jackets while Nick wore a T-shirt and shorts.

Damn it, Nicholai. You couldn't have stolen clothing when you took the boy?

She knelt, positioning herself between him and the judgmental humans. "Are you cold?"

Nick shook his head, but his teeth chattered.

Serena turned and surveyed the passing tourists. A middle-aged couple approached hand in hand. The pashmina wrapped around the woman's shoulders would do for now. "Stay here. I need to talk to these people."

Nick hugged himself and nodded.

"I mean it. Don't move." Her voice came out harsher than intended.

He whispered, "Okay, Mommy."

Serena cringed and strolled to the couple. Between her small frame and expensive clothes, she looked more like a tourist out for a fancy dinner than an immortal capable of stealing their life forces with a touch. "Hi. Do either of you happen to know where to find the Bourbon Orleans Hotel? I'm a little lost."

The man pointed behind her. "It's on Orleans Street."

Serena lowered her voice and laced her words with compulsion. "Be still and don't speak."

The Sinistra Dei, no matter how weak, could compel humans. The strongest among them, members of the High Council and clutch leaders or judges, could compel other immortals.

The couple shared the same wide-eyed expression as they fought the command, but neither could speak nor move.

Serena motioned to the female. "I need your scarf."

The woman removed the pashmina and placed it in Serena's hand.

"Walk away and remember nothing of me or this encounter."

The couple continued along their way without a backward glance.

She hurried to Nick and wrapped the material around him as if it were a sarong.

"I look like a girl." He stomped his foot.

"Nonsense." She tied the fabric in place and fixed his messy curls. Her gaze roamed over his face. Nicholai's hair was a darker shade of brown, but Nick's olive skin and features were the same. No one could deny the boy came from the same stock as Nicholai. He'd grow up to be as handsome as his predecessor.

"But it's pink."

"It's warm."

His shoulders sagged. "Yes, ma'am."

"Let's go. It's not much farther." Serena took Nick's arm and led him down the sidewalk. The child's stomach growled, reminding her she hadn't fed him since the afternoon. The restaurants had all closed. Even if she could find food, they didn't have time to spare. She pressed her lips together, promising herself never to allow Nicholai King to put her in this kind of situation again.

The air around her sparked as if she'd walked into a cloud of static electricity. Serena held her breath and listened. Another immortal was nearby, but who? The clutch had gathered at Lochlain's. Not enough time had passed for the meeting to have ended.

Footsteps echoed on the sidewalk and Serena glanced over her shoulder. A younger couple followed several yards behind. *Petite blonde female. Male, approximately six feet.*

Adrenaline flooded her system. Unlike the humans on the street, they had no aura, marking them as immortal. *Had the representative's entourage arrived early or were they Execrati?*

The immortals stopped walking and stared at Serena and the child.

Shit. Who are they? Protocol dictated that she address visiting members of the Order, but it also stated Execrati, rogue immortals who'd chosen a life apart from the Church as anathema, were to be executed on sight. Serena had killed her fair share of Execrati, but never when caring for a child. How could she keep Nick safe while she fought?

The male took the female's hand and turned down St. Peter Street. Whoever they were, they'd made the decision not to engage her. Still, Serena couldn't shake the feeling that they posed a threat. She had to get the boy to safety.

"Let me carry you." She scooped Nick into her arms. "Hang on tight. We're going to run really fast."

The child wrapped his arms around her neck.

Serena rounded the corner and broke into a run before leaping onto the roof of a one-story building. A shout from below told her that someone had witnessed the maneuver, but she didn't have time to wipe memories. She crushed the boy against her chest and ran, jumping from rooftop to rooftop until she reached the building at the corner of Iberville and Bourbon Streets.

Nick wept against her shoulder.

"Are you hurt?" She rubbed his back to comfort him. The feelings his warm little body stirred up surprised her. He may have been nothing but elbows and knees, but the child had the power to wreck her life.

"My tummy feels weird."

"You'll feel better once you have a snack." Needing to keep her distance, Serena peeled the child from her chest and set him down.

Nick bent and heaved what little he had in his stomach onto the roof and his shoes. She could handle blood and gore, but vomit crossed the line.

I can't do this. I can't raise a child.

Serena knelt to remove his shoes when immortal energy, or *aetherum*, crackled across her arms. Her heart slammed against her sternum.

They followed us.

BLOOD VOWS CHAPTER 2

"In the irreverent words of Mel Brooks, *it's good to be the king*." Nicholai leaned forward, set his elbows on the table, and pulled his winnings close. One lucky hand had earned enough money to keep a roof over his family's head and food in Nick's belly for a year.

"How much did you win?" Heather lingered near Nicholai's side, running her finger over the rim of her glass.

Adrian, Heather's *guardian*, would hang Nicholai by his entrails if he found the girl in Luxuria. Technically, she was in the backroom of the gentlemen's club. Due to her age, Nicholai had slipped her in through the employees' entrance to avoid the ID check at the front door. However, the distinction wouldn't make much difference to Adrian. The girl, his human descendant, would become immortal soon. Until then, Adrian had made it his life's goal to keep her safe.

Nicholai finished his scotch and set the glass on the table. "It's never polite to ask how much someone won before the end of the game."

Tension rose in the humans at the table when Nicholai paid the big blind. The dealer dealt the next hand, and the players peeked at their cards with blank expressions. Nicholai studied their reactions, searching for tension in a jaw, a downturn of a lip, the drumming of fingers. Each player had a tell—a clue that hinted at their hand.

Heather interrupted his focus. Pouting, she leaned close to whisper, "I thought you said we needed to talk?"

"We do. I'll be finished soon. They're almost broke." Nicholai chuckled and knocked on the table. "Unless you three plan to gamble your return ticket home?"

The men stared as Heather sauntered to the bar. Nicholai might have invited her to a place of questionable morals, but he didn't care for the way they looked at her. She'd grown into a beauty, all legs and long blonde hair, but he'd held her in his arms days after her birth and watched her grow into a young woman. "Eyes on your cards, gentlemen."

The player to his left smirked. "Why bring a distraction if you don't want her to distract?"

"She's not—" The guy had a point. "She's family."

"Enough said." The human glanced at Heather and then to his cards.

Nicholai peeked at his hand. He had pocket kings. Not bad. Plus, he'd run the table the entire evening. His opponents' weary expressions had become downright grim. Two folded. The third player nursed his drink as he stared at his cards.

"I call." The man pushed his chips to the center of the table. Hands trembling, he turned a pair of queens.

The dealer nodded. "All-in."

"I'm in." Nicholai moved his chips forward and tossed his kings on the table. It all came down to the flop. Three of a kind beat a pair, no matter how high the card.

Adrenaline coursed through Nicholai's veins. His pulse raced, but the tension in his shoulders eased. The rush of the game beat any drug. Highs and lows, wins and losses, the unknown outcome—he craved it all.

The dealer turned the ace of spades, three of hearts, and two of spades.

Come on, sweetheart. Give me something good.

She dealt a seven of clubs.

Nicholai tapped his cigar and eased his finger toward the cherry. The pain increased his anxiety, raising his tension. *One more, baby. Make it count.*

The man licked his lips as Heather returned to the table.

"I'm bored." She wiggled into Nicholai's lap.

The dealer turned the last card.

The humans who'd folded cheered, while the other stared in disbelief.

Shit. Nicholai repositioned Heather and double checked the card. *Queen-of-fucking-hearts.* He motioned to the barmaid for another scotch as his opponent claimed his winnings.

"Well played." Nicholai sat back and exhaled long and slow. The highs made a man dream. The lows made him desperate. The marriage of the two created an obsession.

Heather pushed her lower lip out, a move she'd mastered in early childhood. "Why don't you use your gifts?"

In hundreds of years of playing cards, Nicholai had only cheated once. The dishonesty had cost him more than his life. After taking a sword to the heart, he'd woken as an immortal slave to the Holy Mother Church. A fledgling member of the Order of the Sinistra Dei, he'd been sentenced to spend the next century in training to become whatever-the-fuck the Order needed him to be.

He leaned forward to stamp out his cigar. "I don't cheat. It always comes back to bite—"

Serena burst into the room with his newly adopted son in her arms and bouncers following. The woman's anger hung in the air as thick as the tobacco smoke, but deadlier. She turned her dark eyes to the blonde in Nicholai's lap and froze.

Damn, she's beautiful when she's angry, like some Egyptian goddess of vengeance and sex.

She assessed the situation with a warrior's stare.

Nicholai recognized the look in her eye and went on the defensive. He'd screwed up and he knew it. "Whoa! You can't bring the kid in here."

The woman he'd loved since the New World was born smiled. Outsiders may have taken her expression as a sign of encouragement, but Nicholai recognized it as a promise of pain to come.

Nicholai cleared his throat. "Heather, you should get up now."

The girl's gaze moved over Serena from head to toe.

"We need to talk. Alone," Serena said.

Nicholai eased Heather from his lap. "Why don't you take Nick into the other room for a little while?"

"I gave up time with my boyfriend and you want me to babysit?" The girl put her hands on her hips. "Seriously?"

"No." Serena spoke as if she were ordering dinner. "But you should go home and explain to your guardian why you were in a strip club, sitting in Nicholai's lap." She paused. "Unless, of course, you work here. Adrian never mentioned you were good on a pole."

Damn, damn, damn. This isn't going to end well for Heather—or me for that matter. Nicholai glared at the waitress. "Where's my scotch on the rocks?"

Serena ignored Heather's red face and balled fists and met Nicholai's gaze. "Tip the girl so you and I can talk alone."

The human who'd won the last round chose that moment to speak. "Come here, sweetheart. I'll tip you. I doubt he can afford it."

Heather stamped her foot and growled like a two-year-old deprived of a cookie. "Are you going to let them talk to me like that?"

Nicholai took the drink from the waitress and knocked it back. "Keep 'em coming, sweetheart."

Nick giggled. "Keep 'em coming, sweetheart."

"Everyone out." The room cleared at Serena's command. Not even Heather, in a full-blown temper tantrum, could resist the compulsion.

Nicholai stood. "Serena—"

"Don't." She set Nick on a stool, moved behind the bar, and filled a bowl with pretzels. "What would you like to drink?"

Nick rubbed his eyes. "Scotch on the rocks, sweetheart."

Serena shot Nicholai a dirty look and filled a glass with juice. "Daddy and I need to have a talk. Are you okay here?"

"Uh-huh." Nick stuffed a handful of pretzels into his mouth.

Nicholai sighed as she joined him at the table. "You're good with the kid."

Serena stiffened her spine. "Lochlain has been trying to get a hold of us tonight. I received his pages, but the house phone was disconnected again."

"You know I turn my beeper off while playing. What does he want?"

"The Order is sending a councilman to interview Heather before she's imbued. Lochlain called a meeting hours ago. We're expected to see him tonight and he's not happy."

"That's odd." Nicholai had a good idea what would bring the Order to New Orleans, but if the shit hit the fan, the less Serena knew the better.

Serena nodded. "This isn't a good time to have a mortal child. Lochlain isn't going to be happy when he finds out."

"He'll get over it." Nicholai reached for her hand but she pulled away. "Look at me. Let me explain what you think you saw."

"That can wait. I ran across two immortals tonight. I thought they might be part of the group coming from Rome, but they didn't introduce themselves." She glanced at the kid and lowered her voice. "They followed Nick and me here tonight. I'm not sure if they're still outside."

The change of subject left his head spinning. "What? No, it's unlikely they're Execrati."

"I didn't *stroll* here after I saw them. I picked the kid up and ran across rooftops. Why would a couple of paper pushers from the Vatican follow me?"

"I'll take you and Nick home, then go to the meeting." Nicholai ran a hand over the back of his neck. Third in the chain of command, he had a duty to report the incident to his commander, but first, he'd make sure his family was safe.

"No. I've never let you speak for me and I'm not about to now. This is my responsibility. My reputation." She motioned to the cards on the table. "Your bad decisions are affecting me as much as you. What do you think others say about me behind my back when you gamble away our mortgage money? Or when you allow a young girl to sit in your lap? Adrian's descendent, no less. How do you think he and Fare will feel when they find out you had Heather in a strip club?"

"Who cares what others think?"

"I do." Serena folded her arms. "Are you sleeping with her?"

Nicholai's mouth fell open from the verbal jab. "How can you ask me that?"

Serena looked away.

"I don't cheat at cards or on my woman." Nicholai ran his fingertips over her cheek. "*Cara, amore mio*, please."

"Don't call me that." She pulled away. "Your charming Italian routine isn't going to work this time."

"I asked Heather here because I wanted to speak to her about helping out with Nick."

"She's about to become immortal and be shipped to Rome for training. Besides, she's not suitable to care for a child. Then again, the back room of a strip club isn't conducive for interviewing potential nannies, either."

"It's important that Nick bond with her. He's going to need young immortals around him when he's imbued."

Serena stood and waved her hand. "Rather than worrying about what may happen twenty years from now, let's worry about tonight."

"You're going to need help taking care of him."

Serena's eyes darkened.

Nicholai eased back. He'd pushed her too far. It'd take some serious finessing to smooth this one over. "We should report what happened tonight to Lochlain. The last thing we need are Execrati in town during a visit from the Order."

Serena shook her head. "Not before I've said what I came to say. I'm going to speak and you are not to interrupt me until I'm finished."

"Yes, dear." Nicholai motioned for her to unload. Serena had a temper like a geyser. It simmered beneath the surface as the pressure built. When it reached a certain point, the only thing left to do was stand back and let it blow.

"We have no food to feed the child you insisted on bringing home.

We have no clothing for him, or toys, or anything else children need. He's too young to be away from his mother—"

"You're his mother now."

He could all but hear her counting to ten when she closed her eyes and drew a breath.

Serena lowered her voice. "And if I refuse?"

Would she do that? He hadn't stopped to consider the possibility. "Then I'll raise him alone."

"Why? What happened to Angelina?"

Nicholai's throat tightened. He looked away before she could question the tears stinging his eyes. "I have my reasons."

She took his hand. "What reasons? You never explained. You just came home with a five-year-old, announced he was ours and left."

He cleared his throat. "Angelina needs me to care for him."

"Did she get married? You mentioned something about her dating. Do you disapprove of the guy?"

Memories of Angelina, his human descendent and the mother of the last male in his bloodline, would haunt him for the rest of his life. "I wouldn't willingly deprive Nick of his mother, not after losing his father so young."

"Tell me what happened." She leaned close.

He turned from her pleading eyes. "I can't. Not yet."

"I love you, but I cannot and will not live like this. I think we should split up. It's just not working." Serena stood and stared at Nick. The boy had fallen asleep with his head on the bar like a miniature alcoholic.

"Serena, wait." Nicholai's brain stuttered to a halt at the idea of a life without her. *She can't be serious. Can she? I'll be damned if I let her walk out the door without giving me a chance to explain the situation.* "Sit. Let's talk. You mean the world to me. I can't do this without you."

"Do what?"

Nicholai motioned to the child.

She threw her hands up. "I need to go before I say something I'll regret."

The pain in his chest reduced his voice to a whisper. "You haven't already?"

"Goodbye, Nicholai." She stood and headed for the exit.

"Stop."

Serena's spine stiffened, but she stood motionless. Her hand flew to her mouth and the color drained from her face. "Did you just *compel* me?"

Blood Vows is available on Amazon and Kindle Unlimited.

ALSO BY KATHRYN M. HEARST

Tessa Lamar Novels
The Spirit Tree
Twelve Spirits of Christmas
The Spirit Child
The Spirit Walker
The Spirit Dancer

Immortal Reign Series
Blood Vows
Blood Awakening
Blood Rising
Blood Coup
Blood Reign

Paranormal Romance
Dragon Glass
Dragonstruck

Bourbon Street Bad Boys Club
Absinthe Minded
Highball and Chain
Single Malt Drama
Hot Momosa
Gin and Trouble

Contemporary Romance
Doctor Heartbreaker

ABOUT THE AUTHOR

Kathryn M. Hearst is a southern girl who seasons her romances with sprinkles of humor, mystery, and suspense. Her second book, The Spirit Tree, won the Kindle Scout competition, and her work has been featured in Chicken Soup for the Soul. She has been a storyteller her entire life. As a child, she took people watching to new heights by creating back stories of complete strangers. Besides writing, she has a passion for shoes, vintage clothing, antique British cars, and music. Kate lives in eastern North Carolina with her three dogs, Jolene, Roxanne, and Jagger—whose names were chosen based on popular tunes—because everyone needs a theme song.

Never miss a new release! Sign up for Kate's Reader's Club or visit her website www.kathrynmhearst.com

Stalk Kate here: BookBub, Amazon, Facebook, Pinterest, and Goodreads

Made in the USA
Coppell, TX
26 November 2022